D1176239

M. S. Power was born in Dublin and educated in
Ireland and France. He has worked as a TV producer
in the United States, but now lives in Galloway,
Scotland, where he devotes his time to writing. His
story, MR APPLE SEEKS THE LIGHT, was the
winner of the Hennessy Short Story Award in 1983
and his first novel, HUNT FOR THE CLOWNS
was published in the same year to critical acclaim.
His three novels comprising the children of the North
trilogy, THE KILLING OF YESTERDAY'S
CHILDREN, LONELY THE MAN WITHOUT
HEROES and A DARKNESS IN THE EYE, and
his most recent work, BRIDIE AND THE SILVER
LADY, are also available in Abacus.
Also published this year in hardback, are CRUCIBLE
OF FOOLS, A SHADE OF DEATH and THE
SUMMER SOLDIER.

THE CRUCIFIXION
OF
SEPTIMUS ROACH

M. S. Power

AN ABACUS BOOK

First published in Great Britain
by Bloomsbury Publishing Ltd 1989
Published in Abacus by Sphere Books Ltd 1990

Reproduced, printed and bound in Great Britain by
Cox & Wyman Ltd, Reading

ISBN 0 349 10137 X

Sphere Books Ltd
A Division of
Macdonald & Co (Publishers) Ltd
Orbit House
1 New Fetter Lane
London EC4A 1AR
A member of Maxwell Macmillan Pergamon Publishing Corporation

This book was always intended for my friends Michael and Rhona Kenneally, and to them, indeed, it is dedicated with affection and thanks.

But since they knew and loved her I know they will not mind sharing the dedication with the memory of my beloved Nina who died on August 30th, 1987. Without her encouragement and faith I doubt I would ever have written a book; without her love I would never have known the happiness I did; without her beside me I am, still, desolate.

Of human striving there's no symbol fuller:
Consider, and 'tis easy comprehending –
Life is not light, but the refracted colour.

Goethe: Faust, Act I

Prologue

He was walking somewhere with his nurse, holding her hand, behind them the only thing allowed to share their pilgrimage: a wooden pony on wooden wheels that he towed through the dust by a string.

– Where are we going, Nnanan? he asked.

– To the light, child.

– What light?

– The light of knowledge.

– Why there, Nnanan?

– So that you may be prepared.

– Prepared for what?

– For the coming of the man.

– What man, Nnanan?

– The redeemer.

– What is a redeemer, Nnanan?

– One who suffers for others. One who dies for others. One who is sacrificed for others.

– And will that happen?

– Yes.

– When?

– That is not known. Maybe today. Maybe in a year. Perhaps in a thousand years. But at some time it will happen.

– How will I know that person?

– That is why I take you to the light, child.

And by degrees they reached a village that seemed to be far from his home, a village set on a plateau between two mountains whose peaks were like spires proclaiming a place where God might choose to dwell. It was very quiet; several people, most of them old and wizened men, sat in a circle in the square formed by the huts of mud.

– You bring the child?

– I do, Nnanan answered.
– He is the son of Lagreze?
– He is.
– And he is to be received?
– He is.
– Will he be worthy?
– He will be worthy.

The houngain macoute took a small inlaid container like a pillbox from the folds of his robe. He dipped his thumb in it and smeared something on the boy's forehead, pressing his thumb down hard as though attempting to leave an indelible imprint.

It was possibly his imagination, or some mild delirium brought on by the sinister aura that pervaded the place, but the boy felt a frightening surge within him as though his blood were boiling. Come, child, the houngain said kindly, and Gilles followed him. Sit here: and Gilles sat, squatting cross-legged on the floor of the dark little hut, the houngain opposite, also cross-legged, holding his hands in his, covering them completely. Then the houngain started to chant, closing his eyes and throwing back his head, wailing like a muezzin in a language Gilles had never before heard. Suddenly he stopped and commanded Gilles to close his eyes; then he placed both hands on the boy's head, palms down, again pressing forcibly. Now, child, he said almost in a whisper, tell me what you see.

It was uncanny; it was mesmerizing. In his mind's eye Gilles, at first, could only see what seemed to be darkness, but a darkness which he, standing in the light, was peering into, as into a vaulted cavern. And from this cavern someone walked, materializing with dreadful irregularity, the features piling up layer upon layer as he moved closer, making the apparition appear to be several people in search of an acceptable composite. As Gilles's comprehension grew he could discern that it was definitely a man, tall and gangling and gaunt, the face grey and lined and infinitely sad . . .

One

When Monsieur Gilles Lagreze smiled, and he smiled often, it was like a wide, white hammock slung between his small, delicate, Negroid ears. He was smiling now as he followed his companion's gaze, and stared at what so fascinated him. Below the hotel veranda on which they sat in high-backed cane chairs, beyond the swimming-pool (only half-filled, the water stagnating, leaves and sheets of newspaper floating on the surface), a solitary man danced with his shadow on the weed-strewn hard tennis court. Curious though his actions appeared, he gave the impression of being happy and perfectly sane. Dressed in dark trousers that sported elaborate braiding down the seams, and a scarlet singlet, his feet bare, he swayed and contorted his amazingly supple black body in rhythm to some music that existed only in his mind. He spread his arms wide and waved them as gracefully as a great bird seeking flight. Then, slowly, he brought his arms together and folded them across his chest, at the same time sinking gently to the ground, so that he appeared to have been sucked into it, gathering his shadow within him.

'Incredible,' Oscar Nicholson heard himself exclaim.

Monsieur Lagreze cocked an amused eyebrow, using the gesture to replace the smile that perforce vanished from his face when he spoke. 'You surprise me,' he said. 'I would have thought you had been here long enough now to know that many of our people consume their shadows at noon, taking them with their flesh to the shade to escape the burning sun.'

'I'm sorry? Oh . . . No.' Oscar Nicholson shook his head and became instantly attentive. 'I wasn't referring to . . .' He waved his hand in the direction of the dancer, who had moved to the impoverished shade of a stunted dartura tree and was dozing contentedly under the huge, pendulous flowers, his body curled in the womb of his dreams. 'I was thinking of Father Roach.'

3

'Ah,' Gilles Lagreze sighed, and nodded understandingly.

'Quite incredible,' Nicholson said again, as though the repetition would make the thought more believable.

'Indeed,' Monsieur Lagreze agreed. 'Quite incredible. To some,' he added, removing a small lethargic bug from his nose with a meticulously manicured finger on which he wore too many rings. 'But not to everyone, Oscar. Not to all of us, I regret. It was a tragedy, of course. But it was also most inevitable.' He sighed again. 'His particular ordination included – ' He broke off and scowled for a moment. 'You do understand what I am trying to say, I believe?' he concluded, turning a baleful eye on his friend.

They had been playing chess, not very earnestly, and as Oscar Nicholson rose he caught the corner of the slatted table with his thigh, sending most of the chessmen toppling to the ground. 'Oh, dear. I am sorry.'

Monsieur Lagreze shrugged. 'Not to mind,' he said, adding solemnly, 'I would soon have checkmated you in any case.'

'Probably,' Nicholson conceded. He walked to the edge of the veranda, accompanied by a wave of boisterous laughter from the foreign journalists assembled in the bar, and gazed down at the city that sprawled beneath him: Port au Prince, lying sulking and sweating across a low, steaming, tropical plain at the head of a bay flanked by soaring mountains. Oscar shielded his eyes from the glare of the sun with one hand. What a wild, infernal, chaotic city it was! The streets lined with flamboyants and peppered with half-completed, already decaying public monuments; the stench of fish and ash, perspiration and excrement hanging low over every-thing, menacing even the grandiose government buildings and, with considerable impertinence, the Presidential Palace (so white, such an insulting, immaculate contrast to the shanty towns on the water-front). Then, of course, there was the Hotel Ollofson: that incongru-ous haven of Western, Hiltonesque comfort, that outrageous filigree mansion draped in bougainvillea, reeling now under the babble of intoxicated foreign tongues as reporters waited to communicate the aftermath of the President's flight to luxurious exile. There was what amounted to a legend that the hotel managed to adapt itself to the ever-shifting mood of the city: in the early daylight it gleamed, fragile and pretty, its fantastic turrets and towers, cupolas and minarets decorated as if with lace: it smiled, serenely welcoming. By the afternoon it had fallen into desuetude, the timbers panting and sweating in the moist, sapping heat, some walls revealing long fissures like undoctored sores. By night and under a shrouded moon it grew strangely morose despite the inevitable jollification taking place within, staring out over the city with shuttered windows, its impressive gates bound with lianas, the gardens unkempt and wild and grimly threatening, home only for the spirits of the dark – '*pour les perdus*', Monsieur Lagreze had but recently remarked.

Nicholson stretched, heaved himself erect and returned to his chair, casting en route a benign eye towards the cocktail bar that opened off the veranda, scene of so many clamorous nights.

'But you did everything you possibly could to prevent him,' Monsieur Lagreze said, endorsing his consoling statement with a tiny gesture that could have been interpreted as absolution.

Nicholson opened his mouth to reply but was forestalled by an explosion that sent a plume of dark, acrid smoke skywards from behind the *Centre de Psychiatrie et Neurologie*. The cries of the celebrating rioters, which had been steadily subsiding as the heat of the day increased, swelled for a moment, reaching the ears of the two men as a gigantic, enthusiastic moan, and leaving in its wake a strange, eerie buzz that presaged an evening of further turmoil.

Nicholson took advantage of the distraction to offer Monsieur Lagreze a cigarette; when it was declined he lit one himself, sucking the nicotine deep into his lungs. As he exhaled he economically included a sigh.

' – not blame yourself,' Monsieur Lagreze was saying.

'I wouldn't mind, only the wretched man came to the embassy the day before and I warned him,' Nicholson countered peevishly. 'I quite specifically warned him not to even attempt it. To leave things to those who are used to dealing with such matters. To keep his head down. But no. He knew better. He simply would not listen. Insisted on going to the palace. Saying, would you believe – ' He laughed bitterly.

'Saying . . .?' Monsieur Lagreze prompted, leaning forward in his chair.

'That God insisted he should go.'

Monsieur Lagreze leaned back. 'Maybe He did.'

' – ?'

'Or some other god,' Monsieur Lagreze added mysteriously.

They fell silent again, perhaps pondering the odd possibility of some unorthodox deity being involved, perhaps just feeling the effects of the heavy, humid air. Indeed, at one point it seemed as if Oscar Nicholson might have fallen asleep, his head bent to his chest, his body motionless but for the steady rise and fall of his ample, bulging stomach. But he was far from being asleep. Oscar Nicholson, special assistant to the Ambassador (not that *that* was any great shakes as a position) regularly adopted this somnolent attitude when concentrating, retreating into what he jokingly liked to call his 'state of Californian Zen'. Short and stocky, in his late forties, overweight and with a flushed, jowly face, he was, he admitted if only to himself, a dismal failure, a sort of diplomatic jobber, shunted from post to post, usually to remote, outlandish, unexpectedly troublesome places where no one in his right mind would agree to go. Send old Nicholson, was the inevitable conclusion when a distasteful vacancy occurred, and, with equal inevitability, Nicholson would be sent, meek and placid and uncomplaining, repacking his 'essential tack' (a few clothes, a few books, a few photographs, a couple of boxes of pills, a bottle or two of some tonic) and setting sail for pastures or deserts unknown. The great thing about old Oscar (everyone agreed when it suited them) was that he was so very likeable, always willing to comply, always willing to look on the bright side of things, always willing to extricate some incompetent Ambassador from the *faux-pas* he had made. Yet, curiously enough, he *did* always manage to find something 'bright' to cheer him up, regardless of how grim the particular location might be. And after almost three years in Haiti he had grown quite to like the place despite the wretchedness and squalor and appalling corruption, making the best of it as he had made the best of everywhere else he had been dispatched, perhaps drinking too much but never to any real excess.

'I think you loved him dearly. My pardon,' Monsieur Lagreze corrected himself instantly. 'I think you *liked* him dearly. Even still I tend to translate directly from the French.'

Nicholson nodded. 'Yes. In the end I liked him. And, you know, I even found myself admiring him, for all his lunacy. That was the amazing thing about him, don't you think – mad as the proverbial hatter but one was forced to wonder at his courage.'

'He was, I always thought, *un homme triste*. A sad man. But sad only because he shouldered the misery of others, wouldn't you say?'

Oscar frowned: such obtuse observations were not something he cared for much. 'I wouldn't know about that,' he replied brusquely.

Monsieur Lagreze spotted a chessman lying by a terracotta urn in which unrecognisable plants, unwatered, struggled to survive. 'There are people,' he said, easing himself from his chair and retrieving the piece, gazing at it, holding it delicately in his huge fingers, before settling back in his chair. ' . . . There *are* people, you know Oscar, who can only satisfy themselves – fulfil themselves, they call it – I speak spiritually, of course – if they overload themselves with suffering. It is a curiosity prevalent in saints, you will have noticed. Martyrs in particular. And fools. Which could explain why the more comfortable we are with ourselves the further removed we seem to be from God,' he concluded with bewildering logic.

Nicholson gave a tight laugh. 'I would never have considered poor Septimus Roach to have been a saint,' he said. 'Unless madness is akin to sanctity,' he added, as though such a kinship now struck him as a possibility.

Monsieur Lagreze gestured perplexity with both hands, spreading them, palms upwards, the chessman wedged between forefinger and thumb. 'Yet who is to say? We are all, are we not, like this?' He held the chessman aloft. 'All of us pawns in some mightier game.' He smiled at the convenience of the cliché. 'And that, my friend, is why I so delight in behaving out of the ordinary. Like now. Sitting here. Playing chess with you while all about us a small jot of history is being enacted.' Carefully, he placed the pawn on the board, choosing a square that gave him an advantage in the unlikely event of the game progressing with what pieces were left. He chuckled. 'Poor Septimus and I had quite a lot in common, you might have guessed.'

Oscar threw an astonished glance at his companion. He would have guessed no such thing. Then he smiled to himself as he recognised the unlikely suggestion for what it really was: a mildly sinister disguise, a posthumous alliance with a gentle, foolish creature that might distract from a ruthlessness that was probably vital if one was to survive under the unpredictable Duvaliers, *Père et Fils*. And there was no denying that Gilles Lagreze had survived with some panache, his ruthlessness tempered by gestures of extraordinary kindness. Not only survived but prospered, with his pale-grey suit of Italian silk (which mocked Oscar's crumpled, distressed, lightweight, off-the-peg, drip-dry, avocado-green jacket, and baggy, cream-coloured trousers), his Bally shoes so polished that they ricocheted the sunlight like mirrors, the cuffs of his immaculate white shirt (the whiteness gleaming like an advertiser's dream against his black skin upon which it was almost shocking to notice a sprinkling of coarse black hair) displaying gold scarab cufflinks. Yet there was an air of menace about him, a sense of occult power, a feeling that there sat a man who could communicate with the dead as easily and as elegantly as he did with the living.

'Well . . . ' Nicholson said at last, drawling the word and peering at his wristwatch.

'Already? So soon?' Monsieur Lagreze studied his watch also: an enviable half-hunter on the end of a thick gold chain threaded through his lapel. '*Tiens!* How the time does fly!' he sighed, snapping the case shut.

'Not so long ago you told me time stood still here,' Oscar pointed out fatuously, his lips twitching in a mocking grin.

Monsieur Lagreze shrugged. 'Perhaps I lied,' he admitted, returning the grin but making his wider and shinier. 'Or perhaps I – ' He stopped abruptly and stretched, clawing the air before folding his hands on top of his head as if grasping a fleeting thought and manhandling it back into his mind. 'Tell me, did you ever really discover what brought our friend to Haiti? Father Septimus, I mean. After all, it is an unlikely anchorage for a man of his . . . his . . . ' He paused again and grappled for the word, frowning as though vexed by the poverty of his vocabulary. 'His . . . his sensibility,' he settled for, easing the furrows on his brow, seeming almost satisfied.

'No,' Nicholson confessed. 'All I ever learned was what he himself told me, and you know as well as I do that all information from that source was highly suspect.'

'But what did he tell you, pray?'

It was Oscar's turn to dither, and unwittingly he assumed his companion's posture, leaning back in his chair, folding his hands on the crown of his head, closing his eyes. What, indeed, had Septimus Roach told him, pray? There, looming, was the enigmatic priest, dressed in black, always in black despite the relentless heat (so appropriate, black, don't you think, he had asked), peering through those impossibly thick-lensed, rimless spectacles, his gaunt, almost skeletal body stooped but tough and wiry nonetheless, that unsightly birthmark (rather close to an outline of Chile, wouldn't you say?) disfiguring one side of his otherwise pallid face, his curiously conical head topping a scrawny, unnaturally long neck (so decidedly advantageous in crowds, he had joked, and cackled hugely at his little witticism), his long arms and mutilated hands gesticulating haphazardly as he spoke. So what *had* he told him, pray? 'Only that there had been what he termed problems with his bishop.'

'Ah,' Monsieur Lagreze sighed. '*Les problèmes*,' he added, nodding sagely in the manner of a man who knew all about such things. 'I can understand that. He was, I think you will agree, a man who would be given problems by many, not only bishops, and also vice versa.'

Nicholson laughed aloud. 'Oh, on that we can certainly agree.'

'An unconventional man.'

'Decidedly.'

'I keep remembering – now that he is dead – something he once said to me,' Monsieur Lagreze decided to reveal. 'At the time it struck me as being, well – eh, trivial. Now, it merely seems sad. I forget the exact context of our conversation but suddenly, out of the blue he told me about a walking holiday with a friend. In France.' Monsieur Lagreze fell silent and played with one of the rings on his finger, turning it round and round. It was uncanny, but all of a sudden it was as though Septimus Roach had taken up the tale, as though he was sitting there with them, chatting blithely away. Monsieur Lagreze cocked his head and listened. ' . . . You know France, of course, Monsieur Lagreze? Yes. Of course you do. You told me. Anyway, I took this walking holiday with a friend – poor Ignatius – Ignatius Alexander Sebastopol Wyatt – what do you make of that? Sebastopol, can you believe it? – I wonder what has become of him? A very odd gentleman, but a good friend and that's what counts, isn't it? – Anyway, we were in Valençay and we came across a sign outside a small wayside menagerie. It moved us greatly although neither of us could decide why. *On vous prie*, it read, *de ne pas vouloir inquieter, effrayer, ni effoler les bêtes, qui sont là que pour vous faire plaisir.* And that, my black-hearted friend, could apply to all of us, could it not? What other possible reason could God have had for committing us to this dismal earth unless it was to give pleasure? . . . '

'Not,' Monsieur Lagreze said solemnly, 'the sort of sentiment I would expect from a priest.'

'And you don't like that idea, eh?'

'I like the idea,' Monsieur Lagreze confirmed quickly, 'but is it not inappropriate that a priest should think so?'

Nicholson was astonished. 'Whyever should you think that?'

Monsieur Lagreze became sullenly prudish. 'Pleasure, as I understand it, is not to be included in the Catholic way of life. At least, that is what I was taught here – by priests. Suffering, yes. Most decidedly suffering. Any amount of suffering to strengthen the soul against the devastation of evil. But pleasure? I think not.'

'Perhaps he meant pleasure achieved through suffering,' Oscar remarked, intending it to sound facetious, but frowning as the possible truth of his observation surprised him.

'Indeed,' Monsieur Lagreze agreed, nodding vehemently. 'And in that case he would have been a very satisfied man.'

'Maybe he was – in his own crazy way. And now,' Oscar said determinedly, 'I really must get going. The Ambassador will be in the throes of his midday jitters. These are very tricky times, you know, Gilles. Or so he tells me. Very tricky.'

Gilles Lagreze burst out laughing, his rumbling, booming merriment coursing the length of the veranda. A youngish woman in khaki shorts and blouson (an airline bag slung over one shoulder, a camera in its case over the other) glanced up from the book she was reading (*Haiti: Family Business*), and watched them curiously, drawn into their unexplained mirth, her bright blue eyes hesitantly sharing in it. Monsieur Lagreze immediately subdued whatever mild passion rose within him lest he find himself in a situation very much trickier than any that had faced his friend. 'Oh, I can well understand that,' he said finally, taking his eyes off the woman and punctuating his words with a wry chuckle. 'The treacherous natives are restless, *n'est-ce pas*? Always such a trouble when the ordinary people get that first whiff of power. Not to mention the enervating zest of freedom. Ah, yes, your colleagues in Washington must be well and truly anxious. Rebellious natives – is that what they call us? – on their very doorstep waiting to embrace the enchantment of Marx with open arms. Yes, that must be very tricky.'

Oscar Nicholson pushed himself out of his chair and returned again to the balustrade. Diplomatically, although surprised by Gilles's vehemence he ignored the jibe; it was well within the realm of possibility that he might have to call upon the services of his friend Lagreze, if the situation deteriorated on Haiti, as, indeed, it seemed very likely to. He smiled ruefully and glanced sideways at the bland, comfortable Negro who, taking the smile as tacit acknowledgement that his taunt had not been without foundation, smiled back with contented amusement. He might, however, have been somewhat less contented had he known what was running through Nicholson's mind. It was one of the less publicized facts of international diplomacy that always, in every country on the verge of economic or political collapse, there emerged one person of influence who could be called upon to sway the fractious elements into a frame of mind beneficial to good old Uncle Sam. Oscar had seen it time and time again; he had negotiated with such people time and time again, and had enjoyed such bartering; for bartering it was – they simply had to agree a price since everyone had a price, and everything they did had a price. And Oscar Nicholson now wondered what payment Gilles Lagreze might exact for his services were they ever needed. That, as they said, was a puzzlement; for Lagreze insisted that he had no political ambitions, no desire to be installed in a position of power – the usual fee for such assistance. Indeed, he disclaimed, loudly and vehemently, all interest in 'les affaires méchants' as he called them, proclaiming himself to be a simple man who enjoyed small pleasures – a little food, a little wine, chess and birdsong, and reasonable comfort. Of course being enormously wealthy made it a simple matter to avow such modest simplicities, as did wielding such menacing power: he had had the President's ear, had even, some maintained, been the instigator of the President's exile, had certainly been the last person to speak to him before the immense C-141 Starlifter, so thoughtfully flown in from Charleston, South Carolina, had whisked Duvalier and his wife, mother and entourage to France . . .

Below the hotel, this time near the waterfront, another explosion thundered its devastation, accompanied by a rousing cheer and the shrill protestations of women whose washing was being blackened by the smoke. Under the dartura tree the dancer sat bolt upright, listened for a moment, then folded himself up again and returned to sleep. 'I think,' Monsieur Lagreze said quietly, coming to join his friend, 'I think I should accompany you part of the way to the embassy. Just to be safe, you understand.'

Oscar was touched. 'That's very kind of you, Gilles.'

Lagreze shrugged. 'A small kindness perhaps,' he replied. 'It is a difficult time, and we are at trouble to know exactly how people might react.'

'To us Americans, you mean?'

'If only it was that simple. Alas, no. To anyone. They are – how can I say it? – remarkably innocent. They tend to think, still, in straight lines, you see. They do not always allow for the differences in individuals. But it is always so everywhere, is it not, my friend? Individuals are blamed for the stupidities of their governments. And in situations like this – ' he waved an arm to embrace the entire country ' – a minor difference of opinion can be made to look like a major threat. And so it sadly goes.'

Together they left the hotel, both flinching as the full glare of the sun hit their faces, and made their way to Oscar's car. Monsieur Lagreze frowned and hung back, coughing politely. 'Perhaps not,' he whispered, sounding apologetic. 'It would be in preference that we walk, I think,' he went on, raising his voice a little. 'Even such banalities as motorcars have an unpleasant symbolism at the moment.'

'Yes. Of course. I didn't think.'

'Some reveller could summon his friends and together they might overturn us before they realized which persons were inside. Walking, they will see you – and me,' he added, smiling shyly to underline the significance.

'Yes. Yes. Of course,' Oscar agreed returning the smile as he relocked the car door.

'I can arrange for it to be safely brought without interference to the embassy later, unless – '

'Thank you, Gilles. I would appreciate – '

'A pleasure. I had, in fact, intended to telephone you this morning to suggest a postponement of our daily game but – ' he shrugged and tapped the side of his head, looking sheepish ' – it slipped my mind.'

'Thank you,' Oscar felt obliged to say again.

'Fortunately no harm came to you.'

'No.'

'Ah. Now that is how it should be, wouldn't you say?' Monsieur Lagreze asked as they approached the recumbent, gently snoring dancer. 'That is how all our lives should be. Comfortably at peace with ourselves and our dreams. If only we could all shape such placidity within ourselves . . . That was *his* trouble, of course. Father Septimus. Always at the wildest war with himself. Always the furrowed brow. Always the mutterings of doom. Always the battles against what he denounced as *his* devil. *His* devil,' Monsieur Lagreze repeated. 'As though he had some special claim on the power of darkness. Mind you,' he went on, his voice becoming gentler as though he was regretting any criticism of the dead, 'it is possible that he had. The Irish seem to have a way with the supernatural, do they not? They strike me – in my small experience, and that only gleaned from books and one or two acquaintances – as feeling at home in the company of spirits.'

Nicholson made no reply. He grinned to himself, wondering what his mother would have made of such a scurrilous accusation. Images of his childhood suddenly flickered like warped cinematography across his mind: the family rosary every evening, his mother's slow, devout invocations, his own hastily gabbled responses, his father's good-humoured silence; the stations of the cross every first Friday; the Sunday masses; the perpetual supplications to Christ Jesus for help, for money, for happiness, for good results in exams, for work, for health, for –

'It was a pity in the end that he could not have been content to abide with his own spirits and leave our demons to us. Indeed, yes. And, like you, I warned him but he would not listen to me. Leave them alone, I told him. They are not as yours. You cannot hope to understand their bewitchment. But he would have none of that. *Mais non*, with his pious incantations he would defeat whatever evil dared hound him. As if those antiquated prayers could work! Here!' His face creased in genuine bewilderment. 'And yet,' he concluded, his voice filled with sorrow, 'for those mad beliefs he had to suffer so much.'

'Yes. He certainly – '

'Suffered so very much,' Gilles Lagreze repeated.

Oscar Nicholson abandoned his attempt to pass comment and took instead to nodding; he was still at it when they left the hotel grounds and set off towards the embassy, manfully striding down the Carrefour Road. He had been driven along this same frenetic thoroughfare when he first arrived on Haiti. The beaming, perspiring taxi-driver had treated the short journey as a glorious free-for-all, whipping his battered Buick between the stevedores (bent double under their loads of ice and charcoal, furniture and fish), between (but with considerably less abandon, his smile freezing on his thick lips) the occasional brace of Tontons Macoutes, braking every few yards to avoid colliding with one of those kaleidoscopic buses, the infamous tap-taps that careered on and off the roadway in search of yet more cargo, their drivers only sometimes looking where they were going through windscreens non-existent, shattered, begrimed, or so defaced with stickers advertising everything – beer, cigarettes, condoms, Mercedes Benz, stockings – as to be impenetrable. How dazzling it had all seemed, the more so since he had just terminated a nervy stint in dismal Zagreb, and how different now! The bossy *marchand* women, who had stood outside their shops and incomprehensibly extolled the quality of their wares, trying to drag passers-by inside to make a purchase, filling tourists with trivial insinuations of dread, had today gathered in small groups, bitterly surveying their wrecked establishments, bemoaning their looted goods, their exclamations as piercing and weird as a quarrion's squawk. Alas, the beautiful, sultry Dominican girls who had extolled *their* wares, lounging in doorways lined with caladium, had disappeared altogether, yet oddly their heavy, musky perfume seemed to linger in the air, reserving their pitch. The artisans (so involved in their labour they seldom raised an eye as they were photographed, discussed as though they could not hear or, far worse, did not exist) had packed their precious tools and slipped away. Many buildings still smouldered, the smoke itself heavy and damp. Timber, shards of glass and irregular oblongs of rusted corrugated iron were strewn everywhere. Starving dogs, pariahs, scavenged and argued viciously among piles of rotting fruit and vegetables, racing away, chased by the pack, if a morsel of meat was found. And yet, sitting in the gutter amid all this mayhem, as though deliberately determined to maintain a semblance of reason and calm, one man continued to work. His legs were both amputated from the knees. Wearing tattered clothes and a look of complete indifference, a bantam chicken on a string by his side, he conscientiously made shoes from old tyres, wielding his ferocious knife with the delicacy of a surgeon, his skin as black and abused as the rubber he shaped. Monsieur Lagreze observed him also. 'And so life continues,' he said mostly to himself.

'So it would seem.'

'Strange . . .'

' – ? What is?'

'Hmm? Oh, nothing. Nothing of importance. I just cannot ever remember seeing him before.'

'Why should you find that strange, Gilles?'

Monsieur Lagreze allowed himself a small embarrassed laugh. 'I don't quite know. Something . . . I don't know.'

They arrived without incident at the cemetery, a vast acreage of glistening white monuments, some like fantastic hallucinations. Angels in traditional poses abounded, bearing shields and swords, banners and lilies, all in the whitest marble: no stain on these celestial garments! Photographs of the interred had been placed at the foot of each headstone, showing them at their best, their prettiest or most handsome, often cheating the years by displaying long since ravaged images; Oscar had heard that all Haitians had such pictures taken in their prime for just this unhappy inevitability. And by every photograph the flowers, mostly plastic (a monstrous travesty in this land of lush, exotic flora), contorted into crucifixes, hearts, and occasionally some ludicrous conceit of a grieving mind. Now several of the gravestones had been overturned, many more were smashed, the graves desecrated. Monsieur Lagreze sucked air between his teeth, eyeing the scene balefully. 'They have uprooted him, you will have heard,' he said, his voice a whisper in the dismal place, his choice of expression making Oscar assume a barely stifled grin. 'Doctor Duvalier, I mean. Ripped his whitened bones from the earth and hurled them to the dogs.' He sounded shocked but not overly sorrowful. 'His skull impaled on a stake and carried high through the streets, jeered and spat upon as in ancient times.'

'It was pretty inevitable they would react – ' Oscar began.

'But of course. It has amused me how certain foreign journalists found this action so barbaric, as though they had never perceived that in times of great stress, great fear or great joy, people will always return to the consolation of their most primitive instincts.'

'I don't quite – '

Monsieur Lagreze seemed not to hear the interruption. 'Religion, I fear, has a lot to answer for,' he went on, shaking his head. 'That is why they killed poor Septimus in the way they did, of course. They could simply have murdered him, hacked his body to pieces and left it to rot in the gutter. Instead, they bestowed on him what they saw as their most prestigious death.'

'I've no doubt that thrilled him.'

'You think?' Monsieur Lagreze asked, ignoring the sarcasm. 'Yes. He would, I think, have recognized the significance of their gesture. After all, he knew them well enough.'

'Not as well as he thought, obviously.'

As they turned and moved away from the cemetery Monsieur Lagreze linked his arm through Oscar's; a small, intimate sign of affection left over from his student days at the Sorbonne, although not one that Oscar particularly appreciated. Nevertheless he tolerated it, as he did most things to avoid confrontation and fuss, and thus linked they strolled towards the end of the road in silence, passing overturned, burnt-out cars, oil drums (their contents still smouldering), groups of youths who eyed them but kept their distance, their hands behind their backs, rocking on the balls of their feet as if prepared to spring into violent action at the slightest provocation.

None too soon, as far as Oscar was concerned, they arrived at that point where the Carrefour burst into the open, giving a sense that the sea was at hand.

'Thank you for chaperoning me, Gilles,' Oscar said, sounding genuinely appreciative, releasing his arm.

Monsieur Lagreze dismissed the gratitude with a curt nod.

'I'm sure I can manage on my own from here,' Oscar assured him, holding out his hand.

Monsieur Lagreze looked dubious. 'If you are certain.'

'Quite certain. Look, the road is almost deserted.'

Monsieur Lagreze took Oscar's hand and shook it. There were certainly a few people to be seen, but they appeared to be harmless enough, going about their business, offering no sign of a threat. 'I would be happy to come with you if you so wish – ?'

'I'll be okay. It's only down there. Thank you for coming this far.'

'As you wish,' Monsieur Lagreze conceded, reluctant to impose his company, already hailing a touting taxi with that small, all but invisible, gesture normally used to summon a waiter.

'Thanks again, Gilles.'

'You will, perhaps, telephone me later? To reassure me of your safety – and, if you so desire, arrange a meeting for tomorrow?'

'I will. Of course,' Oscar said. 'Nothing must get in the way of our chess,' he added wryly. 'Must it?'

Monsieur Lagreze stepped into the taxi and slammed the door: twice before the catch fell into place. Immediately he lowered the window. 'Remember, you did everything you could to save the priest.'

'Yes. I know.'

'As did I.'

'Yes.'

'We are left to share our sorrow.'

Oscar nodded. 'I'll phone you later, Gilles.'

'Thank you.'

Sitting alone in the back of the taxi as it jounced its way over the rutted, unmaintained road that led to his home in Mariani (that discreet yet magnificent mansion he had designed himself) Gilles Lagreze lit one of those extra-long, tan-coloured, perfumed cigarettes he favoured while limiting himself to five a day. He left it to dangle in his lips, squinting as the smoke attacked his eyes. It was on this very road that he had first encountered Father Septimus Roach, almost knocking him from his bicycle (the monstrous, lightless, saddleless – unless a folded piece of sacking could count as a saddle – bicycle he used as transport, his soutane forever getting entangled in the spokes except when, which was rarely, he remembered to tuck it into the waistband of the rather natty pale-blue linen trousers he wore underneath, his feet scarred in the open-toed sandals which were called into service with grim regularity as the brakes failed). It had not been a propitious meeting.

– Idiot! Monsieur Lagreze roared, jumping with surprising agility from his car, ready to berate the stupid cyclist.

– Oh, I do so agree, Septimus had said with disarming candour. And I also apologise. I was, as they say, a million miles away – which would put me somewhere up there, wouldn't you say? he asked, pointing to the stars. Not paying attention. Something, between you and me, I seldom do, alas. Most remiss. I fear I trust my poor Modestine's judgment rather more than I should, he explained, pointing to the bicycle, then patting the handlebars.

– You could have been killed, Monsieur Lagreze snapped with fatuous logic, his anger deflated by the absurd simplicity of the man.

– Indeed I could. But who would have noticed? More to the point, who would have cared?

Monsieur Lagreze flicked his half-smoked cigarette out of the taxi window, then rolled it up again to exclude the swirling dust. So much for their introduction. Who would have deduced from that inauspicious beginning that two men of such divergent opinion, culture and belief would become ineluctably united by destiny? Who indeed. And yet only five months later, only ten days ago, when he had been given the news of the priest's horrendous death, Gilles Lagreze had wept. He had lost a friend. A dear friend:

enough, was it not, to make any man weep? But it was not so much his personal loss that made him cry. No. He mourned, he decided in the days that followed, the destruction of a man of unique integrity, a clown, a scatterbrain, an apprentice madman probably, but a being nonetheless whose dogged convictions, however quixotic and outrageous they might have appeared, had delivered him safely to the threshold of his fate. Safely from a physical point of view at least (albeit cruelly scarred and afflicted by a permanent limp, one leg an inch or so shorter than the other, which impediment he compensated for by using a stick, an old niblick in fact, the leather binding long since unravelled from the shaft, the metal head firmly grasped in his talonous and nailless fingers); his mind was another matter, constantly culling up nightmares and flashing images of past horrors.

Still, oblivious to all this on their first encounter, Gilles Lagreze, already peeved at being brusquely summoned from his comfortable bed and less comfortable delights of Albert Camus to listen while the President for Life proclaimed his latest ridiculous whim, had taken an instant, uncharacteristic dislike to the gangling, diffident priest; regarding him as yet another abject example of the useless flotsam the Church, in its disinterested wisdom, had decided was good enough for a congregation unlikely, in any case, to be persuaded to abandon its darkly voodooistic practices. Gilles Lagreze had seen plenty such clergy in his time: always old, they sailed in and ambled aimlessly through their circumscribed rituals, content enough that God could understand their intent even if the people couldn't. And when they died, welcoming death from their sanctimonious standpoint as a release from their taunting mediocrity, they left not a single thing behind apart from their rotting flesh and the memory of the smile of tolerant superiority that had been etched on their lips from the moment they arrived. It was, however, a fact (and the memory now brought a sad smile to his lips) that Septimus Roach had disliked him also, regarding him (as he later admitted amid much waving of conciliatory hands and begging for forgiveness for such wanton misjudgment) as a caricature of the rich black who lived in resplendent luxury off the backs of his fellow Haitians. Yet five months later, the last few weeks of which had seemed an eternity of uncertainty, Gilles Lagreze was forced to recognise his genuine grief and deep concern at the foreseeable catastrophe which had drawn them together. Through those months Septimus, without ever prying, without even questioning, had learned almost every-thing there was to know about him, his uncertainties, his fears, his despairs; while he, Gilles Lagreze, had succeeded in learning nothing about Septimus Roach. Or almost nothing.

He paid off the taxi, tipping generously, waiting for it to leave and the dust to settle before walking slowly through the beautiful garden towards the house that gleamed in the high sun. He fanned himself with his wide-brimmed panama, as if to whisk away the doubts that nagged at the hem of his brain. He had definitely tried to restrain the priest, had he not? Certainly he had: patiently, even good-naturedly, he had suffered the interminable rantings long after others (who should have been more inclined to listen, who were, at any rate, supposedly on his ecclesiastical wavelength) had ceased to tolerate his presence. Grunting, he bent and deadheaded a rose, a pungent Enid Harkness, with his long, sharp thumbnail. He had even befriended the wretched man, giving him food and clothes to be distributed among his 'children', arranging for restricted medicines to be delivered to his shanty-town hospice, pleading his cause with the President himself (an action not without considerable personal risk), thus saving him, on more than one occasion, from instant incarceration if not, indeed, a fate decidedly more terminal. Yes, Gilles Lagreze told himself now, he had, in fact 'saved' the priest in every possible sense of the word except, of course, spiritually, which was entirely his own affair. And what had he received in return? Nothing. Not a solitary thing. Not even, as far as he could recall, a word of thanks. He shook his head, still bewildered as to why he had gone out of his way so often to aid the ubiquitous priest. He stared at the seedhead in his fingers, squeezing it as if to extract inspiration from the miracle within, then tossed it away with a heavy sigh. Not that he had wanted nor expected anything; at least, nothing more than that the rebellious lunatic might have shown a little more discretion, a little more thoughful-ness. And, the thought now loomed, been rather less critical of the way he, Gilles Lagreze, lawyer, sometime philosopher, lapsed Catholic, occasional philanthropist, had chosen to live out his life. But for all that, now that he was gone, the crazy priest left a terrible void, decamping from the world with grotesque theatrics (admittedly not of his own devising) and selfishly taking with him something irredeemably precious, something Gilles Lagreze needed . . .

Sighing again, this time deeper and aloud, he opened the ornate front door and let himself in to the welcoming coolness of the long, high, marble hall. The truth was, he admitted to himself, placing his hat on the Dutch marquetry table and gathering up the bundle of letters and periodicals awaiting his attention, he had acquired, unlikely though it was, a kinship, an identity with the befuddled cleric. Like Septimus he strove, as every human did, to ward off the messenger of death; but like Septimus also, he knew in his heart he would welcome it when it came.

– God is so merciful, Septimus had once said in one of his more pacific, rational moods. He whips away our life just at the point when we are about to become useless.

And Monsieur Lagreze, for all his outward show of complacent contentment, had felt useless for some considerable time; had, indeed, been made to feel more so by Septimus himself, his blood-shot, penetrating eyes forever accusing him. Even now, standing in the hallway surrounded by his treasures, without, one might assume, a care in the world, Gilles Lagreze could feel those same eyes burrowing into his brain, presaging a bleak continuance of such harassment, unless –

Gilles Lagreze sighed for the third time, and tossed his mail back onto the table. 'Damn you, priest,' he muttered to himself as he made his way up the wide, carpeted staircase, the luxurious pleasure of a cold shower beckoning. 'Damn you, priest.'

TWO

'*Le prêtre est arrivé*! . . . The priest has arrived!'

Well before the protesting, lumbering freighter *Orlac* had docked, having weathered an Atlantic storm, Father Septimus Roach, standing in the prow, his face ˙scorched a brilliant scarlet by the sun and salted wind, his soutane flapping about him, heard the cry, high-pitched as a ziraleen, skimming off the swell. Ah, yes, he thought, the priest has arrived. They might as well have cried that the fool has arrived, God's untamed jester, with bells ajingle and a missal filled with jolly drollery. For he who has been dispatched to lead you on the righteous path towards God is himself lost, his celestial compass thwarted by the unerring pull of his sad degradation . . .

– Ah. Father Roach! Bishop McKewen kept his welcome diligently formal while his secretary was in the room.

– My Lord, Septimus reciprocated solemnly but with a mischievous twinkle in his watery eyes, genuflecting to kiss the bishop's unusually simple episcopal ring.

– How are you, Septimus? the bishop enquired, sounding truly concerned, as the secretary withdrew and closed the door. Do get up.

Septimus rose as he was bid, pressing both hands on one knee and heaving himself upright with a grimace of pain. Rheumaticky – and anxious, he answered.

– Anxious? Oh dear. Now why should that be?

– Because, Matthew, each time you summon me it is, alas, more often than not to reprimand me for some debatable misdemeanour.

The bishop smiled tolerantly. Blasphemy debatable?

Septimus gave a wicked cackle. Oh. *That*. Yes, well . . .

– Yes, *that*, Septimus. Do you feel up to a stroll in the garden? Without waiting for a reply the bishop made for the French windows and opened them. I always take a small constitutional this time of the evening, weather permitting, he explained. Mind that step, he warned, reaching out to help Septimus. It wobbles. I have been meaning to have it fixed all summer but . . . He shrugged.

They walked along the narrow gravelled path, the bishop leading the way. Septimus, he said without looking round, picking a sprig of mimosa and rubbing it between his palms, we, my superiors and I that is, have decided it is time for you to take a rest. A few months – a year at most – in a monastery has been suggested as most likely to benefit you . . . He passed on the information almost casually.

– The trouble is, Septimus was saying, as I see it – and there is still some logic in these old grey cells yet, believe it or not – the trouble is that it is almost impossible to stick to the law of the church and be compassionate at the same time. A monastery? Oh, I think not.

– It is just to give you the time to –

– I have been studying how I may compare this prison where I live unto the world, Septimus quoted. Poor Richard. Mind you, I do agree it is taking a liberty to substitute monastery for prison, although –

– Septimus! Will you stop chattering for *one* minute –

– And here is not a creature but myself, I cannot do it –

The bishop stopped abruptly in his tracks, placing himself squarely in front of Septimus, blocking the path. For goodness sake will you listen to me, Septimus?

– Yet I'll hammer't out, Septimus concluded. I *am* listening to you, Matthew.

– I want you to try and understand that we are all – the Primate included – deeply concerned about you. The decision was not taken lightly. We are all only too well aware of the terrible ordeal you suffered in Paraguay, how it must still cause you dreadful pain. But we are only trying to help. We are thinking only of you.

Septimus raised his eyebrows mockingly. Of me, Matthew?

– Of course.

– Not of –

– And of the people you have scandalized since your return from South America. I really am sorry, Septimus. I do try and understand what you are going through. God alone knows how what you went through must have affected your –

– Mind?

– life. But really, last week's episode was the final straw.

And the bishop had a point. Even Septimus could appreciate
this although he could also see that, once again, his motives had
been cruelly misconstrued . . . Standing in front of the tabernacle,
having bravely negotiated the prickly intricacies of transubstantiation (in his hands the silver chalice, filled with the wine he himself
had transformed into the blood of Christ, that same Christ for
Whom he had all the love in the world but Whom he had betrayed
time and time again) he paused and staggered slightly as though
suddenly lumbered with an unexpectedly virulent migraine. Behind
him, heads bowed with reverence and indomitable faith, was the
inevitable multitude of worshippers, while to his left, enthroned,
glowered the Papal Nuncio, Cardinal Caspigi, mitred and coped,
resplendent for this glorious Easter ceremony. The entire pro-
Cathedral echoed with the excited, sensual hum he had noticed so
often, in so many languages, in basilicas, in humbler churches of
wattle-and-daub, in converted school houses, in tents, as people
muttered their belated adorations, verbally cleansing their souls to
make themselves worthy to receive the Holy Eucharist. Their faith
was so uncomplicated, so natural; it was as though the Christ they
were about to consume was a very different Christ to the Christ he
had given himself but moments before. Theirs was the loving Christ,
the Christ of compassion and understanding – and swept up in an
uncontrollable longing to share in this he was, grotesquely, guzzling
the contents of the chalice, recognizing it as blood, certainly,
but not Christ's blood that oozed through the awful labyrinth
of his memory, as it trickled from the corners of his mouth.
Weeping beyond control, he reached to the side of the altar and
replenished the chalice, consuming that too. All the while a small
voice, perhaps his own (although it sounded nothing like his own),
begged to be included in the warm gentleness of God; and then
he was screaming, a strangely unmusical sound, and lying on the
floor in front of the altar . . . Yes, I'm sorry about that,
Matthew, Septimus said, bending down to retrieve the mimosa
the bishop had discarded. I don't really know what came over me.
Or, to be truthful, I do, but I doubt if you'd understand. I was
trying, you see, to share in – never mind. I suppose it caused
quite a stir?

– You could say that.

– Yes. I suppose it would.

– You can appreciate why, I hope?

– Oh, indeed.

– And why it was decided that a period of complete rest and calm might be –

– But a monastery, Matthew!

– Can't you see how lenient we are being? The bishop shivered suddenly. Come, let's go back inside.

– Inside? Septimus asked as though he found the word ominous. Oh. Yes. Yes.

– Sit down, Septimus, Bishop McKewen said, closing the windows. He waited in silence until Septimus was seated before moving round behind his enormous mahogany desk and perching himself on the impressive carved chair with its six-inch additions to each leg so that he, a small, plump, puckish man, could appear more prelatic.

– What are we going to do with you, my friend? he asked, shaking his head sadly and idly toying with his handsome pectoral cross. Whatever are we going to do with you?

So, joy of joys, ahem, perhaps no irrevocable decision had been taken on his dubious future. Septimus looked suddenly cheerful. I thought, he stated blandly, hoping that a little levity, a little banter and bluff, might bring about an escape, however temporary, from his predicament. I thought you had decided that I should be to a nunnery gone!

– It is no joking matter, Septimus, Bishop McKewen said, trying to sound severe but failing.

– No, of course not.

– Of all the times to choose –

– I didn't exactly *choose* it, Matthew. It just crept up on me.

– And on top of all that, just when I had succeeded in mollifying the Cardinal, what happens? You come out with your outrageous statements advocating divorce, and –

– Not advocating, Matthew. Suggesting –

– Suggesting, the Bishop, a fair man, corrected.

– and only in special cases.

– Will you not interrupt me, Septimus!

Septimus was taken aback by the Bishop's vehemence, if only briefly. Nevertheless he hung his head and looked properly contrite.

Mea culpa, mea culpa, mea maxima culpa, he intoned under his breath. I'm sorry, Matthew, he said aloud.

– If only your apologies were sincere. If only your sorrow would suffice. I know it isn't all your fault. God knows I have tried to understand. If only you would learn to think before you bombard people with your outlandish concepts, before you rush headlong into situations that really are no concern of yours. But then, I suppose you're incapable of doing that, Bishop McKewen concluded, immediately frowning as though fearing he might have caused unnecessary pain.

Apparently not. Septimus looked quite happy, any unintentional insult having skated over his head. And he would have admitted, if pushed, that his friend, the bishop, had been close enough to the mark. Like the Ancient Mariner, Septimus Roach was consumed by the extraordinary tale he believed he had been ordained to tell; unlike the old salt, however, he seemed to attract only the most adverse attention. Yet it had not always been thus. As an altar-boy at the Tranquilla Convent in Rathmines, impossibly angelic in those days, with golden curls and cherubic face and deep blue eyes that hinted even then at divine secrecy, he had prompted Sister Emmanuel to exclaim in her customary monastic whisper, 'My, what a perfect little lamb he is and no mistake,' to which Septimus, already precocious, retorted unkindly, 'to the slaughter, no doubt.' Even at school, where the Benedictines educated, not taught, educated him – quite a different thing since it meant one learned something that could prove useful in later life rather than having a suffocating curriculum frantically drummed into one's bored consciousness – he had been lauded for his intelligence and perception. And later, as a student at the University of Caen, he had achieved quite outstanding results in his quest for a licence in modern languages, despite a none-too-diligent application and despite, too, the lure of the somewhat meagre fleshpots of St Malo (not to mention the occasional ribald jaunts to Paris, where he ogled the lighted photographs of the nudes outside the seedy bars in the Place Pigalle, wondering, even at that late age – beloved, stultified, terrified Irish youth – what all the fuss was about). Later still, as a steward on the *Durban Castle*, he had been recognised by his fellow crewmen as someone apart; they came to him with their problems, listening to his advice with something akin to awe. And after that? Well, after that he became, as they politely say, lost. He took on a series of outlandish occupations: navvy, itinerant gardener, zoo-keeper, if only of crocodiles – descendants of Sobek bludgeoned by boredom into a state of total lethargy, wallowing in muddy ponds, dreaming of the great Zambezi. There followed, incredibly, a spell as a busker; how he got away with this was anybody's guess, his talent minimal, his voice tuneless, the saxophone (picked up cheap on the Portobello Road) slung from one shoulder, reedless and unplayable, but get away with it he did and earned a pretty penny to boot, sympathy loot it was called. Then, suddenly, and for no good reason he could ever identify, he was smitten by the vocation that had been banging, although quite unrecognized, in his head like a williwaw for as long as he could remember. He returned to Ireland. He entered St John's College in the county of Waterford, not a stone's throw from Tramore and the racecourse where he had seen his first race, taken there at the age of eight by his parents, and backed his first (his only!) winner, a small grey filly called Impeccable.

– All I said, Matthew –

– I know what you said. I was there, Bishop McKewen snapped.

– So you were! Well, then, you can appreciate, surely, why I suggested it was a bit unfair to expect people – people who find it difficult enough to stay on speaking terms with God – to spend the rest of their natural days chained to someone the sight of whom they cannot any longer stand.

Bishop McKewen put his head in his hands and uttered a long groan.

– Anyway, Septimus went on, there must be some little place you could send me? Somewhere I would be of use? Somewhere out of the way. Out of earshot, so to speak. Somewhere whence news of any of my – what did you call them? eccentricities? was it you who said that? – would not be broadcast. Somewhere – He stopped talking abruptly, a look of anguish on his face, as he noticed the bishop already shaking his head. Nowhere? he asked plaintively.

– I'm afraid not, Septimus.

– Nowhere at all?

– Nowhere at all. Unless . . . The bishop's eyes lit up as though by a spark of inspiration.

Septimus brightened appreciably also. Unless? he prompted.

Bishop McKewen fixed his friend with a baleful look that seemed on the point of permanency. Then he opened the centre drawer of his desk and began to rummage, tut-tutting to himself, piling sheaves of paper on to the leatherbound blotter in front of him. Ah, he said at last, smiling in minor triumph, extracting one letter from the collection, and giving it a small wave of victory. I wonder . . . he said, almost to himself, staring at it, tapping it with one finger. I just wonder.

Septimus waited, hardly daring to breathe.

– It's a letter I received – some time ago, I'm afraid – from the Archbishop of Port au Prince.

Septimus frowned. Port au Prince?

– Hmm. Haiti. The bishop studied the letter. He requests, begs, our assistance. He urgently needs priests to –

Septimus was on his feet, his eyes dancing. Why not send me, Matthew?

Bishop McKewen placed the letter carefully on his desk and made a steeple of his fingers; with his elbows firmly planted on top of the letter he used the steeple to support his chin, staring at Septimus, pondering the undoubtedly delinquent implications of any foolhardy decision he might make.

– You *have* to send me, Matthew, Septimus pleaded, becoming agitated, hopping from foot to foot.

– I don't *have* –

– But you *do*, Matthew. Can't you see? Septimus asked, sitting, then getting up again, pacing about the room, gesticulating as he tried desperately to form irrefutable arguments in his mind.

– I was about to say that I don't have the jurisdiction to endorse any such position for you, Septimus. And what do you expect me to see, anyway? More sleepless nights for myself as I worry about what demented theories you are promulgating?

– I will be a model of diplomacy, Septimus promised, donning his most engaging expression. I promise I will –

– Will you just sit down? Please? This prancing about is most, most irritating.

Septimus dropped on to his chair as though shot.

– As I was saying, I, personally, do not have the power to agree to any –

– But you could get –

– It would be a matter for discussion with my superiors.

– Ah, but you could persuade them to agree, Septimus cajoled, keeping his own persuasion flying high.

– Perhaps. Perhaps. But you know what their most virile argument against you will be, don't you?

Septimus certainly did, but he was in no mood to admit as much. What? he asked as innocently as he could manage for the moment.

The bishop smiled tolerantly, in no way hoodwinked. That you have not as yet recovered from your breakdown.

– But I have, Matthew. Fully. Look! Septimus flexed his muscles and thumped his chest.

The bishop smothered a laugh. Have you truly?

– Look at me, Septimus insisted.

– There *are* those in the diocese who believe – well, let's just say there are those who think your ordeal in Paraguay has left too indelible a mark.

– There are those who say, Septimus decided to point out, that I am quite, quite mad.

To his surprise and chagrin Bishop McKewen only nodded his agreement. Septimus went suddenly very quiet. Even as that mute diagnosis of wavering sanity, however mild and harmless and infrequent, rattled in his brain like the forlorn cry of the wishtonwish, even then he knew there *was* a madness that raged within him, a cunning, versatile lunacy that seemed always on the point of exploding, a pain that consumed his mind leaving him gibbering, an incontinent fool, so that on one memorable occasion (for some odd reason surrounded by serious faces staring down at him, faces brown as leather, faces not smiling yet not angry either, faces that analytically studied the process of his torment) he had been reduced to a simplicity that made it feasible to scream 'Pain, pain, go away, come again another day' although even this plaintive brimborium had gone unheeded.

But: what right had anyone, even his dear, kind, considerate, bepurpled friend, the Lord Bishop Matthew McKewen, to suggest that he could not cope with his affliction, or that it would in any way hinder his capability to minister to the needs of others equally afflicted if in other ways, or that it was anything more than just another of life's cantankerous burdens, a special cross he was forced to bear while stumbling along his own particular *via dolorosa*? How could anyone (least of all the well-adjusted prelates in whose hands his destiny now appeared to rest) know what it was like to have the simple face of faith transformed into a metaphysical nightmare that made prayer, his prayer at any rate, seem wilfully redundant, and left him floundering in that region as dark as the House of Usher, unable to forgive God? And all the while tormented by horrific visitations from the spectre of his own derelict unworthiness as he witnessed the strengthening love of Christ being gradually withdrawn.

– Et tu, Matthew? he now asked, sounding bitter and instantly regretting it.

But Bishop McKewen charitably overlooked any such impertinence, and smiled tolerantly in the manner of a man well used to being misunderstood. No, Septimus, he said finally. Of course I do not think you are mad. If I did, well . . . No, but I do believe that there is something within you that is unfamiliar to other men, myself included. Something savage that drives you with such force that it impairs your judgment and obscures the true nature of your vocation.

To the Bishop's surprise Septimus agreed, perhaps only as a belated mark of atonement for his earlier insult. Yes, he agreed flatly, looking towards the window as though trying to catch a glimpse of something that was fast disappearing in the accumulating dusk.

– If only you would tell us what is so tormenting you, perhaps we could be more understanding?

If only you would tell us! Septimus Roach looked very forlorn and vulnerable, his eyes dull and lifeless, failing to locate whatever it was they sought outside the window and instead turning reluctantly inwards on his soul. If only he could! Yet there had been a time when he knew exactly what spurred him on, when the countenance of life had seemed clear enough. But that was before he had suffered the humiliation and anguish of beholding his faith dissemble; it was as though that faith had been his only on a sort of mystical hire-purchase and he had failed to keep up the payments. Yet, as Blake well knew, there was a path through hell, which was a good thing; and from time to time, usually when least expected, a glimmer of his former unquestioning belief and trust returned, and he could hear Christ if only as a tiny wayward roar, out of reach yet within reach, receding or moving generously towards him, always offering, despite his inadequacy, to save him. Then that moment was gone, whisked away, he was rejected, and the blackness of despair would seep into every fibre of his consciousness, and he would cry, and attempt to hide his lonely soul in shadows cast for his benefit, out of pity (out of love?) by a commiserating seraph, and die, all over again, his own pathetic death.

– There is nothing to tell, Matthew, Septimus said, shaking his head as if to dislodge the lie. Nothing whatever to tell.

Bishop McKewen gave a heavy sigh, pained that he was, yet again, to be excluded from his friend's confidence, aware that, if allowed, he could probably help. He thought about switching on the light, but somehow even the light struck him as an intrusion. He leaned back in his chair and watched the darkness roll into the room on soundless padded feet, the tragic priest slipping away from him before he had time to reassure him, to tell him that he too, Bishop Matthew McKewen, the last of the truly paternal prelates no less, had trodden the solitary path of doubt, as all men did, had been saved only by humility, a virtue, alas, unlikely to be forthcoming in Septimus Roach. How eagerly darkness came! Yet not as eagerly, it appeared, as the voice that loomed out of the gathering shadows: You will arrange for me to go, won't you, Matthew?

Bishop McKewen snapped on the lamp that stood on his desk. It is not, as I told you, Septimus, for me to decide. But I will do what I can.

– When will you know?

– A week. Ten days.

– That long?

The bishop suppressed a smile. Yes. That long. You must be patient, Septimus. You must always be patient. Particularly with yourself.

– Patience, Matthew, is a luxury only afforded those with ample time.

– You have ample time.

Septimus shook his head. I'm afraid not. I have – and don't ask me to explain this – I have the feeling that I have very little time.

Bishop McKewen remained silent, waiting.

– You don't, I'm sure, believe in premonitions? Septimus asked after a while, sounding hopeful even as he posed the question.

– I believe that God in His infinite wisdom and mercy sometimes allows us a foreglimpse of what awaits us in certain, critical circumstances, perhaps warning us of the pitfalls that await our indiscretions.

– Ah, Septimus sighed. Pitfalls. Yes.

– Why do you ask?

– Because – Septimus stopped abruptly and frowned, looking acutely embarrassed.

– Because? the bishop persisted.

– Because, Septimus commenced again, once more hesitating, this time to emit a wry chuckle. Because I have this recurring vision of my death.

– Your death? Bishop McKewen sounded perturbed.

– Yes. Not that I understand it. More's the pity. No matter. An hallucination, I suspect, rather than any divine – what did you call it? – any divine foreglimpse of specific eventualities. Fortunately. Still, the *via dolorosa* has been travelled, has it not, so it is not so outlandish an outcome to expect? Perhaps it is inevitable. On the other hand, of course it could –

– Septimus, the bishop called gently.

– Yes?

– I think it is time you went home.

– Home? For a moment Septimus seemed to find the word a puzzlement. Oh. Home. Yes. Indeed, it is, Matthew. High time. I will arise and go now, as the poet had it. He got slowly to his feet. You *will* let me know the instant there is any news – good or bad?

– Of course. As soon as any decision has been taken I'll be in touch.

– Without delay?

– Without delay.

Septimus made his way stiffly across the room and opened the door. There, he paused and turned, and for several seconds stared back towards the bishop, who, feigning annoyance, scowled and demanded: What is it *now* Septimus?

– It just struck me, I don't know why – why at this very moment, I mean, one of your foreglimpses, perhaps – that I have never really thanked you for all your kindnesses to me, Matthew. For all your efforts to understand.

Bishop McKewen blinked and pretended he had just noticed another letter that required his urgent attention.

– Thank you, Matthew.

The bishop looked up. You're welcome, my friend. I wish I could have done more.

– What more could you possibly have done?

And saying that, Septimus smiled: a curious, eager, bright, hopeful smile filled with the promise of salvation, perhaps, or with the hope of salvation which was almost as good, and left the room . . .

And it was with just such a curious, eager, bright, hopeful smile that he disembarked from the freighter *Orlac*, hauling the single suitcase behind him down the swaying gangplank, sniffing the air, and over his shoulder a golf-club that seemed to be the cause of considerable merriment to the crowd.

The traders ranted and screamed for the privilege of replenishing the freighter's stores, hurling samples of their produce towards the gigantic Pole who stood, bearded like a pirate and with feet wide apart, on the deck. Their eyes fixed on his face as he tested their wares, they watched anxiously for that single, all but imperceptible nod that would signify acceptance; then pushing and shoving up the still-thronged gangplank, their merchandise on their backs – in nets, sacks, boxes, baskets, whatever had come most readily to hand. The three half-naked longshoremen called to each other as they wrapped the mooring ropes about the rusting stanchions, walking around them, keeping perfect pace with one another as though it was all a precisely rehearsed tribal ceremony. A dozen or so Tontons Macoutes stood by, unsmiling, some with cigarettes dangling from their lips, their uniforms scruffy, their rifles, held in both hands across their bellies, proclaiming their accessibility to death.

'*Père* Septimus?' His name was lobbed over the clamour by an immensely tall, angular half-caste Haitian, his hair Negro-textured but fiery red, his long bony face covered in rossals, his eyes green and furtive and cunning. He flapped his arms like a seabull's flippers as he signalled Septimus to remain just where he was, then battled his way towards him through the crowd, by performing an extraordinary variety of breast-stroke that succeeded admirably. '*Père* Septimus?'

Septimus nodded. 'Yes. In person.'

The Haitian beamed. 'I am Patrick. I am to drive you to the palace of our Archbishop.'

'Thank you.'

'You are to follow me.'

'Lead on, MacDuff.'

' – ? Patrick. I am Patrick.'

'Ah. Yes. Quite. Lead on McPatrick.'

Obediently Septimus followed his guide back through the crowd which parted respectfully to let him pass. They bowed their heads as he went by, but peeped at him from under their eye-lids and shuffled their feet, so that by the time Septimus had reached his transport they were facing that also, their backs to the freighter.

'This is the motor,' Patrick announced with inordinate pride, opening the rear door of the black Packard that had seen better days, had gleamed off the assembly line in Detroit unaware that its fate was to be the transportation of a succession of Haitian hierarchy along the pot-holed roads of erstwhile Hispaniola. 'I am the only one who drives this excellent motor,' he added, wiping an unwelcome fingerprint from the chrome with his cuff.

Septimus eyed askance the framed reproduction of what someone believed to be a fair image of the Sacred Heart that was affixed to the small maplewood door of what might once have been a cocktail cabinet (but surely wasn't now?). Cosseted in the unaccustomed luxury, the electric partition between himself and the driver lowered, Septimus wondered why it was that all the smiling faces that had greeted him so winningly had also seemed to harbour such a curious menace, had seemed to mock him but in a cheerful enough way as though, at the same time, they were generously trying to warn him; just as, indeed, but without the menace, Bishop McKewen had tried to warn him.

– Well, Septimus, really against my better judgement, I have done what you asked. I have managed to persuade my superiors to let you go to Haiti on loan.

Septimus looked as though he might cry. Thank you, Matthew. I –

– However –

– Ah –

– I must warn you –

– 'The grimmest warning cometh from the friendliest lips . . .'

– Will you be quiet? I must warn you that as far as your missionary work is concerned this is definitely your last chance. If –

– Matthew, I'll – sorry.

– If so much as a hint of a complaint filters back you will be instantly recalled, and from that moment on there will be absolutely nothing I can do to help you. Do you understand?

– I understand, Matthew. I will be constantly on my very best behaviour. I will control all my –

– Septimus: all you have to do is to try and be a good priest.

– Oh, that too, of course –

– *Only* that, Septimus. Nothing more.

– Surely –

– Only that, Bishop McKewen reiterated firmly. Septimus bowed his head. No heroics. No histrionics. No dabbling in local politics. No dubious interpretations of holy doctrine. No criticism of how the Church manages its affairs in Haiti.

– Oh dear –

– And certainly no more episodes like –

– You mean –

– I mean if you start any –

– I won't –

– kind of activity that displeases the Archbishop –

– How will I know?

– you will find yourself straight back here to face the most stringent and –

– Good heavens! –

– *Will* you stop interrupting? Now, the bishop continued, having stunned Septimus into silence, Now. Archbishop Gidron has been advised that you are coming. He has also, I think it fair to point out, been advised that we consider your position there as temporary, and that you *might* be recalled without notice. Do I make myself clear?

– Crystal, Matthew.

– Good. I most sincerely hope so. Bishop McKewen changed his tone from strict to compassionate. All we want you to do, Septimus, is to be the good and caring priest we all know you can be.

– I will try, Septimus promised. I promise.

The bishop sighed. I know you will, but you have made so many promises before.

– But I *do* try, Matthew.

– I know you do. And you mean well in almost everything

34

you do. He gave a short chuckle. It must be the Irish in us that –

'You are Irish, no?' Septimus wrenched himself back. 'You are an Irish person, no?' Patrick asked again, watching Septimus in the rearview mirror.

'Oh. Irish. Yes.'

'I am also Irish.'

Septimus frowned, wondering from what similar words he could have misconstrued what the driver said. Failing: 'I beg your pardon? he asked.

'I am also Irish,' Patrick repeated, grinning hugely.

So there had been no mistake this time, no impish goblin out to baffle him. 'Oh?' was all Septimus could muster.

'My father was Irish.'

'Ah.'

'A magnificent man.'

'I'm sure.'

'A navigator of the oceans.'

'A navigator, no less.'

'You will have heard of William Butler Yeats?'

Septimus jumped. 'Surely not – '

'Oh no,' Patrick interposed quickly, laughing uproariously, a high-pitched cackle that complemented the grinding, protesting springs of the ancient Packard as it swerved to avoid a dejected pony (which should have been of rather more light-hearted an aspect, decorated, as it was, with multicoloured feathers, the harness embellished with chips of glistening glass) hauling a painted cart piled high with melons which stayed in place, seemingly, from sheer optimism. 'Oh no. Indeed no. It was not the great William Butler Yeats who was my father – '

'Ah,' Septimus sighed to himself, gratified.

'But it was from his quotations that I practised my very excellent English.'

Fascinating though this information was, albeit with little evidence, as yet, to support it, Patrick appeared disinclined to expand further, and took to concentrating on his driving, in the nick of time as it turned out; hunching over the steering wheel, peering myopically through the windscreen, he swerved yet again, this time to the right, narrowly missing a ragged cripple who scooted across the road on his buttocks.

Septimus was grateful for the silence; the assimilation of English through the prowess of William Butler Yeats was all very well, quite a remarkable achievement in fact, but it was not a matter startling enough to dislodge the feeling of oppression that had settled on him as soon as the *Orlac* hove within sight of land, an oppression borne towards him, he sensed, by the rolling sea while pelicans, diving headlong into the spume, tried to distract him, or warn him of some outrage long since proclaimed.

'Within five minutes you will be meeting our Archbishop,' Patrick now announced, sharply turning left through an ornate Gothic-Caribbean gateway beside which seven giant palms grew (had grown for hundreds of years, but losing their splendour now, their huge fronds wilting astonished perhaps at the calamity of civilisation that had crept up and surrounded them). He took a peaked cap from the seat beside him, and clamped it firmly on his head with one hand, pressing it down with fingers splayed on the crown, then prodding with his forefinger at a few recalcitrant curls that protruded from beneath the brim, assuming a posture of dignified, haughty servility.

Septimus felt a nerve near his eye start to jump and blinked rapidly. A sense of trepidation overtook him, the same jittery nervousness he had felt when summoned by Bishop McKewen to hear the outcome of the prelate's deliberations, although he told himself, rubbing his eyes, that if the outcome of this visit was as satisfactory all would be well.

'You have been told he is dying?'

Septimus froze, his hands still at his eyes, the nerve thumping worse than ever. 'Dying?'

'Hah! They did not reveal that to you. It is always so. The utterance of such words is forever taboo.'

'I – ' Septimus heard himself utter the single word but instantly forgot with what he had intended to follow it; it hung there, alone and abandoned, waiting to be rescued.

'You will find him very frail and *very* bad tempered. You will not like him, of course,' Patrick predicted flatly, slowing the car to a crawl and chasing off an opaque, long-legged, wide-winged insect that sought to escape through the windscreen, finally finding freedom and zooming away through the side window. 'Nobody likes the Archbishop now. The proximity of his demise frightens them. As if death was contagious,' Patrick concluded with a scoffing snort. Then he added seriously, 'Of course that will not concern you, *Père*, since all can see that you are already afflicted.'

Père Septimus Roach allowed this grim observation to settle in his mind, too stunned, too disconsolate to make a reply. So there it was again, he thought, bowing his head until his chin rested on his chest, and closing his eyes. Yet again someone (and again someone who could not possibly have gauged the depth of his sorrow) had visited upon him the numinous accusation that he was already afflicted with the awesome seal of death; that he was, possibly, already dead, or if not precisely dead as near to it as made no difference whatever.

' – be your consolation,' Patrick was saying, smiling quite encouragingly, stopping the car to permit an elderly peacock to parade across the driveway, glorious feathers undisplayed, making it appear mournfully drab.

Consolation: that sounded hopeful, and Septimus perked up a little. He opened his eyes in time to see the peacock, swaggering now with arrogant bravura, saying, it seemed, 'Look at me. I carry the eye of God on my plumage, but that eye is closed to you, you absurd priest, closed because we knew you were to pass this way', before disappearing into the shrubbery that divided the drive from the lawn.

' – cannot grieve for what one carries on one's shoulders,' Patrick continued blithely, prattling on in veiled parables (and what possible role William Butler Yeats could have played in such chaotic symbolism was anybody's guess). 'You do understand?'

Foolishly, without thinking, Septimus nodded.

'I knew you would.'

'I didn't mean – ' Septimus tried to protest.

'You – like my father, like William Butler Yeats – will be a truly magnificent man,' Patrick announced, ignoring the attempted protest, perhaps not hearing it. 'I can feel it here,' he added, for some obscure reason patting himself on the back of the neck with one hand while manoeuvring the car in an arc with the other, bringing it to a standstill in front of Archbishop Gidron's palace (if a rather modest two-storey house of minimal charm and no architectural attraction could be categorized as palatial). He turned in his seat to gaze quizzically at Septimus, keeping the engine running

37

and gunning the accelerator from time to time with his toe. 'And I am never wrong.'

Septimus gave him a weak, wry smile. 'Then you are indeed blessed. I, alas, am always wrong.'

'Only until now.'

'Of course only until now, although I do not foresee much change for the better in the immediate future.'

'That is because you fear the debt of living, *mon Père*. There will, I promise you, be great changes. We have been waiting so long for you to come. You have been – '

'Waiting? For me? To come?'

'But yes!'

'You mean for a priest to come. Yes. Well, I hope – '

'For *you* to come. Why do you believe so many made their way to the dockside to greet your propitious arrival? We do not welcome *every* priest in this way.'

'But – '

'The wisest, most respected houngain of all predicted your arrival over a year ago and we have been waiting since that day to welcome you,' Patrick revealed blandly, although for a moment a curious faraway, almost sleepy look invaded his eyes. 'And the bokors agreed. We have been occupied in preparing the way for you.'

Septimus, his mouth slightly open, felt hypnotised. He wanted to laugh, but the sinister sincerity of the driver's voice precluded any such levity; he wanted to cry, as he had so often wanted to cry when overwhelmed by unfathomable elements of spiritual treachery, but that most human of reactions also was denied him. He felt, inexplicably, very cold despite the oppressive heat of the early afternoon, felt as if some thirsty, vampiric spirit had sucked all the warmth from his veins, from his heart; most terrible of all, he recognised the entire ridiculous episode as being frighteningly familiar, the chilling prelude to some greater catastrophe: the ominous insinuations couched in the most innocent of terms, even the considerate, thoughtful, scarifying 'preparing the way'. With what had the way been strewn? With hatred? With evil? With . . .

Septimus suddenly toppled sideways in his seat as if overcome by an uncontrollable, all-consuming spasm, his face contorted. Lying there, sprawling, he thought he heard himself scream.

He was positive he heard himself scream: so certain was he that he had screamed that he was about to apologise, somehow to bluff his way out of this latest humiliating embarrassment, when he heard the desolate cry of the peacock come again from the shrubbery. He sighed with relief and leaned back in his seat, widening his smile. Away in the distance other cries could now be heard, disassociating themselves from his turmoil, children mostly.

Septimus sighed again, running his fingers through his hair and giving a small cough as he stepped from the Packard (the door held open by a beaming Patrick) and stared wonderingly about him. Involuntarily he shuddered. Even the landscape, stretching out below the hillock on which His Grace the Archbishop's residence had been constructed, had a tense, disquieting familiarity about it. Beyond the seven palms – the feathery plumes of which could just be seen waving like the wings of some starving nocturnal bird – a Ferris wheel churned relentlessly round, its seats vacant, rehearsing, perhaps, for the carnival in which the unforunate, bedecked pony was doomed to participate. Closer at hand, in the Archbishop's garden, a solitary gardener leaned on his spade and with admirable agility rolled a cigarette with one hand, beside him the dead tree he had just uprooted from the soil, its brittle branches still raised to heaven in mute supplication. Away to the right the mountains, made grander and loftier by the accumulation of dark clouds about their peaks, seemed to sway monstrously as the sun poured molten, shimmering haze on to their slopes, glowering angrily over the abandoned mangrove fields that erosion and careless husbandry had rendered useless. Not unlike, he now thought, the erosion that had taken place in his own –

'You see?' Patrick's voice mercifully penetrated his morbid pessimism. 'You see?' he repeated, stabbing the dial of his wristwatch with the same finger that had earlier punished the wayward curls. 'As I informed you precisely five minutes ago.'

'Ah. Yes. Most punctual.'

'I am never wrong.'

'So you told me.'

'And it is the truth.'

'I expect it is.'

'You will now follow me and I will present you to our beloved Archbishop.'

Behind them the peacock put in another appearance, emerging from the shrubbery in a sort of break-dance. It spread its fantastic tail, almost overbalancing from the weight. Septimus stared at it: perhaps God was keeping an eye on him after all.

Three

Monsieur Lagreze seldom drove his own car, an expensive new BMW similar to that favoured by the President; he preferred to take taxis, believing that this mode of transport kept him in touch with what was going on, listening to the gossip of the drivers, studying the people as he lounged without the aggravation of having to concentrate on where he was going. But when he did drive himself, and he did that particular morning, it would only be to the Ollofson, and he always parked in the same place, in the shade of a wonderful, wide-spreading lime. Thoughtfully he made his way up the alabaster steps of the hotel, stopping to wonder at the brilliant colour of the rampant bougainvillea, a white handkerchief in one hand – at the ready to wipe the beads of perspiration that formed continuously on his wide forehead. For several days the weather had been oppressive, building up, as he well knew, to one of those massive thunderstorms that occasionally plundered his country. While the world celebrated the rituals of Christmas, Haiti seethed with rumours that the bizarre tyranny of Jean-Claude Duvalier was close to an end.

At the top of the steps Monsieur Lagreze turned and looked back at the gardens through which he had just walked: strange, he thought, how even the once lustrous shrubs and tall exotic plants, imported from every corner of the globe, seemed to have become tarnished by the accumulating tension. Still stranger was the unheralded vision of Sartre that took shape in his mind. Yet perhaps it was not so rummy since of all the things he would confess to missing, the five Christmases he had spent as a student in Paris remained, without question, the most nostalgic, fondly remembered every so often if only to reassure himself that there had indeed been a time when human life was more than just an inconsequential hazard to be snuffed out on some lunatic whim. And it was as though Jean-Paul Sartre, peering with those bulbous eyes through the thick lenses of his cheap spectacles (as the young Gilles Lagreze had seen him do so many times), was alongside him, saying, '*Regardez-vous*, see how sadly nature can prognosticate the coming of death. Consider the perfume of the wilted rose. Consider, too, the agony of the thorns. Consider – '

'Are you all right, Gilles?'

Monsieur Lagreze shook his head vigorously, dismissing the squat, enigmatic philosopher and his unlikely considerations.

'I've been watching you. You definitely seem queasy.'

'No, I am not unwell, Oscar. Just thinking.'

'Oh.' For some reason Oscar Nicholson sounded almost disappointed.

'The treachery of pleasures recalled.' Monsieur Lagreze frowned. 'Whose words are those, I wonder?'

'No idea, I'm afraid.'

'Nor I. They might, of course, be my own,' Monsieur Lagreze suggested with a timid smile. 'But come. You have been deprived for long enough of the pleasure of our game.'

'Yes,' Oscar agreed. 'And today I will win.'

'But of course.'

'I mean it,' Oscar insisted.

Monsieur Lagreze gave the smile on his lips time to disappear before replying. 'If only events worked out as we would have them do,' he said wistfully, taking Oscar by the arm and steering him to the far end of the veranda where, on a white-painted, latticed table, the chessboard had already been set, armies ranked.

But an hour later, his warriors, carved in Mingish images, massacred to the tune of three battles to nil, Oscar Nicholson groaned exaggeratedly and leaned back in his chair as though he himself was mortally wounded, and waved a white paper napkin in the air by way of surrender.

Monsieur Lagreze summoned the waiter – the same elderly mulatto called Hispo who always served them, hovering by their table, instantly busying himself but doing nothing as soon as anyone else tried to catch his attention – with a vague wave of his handkerchief, and ordered: a large bourbon and, for himself, a *crème de menthe* in a tall glass with crushed ice and a straw. 'You were simply not concentrating, my friend. Not concentrating at all this morning,' he admonished Oscar as the waiter withdrew, bending his body at the hips to glide between the tables.

'Oh, I was concentrating all right. You're just too damn good. In the, what, three years? – dear God – I've been trying to beat you I've only succeeded once. And then, I suspect, only because you let me win.'

'Your thoughts have been on other affairs,' Monsieur Lagreze insisted.

'Well, maybe this morning they were,' Oscar conceded after a moment's thought, during which he eyed his companion almost suspiciously.

'Aha,' Monsieur Lagreze responded, or possibly it was the arrival of Hispo bearing their drinks on a silver salver that made him exclaim with such gusto.

As ever, of course, the cunning devil was correct. Oscar Nicholson's mind had definitely been preoccupied with other matters.

– A storm is brewing, Oscar, the Ambassador said. You mark my words. The Baby is losing his grip. Dammit. Life was such a helluva lot easier when the old Doc was alive and in power.

– Easier for us, maybe.

– Who the hell else counts?

Nicholson diplomatically refrained from commenting on this flippancy. He disliked the ambassador. He found him both gross and insincere, both vulgar and offensive, a wealthy hillbilly out of his depth. But he was also amused by him; he always found it entertaining and ironic to witness someone who exuded such lofty self-importance striving so obviously for notoriety. Still, Oscar sometimes reflected but only when things were going really badly, the ambassador and he had one thing in common: they were both pretty well disillusioned. Having poured millions of dollars into the current President's campaign fund (twice) it must have been galling and something of a shock to find oneself banished to the Court of Duvalier when the Court of St James had been what he had set his heart on; while he, Oscar, well . . .

– What have we got on those riots in Gonaives, Oscar?

– Protests, Mr Ambassador.

And that was another thing: his insistance on being addressed at all times as 'Mr Ambassador' by all the staff, most of whom were career diplomats who had seen ambassadors come and go as the powers in the White House altered their favours or were shunted out of office.

– Bloody riots, the Ambassador insisted.

– Three students were shot. There was bound to be some re-action.

– Not in Papa Doc's day there wouldn't.

– Times change.

– Never for the goddam better.

– That depends on your viewpoint, Mr Ambassador.

The rebuke skirted the Ambassador's intelligence. We'll have to notify Washington, he said.

– Of course.

– If this spreads, the Ambassador went on, wrinkling his nose as though discussing some viral epidemic, Christ alone knows what shit we'll find ourselves in.

Oscar said nothing.

The Ambassador raised his eyebrows. What do you make of it?

– I think it's rather too early to panic.

– Nobody's panicking, the Ambassador was a little too quick to insist.

– What I mean is that it *could* be just an isolated incident. It could, if handled properly, just fizzle out and stop there.

– You think?

Oscar shrugged.

– You think it will? the Ambassador demanded again.

– Possibly.

– Damn students.

– Just students, Mr Ambassador.

– Some bastards should never be bloody educated.

Oscar just stared at his superior.

– Hey, you have friends – Haitians – well placed, in the know, don't you, Oscar?

– I have some Haitian friends. Yes.

– What do they think?

– I haven't asked them.

– Well you better. Sniff about. See what you can find out. No harm in being prepared if we're in for a full-scale revolution, is there?

Oscar gave a tight, sardonic laugh – the hint that he was now classified as a sort of hound-dog sniffing things out not escaping him. I doubt very much if they'd tell me anything of importance, Mr Ambassador. We Americans are not exactly flavour of the month, you know. We're probably the last people on earth they would trust with any genuine information. They won't help *us*.

And yet: 'If you have any problem with which you think I might be able to help, you have only to ask, my friend,' Monsieur Lagreze was now offering generously, not looking at him, quietly, methodically replacing the dead chessmen in their felt-lined coffin.

Oscar gave him a grateful smile. 'To tell the truth, I have been asked to do some sniffing. To try and establish how you feel.'

Monsieur Lagreze slid the wooden cover into place and put the box carefully on the table beside the boards, pushing them both to one side. He picked up his drink and sucked on the straw, watching Oscar over the brim of his glass. Then, his thirst quenched, he placed the glass on the table also, and wiped his fingers, one at a time, with his handkerchief. 'About what should I have feelings?' he asked.

'About the disturbances in Gonaives.'

'Ah. Those.' Monsieur Lagreze scowled. 'And why should anyone care how I feel?'

'I didn't say anyone *cared*, Gilles. I was told it might be productive to pick your brains.'

Monsieur Lagreze burst into one of his deep, rumbling laughs, his entire body shaking and participating in the merriment. 'I see.' He continued to laugh, wagging a mocking, warning finger. 'You must learn the art of the devious, my friend. Such forthright honesty has no place in diplomacy.'

Oscar grinned before asking seriously, 'What *do* you make of it, Gilles?'

'Gonaives? Who can say?'

'Will the violence spread?'

'It may.'

'And if it does? What then?'

'The usual slaughter that follows such things.'

'There *are* those who say Duvalier has lost control . . .?'

'There are *always* those who say the person in power has lost or is losing control. You should know that.'

'Has he?'

'Why do you ask me?'

'Come on, Gilles. You know him better than anyone. You're one of the few people he trusts.'

'You flatter me,' Monsieur Lagreze said in an odd simpering

voice, clearly basking in the compliment. 'I'm not so sure our President trusts anyone.'

'But you *know* him.'

'Even that is, perhaps, exaggerating my access. I meet him from time to time, certainly. When he sends for me. And we discuss matters. He has even, it is true, asked my opinion on occasion – not, mind you, that he paid it much heed. But as to knowing – '

'Gilles – is he or isn't he losing control?'

Monsieur Lagreze gave an enormous shrug and spread his hands wide. 'We will all know the answer to that within the next few weeks, will we not?'

'And supposing he is?'

'Ah, in *that* case, we are heading for troublesome times.'

'Meaning?'

'Meaning – well – let us just say that if our President *is* losing his grip he will not, I imagine, stay here to see the outcome of his weakness. And should he go – *sacrebleu*!' Gilles Lagreze suddenly exclaimed (the words sounding absurdly theatrical to Oscar even though he had heard them used on many occasions by his friend) staring open-mouthed in the direction of the swimming pool as though the prophesied troublesome times were already marching in his direction.

And possibly they were. Making his way round the perimeter of the pool, placing one sandalled foot directly in front of the other, holding his ridiculous niblick before him with both hands as though balancing himself on a tightrope, was Father Septimus Roach.

Oscar Nicholson followed his companion's gaze. 'Ahah,' he remarked. 'Behold the meddlesome priest.'

'I must go,' Monsieur Lagreze said quickly, already making to stand.

'Oh, no you don't, Gilles. You're not leaving me here alone to face – '

'He drives me so crazy,' Monsieur Lagreze interrupted, tapping the side of his skull, but nevertheless easing himself back into his chair.

'He makes everyone crazy. But – '

'I cannot abide – '

' – is greatly loved, you know.'

'I know. I know. But he is a menace.'

'He is kind.'

'He is a nuisance.'

'He is selfless.'

Monsieur Lagreze snorted through his nose.

'They worship him at the hospice he runs in the slums of the Cité Brooklyn.'

'I know they do,' Monsieur Lagreze snapped. 'But it is *me* they should worship. It is from me the wretched man has begged, demanding clothes and food and medicine and money. Tcha. I was a wealthy man before that Septimus Roach set foot on Haiti, but now . . .' He stopped talking and adopted a woebegone, plaintive air, but smiling, advancing the smile to a chuckle that cascaded over the words as he continued, 'I sometimes wish our first encounter had been somewhat more terminal.'

Oscar laughed. 'You're not alone, Gilles. He has the embassy staff driven to distraction with his endless cajoling.'

'Is no one spared?'

'It seems not,' Oscar replied, watching Septimus continue his hazardous exercise, pacing along the pool yet oddly enough not appearing to draw any closer to the veranda.

(– That priest is here, Mr Nicholson, his secretary informed him, her voice brimming with consternation.

– What priest?

– Father Roach, from the hospice – I told you about him.

– Oh. Yes. I remember. What does he want now?

– To see you.

– I can't see him now.

– He insists. He says he won't move until he does see you. He's sitting on the floor in the lobby and says he'll stay there until –

– Well let him stay there.

– I can't do that, Mr Nicholson. He's causing havoc. He's singing and –

– Then get security to throw him out.

– He's a priest, Mr Nicholson.

– So?

The secretary looked mortified. You can't just throw a priest out, Mr Nicholson.

– Whyever not?

– Because – because he's a priest.

Oscar Nicholson shook his head in exasperation but smiled just the same at the illogical logic. Oh, let him come up then. But don't you dare leave me alone with him for more than five minutes.

– I need help, Septimus Roach announced without ceremony.

– Don't we all? Oscar parried, lighting a cigarette.

– Indeed we do – but some more than others.)

Such was their introduction. In the months that followed they met frequently, always when Septimus wanted something; their relationship remained superficial, although amicable enough, as Oscar surreptitiously if legitimately skimmed modest financial donations from a variety of 'contingency funds' which Septimus accepted, usually eyeing the currency balefully as if it always fell well short of what he had anticipated.

'But now that he is here,' Monsieur Lagreze said, crouching as low as his bulk would allow as though hoping this furtive action would withdraw him from the priest's line of vision, 'it is the priest you should ask if you want to know the mood of the people.'

'Oh, I intend to. It's damn well about time he did something for me. The question is: will I be able to get any sense out of him?'

Monsieur Lagreze looked doubtful. 'Probably not unless you are privy to his – '

'Brace yourself, Gilles. Here he comes.'

And come Septimus Roach did although none too directly, weaving his way towards them in a meandering line as if following a particularly tricky invisible path, halting frequently to study some small miracle unfolding at his feet, then advancing a few wavering paces, stopping again, peering skyward, shielding his eyes from the glare of the sun, his niblick tucked under his arm. Thus blinkered, his gaze affixed itself to the ornate façade of the hotel. It could have been that he was silently, mournfully comparing this opulence, already well down the slippery slope of decay though it was, to the dismal squalor of the slum where he had set up his hospice – somewhat of a misnomer since it was but a run-down, dilapidated structure, little better than the hovels which surrounded it, although redeemed by the undimmed cheerfulness of Sister Mary Dowling (who appeared one morning, bustling in for all the world like a nunnish Mrs Tiggywinkle, announcing that the Archbishop had sent her 'to keep an eye on things' as she put it, her bright eyes indicating that Septimus himself was one of those things, and rolling up her sleeves, setting to, scrubbing the floor and washing down the walls with disinfectant, badgering some astonished layabouts, most of them sailing peacefully on a tide of marijuana, to assist her, and generally transforming the place). The Cité Brooklyn was another gross misnomer with its rather less refined edifices constructed of cardboard and newspaper and some, more grandiose, of corrugated iron (although these had their drawbacks, having to be vacated in the heat of the day, the occupants squatting outside, never straying far in case their homes were usurped, just waiting, their outlook derelict, for the night to descend and the metal to cool); with its open sewers, the stepping-stones over these sewers slippery and treacherous with excreta, the appalling stench of urine, of poverty, of hopelessness, of festering disease, the perpetual wailing of famished children, their stomachs bloated, the wailing women, their eyes distended, the silent moaning men, their minds bludgeoned, the not so silent groaning of ghosts that had requisitioned the slum as their habitat. But it was Archbishop Gidron's voice, no ghost's, that now chattered in Septimus's head.

– So this is what they have sent us, he said in surprisingly unaccented English.

– That is so, Your Grace. I'm afraid so, Septimus concurred apologetically, eyeing the old man, whose black skin already carried the grey pigments of death, with some amusement.

– Hah! You'll be of no more use than I.

Patrick, standing behind the Archbishop, signalled Septimus to remain silent by pressing a finger against his lips.

– What troubles you must have caused to be exiled here! the Archbishop went on, curiously enough in a voice that somehow hinted that he had a sneaking regard for troublesome clergy.

Ignoring Patrick's warning, determined to sidestep the truth, Septimus defended his arrival. Actually, my Lord, I asked to come.

– Asked to come? Here? You hear that, Patrick? He says he asked to come. He must be mad.

– I understand Father Roach *did* ask to come, Patrick put in.

– Then we must ask ourselves from what it is that he is trying to escape, the old prelate announced as though he and Patrick were discussing an absconding prisoner.

– The twilight? was Patrick's outrageous suggestion, possibly misconstruing the unfortunate Yeats.

– Or himself?

– Or what he *thinks* is himself.

The Archbishop approved of that. Ah, he said, brightening. Now that *is* a thought, Patrick. What would you say to that, Father Septimus Roach?

Caught on the hop by his sudden inclusion in this weird dialogue, Septimus could think of nothing to say.

And he could think of no immediate reply, either, to the question that was now volleyed at him from the hotel veranda by Monsieur Lagreze.

'I'm sorry?' he queried, playing for time.

'I only asked if you were seeking the elusive spirit of youth,' Monsieur Lagreze repeated, regretting he had ever asked the facetious question, and irked that his little dig had gone awry.

Septimus shook his head. 'No,' he replied seriously. 'I was thinking of what difference there might be between what is oneself and that which one thinks is oneself.'

Oscar smiled and winked at Monsieur Lagreze. 'And did you reach a conclusion, Father?'

'Alas, no. Not yet at any rate. But I will. I will.'

'It is odd that you should choose here,' Oscar waved a hand, 'for such profound meditations.'

'I didn't actually come here to – I came to see you,' Septimus said.

'Me?' Oscar sounded alarmed.

Septimus grinned delightedly. 'Yes. You.'

'I – Oh, God,' Oscar moaned in mock agony, which made Gilles Lagreze beam with sadistic pleasure and straighten up slightly in his chair, an action, as it turned out, somewhat premature.

'Or you, my dear Monsieur Lagreze,' Septimus added with a crafty leer.

'Me?' Monsieur Lagreze gasped, unintentionally filching Oscar's exclamation, borrowing, also, his agonized groan.

'I need advice,' Septimus confided, causing both men to glance at each other simultaneously; advice had never before been one of the priest's requisites.

'Ah. Well. In that case Monsieur Lagreze is the man you want,' Oscar said gratefully. '*His* advice would be far more beneficial than any I could offer.'

'Nonsense,' Monsieur Lagreze protested hastily, impaling Oscar to his seat with a furious glare. 'I am but a simple man who has not yet learned enough to be in a position to advise others.'

'You, simple? Hah!'

'Most simple.'

'Gilles, how you can sit there and – '

Monsieur Lagreze raised a hand. 'It is all academic until we know what advice it is that is needed.'

'All immaterial,' Oscar countered. 'Whatever advice is needed you're the one to give it.'

'Again you overrate my capabilities.'

'Rubbish.'

As they bickered Septimus listened, looking sad and befuddled. Once again people were talking over his head, chatting and arguing as though he did not exist, or existed only when they wanted him to exist, materializing on their creative whim.

(– He could replace Père François in the Cité Brooklyn, could he not? Archbishop Gidron asked.

– Certainly. A most excellent decision, my Lord, Patrick agreed, leaning towards the old man as if about to whisper confidences in his ear.)

And:

'Your sudden humility is quite startling, Gilles,' Oscar said.

'I merely state the truth,' Gilles Lagreze insisted.

(– You think they will accept him there? the Archbishop wanted to know.

– They already have, Patrick said.

– Ah. I see. The Archbishop rubbed his bony hands together.)

And:

'Truth, Gilles. In your hands, Gilles, truth is a master of disguise,' Oscar retaliated.

'Again I must disagree. Truth always makes itself evident. It is man's deceitful interpretation that masks all verity.'

(– You will be so kind, Patrick, in that case to see that all arrangements are made for his accommodation?

– All has been seen to, Patrick replied. He will have Père François's room at the convent.)

Or:

– What you lack, my dear friend, is that sincere simplicity that allows God to make His will known, Bishop McKewen had said. Adding: You must never expect to know God. What would be the point of faith if you did?

'You would agree with that, would you not, Father?'

Septimus, looking justifiably fantod, wrestled himself away from eavesdropping on the assorted voices that crackled like mutilated atmospherics in his mind, staring at Monsieur Lagreze (who stared hopefully back, giving small jerks of his head as though to encourage a response), trying desperately to extract from the now fading mutterings some indication of what he would or would not tend to agree with. He had heard, with dire misgivings, the word 'truth', and it pierced his soul like an arrow: truth for Septimus Roach, was a figment on which he would rather not dwell. Not at the moment anyway. Deviously he latched on to another word that isolated itself from the babble: masks. The essential paraphernalia for actors and priests and all such dabblers in mystifying make-believe. Illusionists. Magical conjurors plucking promises from hats, birettas, mitres even, flummoxing the innocent onlookers (and themselves) but mostly themselves. Oh, yes: Septimus knew all about masks; donning them with dexterous virtuosity he could, and had, played all the roles of hypocritical deception – the lowly rasophor, the humble mendicant, the thirsting seeker after truth (how the word persisted!), the sadly misunderstood. Yet always, as at this moment, when faced with a straightforward question that demanded no great commitment, merely an opinion that would keep the conversation intact, he panicked, resorted to the most extraordinary prevarication, as he was certainly about to do, wasn't he, or turned his back on it, as he might even yet decide to do, and strode away with dented pride to take a tilt at some less formidable windmill.

'Would you not?' Monsieur Lagreze asked again.

'Is it important?' Someone snatched the words from Septimus's mouth and tossed them hopefully as dice.

'Truth? But of course.'

Again that word. 'Whether I agree or not, I meant,' Septimus *heard* himself say, not without difficulty however since his thoughts (like erudite dons placidly strolling along the bank of his mind, nodding, chatting to each other – 'not altogether impossible' – 'nothing is' – 'unless, *inter alia*, it becomes . . .') were posing questions of their own: God knows, they were insisting, we have been through all this absurd rigmarole before. You are eschewing the point again, veering from the rightful path and making your lonely way down the dusty, rutted track where only the abandoned walk, where, by the forlorn wayside crosses that mark some tragedy greater even than yours, the unrepentant pilgrims beg, rattling their tins, like, incidentally, that crippled cobbler with a face that bears an uncanny resemblance to Toussaint L'Ouverture, although you cannot fairly be expected to appreciate that, crouched beside that splendid motorcar in the carpark under the lime tree: you remember him, of course.

It was true; it was almost eldritch; there *was* someone squatting by the gleaming BMW in the carpark, shaded by a lime tree. Septimus settled his gaze on the cripple. Of course he remembered him. Like some horripilant caricature of his own soul, the cripple haunted him, appearing without warning in the Cité Brooklyn to crawl on to the porch of the hospice and set up shop, making shoes from unremouldable tyres, a chicken on a string beside him.

' . . . advice?'

Septimus turned and faced Oscar Nicholson, staring through him, his lips quivering.

'You said you wanted advice, father.'

'I – ah, yes. I did,' Septimus said vaguely.

'Well?'

As he was about to respond, the words already forming in his vocal cords, Septimus felt the eyes of the crippled cobbler probing his skull. Reluctantly he turned back to look at him. He was still there, crouched by the car, stroking the neck of the chicken he now held on his lap. 'Behold,' he seemed to cry, 'behold my affliction, but it is as nothing compared to yours: my withered limbs were severed and cast away; but your malaise, my poor benighted friend – and we are friends, are we not? – your malaise is a withering of the spirit, your soul is wrapped in darkness and is strangled as by the caotchu succulent which, like so many other things you have yet to encounter, is pointed and sharp and has sap that burns. Your soul is worthless, a cancerous appendage to be jettisoned without delay, leaving your mind free and uncluttered and ready to receive the only possible words of redemption that will come, not from those of whom you now stupidly seek advice, but from the mightier power the existence of which you have long since suspected.'

'Father?' Oscar Nicholson called.

– Father, the cripple called.

– Father, a voice emanating from the past called.

And from the past, too, came skipping a motley, clamorous crew, all of them calling his name, demanding his instant, undivided attention, their voices merging into an all but indistinguishable cacophany so that, as he listened (avoiding, quite successfully he reckoned, the curious stares of Oscar Nicholson and Monsieur Gilles Lagreze, but unable, alas, to escape the unblinking, mordant gaze of the cripple), each hysterical plea fondled the next, becoming a terrifying unity of horror, becoming one, elongated pule of utter desperation. 'You must save the child . . . Answer the question, priest . . . You think your God will save you now? . . . *Wer immer strebend sich bemuht* . . . The soul is carnivorous . . . You must catch the next bus . . . I tell you, priest: your cruel creed has bedevilled us more than all our poverty and sorrow . . .'

'Father Septimus?'

It was Monsieur Lagreze, leaning anxiously forward, who now called his name.

And from the whirling cerebral chaos there emerged an orderly if totally baffling reply: 'They killed the child anyway, of course.'

Oscar and Monsieur Lagreze gaped at each other. Monsieur Lagreze shook his head; Oscar Nicholson shook his head also, adorning his action with a shrug and a wispy smile.

As for Septimus Roach: oblivious to the confusion his remark had generated, the advice he once sought either received or forgotten, he left the veranda and made his way slowly back down the steps, tapping them with his golf-club as though testing their sturdiness and, with his lopsided, inimicable gait, set off down the driveway, deep in conversation with himself, wagging his head.

'What on earth was all that about?' Oscar wanted to know.

Monsieur Lagreze did not immediately reply. He frowned deeply, drumming the fingers of one hand on his knee in what looked like a scherzo. Something about the priest, something more than the obvious eccentricity, worried him. While he could dismiss Father Roach's whimsical antics as an amusing, rather sad play-acting brought about by the implacable strictures of his religious life, there was something . . . Monsieur Lagreze clicked his tongue against his teeth and stood up, peering in the direction the priest had taken for several minutes before sighing and sitting down again. He was on the point of abandoning his reflections, of suggesting another game of chess, when it came to him. It was as if, and the sudden realization appalled him, he had been allowed, by some strange contrariness, to glimpse in the priest's eyes his own poisoned happiness; as if Septimus Roach had, for the briefest of fleeting moments, mirrored his own meagrely suppressed guilt and sorrow at a wasted life. And there was even more to it than that: as he had receded down the drive Septimus had cast no shadow, and to Gilles Lagreze, a man who vehemently disclaimed all manner of the occult, that was of awful significance. Involuntarily he shuddered, hearing, he imagined, the wailing spirits of the houngain macoute already plotting the priest's downfall.

'Gilles?'

Monsieur Lagreze jumped. 'Ah. I apologise, Oscar. I was, I fear, thinking again.'

'Oh, I guessed that much. About our friend?'

Monsieur Lagreze nodded. 'Yes. About our friend, as you put it.'

'Why look so serious? You look positively mournful.' Oscar stretched himself, and for a time the two men watched each other in silence.

'Ryder,' Monsieur Lagreze tossed out unexpectedly.

It was Oscar's turn to jump. 'Ryder? For God's sake don't you start, Gilles. Who's Ryder – if it is a person?'

Gilles Lagreze was no longer listening. He was nodding away enthusiastically to himself. 'Albert Pinkham Ryder. You've heard of him?'

'Should I have?'

'He was American.'

'There are one or two of those I haven't yet met.'

'Oh, you wouldn't have met him I don't think. A rather eccentric artist. A painter.'

'Gilles, what in heaven's name are you rambling on about?'

'About Albert Pinkham Ryder. He never completed anything. Did and redid every canvas until they were so richly textured with oil and candlewax and alchohol and varnish that they collapsed under his manic, unrealistic desire for absolute perfection.'

'Oh *that* Ryder. *Now* I understand,' Oscar said sarcastically.

Monsieur Lagreze chuckled. 'What I am trying to tell you, Oscar, is that our friend, Father Septimus, suffers from the identical ailment.'

'Yes . . . well, I'm sure you're right, Gilles.'

'And it is because he seeks absolute perfection that he is in such terrible danger.'

'Danger?'

'Of being misused. Abused.'

Oscar laughed. 'Lost me again, I'm afraid.'

'This battle for perfection only weakens the spirit,' Monsieur Lagreze went on, but quietly, as though discussing the matter with himself. 'No peace exists but that we must pay full toll in hell.'

'What you need – what we both need – is a drink.' Oscar summoned Hispo, as ever lurking nearby, for two more of the same. 'Perhaps we should have offered the priest a tipple?'

Monsieur Lagreze nodded abstractedly.

'You know, Gilles, that could be just what the old fellow needs, a really good bender.' Oscar laughed aloud, visualizing a tottering, ribald Septimus, a singing Septimus, a Septimus carefree and unashamedly gay, as he himself had once been carefree and unashamedly gay, but that was when –

'I think not,' Monsieur Lagreze said. He stood up and walked again to the edge of the veranda. Then he turned suddenly and said, 'I would like you to promise me something, Oscar.'

'What might that be?'

'That you will tend the priest.'

'I – ' Oscar was about to protest that he could hardly promise such a thing, could hardly be expected to keep an eye on the recalcitrant priest if that, indeed, was what Gilles Lagreze meant by 'tending', when he noted the genuine concern in the Haitian's face. 'What on earth makes you think he needs . . . tending?'

Gilles Lagreze turned away, and leaned his pelvis against the balustrade, his hands deep in his pockets, jangling his coins. Perhaps it was just the gloominess of his thoughts that made him wonder if the weather was about to change for the worse, falling, as it were, into line with impending tragedy. It certainly looked as though a storm was on the way: those black portentous clouds surging from the waters of the Golfe de la Gonave, stretching as far as the eye could see along the horizon, probably all the way to the Ile de la Tortue – de la Torture as the wags had christened it solemnly. He sniffed the air, believing he could smell rain, although it was most unlikely to rain at this time of year, and the silly idea careered through his head that he would enjoy nothing more at this moment than to be caught in a cloudburst, to walk majestically through the deluge, while all about him lesser mortals scattered for shelter, leaving the world to him alone, getting wetter and wetter. He watched the clouds change formation, shaping the images of some celestial surrealist: shrouded images of mental aberrations. Yet there was no denying their beauty; no denying the beauty of Haiti itself, the nearest thing, he often thought when moved by his country's decline, to earthly paradise. Sadly, like Adam, he had abused that paradise. Worse: he had done nothing, unless the acquisition of a few friends, a Cuban mistress of some magnificence and unquestionable sexual prowess, and numerous items of exquisite antique furniture could be said to count as something. On the other hand, he had, fortunately –

'Did you hear me, Gilles?'

Monsieur Lagreze looked over his shoulder, nodding quietly. 'Yes, Oscar, I heard,' he said again quietly, and turned away again, hoping to recapture the thread of what had hinted at his more redeeming features.

Oscar Nicholson finished his drink, tossing it back in a single gulp, and joined Monsieur Lagreze, leaning his hands on the balustrade.

'You really *are* worried about the priest,' he said.

'Yes, Oscar, I am,' Monsieur Lagreze admitted.

'Why should you be?'

'I'm worried about many things. Many things. But mostly, as I say, about the priest. He has already acquired the look of death.'

Oscar gave a harsh, snorting gasp. 'Jesus!'

Using his handkerchief like a Zulu chief's whisk (a carefully monogrammed square of white linen – a gift, with eleven others, from the Sisters of the *Sacré Cœur* Convent in recognition of his continuous generosity – that had started the day, like himself, crisp and fresh, but was now limp and crumpled), Gilles Lagreze discouraged a battalion of irate storm-midges that all of a sudden swarmed about his head and laid siege to his face. Below him, in the port, the ships, tankers and freighters for the most part, sounded their melancholy sirens, the variety of tone reminiscent of the gargantuan, chugging steam-trains in the American midwest (visited once when Doctor Duvalier had dreamt that agriculture was to be the saving of Haiti, and sent Gilles as his emissary, although how that vast grain-belt could have offered anything to Haiti was never explained). The wind rose abruptly, remarkably chilly, making him shiver, then soughed away. The cold, grey aquilon of Ajax, he thought for some reason; and for some reason that also eluded him, he said aloud: 'He has been marked with the thumb of Zangbeto.' He placed a hand on Oscar's shoulder, and added, 'Now I must go,' as he observed Oscar about to question his curious statement.

'I need a few hours' rest. I have been summoned to dine at the palace this evening,' he explained. 'So I shall see precious little of my own bed this night.'

Nicholson watched the impossibly handsome Negro walk away from him, still feeling the comradely squeeze on his shoulder that had been given by way of farewell, still seeing the deep, perturbed look that had shadowed the dark, usually emotionless eyes. The thumb of Zangbeto no less – whatever nonsense that was. Some absurd voodoo spirit no doubt, but what role such a creature played in Gilles's domestic drama was anybody's guess. Zangbeto Lagreze – the name filtered into his mind. Oscar whistled to himself, a few bars of the waltz from Swan Lake, and shook his head. The thumbprint of Zangbeto! It certainly had an ominous ring to it. The Bride of Frankenstein. The Hands of Orlac. The House of Usher. The Thumb of Zangbeto . . . Zangbeto Lagreze, he thought again. That had a ring to it also. He gave a short chuckle. Then, abruptly, he ordered another bourbon, lit another cigarette, and, selecting a reclining steamer chair that caught his eye, settled down for a few moments' peace.

Four

HOSPICE DE – The sign (hospice of what hidden beneath an old, synthetic-fibre string vest, draped to dry over that enlightenment), hung from two short lengths of rusting chain, one a link or so shorter than the other. This should have made the suspended nameplate lopsided, but the building itself leaned sideways at such a precarious angle that the sign appeared magically horizontal. It was constructed of timber and uplifted on low stilts, with a new felt and shingle roof, gaping sockets where the windows would have been if not for the fact that Septimus had got the measurements wrong, using inches instead of centimetres and not bothering to mention this small matter.

Eyeing his handiwork, for it was he who had laboriously painted the notice (making a meal of the exercise, even donning a smock – half a blanket with a head-hole snipped out – and standing back every few minutes to view his artistry), Septimus Roach struggled along the deeply rutted, slippery roadway, a crucifix, close to life-size and acquired after some sharp dealing with the Mother Superior of the convent where he lodged, over his shoulder. The belly of the ethnically ebonised Christ nestled against his cheek, while one hand clutched the cruelly nailed feet, and the other, in a singularly awkward arc over his head, the horrific crown of thorns. His niblick was thrust like a sword – poor Damocles – into the thick leather belt he wore about his waist. He stumbled into a pothole and came to a standstill, and for an instant the world stopped also: the child half-born, the tear poised to fall, the damned suspended in their downward hurtle, the voice that warned – why should *it* be exempt and continue to function? – do not adjust your mind, there is interference with reality.

'In the name of heaven, father,' Sister Mary Dowling exclaimed, bringing reality back into reasonable focus. 'What have you brought with you this time?'

Septimus stepped from the pothole and shook each foot in turn, like a cat, dislodging the slime that had seeped into his sandals.

'Christ,' he said, most probably by way of explanation, while Bishop McKewen frowned disapproval in his mind. He negotiated the four steps of the porch and leaned the cross against one of the rough-hewn poles that supported the overhang. Then he stood back and stared at it, rubbing his shoulder.

'And where, might I ask, do you think we're going to put it?' Sister Mary demanded.

'Why, in there. In the hospice, of course.'

'There's no room.'

'No room?' Septimus sounded astonished.

'No room.' Sister Mary was adamant. She wiped the grime from her hands on the blue and white butcher's apron she wore over her habit, then plonked them pugnaciously on her hips, assuming a stance that defied further argument.

'On the wall, surely . . .?' Septimus tried, glancing at the crucifix, getting God on his side.

Unimpressed, Sister Mary asked, 'And have the weight of it bring the whole building down over our heads?'

'On the floor *against* the wall?' Septimus ventured with that smile he had found, on occasions, winning.

It seemed to work. Sister Mary relented. She returned his smile, her small eyes (made even smaller by permanently drooping lids, an affliction found in people who have spent years squinting against tropical light) twinkling. She took off her apron, getting the tie-strings entangled in the rosary that hung from a white corded rope about her waist, muttering vexations to herself, and patting the beads, once released, by way of repentance for any imagined sin of anger. Although confused, and often shocked, by the antics of Father Septimus, she held him in some esteem; or rather, she held what she saw as his restless agony in some esteem. As he celebrated Mass each morning in a side chapel – the High Altar presided over only by the resident chaplain, Father Placid, a young Haitian whose rather frenetic approach to the liturgy belied his name – with a truly beautiful stained-glass window, erected at enormous expense by Monsieur Gilles Lagreze in laconic memory of his parents who were depicted as dusky guests, or maybe refugees, at the throne of a smiling benevolent God the Father, she shared with him an aching panic that God was not listening, that He had other things to do, that the sacrifice she had made, not to mention the sacrifice taking place before her eyes, was perhaps, after all, a bitter waste. Yet there was something about this strange priest's fervour, something about the yearning intensity with which he invested the awesome words of holy transubstantiation as he implored Christ to change the bread and wine into His body and blood so that all who partook might be saved, that moved her, that made her long to join him on his lonesome trek through the morass of doubt and into the shining peace of humble acceptance, a journey that would make her lonely, celibate life fulfilled, or give it, at least, a semblance of sanity.

– Little Brigid's going to be a nun! Her mother's voice twittered into Sister Mary's consciousness sounding, as it had at the moment young Brigid Dowling had announced her decision, holier than it had ever done in prayer, as though she, in some intricate, round-about way, expected to reap a share of whatever spiritual benefits might accrue from her daughter's vocation, sounding faintly superior too as she disclosed the news to her friends, her acquaintances, anyone who would listen. Little Brigid's going to be a nun.

– Are you, Brigid? asked her father, the small town's senior solicitor, aware of his wife's tendency to exaggerate anything that delighted her.

– I'm going to try, Daddy.

– You have thought about it carefully?

– Yes. Very carefully.

– And you're certain you have a vocation?

– I think so.

– It's a very big step to take if you're *not* certain.

– I can't be absolutely sure. Not yet. Not until I've tried.

Daddy shook his head.

– I thought you'd be pleased.

– I *am* pleased. But if it turns out that you do not have a vocation. What then?

– Then I'll have to leave.

Daddy mumbled something about a terrible stigma.

– At least I'll have tried.

And try she did, desperately; overcoming the inevitable pangs of doubt, insofar as any religious overcomes such monstrous hurdles, doubt about her worthiness, about her motives, about her ability to withstand the lonely, chiding cries of her empty, barren womb – brought so virulently to the fore when the cries of children wafted their tearful way over the convent wall into the contemplative stillness – doubt, even, about Christ Himself. And renouncing all pleasures of the flesh, all pleasures, some said, perhaps envious, of the mind, renouncing her siblings, her parents, her few friends, even Peter Clark – kind, sweet Peter who loved her dearly in his silent, fumbling way: poor Peter who actually wept when he heard of her decision and sought solace in one magnificent bender, but who nevertheless continued to write to her long after she had taken her final, irrevocable vows, still guaranteeing his undying love. And for a moment it was as though it was *his* voice that coaxed: 'Be a good little nun and grab God by the feet while I take hold of His head.'

Then another voice replying: 'Permit me to uplift you, father.'

And the first voice again: 'Ah, thank you, Patrick.'

'I came, in any case, to seek – '

'How timely your arrival. I – '

' – you out. The Archbishop would – '

' – thought for a moment, a terrible moment I might add, that you were – '

' – like to see you.'

' – figure risen from the cross. See me? The Archbishop?'

'As soon as possible.'

Sister Mary watched the two men manhandle the crucifix through the doorway of the hospice. She stayed on the porch, listening to their disembodied voices, listening, too, to Peter Clark trying valiantly to make himself heard.

'Be careful here,' Father Septimus said.

'I am caring,' Patrick replied sharply.

– Don't you care about me? Peter Clark pleaded.

'*That* corner, I think, Patrick.'

'If you desire it there.'

'I desire it there. Why should the Archbishop want – '

'He did not say.'

'But you know, don't you?'

– Don't you know I love you, Brigid?

'I repeat, I have not been told.'

'You don't have to be told. Not too steady, is it?'

'It will not fall. I am to drive you to the palace. That is all I know.'

– All I know is that I cannot live without you.

But he had lived without her, and married another girl, fathering five children, each blue-eyed, fair-haired child bearing witness to her aching for motherhood. On each short visit home (first from Rhodesia, then Uganda, then Chad) she had visited them all in the village of Murroe, he still calling her Brigid, still clinging to her hand many minutes after he had welcomed her; his wife, a fine, plain girl of enormous heart and kindness, embracing her as though she understood and shared her husband's yearning and was determined to be part of it –

'We must consult the oracle. Sister Mary?'

– and when the dusk of those summer days faded into darkness, and the lights were switched on, it was as if they had all, together, vanished without trace into the brightness.

'Sister Mary?' Father Septimus sounded tetchy.

Sister Mary moved slowly across the porch and entered the hospice.

'Ah. There you are. What do you think?'

'Very nice', she had said vaguely, the comment still striking Septimus as decidedly odd as he sat in the Packard being driven to his audience with the Archbishop.

' – want to say in front of the reverend nun, but he has only a day or two left with us.'

Septimus leaned forward. 'I'm sorry?'

'The Archbishop. He is failing most rapidly. Two, three days at the most, and he will be dead,' Patrick explained, generously allowing the dying prelate the benefit of an extra twenty-four hours.

But Archbishop Gidron looked nowhere near that approximate to death, although there was something curiously final about the way he took Septimus by the hand, dropping it carelessly as if irritated by the futility of any prolonged contact with life. He looked well enough however, almost animated, his wheelchair the only indication of his murderous ailment, his eyes still bright and watchful. 'You will, please, give Father Septimus a sherry, Patrick. And then leave us,' he said, tugging at the astrakhan rug that covered his legs. 'You have settled well, I hear,' he went on as Patrick withdrew looking, Septimus thought, quite miffed.

Unable to decide whether the Archbishop was expecting a reply or not, Septimus elected to say, simply, 'Thank you, Your Grace.' The old man made a flickering gesture of annoyance, his hands jumping beneath his rug, his wide, flat nose wrinkling. 'Your Grace,' he snapped, mimicking Septimus. 'What a stupidity. High time we abolished such flamboyant titles. The Almighty is unlikely to be impressed when – I've always hated them. My Lord. Your Grace. Your Eminence. So foolish. So arrogant. Barriers between ourselves and our flock.'

For no particular reason Septimus suddenly felt uneasy. The Archbishop, spotting this, clearly found it amusing; he gave a wheezing, whinnying laugh, unwisely as it turned out since it instantly brought on a fierce bout of phlegm-filled coughing that bent him double. Still hacking he reached for the spoon and a bottle of raspberry-coloured medicine that stood on the small inlaid table beside him. He extracted the cork with his teeth, and tried to pour the concoction on to the spoon, but such was the virulence of his attack that he found this impossible; impatiently he flung the spoon to the floor, removed the cork from his mouth and swigged from the bottle as eagerly as an alcoholic. 'Pardon,' he apologized with an impish grin as though, indeed, he had been caught having a surreptitious tipple, recorking the bottle and returning it to the table, wiping his mouth with the cuff of his purple-piped cassock. 'Such a nuisance this business of dying.'

Septimus rose to retrieve the spoon from the floor, placing it carefully on the table by the medicine. 'Can I – ' he began, in truth with no idea what he was about to offer.

Fortunately the Archbishop seemed to know and shook his head. 'Thank you, no. You have settled well?' he repeated, this time making it a question.

'Very well. Thank you.'

'Good. Good.'

The Archbishop shifted in his wheelchair, easing himself painfully on to his right buttock, and resting one elbow on the padded arm. 'You know,' he said eventually, 'when Patrick first brought you to see me I had the most terrible doubts about you. Oh, yes.'

Septimus raised his eyebrows in an expression of pain and speculation.

'Oh, yes. You know what I thought?' the old man asked, looking

64

as though he was about to cackle again but fortunately foreseeing the danger in this and settling instead for a conspiratorial smile. 'I thought you were just another of those short-sighted geriatrics they have usually lumbered us with.' He closed his eyes. 'Old men,' he went on almost to himself, 'with minds long since jettisoned. Symbols of archaic religion. Gestures from the Vatican.' He snapped his eyes wide open. 'But you're not, are you? No,' he concluded without waiting for an answer, looking suddenly excited, his old eyes banishing for a moment the tints of decrepitude and sparkling fiercely. 'Are you a fatalist?'

Not meaning compulsive, masochistic depressive by any chance, Septimus thought. Or one of those hapless souls whose weary lot it is to shoulder the baffling huggermugger of – good gracious – tempestuous fortune, and trudge (only occasionally raising a tiny yelp of complaint) along the trenches under life's persistent artillery barrage in much the same way as mules trundled their deadly backpacks through Ypres; all the while longing to lose oneself, simply to vanish, not to die but just beautifully and mysteriously disappear, as the majestic Siberian cranes disappear from the marshy lakes of Poyang, soaring over all the glorious and devastated ages of China on their journey to that secret place man has yet to discover.

'I hadn't thought about that. Perhaps I am,' Septimus decided it was politic to admit, clearly giving the Archbishop what he wanted since he immediately warmed his episcopal smile a few degrees and nodded appreciatively. 'I thought you might be. Patrick was quite certain of it.'

'And he is never wrong.'

Archbishop Gidron laughed gently. 'Ah-hah. You have heard that too? The annoying thing – between ourselves – is that he seldom *is* wrong.' His face went suddenly serious, all trace of amusement dropping away, his eyes narrowing. 'Which is what worries me,' he said, avoiding Septimus's quizzical surprise by shifting on to the other buttock.

Outside on the lawn the peacock, cooling itself under the sputtering sprinklers, its damp plumage clinging tightly to its remarkably small frame, sent up a single, primeval cry, dire and premonitory. As though taking a cue the old Archbishop uttered a cry of his own, a feeble affair, more of sadness than defiance, before warning, 'You must beware of Patrick, you understand. His mind is drenched in the powers of the Vinbrindingue, and I fear he has special intentions for you.'

Septimus stared blankly, his sherry glass poised half way to his mouth.

'Like Mephistopheles,' the prelate went on, speaking with extreme care as if his ruminations were as virulent to himself as they were to Septimus, 'he can seduce the unwary into believing that he has their best interests at heart. And, to his way of thinking, he has.' The Archbishop appeared to be getting drowsy, his voice slurring a little, his eyelids heavy and drooping, his hands less fidgety. 'As, indeed, we all claim to have, is it not so? Always the salve to the conscience. Always for someone else's good.' He managed a wry smile. 'People have said that to you, I am sure. And that is when you must be most on your guard, wouldn't you say? It is the question of perspective, I imagine. And, I suppose, perception. Yes,' he agreed with himself, nodding. 'Mostly, I would say, perception. How we perceive ourselves and all that we deem important.' His chin dropped on to his chest.

For one anxious moment Septimus thought the Archbishop had died, but gentle snoring reassured him, and he drank his sherry, emptying the contents of his glass in a single swallow. He stood up and walked, almost on tiptoe, across the room to the large French windows that opened on to a patio with steps down to the lawn, placing his glass on an octagonal mosaic table as he passed. How we perceive ourselves and all that we deem important! It struck him, gazing out at the superficially lush, deserted lawn, the sprinklers now automatically idle, the peacock retired, a wispy, artificially induced haze gloating over the garden, that Archbishop Gidron's somnolent withdrawal might not have been totally fortuitous; the wily old prelate could very well have sensed sleep overtaking him and served up his intrepid statement as bait knowing that Septimus would have ample, undisturbed time to contemplate its implications. Septimus, however, was not about to do any such thing even if he had wanted to. Something far more pressing was demanding his instant and undivided attention in the shape of a young, dark-haired, light-skinned Indian woman of about twenty, with deep-set sorrowful eyes. On the point of weeping, on the point, too, of being beautiful, she ambled, bulbous and gloriously pregnant, into his mind, then receded, re-emerging younger, flat-bellied, her eyes not yet stamped with that awful sadness, her arms extended in loving

66

welcome, her mouth slightly open, her pink tongue, just visible, flicking . . .

– You are afraid of my body, but you want it, no?

Father Septimus Roach made no answer. The woman was right of course, although she had certainly understated his feelings; he was terrified of her body, its soft warmness screaming his desire, screaming havoc in his mind, and he yearned to possess it more than he could recall ever longing for anything.

– Why will you not take it?

Father Septimus remained silent, not trusting himself to make a reply. Eight years of furtive missionary work in Paraguay, mostly in the province of Caaguazú, had taken the gloss off his naïve zeal and sapped his resistance. What had started out as a genuine and dedicated – slightly glamorized – apostolate (sometimes, innocently enough and without malice, seen as following in the footsteps of earlier visionaries whose exploits, none too deeply scrutinised, had entered the legends of the church) had before long deteriorated into an horrendous, skulking struggle for simple survival in the harsh, all-revealing light of stark reality. The God he had brought (that rather winsome, all-loving, all-forgiving, compassionate God) was, he soon discovered, little short of grotesque in a country where His name was used to sanction inhuman atrocities, where ruthless brutality was the norm, where the *quarani* music of José Asuncion Flores, played at full volume, hammered the night and drowned the screams of the victims of a hypocritically Catholic régime, where people were plucked at random from their homes to be found later, mutilated, floating, like monstrous deadwood, in the swirling brown waters of the Paraná, their faces proclaiming the agony of their death, or worse, vanishing without trace, leaving nothing behind to be mourned but bewildering, uninterred memories.

– You *do* want me, no?

Shaking, some suicidal power driving him on, Father Septimus found himself hurrying through the narrow door and into the one-roomed hut. The girl, smiling, panting, was already undressing, one arm arched behind her neck pulling at the zip of her flowered cotton dress. Septimus groaned in silence, passionately aware of the consequences he would never be able to eradicate from his soul. The dress slipped to the floor, nestling like a crumpled wreath at the girl's bare feet. Her nakedness shimmered with perspiration, drops glistening on her nipples. Again Septimus heard his conscience moan. He wanted desperately to turn and run but he could not. Ludicrous phrases leaped into his mind: Behind me Satan! I have avowed my holy chastity! My body is given to Christ! – So this was it, the first in what would surely be a harrowing litany of betrayals and rejections. He could prevent it even now, but he was too tired, too disillusioned to do anything about it. How glibly the jaded excuses came! He was too weak, too useless to do anything about it. Perhaps the merciful, all-understanding God who had voyaged with him to this unhappy land would offer some advice, would aid him in his escape? Squinting as though in sudden brightness, he peered about the dark little room, listening: no such God had any advice to offer, nor devised a plan of escape, it seemed.

The room itself reflected his sorrow: it was abject. It could have been the disposable lodgings of primitive man, of some hunted being close to extinction, a Kalahari bushman perhaps, were it not for the enormous poster, its proud and arrogant claim on the point of becoming defunct, that was pinned to the wall opposite the doorway. At the head of this poster was a fat, contented, grazing steer, and under it, in fine bold lettering:

FINE CATTLE IN PARAGUAY

Beneath these laudatory words a casserole of the Casa Pupo variety, filled to the brim with nourishing stew, trailings of steam artistically drawn in, was temptingly suspended. Then:

GOOD FOOD IN BRITAIN

Because the grasslands of Paraguay can nourish millions of cattle, a massive meat-packing factory has been built by Liebig's Extract of Meat Company, whose products add both nourishment and richer flavours to the world's cooking, Liebig's, a subsidiary of the Brooke Bond Liebig Group, looks forward to handling an increasing supply of fine Paraguayan cattle, so helping to maintain and improve the economy of the lovely country immortalised by its President, Don Alfredo Stroessner, in one simple but memorable phrase: The People and the Land *are* Paraguay.

And beneath that, in case anyone had managed to overlook the simple but memorable cynicism, it was reiterated in capitals:

THE PEOPLE AND THE LAND ARE PARAGUAY.

Liebig's in Paraguay
Partners in a nation's progress.

The poster had been defaced; along the bottom, not obscuring a word of the proclamation, in red ink, the letters intentionally jagged as though in an attempt to simulate blood, someone had scrawled: The People ARE the Cattle of Paraguay.

– Come to me now.

Silently as sin Septimus moved across the earthen floor of the hut to the cot on which the woman was sprawled, stopping a couple of feet from it. Already naked, the woman flexed her body, pushing with her shoulders, arching her back, gyrating her hips, and the strands of thin metal that supported the coarse horsehair mattress twanged a tune like a loosely strung guitar. Her small, firm breasts stood erect, tempting. Septimus felt himself start to shake again, felt, too, the intoxicating, forbidden ache surge into his loins, and closed his eyes. So this was definitely it: the first rejection of his vows, the first betrayal, the start of his downfall, the imminent perpetration of that act which would shatter the promise he had so presumptuously made at his ordination, that would abort all the trust placed in him. He opened the buttons of his soutane and slipped his arms from the sleeves: the vestment crashed silently to the ground. He could still resist. He unbuckled his belt. Perhaps, even yet, although the possibility grew more and more remote, the God with Whom he had once been so familiar would take pity on him, would recognise his weakness, would come to his rescue. He let his trousers drop, stepping from them, kicking off his rope-soled espadrilles in a single movement. Still no God came to his assistance. He removed his underpants, stooping to disentangle them from his feet. And as he stooped the woman sat upright on the bed and reached out, taking his hard, throbbing penis in one hand and drawing him relentlessly towards her, on to her. Oh, sweet Jesus. She writhed beneath him, sighing and groaning. Her legs, her breasts, her soft voluptuous thighs, her hands with their chipped, work-splintered nails, the coarse black hair that peeped like small animals from under her arms, her entire body – all these things were the materialization of his every adolescent fantasy, a joyous confirmation of his suppressed manhood. But even as he penetrated her, even as his whole being, body and spirit, twitched and jerked with delicious excitement and deliverance, even then the pleasure was draining away from him; he was slipping into a desolate, bleak, abandoned darkness. The moaning, satisfied body beneath him, with its tang of spices and cheap perfume and sweat, became, suddenly, frighteningly, a devastating abstraction, a daemonic apparatus for blasphemous orgasm . . .

Archbishop Gidron snuffled in his sleep but did not awaken. Septimus turned his head and glanced briefly over his shoulder at the dozing old man, then took to gazing out of the window again. Happily the spectre of the woman had withdrawn, perhaps to the shrubbery to delate him to the peacock. As, indeed, she had (although surely blamelessly) betrayed him to the sinister Py-Nandu, her warm, soft flesh ripped and burned and abused with systematic torture. But that had been later, a year, eighteen months later, by which time the child had been born and thrived, despite the poverty and deprivation, into crawling, gurgling infancy; by which time he, Septimus Roach, had come to acknowledge that the temporally deprived had little use for the high-flown promises of spiritual redemption, and had become embroiled in the peasant demonstrations against Brazilian land-buying in the region, excusing his participation (if only to allay his mild remorse at breaking a promise airily made to Bishop McKewen) on the basis that by siding with the impoverished, illiterate peons in their quite legitimate struggle he would remain close to them, be regarded with something approaching respect, and, ultimately, at some favourable date in the future, be able to convince them, if not himself entirely, that God was not so remote, was not, as many of them perceived Him, a suspect idol there to be worshipped as part of an endemic superstition, an ancient pageantry not to be totally disdained lest there should be a glimmer of truth in the myths.

'*Tiens!*' Archbishop Gidron awoke with a start, smacking his lips before explaining, 'It is that evil concoction they force me to take that makes me so sleepy.' He gave a tentative little laugh. 'I believe they are hoping I will die in my sleep. To fit the obituary announcement that they have, without doubt, already prepared, you see. "Our beloved Archbishop was taken peacefully from his sleep to the throne of God." They do think, you know, that it befits my status to pass away peacefully in my sleep. What they will do if I die at any other time I cannot imagine.'

Septimus turned from the window and smiled kindly at the wizened old prelate.

'You look – what is the word? – eh, wistful,' Archbishop Gidron observed, cocking his head to one side and squinting.

Septimus was about to reply, perhaps to agree or offer some explanation for his aspect, when something caught the corner of his eye: a chicken darted from the shrubbery and raced, neck outstretched, across the lawn, a length of string trailing behind it. Septimus shuddered.

'Come and sit by me for a moment,' the Archbishop requested.

Septimus left the window, feeling absurdly elated that the chicken had made good its escape, and made his way back across the room. He was on the point of sitting down by the mosaic table when the Archbishop, sounding testy, snapped, 'Closer. Bring the chair closer.'

Obediently Septimus carried the small mahogany chair with him and placed it beside the Archbishop's wheelchair. He sat down gingerly, folding his hands on his lap. Outside the chicken squawked: alas, recaptured, it seemed.

'Now,' Archbishop Gidron interrupted, frowning a little. 'What were we talking about before I fell asleep?' He pursed his lips. 'Ah, yes,' he went on almost immediately, looking relieved he had remembered, his eyes brightening.

But, for the time being at any rate, he showed no inclination to elaborate on that theme. He sat motionless in his wheelchair for a while, then took to nodding, and mouthing mutely, his hands under the astrakhan rug moving as though he was fingering a keyboard, tinkling a silent tune.

Septimus continued to wait, listening, trying to decipher the words the prelate was mouthing to himself. It was an endeavour crassly interrupted by the unseemly, piercing scream of the peacock (although the Archbishop showed no sign of noticing), a scream, it struck Septimus, that now sounded anything but vain, sounded evil, sounded like mocking laughter at the wretched chicken's misfortune. And, without warning, the room and his entire consciousness was filled with wild, demented laughter, laughter punctuated by sobbing and atrocious cries of pain, cries that Septimus instantly recognized as his own . . .

The windowless cell in the police station at Caaguazú stank of urine and blood and terror and death. Alone, Septimus crouched in one corner, his legs tucked up, his chin on his knees, his back tight against the cold concrete wall, unable to sit for the lacerations on his buttocks. He listened, counting, to the moans that came from other cells, and waited for his captors to make their regular, dreaded daily visit. In an odd, frenzied way he would come to welcome their sinister arrival. When the pain started he would cope; it was the humiliating wait for the unknown that frightened and degraded him, his imagination conjuring up horrors even his abductors could not conceive. But they knew this and always kept him waiting, never visiting him at the same time, day or night. Forgetting, trying to ease the aching from his arms, Septimus tucked his hands under his armpits; the stale sweat stung his nailless fingers, setting them on fire, making his head reel with pain. For a second he relived the dreadful episode when they wrenched away his nails, ripping them from their sockets with surgical pliers, making, with each vicious extraction, a fresh demand that he give them the names of others involved in what they grandly called 'this treason', seeming however to delight in his refusal, laughing their hideous cold Latin laughs, holding aloft each shard of nail in triumph as though it was a valid specimen to enhance their superiority.

The keys rattled outside the cell, and Septimus started to shake uncontrollably. He tried desperately to stand, but could not. He tried to be calm, but the more he tried the worse he shook. Roughly the door was kicked open. It banged back against the wall, its echo reverberating throughout the grim dungeon, its awesome promise of pain making all the inmates of that daemonic place fall silent. Sergeant Colman, swarthy, mustachioed, sleekhaired, swaggering, came in alone. Light suddenly blazed from the ceiling, switched on from the corridor, the single powerful bulb recessed into the reinforced roof and protected by close-mesh wire. It shone directly over the Sergeant's head, making him shadowless, making him seem larger than he was, more menacing. How they had all joked about this Sergeant and his tribulations in trying to arrest them! Huddled together in someone's house, a sentry always at the window watching, putting on faces braver than they felt, they had listened, their wide, friendly Indian faces glowing, as Septimus childishly nicknamed the bullying Sergeant Colman 'Mustard' and explained the derivation, while poor Flecha, now missing, cackled, lips curled, showing more gum than teeth, as the extrovert Ramon Duarte (now hiding in the mountains somewhere, both arms broken, both eardrums smashed by relentless pistol-whipping) practised his meagre English on 'He ees moosturd'.

– Well, priest, Colman asked. Have you become sensible?

Septimus said nothing, but he stopped shaking.

Colman shrugged and tapped his boot with the riding crop he invariably carried – a theatrical hangover from the German propaganda films he had seen and enjoyed as a child. We will get the answers we want in the end, you know, priest. We always do.

Still Septimus held his tongue.

– So? Always the stupid silence?

Septimus shut his eyes and waited.

– Bring the bitch in, Colman ordered.

Septimus froze.

– Is this the man? Colman demanded in Spanish.

– *Si*.

– You know him well?

– *Si*.

– You have seen him with other Communists?

– *Si*.

– He is one of them?

– *Si*.

– And he fathered that bastard?

– *Si*.

– Well, priest?

Slowly, painfully, dreading what he might behold, Septimus eased his eyelids open and looked up. At first he did not recognise the woman: her head had been cruelly shaved, jagged tufts sticking from her scalp like some outrageous punkish cut. Her dress, the one she had stripped so willingly from her body the day he made love to her, had been ripped at the neck and hung shapelessly about her. A raw weal, scabby with dried blood, ran the length of one cheek. One of her deep eyes, eyes that had held for him the promise of ecstatic bliss, had been blackened, the swelling only partially subsided. It was the child Septimus recognized at once. Clasped in his mother's arms, innocently unafraid, he stared at Septimus in serious reproach. Septimus struggled to his feet, sliding his back up the wall for support, but stayed in the darkness of the corner as though to escape the baleful look. He heard Colman laugh. He heard Colman speak but mislaid the first few words.

– your kind not to care for life. But we won't make a martyr of you, priest. Hah, you'd like that, no? It would erase your sin, no? he asked, indicating the child with his crop. Hah. All you damn priests are the same. Hypocrites. Rapists hiding under that black, woman's frock. So –

He hit his boot hard and swung round. He grabbed the child by one leg and started to swing it back and forth, keeping its head only inches from the ground.

The woman, petrified, transfixed, made no protest. Made no sound at all. No whimper. She did not even move. Quite motionless, her arms still raised across her breasts as though holding some disembodiment of her son, her eyes stared at the swinging child, moving with it, witnessing its horrendous predicament, yet all the while expressionless. It was Septimus who screamed: a dreadful, wild, animal cry that seemed to come from some absent being. He felt it well up inside him. He felt it reach his throat, choking him. He felt it leave his mouth. But the awful sound seemed to come from far away, from some part of his soul that had long since abandoned him.

– The names, priest, Colman said simply, sounding almost kind, almost civilly reasonable.

Incredibly the child seemed to be enjoying the appalling game. It gave a tiny chuckle, and hearing it, Septimus believed his heart was bleeding from him. He started to babble, calling out names that sounded Hispanic, dragging them helter-skelter from the recesses of his mind: Caravaggio, Lorca, Peron, Velasquez, Pinero – they rattled from his dry mouth. Goya, Camillo, Gallico, Montaigna. He stopped only when Colman slashed him across the face with his whip. And through the searing pain, through the blood that slowly filtered into his eyes, through the sorrowful vision that accused his moment of lust, Septimus saw the Sergeant swing the child in an arc over his head and open his fingers . . .

'You are unwell?' Archbishop Gidron was asking, leaning towards him, sounding concerned.

'They killed the child anyway,' Septimus heard himself say.

'The child? I do not understand.'

Flustered, confused, Septimus got quickly to his feet. He started to make for the window again, but stopped, wincing, after a few paces. He hobbled back to his chair and sat once more. He bent forward and massaged his mutilated legs, easing the throbbing pain from the wasted muscles with his fingers.

'Of what child do you speak?' the Archbishop persisted.

'Just a child,' Septimus said quietly without looking up. 'A child I once knew. A child I loved.'

'Not here? Not in Haiti?'

'No. Oh no. Long before I came here.'

'Ah,' Archbishop Gidron sighed, sounding greatly relieved.

. . . Their voices came to him, whispering, although this would have been untypical, through the immeasurable abyss of guilt, each of them having something to contribute: Sergeants Colman and Delgado, Lieutenant Romero, and the man in civilian clothes called Gonzalez.

– We cannot kill him.

– We cannot let him live.

– A dead priest will cause us trouble.

– Alive he would cause us more trouble.

– But how?

– It must look like an accident.

Someone laughed.

– No, not an accident. Like a murder.

– Yes.

– That pig Eulalio Gomez –

– I see!

– He is still here?

– Yes.

– And his truck?

– Out back.

– Excellent.

– I think I understand.

Someone else laughed.

– We use the truck to kill him, no?

– Yes.

– And Gomez?

– He cannot deny anything if he is dead.

They all chorused laughter at that.

Colman ordered: Carry him outside. I will drive the truck myself.

He was half-carried, half-dragged to the yard at the back of the police station, and flung into the back of the truck. Delgado and Romero clambered in and sat over him. A boot was nonchalantly placed on his abdomen. Nobody spoke. Delgado lit a cigarette and coughed raucously, spitting over the tailboard of the truck as it bounced and lurched out into the country, its canvas roof flapping, catching the wind like a sail.

Lying on the floor, the sweet smell of Gomez's fruit filling his nostrils, so refreshing after the foetid stink of his cell, Septimus felt no pain. His mind was littered with conflicting thoughts, none of them complete, each leading to the next in a tortuous, inexplicable way, the way of the insane. In his mind too there was music – Mahler perhaps, or Bruckner, probably Bruckner, a mournful melody. Faces hovered over him, none recognizable, each dissembling and reshaping itself as another shadowy profile. Gandhi was there for an instant, or maybe it was Blake, or Lorca, or Wallenberg, or himself, or –

The truck lurched to a halt, its tyres skidding in the dust, sending Septimus skittering across the floor. Delgado scorched his lips with his cigarette and swore. Colman raised the canvas flap and ordered urgently: Get him out.

They pulled him from the truck and dragged him round the side to the driver's door, his feet trailing.

– Up there, Colman said, pointing down the track. And make him stand.

Delgado and Romero manhandled him to where Colman had indicated: some twenty yards from the truck they released him. He collapsed in a heap. Colman switched the headlights on full again. Make him *stand*, he bellowed.

They hauled him upright, cursing him. Swaying, absurdly trying to oblige, Septimus waited to die. He heard the engine growl as Colman toed the accelerator. He watched fascinated as it lumbered towards him, slowly gathering speed, like, the silly thought flickered into his mind, some prehistoric monster on the charge. What a pathetic, ridiculous, undignified way to die! Run down by a rusting, dilapidated fruit-and-vegetable truck in the wilds of Paraguay. Whatever had become of the peaceful death, forgiven by and re-united with Christ, that had been his cherished dream? The lights blinded him, distorting his sense of distance. The truck should have clobbered him by now, but it was still moving inexorably towards him. He should already be dead, but he was still alive. Then he could smell the oily fumes of the overheated engine, even, for an instant, feel its warmth on his face. When, finally and un-expectedly as it happened, it did hit him, he felt nothing. He had the queer sensation of being weightless, of flying pleasantly, of hovering. Even when he thudded into the ground and tumbled down, down into the ravine that ran alongside the road, there was no pain. Instinctively he lay quite still. A light from above shone in his face.

– Is he dead?
– He's dead.
– How can we be sure?
– He's dead all right.
– Maybe we should go down and make certain.
– You go if you want. But he is dead.
– You are sure?
– If not now he will be by the time anyone finds him.

As they moved away one of them dislodged a stone: it crashed past Septimus, bouncing, echoing, hurtling down to the bottom of the ravine . . .

'Into the abyss,' escaped Septimus before he could stop it.

The Archbishop apparently found this remark less disturbing than the reference to a child. He nodded as though he understood and sympathized. 'But there is always a means of escape, is there not?' he asked. 'From whatever abyss into which we may find ourselves tossed. Except,' he added, suddenly pensive, darting a wary look at Septimus, and leaving the word to survive on its own.

Septimus straightened himself up and gazed, frowning, at the prelate, a small, desolate voice warning him that there was more to the isolated word than one might at first suspect. But maybe the voice was just scaremongering since the Archbishop decided to continue, his voice far from premonitory, quite hopeful, in fact. 'Yes. There is ever the exception – to everything.' He leaned forward and patted Septimus on the knee. 'Which brings me to what I wanted to say.' He interjected a kindly, apologetic little laugh. 'It takes my old mind quite a time to get things organized. Particularly thoughts.' He laughed again, this time, however, almost sadly.

77

'When you are approaching death the mind gets cluttered. Memories come sweeping in and, alas, you are forced to recall, most vividly I might add, all the things you hoped to achieve and did not.' He sighed heavily. 'Still, as long as we did our best, eh?'

Septimus fixed his eyes on the bony, claw-like hand that rested on his knee. Gently, as though doodling, he ran his finger along it, tracing the blue vein that stood out like a cord. Astonishingly, he could feel in this wide, high, quiet room that same withdrawn sensation he had experienced in the stinking dark cell in Caaguazú, a curious welcoming of whatever affliction might be in store. As long as we did our best, eh! He became queerly conscious of his presence slipping out of his body; of it standing behind him, glaring down over his shoulder, waiting for some explanation as to why, in fact, he had not given of his best. Happily, this worrying sensation was short-lived, and he was whole again; or almost. Some part of him was at the window again, staring into the garden, fearful yet mesmerized by what might unfold . . . Nothing: the chicken subdued, its master, the crippled cobbler, triumphant, the peacock silently gloating its freedom. But then, suddenly, Septimus felt himself submerged in a wave of remorse and loneliness, a cruel static wave such as men encounter in rapids, that allows them to behold the safety of light yet secures them just below the surface for eternity. Impulsively he grasped the Archbishop's hand and kissed it, then held it tight against his cheek.

Archbishop Gidron didn't seem to mind, seemed accustomed to such demonstrations. And probably he was.

'I'm sorry,' Septimus apologized, looking ashamed but still clinging to the Archbishop's hand though replacing it on his knee and holding it there. Archbishop Gidron gave a reproving tut. 'Why should you be sorry?' he asked. 'It is a kindness you do me. I only wish I could be with you when your agony begins.'

The sense of the words did not immediately clarify itself in Septimus's mind; it was as though he had intercepted a statement meant for somebody else. Then he felt the blood drain from his face, making him giddy. He stared wide-eyed at the Archbishop, who smiled back encouragingly.

'When my agony begins?' Septimus thought he heard himself ask with, he felt, admirable calm.

78

But the Archbishop gave no sign of having heard anything that required an answer. Indeed, if anything, he looked to be relishing the fact that his words had been accepted with such good grace: He squeezed Septimus's hand, and continued, 'In a way I envy you, although I should not sin so close to death. There are so few of us allowed the great privilege of sacrifice. Years from now you will be revered, your name recalled long after mine has faded from some marble edifice. You will be immortal.'

Septimus was stunned. He wanted to get up and go, passionately he wanted to leap to his feet and flee –

' – sacrifice in the name of Jesus Christ,' the Archbishop was saying.

– but the lightness of the prelate's hand on his knee was like a monstrous weight restraining him from any such escape. He wanted to cry out –

' – a glorious bastion against the stranglehold of – ' the Archbishop's voice hummed on.

– that there had been a terrible mistake, a drastic mistake. That he was clearly being mistaken for someone else. That he was, after all, only here in Haiti on loan. That he was simply helping out on a strictly temporary basis. That he could be recalled at a moment's notice. That immortality was definitely not something –

' – glory of dying like Christ Jesus Himself – '

– that was on his agenda. That he had already sustained quite enough suffering in his life. That he was weak and tired and would certainly capitulate, would topple into that one abyss from which there was no escape despite what Blake and Archbishop Gidron or anyone else said, would –

' – shoulder the suffering of all those innocents who could not themselves bear – '

– lie, quaking and grovelling, in the deepest recess of that abyss amid the debris of his life, amid the sins and broken promises, amid the refuse of accumulated despair, probably howling and making an ass of himself.

But Septimus Roach said none of these things: he sat quite passively in his chair, silent and morose, his head swimming, as the wheezy, singsong voice wafted by. Single, isolated words, keen-edged, cut through the blurring bewilderment – 'calvary' – 'inevitable' – 'saviour' (which had a note of comfort in it) –

'scourge' (which certainly hadn't) – leaving Septimus, if not convinced, at least hopeful that he was eavesdropping on words meant for another or on the private ruminations of a sick old man.

And twenty minutes later, sitting in the back of the Packard, a cooling breeze blowing through the open window on to his face, his mind now filled with the very real cries of the market vendors, with the blasting of horns as vehicles tried to manoeuvre their way through the throng of bargaining women, children swinging from their skirts, Septimus began to wonder if he had imagined the entire episode, if, once asleep, the Archbishop had remained asleep, and if the gruesome dissertation had just been some complex crossing of the filaments in his own mind. He sighed and lay back in the upholstered seat.

'*Merde!*' Patrick swore, and swung the car sharply to the left. 'I regret the discomfort,' he apologized, eyeing Septimus in the mirror.

But Septimus did not hear. He was staring out of the window, his eyes fixed on the crippled cobbler who had now made his way safely to the side of the road, the chicken tucked under his bomber jacket. For an instant their eyes met.

'He will be dead tomorrow.'

Septimus, involuntarily, gave a small howl.

'Yes. He will be dead tomorrow,' Patrick repeated. 'It is good that you spoke with him today.'

'Oh. The Archbishop.'

'Of course.'

'Ah.'

'He feels for you greatly. Did he tell you that?'

'Yes. No. He – '

'We all feel for you greatly.'

'I – '

'And we will show our gratitude.'

Somewhere in the distance a bell was tolling. Septimus counted the strokes, using the dolorous tones to focus his mind, to extract some encouragement from Patrick's promise of collective gratitude, an exercise abruptly halted when, as the car slowed to a halt at the top of the alley that housed the hospice, the expressionless face of the cobbler appeared at the window, his eyes tremendously consoling to Septimus, yet commiserating with him too, assuring him that, after all, what had transpired during the past few hours was –

Septimus jumped from the car, using the door to brush the cripple aside, and hurried in a hop-skipping trot to the sanctuary of the hospice.

Five

'Did you know that when they sent poor old Chekhov's body back to Moscow to be buried they shipped it in a goddam boxcar labelled "Fresh Oysters"?'

The boisterous Bronx twang that imparted this lamentable gem of historical fact seemed to find it amusing rather than pathetic however, chuckling breathlessly before shouting, 'Hey, garcon!' with a hard 'c' and hailing a taxi.

Susanna Lichfield, on the other hand, found it bewildering but refrained from commenting on it for the moment. Instead, she dug her heels in, stopped dead, and demanded, 'Solly, what on earth are we doing *here*?'

Solomon Gross watched the taxi-driver put the two suitcases into the boot of the psychedelically painted Buick, and slung the vicuña coat, normally worn over his shoulders like a cloak, on to the back seat. 'You said you wanted to get away for a few days.'

'But *here*. God, you might have asked me.'

'What's wrong with it?'

'It's dreadful.'

'You haven't seen it yet.'

'I've seen enough.'

'You'll love it.'

'I hate it already.'

'You always say that to begin with. Just get in, will you?'

Reluctantly, her lovely face petulant, her wide, generous lips puckering as though she was about to burst into tears, Susanna stepped into the taxi and settled herself in the corner, gazing unseeingly out of the window, sulking.

'Hotel Ollofson,' Solomon Gross instructed, enlarging the words by contorting his mouth as if he suspected the driver to be on the point of misunderstanding him, and squeezed his small rotund body through the door.

82

The tireless keening of the jet-aircraft arriving and leaving François Duvalier International Airport seemed to accompany them as they were driven to the hotel. Susanna shivered a little, before suddenly abandoning her vexation. 'Anyway, what has Chekhov got to do with anything?'

'Not a lot.'

'Why did you mention him?'

'I thought it might amuse you.'

'Oh.'

'Another flop.'

Susanna laughed. 'I'm sorry. It's just – well, when you said we were going away for a few days I thought at least Bermuda.'

'I should have told you. I admit.'

'Yes. You should. My God – Haiti! What in heaven's name made you choose here?'

Now Solomon laughed. 'I don't know. I thought it would be different.'

'Oh, it's certainly that.'

'Or maybe I thought: Fonteyn goes to Panama so we'll go – '

'That's quite different.'

'Look, if you still hate it tomorrow night we'll leave, okay?'

'All right.'

Ashamed at her childishness, aware that she was still playing the internationally acclaimed ballerina whose temperament had always been suspect, Susanna stared defensively out of the taxi window, trying (if only to convince herself that she was upholding her end of the bargain) to absorb what brochures would undoubtedly call the 'local colour'; trying, too, to raise her mind from the curious torpor into which she had descended ever since her official retirement. She drew a deep breath. Immediately she frowned as an unexpected sweet smell of incense assailed her. ' – parade,' she heard Solomon say.

'I'm sorry?'

'It looks like a parade,' Solomon repeated.

'Oh.'

And in a sense he was correct: the funeral of the late Archbishop Gidron had all the trappings of a festive parade. It was at first glance, Susanna thought, like Mardi Gras in New Orleans; only when one looked again more closely could one could detect something mournful.

'You want to have a look?' Solomon asked, already leaning forward and tapping the driver on the shoulder.

Susanna stepped from the taxi and followed Solomon, allowing him to push a path through the crowd that lined the Carrefour. The scene was breathtaking: an incredible panoply of light and colour and sound.

'Jeez,' Solomon said under his breath. 'It's a funeral.'

Susanna felt icicles zigzag down her spine.

' – *Évêque*.'

'What's an eveque, Susanna?' Solomon wanted to know.

'What's what?'

'An eveque. The cabby says they're burying an eveque.'

'Oh. Bishop, I think.'

'Well, that's who they're burying then. A bishop.'

And burying him in some style! Down the Carrefour the cortège came, headed by children dressed in white tossing flower petals on to the road, paving the way of the dead with delicate scents. Behind them the women, dancing a strange nubile step, their rhythm transforming a dirge into something unbelievably sensual, their loose-fitting, multi-coloured dresses seeming to float about them like immense and gorgeous butterflies, a hurricane of sunny pastel shades, their faces, grave but not sorrowful, displaying a deliberate, serious joyousness as they celebrated the fact that someone they respected had been swept away to another, less troublesome world; then the men, sober and austere in black, all clapping their hands to the beat of the music, all wearing hats that sported black streamers; then the band, the jaunty musicians sweating as they blew into the mouthpieces of their instruments, their cheeks puffed out, their eyes bulging, the brass and silver trumpets, cornets, trombones and clarinets swaying with each stride of their slow, curiously tempoed march; and finally the hearse, a black Chevrolet bedecked with ribbons, with white and scarlet flowers, with tinsel, with tiny effigies, with small, orange-coloured net bags containing coins, and little fruits – a fig, some dates, a few grapes.

'What a way to go,' Solomon observed, although whether he approved or not was impossible to tell.

'Can *we* go?' Susanna asked, already turning her back on the funeral and pushing her way through the crowd towards the waiting taxi.

'That was *something*,' Solomon said, clutching the edge of his seat with both hands as the taxi dived down one of the alleys that led off the Carrefour.

'It was horrible,' Susanna retaliated.

'Why horrible?' Solomon sounded surprised.

'All that razzamatazz. It's unseemly.'

Solomon laughed. 'Unseemly yet! You do come up with some real beauties.'

Away from the Carrefour the streets were deserted, giving the city a faded melancholy, everything shuttered yet somehow expectant, one wary eye kept open. A lone pariah dog, red-eyed and slavering, lay in the gutter, panting; it got cumbersomely to its feet as the taxi passed, stared at it, stumbled a few paces then slumped down again and took to scratching itself behind one ear. Susanna's heart went out to it:

– But mother, it's been hurt.

– I don't care, Susanna. I'm not having any stray dogs in my house. And that's final.

– It's only a puppy.

– Get rid of it this instant.

– Couldn't we –

– Get it out of the house *now*!

Susan bridled: – Daddy would have let me keep it.

Mother's eyes flashed: – Your father would have let you do a lot of things, and you'd have ended up like him too.

Mother wrenched the quivering puppy from her arms and threw it outside, slamming the door. All through the night it howled pitifully. In the morning it was dead on the doorstep. Mother gathered it up in some old newspaper and dumped it in the garbage can . . .

Suddenly, the detour negotiated, they were on the Carrefour again, the funeral behind them but the music still clearly audible, seeming to be following them rather than receding. Yet, amazingly, the moment the taxi swung through the gates of the Hotel Ollofson the world became soundless save for the crunching of tyres on the gravel. Even when she got out of the taxi and listened intently she could detect no whisper of the boisterous funeral. All was totally quiet. No birds sang. No insects hummed. She took in the hotel in a long, disenchanted look – the ridiculous fantasy that might have been a stage set, an amateur production of the Sleeping Beauty perhaps, the long, cool veranda deserted, waiting dismally for the entrance of the players.

She followed Solomon into the hotel, hitching her skirt as she mounted the steep alabaster steps, looking as though at any moment she might change her mind and flee the eerie, depressing scene, just as she had flown (true, for quite the opposite reason) her home, leaving her mother screaming coarse, abusive valedictions from the doorway.

The foyer, too, was empty. Or rather, with only a cursory glance it appeared to be. Blinking myopically in the sudden gloom Susanna discerned a figure moving towards them, gliding rather than walking, his arms kept stiffly by his side. She heard, without listening, Solomon start to speak. The man bowed and then swung away, retreating behind the reception desk. Solomon followed and leaned on the counter, still talking, talking to himself possibly since the man didn't seem to be listening. Susanna meanwhile stood in the centre of the lobby, not daring to make a move, watching for the adversary she felt certain was lurking nearby, the droning of the airport still with her (somehow emerging as a synthesized, secondary motif of the funeral music that replayed itself also), and with her too, the strident voice of her mother as it hammered home its vile accusations. She forced herself to walk a few paces and sit down in one of the many heavily carved, over-upholstered chairs (possibly purloined from some Bavarian Schloss) that lined two walls of the foyer. She saw she was mistaken about the receptionist; he was paying considerable heed to what Solomon was saying. That is, while doubtless having some difficulty in understanding everything Solomon said, he was writing something down, occasionally nodding, his mouth opening a fraction from time to time as though about to interrupt, but closing it again as the opportunity to submit his pennyworth receded. Susanna wearily closed her eyes. Almost instantly a bell sounded, and another figure appeared through the glass door artfully concealed as part of an enormous mirror, a sleek dark youth, his hair flattened and glistening with pomade, his countenance cocky and giving notice that servility had no place in his makeup.

'What do you think now? Not bad, eh?' They were in the bedroom, and Solomon was already stripping off his clothes, ready to take a shower.

Susanna made no reply. She stood by one of the two windows,

staring down at the gardens below. One could still, just, make out how truly magnificent they must have been when properly tended. How her father would have adored them! How he had always hankered for a garden (a *proper* garden) of his own – a throwback to his English grandparents, he had explained with a wry smile. Poor, poor father: how absurdly sensitive, how absurdly foolish he had been.

Behind her Solomon gave voice in the shower: a wailing, out-of-tune version of some ethnic lament. Below her a car turned into the hotel grounds, stopped, then moved into the area set aside for parking. A man, tall and stooped, got out and gazed about him, and, miraculously, it was her father who now made his way on foot along the narrow path to the hotel entrance, responding generously to the wonder of each flower he passed, gently touching one or two, perhaps enquiring after their health, showing concern, encouraging them, telling them that life wasn't really quite as bad as it seemed, her father whose reckless and peculiarly abstract habits still smacked of good-natured insanity. He disappeared briefly behind a huge oleander, and his place was taken in her mind's eye by the only photograph she had of him (very small, somewhat out of focus, turning sepia at the edges, framed in silver and carried everywhere, displayed in dressing-rooms throughout the world and kissed affectionately before every performance).

'Aaaahhhhhhhh. That's better,' Solomon announced, coming from the shower, smelling of deodorant, towelling his buttocks, vainly trying to diminish his paunch by flexing his unused muscles, his hair hanging in thin strands over his eyes.

Susanna ignored him, her eyes held by the stranger in the garden below who emerged from behind the great shrub and glanced up for a moment, staring directly at her, something close to a smirk on his angular face. How on earth she could possibly have mistaken him for her –

'I need a drink.'

Susanna swung round. 'That's the first intelligent thing you've said all day.'

Solomon grunted good-naturedly.

'Just let me have a quick shower and change into something a bit cooler.'

The tepid water washed over her smooth, tanned skin. She directed the jets on to her breasts, keeping her face averted from the downpour. She detested water on her face, saying that it encouraged wrinkles but only too aware of the true reason, a reason she constantly challenged but was unable to overcome:

– The long, lazy rollers still advanced as though nothing untoward had happened, rising imperiously and crashing down to slither, sinking, in bright, mocking ellipses over the shingled sand, never quite reaching the pathetic bundle of clothes, carefully folded and piled neatly, each garment placed in the order they had been removed but topped by her father's silly fedora, a pipe protruding like a misshapen tongue from the pocket of a tartan shirt.

– You say he came here every morning?

– Yes.

– What for?

– To walk. To think.

The officer looked bewildered. Not to swim? he asked as though the only logical reason he could conceive for coming to this Pacific cove was to swim.

– No. He never swam. He couldn't.

The officer eyed the clothes. He did this morning.

Susanna stared angrily out over the ocean; the gannets and gulls, unperturbed, circled, screaming their raucous yearning for food, swooped, hunting, soared, swooped again, moving with the controlled precision of celestial bodies, gathering their nourishment from the seas that had cruelly consumed her father. Why? Oh, dear God, why? –

'Ready?' Solomon's voice, impatient and gruff, generously interrupted her thoughts.

'As ready as I'll ever be.'

Dressed, then, in a lightweight, beautifully tailored suit of white silk with a navy shawl collar, and navy court shoes to match, her small handbag, by contrast, bright carmine, her face only lightly made-up, Susanna followed Solomon down to the cocktail bar.

'What will it be?'

'Something long and cool. A Pimm's, I think.'

The gloom that she had encountered on her arrival had been dissipated. The bar was almost full: foreigners, journalists, cameramen, but they kept their conversation in low key as if still overawed by the sumptuousness of the Archbishop's interment from which they had obviously come. Some turned and stared at her, one in particular who held a cigarette in his fingers and waved it as though trying to stimulate his brain into putting a name to the face he was certain he recognized. Deliberately Susanna looked away, automatically posing, her neck arched, her nose wrinkling a little, adopting the haughtiness of someone who suddenly finds herself in the midst of riffraff.

'Here we go,' Solomon said, yet again rescuing her, handing her a Pimm's.

'Let's sit out on the veranda.'

The conjectures followed Susanna as she made her way across the bar and out through the glass doors. She placed her drink on the table Solomon had chosen, patted the cushioned seat of the wickerwork chair and sat down, crossing her legs. Then she lit a cigarette and inhaled it deeply, half-closing her eyes in an expression of exaggerated ecstasy. Instantly she snapped them open again in astonishment, scarcely exhaling the slow, billowing smoke from her mouth and nostrils, and stared incredulously down the veranda at the two men who were bent over a chessboard, one a broadshouldered, elegantly attired Haitian, the other – It simply couldn't be! She waved the smoke from before her eyes and blinked. 'It can't be,' she said aloud in a strained whisper, stubbing out the cigarette with nervous, brutal jabs in the glass monogrammed ashtray, and reaching for her drink.

'Can't be what?' Solomon wanted to know, not looking up, intent on filing down a jagged sliver of nail.

Her eyes still fixed on the two chess-players, Susanna removed the sprig of mint from her drink and dropped it into the small ceramic bowl that had been emptied of nuts by a previous customer.

'Can't be what?' Solomon asked again, placing the nailfile in his top pocket, his voice displaying tolerant rather than genuine interest.

Susanna shook her head. 'Nothing. For a moment I thought I recognized someone.' She gave a little titter, and took a sip from her glass. Over the rim she saw the Haitian move his queen the length of the board and lean back in his chair, folding his hands across his stomach, a benign, satisfied grin gleaming across his face. His companion chose to move his rook, did so, then spotted the futility of the manoeuvre and threw up his arms in mock exasperation. Then he said something which made them both laugh.

'Miss Lichfield!' a voice called sharply, and a camera clicked repeatedly, its motor whirring, the brilliance of the constant flash freezing everyone in attitudes of surprise.

Oscar Nicholson looked up abruptly, focusing first on the young photographer (barely, it seemed, out of his teens, a rookie probably, intent on snapping anything that might conceivably enhance his career) before seeking out the subject of all the attention. Then he saw her. He did not, however, immediately realize who she was; she had looked away from the prying lens, studying the flowers that lined the driveway, offering only her profile to his gaze and that a little blurred because the sunlight, slanting through the trees, was behind her. He was on the point of turning away, on the point, indeed, of remarking to Gilles Lagreze that things were looking up if the dazzling lady was anything to go by, when something seemed to disturb her and she settled back in her chair, leaning forward as though to speak to her companion, but staring straight at Oscar. 'Good God!' Oscar heard himself exclaim.

Monsieur Lagreze raised his eyebrows questioningly.

'It's – it's Susanna.'

Still holding the well-intentioned, demoralized rook in his fingers, Oscar scrambled to his feet and walked across the veranda. He stopped beside her, looking down at her smiling upturned face. For a moment neither of them spoke, until eventually Susanna held out her hand and said, 'Hello, Oscar', quietly and calmly as though they had been parted for but a few days.

'It *is* you.' Oscar took her hand.

'Oh, yes. It's me.'

'I can't *believe* it.'

'Have I changed so much?'

'No – no, you haven't changed a bit. It's just – well, you're the last person I expected to see.'

Susanna laughed. 'You know Solomon?'

'No. I – '

'Solomon Gross – Oscar Nicholson.'

The two men shook hands, a perfunctory gesture, restrainedly antagonistic, the awkward moment salvaged when Susanna asked, 'What on earth are *you* doing here?'

'I work here.'

'Here? Oh.'

'At the embassy.'

'Of course,' Susanna said, turning to Solomon and explaining in a bantering way, 'Oscar is a leading light in the diplomatic corps.'

Solomon grunted.

Oscar overlooked the exaggeration, and asked, 'And you? What brings you to Haiti?'

'I wish I knew. A holiday supposedly. One of Solly's little surprises.' She tacked on a small affectionate smile and patted Solomon's hand as she noticed him glowering.

The total unexpectedness of their encounter evaporating, Oscar leaned down and kissed her lightly on the forehead. 'God, it's good to see you again. You haven't changed a bit.'

Susanna laughed gaily. 'You're quite wrong, you know. I have changed. Changed a lot.'

'Not that I'd notice. How long are you staying?'

Susanna hesitated.

'A couple of days,' Solomon interposed quickly.

'Only a couple of days?'

'Susanna doesn't like it here.'

Susanna threw him a vexed look. 'It might grow on me,' she told Solomon sharply. 'It's my privilege, isn't it, to change my mind? We haven't decided,' she said directly to Oscar. 'It depends,' she added.

'Look – I'm with someone. An old friend. Why don't you both come and join us?'

Susanna got to her feet. 'Come along, Solly.'

Solomon built himself to his feet, downing his drink. 'You go on. I've a couple of phone calls to make. I'll be back in a minute.'

Monsieur Lagreze stood and bowed politely when Oscar introduced them. He stooped over Susanna's hand as if to kiss it, his eyes twinkling when he straightened and said, 'I did not know my good friend Oscar knew such an eminent artiste. He has kept that knowledge concealed from me most unkindly.'

'He's very secretive, isn't he? We're old friends.'

'They are the best,' Monsieur Lagreze said wistfully, retrieving his panama hat from the fourth, vacant chair by the table. 'And old friends must always be allowed the preciousness of time to themselves. So I will, if you permit, leave you.'

Oscar, suddenly embarrassed, protested. 'Gilles – you really don't have to – '

Monsieur Lagreze smiled and nodded. 'I know you would make me welcome. But I regret, I really must go – difficult though it is to tear myself away from such delightful company. I have so many things that must absolutely today be attended to. Letters I should have long since written and have not. Some small but necessary businesses to attend to. Besides . . . ' He widened his smile, showering its glitter upon Susanna, and shrugged.

'Another rematch tomorrow?' Oscar asked.

Monsieur Lagreze looked pensive, his eyes filling with the doubtfulness of an intruder. 'We shall see. We can decide about tomorrow later on the telephone, no? It is, I foresee, possible that you will have greater delights to attend to. At least I believe you should.'

Oscar dismissed the suggestion with a small snort. 'I'll phone you later, then, Gilles.'

'Very well.' Monsieur Lagreze gave one of his courteous, oldfashioned bows to Susanna. 'Madame,' he said. 'It will be most pleasurable for me should we meet again,' he added, and bowed again, backing away a few paces before striding off.

Alone, absurdly and childishly bashful, Susanna and Oscar used the retreating figure of Monsieur Lagreze to hold their gaze, steadfastly watching him as he made his way towards the car-park where a hopeful taxi waited. He stopped once to pick up a crumpled cigarette packet from the grass verge and deposit it in a nearby wheelbarrow, then wiped his fingers in a handkerchief that he used, also, to summon the taxi and, spinning round on his heels, to wave towards the veranda.

'He's adorable,' Susanna remarked. 'However did you find him?'

'He found me.'

'Lucky you.'

'That's truer than you think . . . Honestly, Susanna, I just don't *believe* this.' Oscar caught Susanna's hand as it descended from returning Monsieur Lagreze's wave, and kissed it. 'I wish I'd known you were coming, though.'

'*I* didn't even know I was coming. Like I told you – Solly planned it.' She laughed gaily. 'I bet he's sorry he did now.'

'Why?'

Susanna grimaced prettily. 'Because you're here, silly.'

'He doesn't know me.'

'He doesn't have to. I've told him about you. Anyway, he saw the way you looked at me. He's not a fool, you know. Very shrewd is my Solly.'

'I –'

'*And* very jealous, poor dear.'

'Can't say I blame him for that.'

Oscar finished his drink and glanced about him for Hispo, caught his attention, and then, with his eyes only, invited Susanna to join him. She shook her head. 'Not for me. You have one. I'll stick with this.' She popped the cherry into her mouth and sucked·on it, breaking the little stick on which it had been skewered in two and playing with it, drawing circles on the table as though with a compass.

Waiting for Hispo to return with the bourbon Oscar had ordered, they sat in silence, facing one another. Oscar, his elbows on the table, his chin cupped in his hands, stared at her, delving for the secrets behind the half-lowered eyelids.

. . . There they were, Susanna and he, sauntering along hand in hand, basking under the brilliantly spangled cosmetic sky, blissful lives and unquenchable love stretching gloriously and contentedly in front of them. How quickly, how treacherously all that had changed! She had taunted him, taunted him still, from the covers of glossy magazines, her name linked (with less than complete objectivity) with Ulanova and Plisetskaya, her talent immortalized as the creator of such roles as Desdemona and Lizzie Borden and the demented Blanche Dubois, unbelievably, at forty-six, only now retiring. Oscar flicked the remains of his cigarette away, attempting to clear the rail of the veranda but falling short: instantly Hispo was there, materializing like a scolding warden, like – gracious – like Auntie Jeanne, who whipped away ashtrays the second cigarettes were extinguished (and plumped up cushions the moment one was foolish enough to stand), brushing the smouldering stub into a contraption of silver-plate that resembled an old-fashioned crumb-tray with a lid that snapped to as viciously as any venus fly-trap.

– Wasn't she exquisite?

– Very good.

– Very good? Really Oscar! She was out of this world . . . The neon script advertising the Ristorante Rigoletto flickered on Susanna's ecstatic face as they walked through Covent Garden. Under sufferance, still anchored to his narrow American machismo that deemed ballet an effeminate indulgence, he had taken her to see Nureyev and Fonteyn dance *Giselle* in the hope, vain as it soon became clear, that thus fortified and enthused by her passion, she would discuss more reasonably their floundering relationship.

– I thought you'd be pleased for me.

– I *am* pleased for you, Susanna.

– It's the chance of a lifetime. It's what I've always wanted.

– I thought *I* was what you always wanted.

– You are, darling. You know you are.

– Then you'll stay?

– Oh Oscar. How can I?

– Just tell them you don't want to go for a year.

– A year is –

– I go back to Washington in eleven months. You know that. We could go back together.

– They won't wait a year, darling. They want me now.

– I want you now too.

– Don't make it more difficult for me than it already is, Oscar. Please?

He had, of course, surrendered, had even put on a consummate act of deception, talking about a year hence as though it was just tomorrow, taking her to Heathrow, standing dejectedly by the PASSENGERS ONLY barrier but smiling, smiling, smiling while his heart was breaking, smiling as she walked through PASSPORT CONTROL and on in that wonderfully graceful way that gave the impression she was floating, through the swinging doors to the boarding lounge, turning only once to wave and transmit a kiss, blowing it from the tips of her fingers, irrevocably out of his life.

Oscar cleared his throat and took a sip of the bourbon, holding the brash, burning alcohol in his mouth for several seconds before swallowing.

Spectacular . . . Dazzling . . . Ethereal . . . Heavenly . . . Breath-taking . . . Sublime . . . dear God, every printed utterance of extravagant praise had removed her further from his reach. And not only out of his reach but, it appeared, if all the press photographers could be believed, into the arms of Solomon Gross, a sort of upstart Sol Hurok, her manager he was euphemistically titled, guiding her career from San Francisco to New York, via Dallas and Boston, bedecking her with all the jewelled trappings of success and fame, isolating her in a privileged world wherein there was certainly no place for him . . .

'God, you can't imagine how wonderful it is to see you again,' he said quietly.

The words, so well intentioned, should have made her happy. But instead she could feel the smile slipping away as love had slipped away, and she struggled to keep back the tears. 'You could have written, you know,' she found herself saying.

'I did.'

'I never got any.'

Oscar smiled. 'You answered two of them.'

'Oh. I'd forgotten. It was so long ago.'

Hispo arrived with the drink and placed it on the table between them.

'Thanks, Hispo. You're sure you won't have something?' Susanna shook her head. 'Cheers, then.'

'Cheers.'

There was another silence. Then Oscar said, 'I was just thinking about us in Covent Garden.'

Susanna swung her legs from under the table and stood up in a single lithe, feline movement. For a moment, she stared down at Oscar, then turned and walked slowly to the balustrade. Covent Garden! The words clutched at her heart.

She watched his reflection in the glass veranda doors. He was twisting his glass round and round in his fingers, smiling to himself; yet in that smile she could detect the sorrow with which he had invested the smile that bade her farewell at Heathrow all those years ago. Surely, after all these years, they couldn't . . . The thought withdrew wearily, leaving a vision of their love as a forlorn animated spectre wandering disconsolately over the desert of their separation. Susanna jumped as someone touched her shoulder. 'My God, Solly, you frightened me to death!'

Solomon studied her face with one of his deep, hurt, quizzical looks. He was holding a flight timetable in his hand, his thumb marking the page he needed. He gave a small chuckle devoid of mirth. 'Well, that solves that. I've got to get back to New York tomorrow, so you won't have to stay here after all.'

Susanna stared blankly at him for several seconds, then frowned. 'I thought you'd be pleased.'

'I am – '

'Good. Three days in New York and then I'll take you anywhere you want. You can choose this time.'

'I – ' Susanna began, noting Oscar's woebegone look, the same look that had once filled her with guilt: a steady, unblinking, confused gaze now directed not at her but at something away to his right. She felt a sudden dread that he might turn his head and bestow it on her again.

' – name it,' Solomon was inviting. 'Paris. Rome. Venice. It was thoughtless of me to bring you here.' He peered at Oscar over the top of his timetable. 'There's a flight at ten thirty-five,' he announced.

'Oh.'

Susanna felt Oscar's eyes pleading with her. Damn it all, you can't just up and away now that we've found each other again, he seemed to be saying, reasonable as ever. Surely you can appreciate that it is much more than mere coincidence that places us both here at this precise moment, and if you insist on abandoning me once again, winging off into the sky as you did once before, how can I possibly tell you that I still love you? But if you do stay, even for a few days . . . ah, then, perhaps . . .

'You do still *want* to leave, don't you?'

'Yes, Solly, but – '

'But?'

Susanna tried to smile kindly at him, almost succeeding.

Solomon Gross smiled wearily back, looking dejected and disappointed but understanding nevertheless. 'It's him, isn't it?' he asked, jabbing the timetable in Oscar's direction.

'No,' Susanna lied. 'Yes,' she confessed. 'Oh, Solly, I don't know. Please don't – '

Solomon closed the timetable as though closing another chapter in his life, and stowed it safely away in his jacket pocket with a sigh of resignation. He recognized the signs. Only now – now he knew this was different. On the one hand Susanna was too serious. There was none of the girlish enthusiasm she had always betrayed when about to launch herself into one of her frivolous affairs, none of the coquettish banter with which she had, quite openly, quite insensitively too, made him aware of her intentions. On the other hand, the man, that plain, unglamorous, ageing Oscar Nicholson of the diplomatic corps had none of the qualities Solly associated with Susanna's little dabblings; her preference for young men, musclebound and bronzed and usually moronic, was something he could accept and cope with, the difference between them and himself so vast they represented no threat. But Oscar Nicholson was an entirely more dangerous matter. They were, for instance, approximately the same age, of similar intelligence, both, alas, most blatantly in love with Susanna. And so, for the first time feeling defenceless, Solomon opted for the only way he knew to deal with the problem: he smiled again and nodded.

'Oh, Solly – '

Solomon stopped her with a boyish wink. He took her hands in his. 'You don't have to decide this minute, you know. I can book the flight and if you change your mind I can cancel it.'

'Damn it, Solly, I wish you wouldn't always be so understanding.'

Solomon shrugged. 'So what should I do? *Demand* that you come with me maybe?'

'Solly – '

'Forbid you to speak to him?'

'Solly – '

'Lock you in your room like a naughty child?'

Susanna looked away.

'You'll do as you please in any case so what's the point in my making this difficult?'

'You *are* making it difficult by being so – so damn *nice*.'

'Okay, so I'm nice. Maybe that's why you always come back to me. Look, I really do have to leave tomorrow – it's not just an excuse to get you away. If you want to stay for a few days, to get it out of your system, you stay. You know where to reach me. I'll wait.'

'Whatever would I do without you, Solly?'

Solomon laughed, a quick, brittle chortle. 'Oh, you'd manage. I'm the one who'd be lost.' He patted her hand gently and went off back towards the bar.

'I have a feeling – ' Oscar began as Susanna returned to the table.

'Solomon's leaving tomorrow,' Susanna interrupted. 'He wants me to go with him, of course.'

'That's more or less what I felt. And will you?'

'I don't honestly know.'

There emerged from the hotel the sound of music, someone singing, the voice crackling from a scratched recording, Billie Holliday or Sarah Vaughan, maybe early Ella Fitzgerald, it was difficult to tell: '*I hold out my hand and my heart will be in it . . .*'

'Feel like a stroll in the garden?'

Susanna brightened. 'Yes. Yes, I'd like that. I seem to have been sitting down for days on end.'

'Let's go.'

' . . . *For all we know we may never meet again . . .* ' the husky singer seemed to warn them as they walked, arms linked, down the steps. *'For all we know we may part again, and then . . .'* Susanna fumbled in her handbag, found a pair of dark sunglasses and put them on. Oscar held up one finger in dubious greeting to an individual (reminding Susanna, briefly, of one of her weekend stands, a treacherous creep called Nigel with the deceitful, calculating eyes of an estate agent and the thin, sulky mouth of an unsuccessful parasite) who hurried past them saying 'Oscar' as though accustomed to the familiarity, and giving Susanna a mildly lecherous stare.

'Who was that?'

'No idea.'

'He knew your name.'

'Good for him.'

The sunlight blazed down on them, blazed on the swimming pool, turning the sullied water momentarily into a giant reflector, blazed on the flowers that seemed to pant, dipping their brazen colourful heads. Sitting in the full molten glare by a circular flowerbed, oblivious to the intense heat, a cripple sliced slivers from a potato and fed them to a chicken by his side. Susanna, appalled by the man's deformity yet amused by his rare preoccupation, giggled nervously. The whole scene about her – the flamboyant, jaded flowers, the listless water in the pool, the melancholy music, the legless cripple gratifying his greedy, beady-eyed fowl – struck her, passionately, as horribly familiar. It was not so much that she had experienced any such setting before; more, it seemed, that at some time, probably in a moment of great anxiety or sorrow, she had imagined that only in just so harrowing a place could she find the solace she sought.

'You remember I sent you a bunch of those?' Oscar, with his free hand, a cigarette long since extinguished and forgotten dangling from his fingers, was indicating across the expanse of lawn the cluster of tall, brilliant, wax-like plants, their single ribbed petals scarlet, a small, chunky, yellow protuberance jutting from them like the devil sticking out his tongue. 'Very expensive they were, I recall. Here they grow like weeds.'

'I remember.' Susanna bit her lip, feeling again that she was about to cry.

On they strolled, emerging at length from the shaded walk

bounded on either side by cypress trees, their fronds dull-grey with dust: Susanna was grateful for the magic of the panorama before them. They stood, silenced, absorbing the heat-drenched scene. The garden fell away from them in layers of shifting colour to a stream on which five black swans swam languidly, their arched necks swaying. In the distance the mountains commenced. their majestic soar, emerald at the base, changing, as the eye scaled their rugged heights, to deep blue, to purple, their peaks still darker. Susanna folded her arms and breathed deeply.

'That's odd.'

Oscar's comment made her jump. 'What is?'

'I could swear I saw Father Septimus.'

'Who? Where?'

'Over there.' Oscar shielded his eyes and peered in the direction of an isolated dartura tree. 'He seemed to be extracting sap from the bark. Letting it drip into a little tin mug.' Oscar laughed. 'He was wearing a ridiculous cap. Made him look like one of those Tudor barber-surgeons.'

'Really, Oscar! What on earth are you talking about?'

Oscar laughed again. 'I'm sorry.' He put his arm about her shoulder, pulling her closer to him. 'That's one person you must meet before you leave. Our Father Septimus, I mean.' He chuckled. 'Our *bête noire*, as Gilles calls him. He's our mad priest – '

'I gathered that much – that he was a priest.'

' – who sends us all berserk. He runs a hospice in the slums, and badgers us all into supporting his efforts. Camps in the embassy lobby until I agree to see him. Gilles says he stalks him – Septimus stalks Gilles, I mean, not the other way round – and poor Gilles keeps trying to avoid him.' He kissed her hair. 'On second thoughts, maybe you'd better *not* meet him.' He laid his cheek lightly on her head. 'The trouble with him is,' he went on seriously, 'that despite his craziness there is something very frightening about him. He seems to *know* things. Gives you the feeling he knows more about you than you do yourself.' Oscar gave an exaggerated shudder.

'Oscar, you were right the first time, I must meet this priest before I leave.'

Leaving the swans, they wandered along a narrow pathway, rough-hewn from the harsh, rocky earth, slightly humpbacked in the middle where drains had recently been laid (causing them to walk either side of the hump) that led back to the hotel from the rear, the stillness shattered by the clatter of cooking vessels from the hotel kitchens, the heady perfume of flowers swamped by the smell of cooking.

Susanna sniffed. 'Lord, I've just realized how hungry I am. I could eat a horse!'

'You might have to.'

'Don't, Oscar!'

'I'll buy you lunch.'

Susanna stretched her hand across the path, reaching for his. 'Thank you Oscar, But no. I think I'd better lunch with Solly. You understand, don't you?'

Oscar gave her a sad look, but nodded.

'You can buy me another drink, though.'

Oscar cheered up. 'Done.'

Still holding hands they rounded the corner of the hotel and started to mount the veranda steps. Oscar suddenly stopped. 'You go on,' he said, releasing her hand. 'I'll join you in a tick. Won't be a minute. I promise.' He jumped from the steps and went off at the trot, back the way they had come.

Susanna, puzzled but amused by Oscar's antics, glanced about the veranda. The table they had vacated was now occupied. Oddly, this filled her with resentment: how dare those three men sprawl themselves about the table where she, but for a moment, had recaptured – She snickered to herself, mocking her stupidity, choosing a table at the opposite end of the veranda and sitting down. An impulse, sudden and not quite explicable, to get up and race into the hotel, to find Solomon, to throw everything back into her suitcase, to scream 'Get me out of this awful place *now*', surged within her. Someone shouted a name – Conquy it sounded like – and the impulse ebbed, to be replaced by a mood of tragic sombreness. Instinctively she set her face in lines of sorrow. She wanted Oscar, when he returned, to find her abandoned, vulnerable as a child. But (shaking her head as Hispo – generously admitting her to what he regarded as his personal clique – approached, watching him bend at the hips and swerve away looking somewhat affronted by her refusal of his services) she abandoned her fraudulence and, for an instant, forgot Oscar. It was all so unsettling. She was *meant* to be here, and here *now*. The cripple moved his head in a wild gesture and, even from that distance, seemed to be staring at her, warning her, destroying the illusion; now he looked less like fate than some mummer lampooning by his deformity the wretchedness of her unfulfilled life, her unrequited love; and there, moving across the lawn towards the cripple, a limping figure, swinging a – good heavens! – a golf-club, dressed in a black soutane, stooping now and appearing to tickle the chicken under the chin, even he seemed to fit –

'Oooooooooooooooo!' now issued from the cocktail bar: a good-natured, ruffianly, ribald scoffing, starting low and rising to a falsetto. 'El Conquistador,' a voice called. 'Act one, scene one of the great seduction,' another voice, clearly British, offered, this followed by loud laughter that submerged yet another jolly taunt. There was a moment's tentative silence, and Susanna, listening although pretending not to – the pretence unnecessary since she was alone now on the veranda, the others drawn into the bar by the jollifications – was certain she heard Oscar's voice speak. 'A likely tale, dear boy,' the British voice quivered gleefully. Then: 'I tell you, matey, you just go on with what you're up to. Ignore these bloody buggers.' Another cheer greeted this advice and followed Oscar, who appeared at that moment on the veranda, looked about him, spotted her and moved quickly to the table. 'I got these for you.'

Susanna stared at the bunch of flowers, tears welling in her eyes. 'Not too expensive this time, I hope,' she managed to say with a small smile.

'Actually I stole them.'

'Oscar!'

'I stole them first then offered to pay.'

'Oh. That's all right then. They're lovely. Thank you.'

Oscar winked his welcome. 'It's funny – when I was picking them it struck me we'd come full circle: almost.'

'Almost,' Susanna said quietly through the flowers.

'Have you – oh, Lord, watch out – made up your mind about leaving?'

He came hobbling across the veranda, Septimus Roach, his golf-club to the fore as though he was blind, his gait more or less in step with the chacha music that had taken over from the drunken choir, but his face solemn.

Without a word, hardly looking at them but clearly embracing their presence nevertheless, he eased himself into a chair at their table and, after carefully placing his golf-club on the ground, tucked his hands up the sleeves of his soutane and bathed them in a wild if friendly enough smile.

Susanna, still discomfited by Oscar's gift and his unanswered question, experienced the odd feeling that the priest, commissioned by some considerate angel, had come to rescue her. 'And just in the nick of time,' she heard herself say aloud.

Oscar regarded her askance, his eyes widening in surprise. Septimus, however, gazed at her without expression as she manipulated her confusion into a low, tuneless hum, then looked lovingly at the flowers that she cradled in her arms like she might an infant. She prayed that Oscar would say something.

'It has always struck me as particularly unimaginative that flowers are offered as a declaration of love.' But it was the priest who made the bantering, disturbing statement. 'After all – when all is said and done, that is – they die, do they not? So very short-lived. One might have hoped that man, with all his supposed intelligence, could have devised a rather more long-lasting symbol of his affection,' he added, eyeing the bouquet with reproach.

'Love dies just as rapidly,' Susanna said, again unintentionally, again regretting her impulsiveness. For a moment it looked as though she might try and explain it away; but she relapsed into silence, making a tremendous, conscious effort to control that silence as words spewed into her mouth, screaming to be voiced. What she could not deny was that Septimus Roach, the ludicrous disciple of God she had already locked away in the glory-hole of her mind (but hanging the key on a convenient cerebral nail just in case), was frighteningly familiar. Not as he was now, sitting there, silently rational: no, that wasn't it at all. He was, she thought, familiar in the sense that she had imagined, known really, that at some time someone would suddenly intrude into her life, someone who – how silly – would save her.

'I thought it was the thought that counted,' Oscar interjected tritely.

'Of course it is, darling,' Susanna agreed, grateful for the interruption.

'Of course,' Septimus, surprisingly, agreed also. 'By the way – I'm Septimus Roach.'

Oscar cleared his throat. 'I'm sorry – I should have – Susanna, Father Roach. Septimus – Susanna Lichfield.'

Incredibly, for the first time since he had taken his place at the table, their eyes met. For no more than a second, for eternity, they held, parting only when Oscar, in reparation for his oversight, offered: 'A drink, Septimus?'

'Hmmm. No. Oh no, thank you. Just passing, you might say.' He flicked his eyes back to Susanna's face. 'Answering a muted call,' he said mysteriously, before cackling, his body shaking with mirth, and standing up.

'Oh stay. Don't leave. We have so much to say!' Susanna wanted to cry. 'It was nice meeting you, Father,' she said, shrinking from the banality of her words.

Septimus held up a finger. 'We will meet again,' he said.

'I hope so.'

'I'm certain we will.'

Ignoring Oscar, ignoring Susanna too, he wheeled and walked with surprising speed across the veranda and vanished, literally, down the steps.

Oscar laughed nervously. 'I told you he was mad.'

'Who is – who is – ' Susanna faltered. She craned her neck to peer over the balustrade; there was no sign of anyone, even the cripple had forsaken his post and disappeared.

'Septimus, of course.'

'Oh. That's not – Yes. Of course.'

'Susanna, whatever is the matter?'

'Nothing. Honestly. Nothing. You were perfectly right. Quite, quite mad obviously.'

Oscar eyed her sceptically.

'Only – '

'Only?'

Susanna shook her head and shrugged. 'Nothing,' she said again.

'Gilles has a theory . . .' Oscar paused to light a cigarette. 'A. . . theory, well not really a theory, a sort of premonition, that poor Septimus is scheduled – '

'Stop it, Oscar!'

Oscar stopped, the lighted match still in his fingers. Confused and embarrassed he stared at the flame, letting it burn down almost to his flesh, then reversing it, holding the burnt head, mesmerized as the match consumed itself. He tossed it into the ashtray.

'I'm sorry, Oscar.'

'No need to be.'

'There's something about him – '

'He *is* a creepy old devil. Frightens us all to death.' Oscar laughed. 'You should see the look on Gilles's face whenever Septimus hoves into view.' He laughed again, a sort of whinny. Then: 'Have you made up your mind about leaving?' he asked again.

'Yes. No. Not yet.'

'Stay. Don't go. We have so much to say.'

Susanna sat bolt upright in her chair, Oscar's words, *her* words, the words she had longed to scream at the priest, echoing in her mind. She could feel the giddiness overtake her; she buried her face in the flowers.

Oscar seemed unaware of anything untoward: he leaned back, waiting patiently for a reply; or perhaps not so patiently. His brain chivvied him: waiting, always bloody waiting, waiting for the phone to ring, waiting for letters that never came to come, waiting for goddam Godot, waiting for – ah, for love. He burst into a self-deprecating laugh that became a cough.

' – would be the point?' Susanna was asking.

'I'm sorry. Of what? The point of what?'

'Nothing, Oscar.'

And deliberately as she had so often done, slowly seeing her face transformed by the heavy theatrical makeup into someone else's, and with each stroke of mascara and daub of rouge her own character being devoured, metamorphosed into the Odiles and Giselles (how wan they were!) she portrayed with such exquisiteness, Susanna forced herself out of the present situation: she thought about her final performance, remembering her last poignant glimpse of her faithful audience before the curtain swooped down to obliterate them, leaving her – She placed Oscar's flowers on the table and stood up, stretching. The bar was silent now save for the clink of glasses as someone cleared the tables; the sound reminded her, confusedly, of little bells, sleighbells, Vermont pretending to be Saint Moritz, before she met Solomon, and when she had half imagined herself to be totally in love with 'art' (as some of her chic acquaintants described almost everything they could neither appreciate nor understand, following her everywhere, circling her like scavengers waiting to cream off some of the glamour that accrued to her) but ever accompanied by an unwanted spectre that constantly bemoaned the proximity of possible tragedy.

'Susanna,' Oscar called quietly, waiting for her to turn and face him before continuing. 'You didn't say. Have you made up your mind about staying?'

Susanna shook her head.

'Stay – please.'

She felt her indecision melting. A sense of a ridiculous, shared, devil-may-care pact seemed, at that instant, to be sealed between them. She tucked her handbag under her arm and gathered up the bouquet, suddenly lighthearted and barely conscious of what Oscar was saying. She held out her hand, smiling, and hand in hand they walked as far as the doors leading into the bar. 'Will you join Solly and me for dinner tonight?'

'I'd love to if Solomon won't mind.'

'He'll mind. Eight?'

'Fine. Susanna: I still love you.'

'I know you do. I'll see you at eight.'

Oscar kissed her on the cheek, then kissed his own forefinger and pressed it gently against her lips. 'A date sealed with a kiss is a date that cannot be broken.'

Susanna watched him leap boyishly to the bottom of the steps and swagger off down the drive, the years, all those wasted years, dropping from his shoulders. Oddly enough his puerile behaviour made her feel delightfully young also. She held the flowers tight against her breast, closing her eyes. When she opened them, expecting to see Oscar frolicking away, hop-skip-and-jumping, doing somersaults even, intending to wave merrily to him (she had already set aside her handbag and the flowers on the dumbwaiter, used, possibly for some deeply embedded religious reason, only on Sundays to display a lavish cold buffet), she found herself instead staring into the upturned face of the cripple, whose head showed above the bougainvillea. Her smile, so passionate, so endearing, froze to a ghastly leer. The cripple grinned at her; his teeth, stained to the colour of nutmeg, were all pointed, canine almost, but very regular as though they had been purposely filed to their vampiric design. Yet his smile for all its devilish aspect was encouraging. 'Ah, he seemed to be saying, so it *is* you. I nearly gave up hope that you would come. And then I saw you, down by the stream, down there by the stream where the black swans glide – although by now you will have noticed that they are not the docile, elegant creatures you supposed, but treacherous beasts, their beaks not naturally red but bloodied on the corpses of suicidal love – gazing at the mountains, and even then I was not certain which is why I am here to make a closer inspection . . . Why has it taken you so long to – '

A great clatter came from the hotel as someone dropped a tray laden with crockery. Susanna, jumped, automatically cowering from the noise, bowing her head. When she straightened the cripple had gone. She grabbed her handbag and dashed into the hotel, leaving the flowers, already withering in the heat, on the dumbwaiter.

Six

An old woman with the face of a scorched Hecuba gave her directions, although at first reluctantly, shaking her head and rolling her bulbous eyes as if she had been asked the road to the castle of Dracula. '*L'hospice de Père Septimus?*' she demanded, rather over-acting, taking in Susanna's finery at a glance. '*Mais non, madame.*'

'*Mais oui,*' Susanna insisted. It was extremely hot and she was feeling distinctly tetchy. Besides, her decision to visit the priest was pretty indecisive; something drew her towards him, urging her on but against her will, hence anything that appeared to dissuade her was welcomed, yet in welcoming it she was showing her usual old weakness, and the recognition of this weakness irked her.

'*Mais c'est pas pour vous, madame. C'est un endroit bien malheureux.*'

Uncomprehending, Susanna tried again. '*Le Père Septimus?*'

'*Oui. Le prêtre.*' The woman took to cackling as though some enormously amusing joke had been cracked. '*Bien,*' she continued once her merriment had waned, now giving the impression she had been laughing at something different altogether. '*Venez.*' She took Susanna by the arm and steered her down a narrow road, sidewalkless, that ran with increasing steepness downhill, the shops, stalls more like (looking ridiculously makeshift, suggesting, falsely as it happened, that they were folded up at night and transported elsewhere the following day) offering harness and fruit, meat and fish and charcoal, all besieged by enormous bluebottles that far outnumbered the customers. Strings of tiny sausages, *saucisson sec*, of garlic, of aromatic spices (tied in little white muslin bags) festooned the façades like carnival streamers. Everyone bartered, roaring their compromises in fierce good humour. Children watched, sharp-eyed, mastering the art. Even the alleys that

107

spindled off the road every fifty yards or so were the scene of considerable jollity as women harvested their laundry, dumping the dry garments and blankets into huge panniers that they then hoisted on to their heads, talking all the while as they waddled off, their immense buttocks wobbling. Infants swarmed about the women, clinging to their skirts, trotting beside them, their legs rickety, their feet bare. There was the constant humming babble that is part of the makeup of hot climates: it was as though the women were bemoaning, but in a sunstruck, lackadaisical way, the universal plight of the overworked housewife. Sometimes they gave Susanna a glare that accused of intrusion, then they spotted the old woman and looked away, pretending never to have seen her at all.

'*Et voilà!*' The ancient hag (who all the length of the road had clutched Susanna's arm, leaving on it small painful indentations where her sharp nails had pressed into the flesh) came to a standstill and pointed down a particularly abhorrent, dirty alleyway.

With some trepidation, again regretting her rash decision to come, Susanna made her way towards the hospice, sidestepping the pot-holes (cynical testimony to the continuing deadlock between the President and the Municipality as to where American aid should be allocated), the heels of her expensive Bruno Maglie shoes sinking into the sludge. The stench was appalling: she took a small, lace-trimmed handkerchief from her sleeve and pressed it against her nose. A youth, wearing only trousers that looked like pyjama bottoms, laughed at her discomfort, lounging against an upturned cart under which someone slept, his legs protruding. Immediately others, all men for some reason, seized upon the sound and joined in, their laughter becoming more frantic, more shrill as they forced it from their lungs. Then, as quickly as it had started, it was switched off as if at some daemonic mains. The alley became deadly quiet. The men, who but a split second before had been rolling about in cruel merriment, jiggered into frozen attitudes of struggling shame.

'Well, glory be to God!'

So unlikely were the words that Susanna, at first, thought she had imagined them, thought they were but another trick of her frightened mind. But –

'Glory be to God!' the voice said again, this time without the brittle edge of surprise.

'Oh. Hello. I was looking for Father Septimus.'

Sister Mary, the skirt of her habit tucked up, leather pads strapped to her knees, wearing galoshes on her socked feet, came bustling down the steps from the porch. 'Dear God, child, you should never be wandering about this place on your own like this.'

'I wasn't exactly wandering,' Susanna replied self-righteously, the word 'child' vexing her.

'Well, whatever you were doing don't ever do it again.'

'I don't intend to.'

'Good.'

'Is Father Septimus here?'

Instantly Sister Mary was on her guard. 'Why?'

'I want to see him.'

'Does he know you?'

'We've met, yes. Is he here?'

'Not yet. He will be though. At least he should be. Soon, I sincerely hope.'

'Do you mind if I wait?''

'Of course you must wait. You don't think for one minute that I'd let you go meandering – '

'Thank you,' Susanna interrupted, still irked.

'In fact a friend – Mister Lagreze – '

'I've met him – '

' – sent us – have you? – some coffee and I've just made a potful.'

'I can smell it.'

Even above the stench of the alley, above the clinical smell of disinfectant that saturated the hospice, the aroma of fresh coffee came through victorious. And from her chair just inside the entrance (placed there by the fussy nun) Susanna gazed about the room. Unbelievably it was spotless. The floor, rough hewn planks of varying sizes giving the effect of crazy parquet, gleamed freshly polished – which explained the knee-pads. There were eight beds, a white sheet on each, a brown blanket, folded military style, stretched across the foot. Only one bed was occupied: in the furthest corner an emaciated woman lay so still she could well have been dead. Only an occasional croaking gave evidence that life, however tenuously, still lingered. There were three pictures on the walls: inevitably, perhaps, Christ blandly indicating His bleeding heart, rupturing it further with His forefinger; His mother, the Immaculate Virgin, looking impossibly serene, even off-hand, squatting in a physically improbable position, her dead Son stretched across her knees; between these two, incongruously, an enlarged photograph of the phosphate mines in the Jordan valley. But dominating the room although placed at a precarious angle in one corner, was a huge crucifix, Christ, black as the ace of spades, securely nailed to it.

'That,' Sister Mary explained, following Susanna's gaze, her voice sniffing, handing over a mug of stiff steaming coffee, 'that was Father Septimus's bright idea.'

'Oh.'

Sister Mary plonked herself down on one of the beds.

Susanna flicked her a nervous smile. 'I don't want to interrupt – '

Sister Mary dismissed the apology. 'Everything's done for the moment. We only get busy in the evening. They' – she pointed over her shoulder towards the alley – 'only bring in their dying at night.' She sighed understandingly. 'They cannot be seen to abandon them, you see.'

'But good heavens, their families must know what they're doing.'

Sister Mary smiled tightly. 'It's not their families they're concerned about,' she said enigmatically. 'You say you know Father Septimus?' she then asked, her calm face belying the mild surprise in her voice, her eyes probing.

'I met him the day I arrived. Four days ago. Although – ' Susanna fell silent and made as if to sip her coffee. It was still too hot; she lowered the mug to her lap, cupping it in both hands, fixing her eyes on it.

'Although you felt as though you'd known him all your life?' the little nun remarked almost casually.

'Why yes!'

'He has that effect on most people.' Sister Mary gave a thin smile. 'He had the same effect on me when we first met,' she confided in a voice that clearly intended to make little of the phenomenon.

What appeared to be a serious disagreement was developing outside, although the singsong voices seemed unsuited to violent argumentation. Something splattered on to the porch. Immediately Sister Mary was on her feet, darting into a walk-in cupboard that led off the dormitory (the kitchen, Susanna later discovered) and reappearing with two enormous terracotta ewers. With considerable speed (her habit now released and trailing to the ground, giving the impression she was floating, although the muffled thudding of her galoshes did their best to destroy the illusion) she scuttled into the alley.

'Water. Holy water. *Good heavens!*'

Septimus Roach, soaked and dripping caught unawares by the vision of Susanna Lichfield smiling with considerable amusement at him, came to a skidding halt in the narrow passage between the beds. To his credit, he recovered his composure with a minimum of fuss. 'They only switch it on for a couple of hours, you see. The water. From some municipal tap. Waste not, want not, I suppose. But that only applies to those that have not. Those who have, want not, don't you think?' He glanced absently back towards the porch. 'Mind you, those that want not could find themselves in a pretty pickle,' he added, turning towards Susanna again, and fixing her with a steely glare. 'We have met.'

'Yes. At the hotel. The other day.'

'I know,' Septimus said sedately.

'Oh. I thought you were asking.'

The querulous voices outside the hospice changed suddenly to hectic laughter. Jets of water, splayed like slivers of coloured crystal, arced into the humid air as the men (some of them very old but acting like children) drenched each other from hosepipes. Septimus spotted a pair of woolly footpads near the cupboard door and donned them; he chuffled about the floor giving an infantile impression of a steam-engine, interspersing his guttural hissing with a line or two from a mutilated nursery-rhyme. 'The little red train went over the hill, hooray, hooray,' he sang, the inconsequence of the words all the more ludicrous because of the seriousness of their interpretation. But the train, alas, ran out of control if not steam, and he collided with the crucifix, hissing to an abrupt halt, his golf-club, called into service as a piston, reverting to a walking-stick and aiding the priest towards a bed. He sat down, puffing. 'Asking what?' he demanded, somehow keeping his conversation at least on the same track.

'If we had met.'

The reply appeared to flummox Septimus: it bore no relation to the question he had asked. So what if they *had* met? What possible difference could it make to anything if they had met? Except – Septimus took a surreptitious glance at Susanna, using the thick lenses with some effect to cover the intensity of his gaze. Except: for one moment (a moment quite long enough by any standards but particularly by his notoriously manipulative ones) by the tilt of her head, by the slight movement of her hand as she fingered a wayward strand of hair from her face, by the odd way she parted her lips, revealing the rows of small, white, improbably even teeth that spoke reams for the skill of her New Haven dentist, by the way her eyes tried so desperately to be calmly deliberate, to suppress the passionate sorrow and longing that welled within them, for one infinitesimal moment she became –

' – back another time.' Susanna was already on her feet.

Her voice, alas, pummelled by others that demanded his attention, failed to make the short cosmic trip to his brain. All he heard was a kind of seething from which, as from the persistent shouting and remonstrating of the men outside, occasionally a lone, distraught voice managed to dissociate itself:

– You've really overstepped the mark this time.

– You're on your own now, Septimus, my lad.

– A monastery, I think.

– A madhouse, I think.

– An asylum, I think, but for your own good, of course.

– Of course!

– Of course!

– The gibbet *I* think. He did, after all, it must be admitted, he *has* admitted, ultimately kill the child.

'I won't let you.'

Ah, that was better! Septimus, from the clamouring hobgoblins, recognized Sister Mary's adamant tones.

'I came by myself so I can get home by myself.'

Oh, dear. Not so good. Almost familiar. Definitely heard before, but –

'Father Septimus, will you speak to this young lady?'

Septimus swung to an upright position, planting his feet firmly on the floor. He adjusted his spectacles. 'Certainly I will. And what would you have me say?'

'Tell her she's not to attempt walking back to the hotel alone and by herself,' Sister Mary instructed, her containers of water by her side, her body blocking the door.

'You are not to attempt walking back to the hotel alone and by yourself,' Septimus pronounced obediently.

'Tell her you'll see her home.'

'I'll see you home.'

'There's really no need. Honestly,' Susanna protested hastily, feeling small waves of hysteria sweeping over her, wanting, now, only to extricate herself from the silly pantomime being enacted before her, while she, relegated to a cameo role, was being all but overlooked.

'Insist,' Sister Mary ordered.

'I insist,' Septimus insisted calmly.

'One does not, unless one is very foolhardy, argue with the most formidable Sister Mary,' he explained a few minutes later, sounding quite reasonable, as they walked along the alley down which she had so recently come.

'I can see that.'

'You can? Oh good.' He administered a blessing to an elderly man who lay on a mattress outside his shack, one foot suppurating horribly. The man ignored him. 'What I mean is, of course, as I'm sure you'll have gathered also, that you always appear to give the good woman her own way. Whether you actually fulfil her demands is another matter. Whether you fulfil any demands except those you impose on yourself is another matter for that matter. Mind you – ' Septimus paused to take a closer look at something that interested him in a puddle, probing the filthy water with his niblick. 'Mind you,' he went on, enlightened or simply losing interest, 'one has to take care that one does not demand too much of oneself, eh?'

The question, bowled underarm, traversing the alley which, for no good reason, they negotiated on opposite sides, had a distinct edginess about it; as, indeed, did the dozen or so young men, their Rastafarian dreadlocks giving them a superior, sinister air, who had gathered on the corner where the alley joined the market road. None of them stood still: they all moved nervously on the balls of their feet as if, Septimus thought, they were preparing to receive a particularly malevolent serve at tennis. Their leader, oddly enough the smallest of the group, crossed the alley and made as if to accost Susanna, swaggering towards her, his distressed jeans and T-shirt that professed his love for Jimi Hendrix enhancing rather than limiting his menace. In a flash Septimus placed himself between them, brandishing his niblick like a rapier, even taking the bent-knee stance of a duellist.

The youth, slowly becoming aware that the white American woman who had seemed an easy enough target for harassment and this unexpected musketeer were in company, coped with considerable aplomb; losing face uppermost in his mind, he made a joke of the episode, sticking two fingers in his mouth and pulling it wide, grunting and hopping about like an ape before swinging away and returning to his clique, his ego salvaged and bolstered by their applause.

Susanna walked cautiously to the priest's side and slipped her hand into the crook of his arm. Septimus patted it.

'That was very brave of you, Father.'

Septimus pooh poohed the idea. 'They are only children. Envious that you appear to have money. The haves and the have nots again, I fear. I don't think they would have done you any harm,' he told her consolingly. 'Not yet, at any rate,' he added, sounding thoughtful.

The incident behind them, they turned left out of the alley. For Susanna, however, it was not quite left behind. The sullen, glazed, angry look in the young Haitian's eyes still hankered to be remembered in her mind; as, suddenly, did another event, quite dissimilar from this but with the same painful, lingering aftermath. Her father, in a state of great agitation, had taken her to a museum and stood her in front of a large glass case containing a skeleton. – Look, child. Look. Behold one man's greatest sacrilege. Behold the Princess Truganinni.

Susanna looked, nonplussed. – Who was Princess Truganinni?

– She is the ultimate horror of one George Augustus Robinson.

– Thank you, Daddy.

– Allow me to explain, her father said in his accustomed bellow, making heads turn and a minion in uniform wonder what he should do about it. – Our friend, Mr Robinson, was the most dastardly rogue, a religious rascal, not satisfied until he had seduced the last Aborigine in Tasmania – the royal bag of bones you see before you – with his godless claptrap. He lowered his voice and bent his head conspiratorially. – If it is any consolation you can be quite sure George Augustus got his comeuppance. Word hath it that he was well and truly hurled from the Sephirotic tree to suffer the eternal and dreadful torment in Oliphoth. The land of Husks and Demons, you understand. He became thoughtful, even mournful – On the other hand, of course, he might have rather liked it there. Felt at home, I shouldn't wonder. Hung up his hat and put the changeable cat out at night.

'Mind your step – ' Yet it was Septimus himself, despite his warning, who stumbled and almost fell.

'Are you all right, Father?'

'Perfectly.' Septimus straightened himself. 'It comes from having this leg – ' he whacked his left leg severely with his golf-club ' – some few inches shorter than the other. I still cannot calculate distance correctly. Two inches, say, for each pothole, but an additional three in the mind. That's the hard part – getting things right in the mind,' he concluded, still holding one finger and the thumb of his left hand some three inches apart. He eyed them as they closed.

'*You'd* better take *my* arm.'

Septimus put on a great show of being shocked. 'Whatever would they say?' he asked, casting both arms wide in mock horror.

'Who?'

'My flock. Seeing their priest on the arm of a beautiful woman, a *most* beautiful woman, would scandalise them as they never before have been . . . Speaking of flock – clerically, of course – did you know that Beethoven confessed that the thing he missed most was not being able to hear the shepherd sing? Pretty rummy that, wouldn't you say, or would you?'

Susanna gave a tinkling laugh. 'You sound like Solomon.'

Septimus came to a halt and stared at her, mystified.

'Oh. Not *that* Solomon. *My* Solomon.'

'You have your own Solomon?' Septimus was definitely interested.

'A friend. At least I *hope* he still is. He's always telling me – ha – parables. Chekhov was his latest. Or Ibsen. No, Chekhov, I'm sure.'

None of which seemed to be making much impression on Septimus; now that Solomon had been reduced to mortality he had turned his attention to a man carrying birdcages (the cages themselves attached to a long, thick, bamboo pole he wore across his bare shoulders like a yoke). Septimus was particularly taken with a cardinal: grappling behind him with one hand, still bent over the cage, he summoned Susanna to share his interest. 'You know what they call the cardinal here? *L'oiseau flambé*. The flame bird.

Actually, the bird on fire, to be quite literal. Apt, wouldn't you agree?'

Susanna's heart bled for the terrified bird that (hardly surprisingly with Septimus all but poking his long nose between the bamboo bars) beat its wings frantically, beat its imprisoned passion in the cruelly confining space before collapsing on the floor and lying there, beak open, gasping. 'How cruel,' Susanna said.

'*Nous sommes tous les prisonniers*,' Septimus remarked, perhaps in reply, perhaps abstractly consoling the unfortunate bird.

'How much is it? – Oh, never mind.' Susanna rummaged in her handbag and produced a five-dollar bill, shoving it angrily towards the bird-vendor, and unhooking the cage from the yoke as soon as the money had been snatched from her fingers. Gently she caught the bird and held it for a moment in her hand, feeling its tiny, terrified heartbeat, feeling a part of her spirit enter the small, warm body. Then she released it and watched it soar away, taking that fragment of her soul with it . . . She was ten, or eleven, or nine, or ageless, and she was sitting in a small cosy room. Her father was there and another man. The walls were covered in prints, paintings and photographs of immortal thoroughbreds: Sea Bird, Persimmon, The Tetrarch. There was a fireplace, inglenook, wide and open, with a log fire blazing. Arcado – that was his name. Erik Arcado! How could she have forgotten. Dear Erik: her first love. No! That was silly. Her first childish crush but no less heartrending for that. Erik Arcado, like her father, a stultified maverick, his field, as chancy as the ponies, poetry, sitting there in the high-backed Windsor chair, a stuffed lamb draped about his neck like a grotesque Taureg lytham (often solemnly consulted and gratuitously lumbered with the name of Clarence). He, like the scarlet-breasted bird she had just released, had sought freedom, and perhaps, who could tell, found it. One night, without a word, he had simply packed up and vanished. And years later, quite by chance, she had come across what was, in a sense, an obituary, an offhand scanty footnote that stated briefly a man identified as Erik Arcado, a poet, an American national (which seemed far more important) had shot himself in Dakar . . . She was watching Septimus, who now carried on an animated conversation with the bird-seller:

' – *la liberté* – '
' – *la beaute* – '

116

' – *pour faire plaisir* – '

' – *pour manger* – '

Susanna shuddered. 'Can we go now?'

'Forward. We cannot, after all, go back.'

The throng had dissipated: the shoppers, with their loud, ebullient dresses that had lent such colour to the drab scene, were gone, their purchases completed, their laundry reaped for another day, their absence unveiling the true poverty and degradation of the street. Four men, sitting under the awning of what was once a mobile soft-drinks wagon, but now irrevocably rooted to this one spot, its wheels gone, its axle embedded in concrete, played a boardgame, but not chess; backgammon or draughts or some epileptic offspring of both perhaps. Even the normally boisterous shopowners seemed to have lost their appetite for merchandizing, sitting on small, canvas, collapsible chairs outside their premises, women knitting, men smoking and staring at nothing. A few children made mud-castles then hurled them at each other. A donkey, tied to a warped stanchion, nodded its head continuously to rid itself of the flies that swarmed about its eyes seeking liquid from the ducts.

'Why did you come?'

'It was one of Solomon's – *my* Solomon's – bright ideas.'

'Why should your Solomon want you to come?' Septimus asked, looking a little confused, although not so confused to prevent him taking a somewhat soiled handkerchief (smeared with black oil as though used to wipe dipsticks) from the pocket of his soutane and, tucking it securely into the headband of the donkey's halter, spreading it as best he could over the beleaguered beast's eyes.

'It was supposed to be a break. A short, getting away from it all holiday.'

'I see,' Septimus said, taking off his spectacles and wiping them casually on his sleeve. But clearly he didn't see. He knew they were talking at cross purposes – nothing too very unusual in *that* as far as he was concerned; he could even appreciate that, by and large, it was not entirely down to him that the confusion was taking place. Nevertheless he was loath to try and correct the imbroglio, to meddle with what fate had seen fit to present: one never knew, did one, what might loom from the ashes of any unwise tinkering? He gave the donkey a friendly pat on the rump and was rewarded with a bad-tempered, ill-aimed cow-kick. However, all was not lost. An alternative reward was at hand; it dawned on Susanna what the priest was getting at. 'You meant why did I come to see *you*, didn't you? Not why had I come to Haiti?'

'Well, yes, actually.'

'Heavenly shades of night are falling, it's twilight time' – the unmistakable voice of Tony Williams (the Platters hoo-hooing in the background) floated from a jukebox installed in a makeshift hut of its own, the electric bulbs that should have been circulating behind the coloured glass panels blown; a man, and a woman far older than he, danced, but only from their hips upwards, their foreheads pressed together, their arms resting lifelessly on each other's shoulders, hands dangling, their feet not moving an inch.

'Would it sound terribly silly if I said I didn't know why?'

Septimus shook his head. 'No.' He gave a dry little laugh. ' 'Tis a symptom most familiar. Does tend to land one in kettles of fish, mind,' he added with a friendly, warning scowl. 'To coin a phrase. Funny things fish, don't you think? Never quite did see the point of them.'

' – even sillier if I admitted that I did know when I set out to find you but have since – '

' – just to be eaten. So dreadfully soundless. The only uncomplaining creatures devised by God, I remember reading somewhere. Unnerving that anything should have to suffer – and indeed rejoice – I presume fish *do* have the odd occasion to rejoice? – in silence.'

'I needed your help,' Susanna longed to tell him.

'Pisces, piscatorum.'

'I still need your help,' she wanted to cry.

'Pis-ca-tor-um. Pssssssss.' Septimus had spotted a cat pussyfooting towards them. 'Must have heard us,' he remarked to Susanna. 'Did you say help?'

Susanna was stunned. She kept her eyes fixed on the cat as her mind raced back trying to remember if, by chance, she had spoken aloud. She crouched down on her hunkers, rubbing her fingers together, holding her hand towards the cat, encouraging it to come closer. 'Help?' she asked, looking up at Septimus, squinting as the sun's glare struck her face.

'I thought – ' Septimus frowned, and jerked his head to one side several times in the manner of a swimmer dislodging water from his ear.

'Why should I ask for help?'

The cat, at first curious at the priest's antics, became bored; it looked about it for a moment, then turned and sauntered off, its tail held high.

'I thought – ' Septimus said again, frowning but keeping his head still.

'I never said a word,' Susanna replied, truthfully she hoped. She stood up and rubbed her hands together as if dusting them off.

'Ah, well,' Septimus sighed, looking a little abashed but eyeing her sceptically nevertheless. 'Perhaps someone said it for you.'

Almost at a trot, moving quickly a few strides ahead of Septimus, Susanna tried to conceal her alarm. They were now within sight of the hotel, the tips of its outlandish cupolas like strange sugar-coated fruit on the uppermost branches of the great trees that hid the main structure of the Ollofson from view. For one glorious moment Susanna thought she saw the cardinal about to alight – he, too, perhaps fooled by the illusory candied fruits. But there was no cardinal. No escape either from the priest who had made up ground and joined her as she waited for a loaded vegetable lorry to trundle its way past. 'It is quite amazing, you know, how often that happens,' he said, so close to her now that she could have sworn his lips brushed her ear.

'What?' she snapped, unreasonably angry, mostly with herself.

'That some being, some caring angel possibly, or some other celestial nymph, takes it upon itself to transmit a message we ourselves are too timid to utter.'

'Really.' The word came out flat, hard, sarcastic.

Septimus was busily nodding. 'Oh, yes. Really. Sometimes very really real. And a good thing too.' He stuck his niblick out in front of him, making a covey of cyclists swerve, and helped Susanna across the road.

'I'm sure it is,' Susanna said to keep the peace.

Septimus came to a sudden standstill, about-faced and stared at her. 'What would have become of you if I hadn't been told you needed help?'

'Don't be so damn stupid!' Susanna wanted to say. 'You really are as mad as I've already been led to believe,' she wanted to yell.

But she said neither of these things. She said nothing at all. Once more – how extraordinary that his ghost should be exhumed twice in one afternoon and within a matter of minutes! – the late Erik Arcado took hold of her thoughts. Yet not so very extraordinary. While the person of the freedom-seeking poet had remained secreted in her mind, not forgotten exactly, just unthought of, the circumstances of his death had made a defiant, indelible impression on her mostly because when she read about the suicide – how sad, how dreadfully sad that a human life could be so brutally reduced to no more than a mere footnote in a newspaper! – she realized she had known all along that his gruesome choice of deliverance was inevitable, known even when, as a child, she had listened, enthralled, to the utterly fantastic tales he wove. And, my goodness, they certainly had been fantastic! By no possible stretch of the imagination could he have been the leader of that heroic band of stuntmen who had survived the rapids while shooting MGM's calamitous *Trail of '98*; nor could he have been the astonished sparks in Buenos Aires who received Captain Hans Langsdorff's uncoded message from the *Graf Spee* requesting assistance for the crew of the *Clement* which he had just sunk; no more than he could have been the only living mortal who knew the true identity of the notorious Black Dahlia murderer, or given Jack London the idea for *Sea Wolf*. It was as though, even then, he had been yearning to join those whose lives he filched. And without consciously admitting it, without, in truth, being quite aware of it, an element of this curious, unstable search for vanishment had dogged Susanna, making her, at times, romanticize death as her choreographers romanticized it, dying broken-hearted, dying loved but always untold she was loved, always betrayed or seemingly betrayed, each mythical lover an Albrecht by any other name.

'Well, I'm afraid your nymph has got it wrong this time,' she told Septimus, heaving a grateful sigh as she rounded the bend in the road, slightly ahead of him, and saw the gates of the Ollofson only some fifty yards away.

'It is always possible, of course. But not – '

'Thank you for seeing me back safely, Father,' Susanna interrupted quickly, watching the long black limousine that glided past them and came to a halt a few feet away, rocking on its over-zealous springs.

' – very likely. No *reason* for them to get it wrong, you see.'

Susanna waved a hand before her face to disperse the dust that rose from behind the car before holding it out. 'I'll say goodbye, Father,' she said, the words appropriately punctuated by the slamming of the car door.

Septimus, overlooking her hand, glanced towards the noise. His eyes lit up. 'Talking of getting things wrong – now here's a genius who never gets *anything* wrong,' he said, holding up a single finger by way of salutation. Then, raising his voice: 'I am right, am I not, Patrick?' he called.

'*Mon Père?*'

Septimus waited for Patrick to join them. 'I was just telling my charming companion how it is that you always get things right.'

Patrick bowed his head modestly in agreement.

'It came up since we were talking about – '

'I really must go now, Father.' Susanna started to back away.

'Must you? Oh, dear. Ah, well. Another time. There will, of course, *be* another time, you know.'

Susanna gave the priest a tired smile and nodded curtly to Patrick before spinning on her heels and hurrying towards the hotel. She felt uneasy, almost frightened. She should have followed her original instinct and insisted that Solomon take her away from Haiti the moment they had arrived. She should certainly have gone with him when he left. It was so *stupid* to imagine that anything good could have come out of this menacing, festering place. But you saved me, the cardinal sang in her ear. She turned in through the massive iron gates and started up the drive.

'Yes, I saved *you*,' she said aloud, feeling a brief elation. Then her heart sank. Before her, on the ground, its wings spread as though in flight, lay the dead cardinal. Almost blinded with tears she bent and picked it up, holding it close to her. It was still warm. She looked about her as though expecting to see the spirit of the bird hovering close by. 'Poor, poor little creature,' she whispered to it.

Strangely enough, that was more or less what Septimus was saying to Patrick. 'Poor, poor child,' he said, still staring up the road along which Susanna had gone.

Patrick nodded solemnly.

'If only the human spirit would learn to admit its limitations.'

Patrick continued to nod, rather less solemnly, his face contorting in slight pain as he doubled up his action to include an easing of a nagging crick in his neck.

'What was that you said?'

' – ? I said not a word.'

'I thought – ' Septimus cocked his head, listening. Then he shook his head, clearly bewildered, but almost hiding this behind an embarrassed smile. 'I thought I heard you say I had saved you!' He snorted, still wagging his head. 'Not, I know, that *you* need salvation. How goes it with you anyway?'

'Sadly.'

'Oh dear.'

'Things are different.'

'They always are.'

'Since our Archbishop died.'

'Ah, yes.'

'They have come and stripped the house of his presence.'

'Well, they would.'

'Everything that was his bundled into boxes and swept away.'

'Oh dear,' was all that Septimus could think of to say. 'And you? Are you to be swept away also?' He managed a naughty chuckle.

Patrick drew himself up to his most magnificent height. 'Of course not. I am irreplaceable. I must remain to serve the new Archbishop when he is enthroned.'

'I didn't really mean to offend you.'

'You meant to mock, no?'

'A little.'

By the expression on his face one could assume that Patrick was considering whether or not to take offence. He decided not to, waving away the mockery with a delicate flick of one hand, a hand that curved away into his inside jacket pocket, and reappeared holding a letter. He offered it to Septimus. 'I was instructed by our late Archbishop – the evening he died – to make it my personal responsibility that you received this into your hands.'

'For me? From the Archbishop? How extraordinary.'

'Yes,' Patrick agreed archly. 'I thought so also.'

'No message – just that?' Septimus pointed nervously to the letter but made no attempt to take it.

'No message. Just this.'

Septimus, with an effort, forced himself to take the long manilla envelope. He studied the late Archbishop's unbroken wax seal: a tiny mitre with crossed keys unrampant.

Patrick waited, his eyes narrowing.

Septimus turned the envelope over and read his name.

'You will read it?' Patrick asked, his eyes widening and filling with curious expectancy.

'Read it? Why yes. Of course I'll read it.'

'Now?' Patrick encouraged.

'This minute?'

Patrick inclined his head.

'Oh no. Not now. Not this minute.' Septimus peered up and down the road before leaning forward towards Patrick and explaining quietly: 'Not the sort of place to read a letter from an Archbishop. Especially a dead one, is it? On the side of the road. A card from a friend on holiday in Dingle or Skibereen could be glanced at without fear of retribution, I'm sure. But a letter such as this' – he waved the epistle (for that was the word already looming in his mind) under Patrick's faintly wrinkling nose – 'must be read in private. In a holy place, I should think. If one can find such a place.'

. . . He found the chapel empty. The nuns had finished compline and the tones of their chant stayed faintly behind them. The flowers on the altars had already been freshened for tomorrow's masses. The parquet transept had been polished with beeswax, and the smell of this wax and the flowers and the waning pungency of incense gave the chapel a pleasant, comforting, homely atmosphere. Septimus settled himself on a small, plastic-seated chair (one of ten stacked optimistically to seat any unexpected overflow of the devout). Light from the window of unstained glass fell on the letter as he removed it cautiously from the envelope. He adjusted his spectacles before unfolding it, and cleared his throat. There were four pages of thick, expensive notepaper, parchment almost, each covered on both sides with the spidery writing of an ailing hand, each word joined to the next by a loop as though the effort of lifting the nib from the paper had proved too much. It did not appear, from the introduction, to be a letter at all, rather a sort of dissertation, a sermon, but an intimate one. Glancing down the first page Septimus spotted his own name and felt a sudden qualm; how ominous, he thought, that his name should leap at him from this missive from the dead. For a moment he felt an urge to return the letter unread to its envelope, but the vision of the old Archbishop so laboriously writing, even as death tapped him on the shoulder, forced him to concentrate and read:

I salute you, my friend, strange though it will doubtless strike you that I feel the compunction to address you at this moment when I should be directing all my thoughts to God, when I can surely hear death approach on stealthy padded feet. Such a sly fellow, death! Why he creeps upon me so ashamedly I do not know: I welcome him with open arms – he is, if he but knew it, my most beloved friend. As he will be yours, but that is something you must take from me on trust. I can but tell you that it will be so, and warn you that his advent will take place not too many months after my own demise. Hah! – how can the old fool say such things, I hear you ask. How can the old idiot know? There are, believe me, more things in heaven and earth than are dreamt of in our philosophy. Our minds are so tunnelled towards the concept of one God, that we are blinded to the escapades of other deities that grapple with equal vigour for the souls of men: no benevolent, all-forgiving spirits these – wily, rampant demons hell-bent on self-preservation. And they are winning, feeding on the eternal sorrow that never sleeps of my unfortunate Haiti. I have tried so hard to combat them but have grown weary, weakened by their constant shrieking even when I sleep, their voices gibbering outside my window, my name defiled by each new wave of spectral terrorism. And what do they scream? They scream that I have betrayed them since they are the real spirits of Haiti, born from the matings of rock and soil, wind and sea. And in an awful sense this is the truth: for I, my dear Septimus, I am a child of Haiti, my soul claimed, even before I was born, by the most ancient theogony of my country. And although I have carried my love and belief in Christ Jesus into the misericordes of a thousand sanctuaries in Rome and Nazareth and Gethsemane, seeking shelter and comfort and peace, they have always unearthed me, invading my turmoiled mind, scoffing at my impotent God, their putrid breath so vibrant it makes me retch, and I am doomed to give them heed. I cannot escape. There is no escape. In truth, I have been forced to believe that I do not want to escape for there is a strange palliation in their familiarity, a genial analgesic in the words they speak, words not comprehended by the brain but by that latent consciousness of my race which hovers, patient and consolatory, on the outskirts of credence, waiting, sometimes calling but mostly waiting in vaporous silence, its occasional dry cries more like shunting echoes spewing from the belly of hell. Yet for all the cloying power, for all their hereditary vigour, I recognize these grey, laconic spirits to be false, rogues of another world, conquerable only by someone who is unmanacled by centuries of suppurating witchery, someone who understands the power of suffering, someone who has suffered as most men never suffer, someone who –

'Is everything all right, Father?'

A sister came to his side on soundless feet, a bunch of keys in her hand, one – which she held separated from the others – huge, medieval, sinister.

Septimus looked up slowly. 'Oh. Yes. Just – ' He held up the letter by way of vague explanation.

The nun nodded. 'It's the nicest time to be in the chapel, isn't it?' she asked, her tone nonchalantly conversational. 'I often spend a few minutes alone here in the evening after I've locked up.'

'Locker-uppera ecclesia,' escaped Septimus before he could muzzle it.

The nun didn't seem to mind. 'Exactly. Of course we never used to, you know. Lock the doors at night. But now – with the rumours of trouble and what have you, Mother Superior thought it better to be safe rather than sorry.'

Septimus stood up.

'Oh, you don't have to leave, Father.'

Septimus eyed her.

'I have lots of little jobs that need seeing to in the sacristy. I can let you out when you're ready.'

'Thank you, Sister. But I'll – I wonder what God thinks about it?'

'I'm sorry?'

'Being jailed overnight.'

'Really, Father!'

Septimus sighed. 'Just a little joke, Sister. I think,' he added with a melancholy smile.

Unsure of her ground, wondering whether or not to share the amusement supposedly contained in the mild blasphemy, the nun chose to refrain from further comment and made her way like a shadow back to the sacristy.

– someone who himself is beleaguered not by the ethnic menace of

*voodoo spirits but by the appalling trauma of a fall from grace. Which
is why I write to you, my dear friend, my poor Septimus. I –*

Septimus Roach began very slowly to fold up the letter again,
frowning, an odd light in his eyes, smoothing the creases between
finger and thumb before replacing it in the envelope. He stood
there, waving the envelope slightly as though debating what to do
with it, staring, deeply abstracted, about the chapel. In the brief
time it had taken him to read as much as he had, the atmosphere
had subtly changed: it was as if Christ, for the moment, had forsaken
the chapel, gone off about some other, more pressing business,
leaving the congregation to discover how ill they could manage
without him. (For now, indeed, a congregation of sorts had gathered, hard to distinguish in the dimming light, shadows, outlines,
not kneeling as one might have expected but meandering about,
apparently searching for something although not all that bothered,
passing through each other as they wandered, respectfully quiet,
each, it seemed, unaware of the others. From time to time a familiar
emerged, fleetingly, gazed at Septimus with dull eyes, then glided
off again: Archbishop Gidron, followed by Patrick, emerged from
the spectre of a gigantic Haitian, stared, and withdrew; Sergeant
Colman, smiling his sinister smile, passed by; a gaunt, haggard
young woman, carrying a headless child in her arms, tried to make
her way towards him but was prevented from so doing by the
shadows encircling her.)

'All finished, Father?'

Septimus jumped: the shadows and the slightly sulphurous smell
vanished.

'Ah. Sister. Yes. Quite finished. Thank you.'

'I'll lock up after you then.'

'Is Christ back?'

' – ?'

'I see He is.'

Outside, the air cooling under the promise of rain (a promise
invariably broken) made Septimus shiver. He was about to shove
the letter into his pocket when, with sudden determination, he
raised it in both hands high above his head, offering it to whatever
spirits might be in attendance. Beyond the convent wall there was
a small explosion as a firework was lit: it whooshed into the sky,
disintegrated, sent myriads of brilliant sparks cascading into
the blue darkness. Septimus tucked the letter up the sleeve of

his soutane. The beautiful sparks extinguished themselves before falling invisibly to earth. A breeze like a sigh sprang up, then died away. Behind him a key turned importantly in the chapel door. Over the city a strange, throbbing hum eased its monotonous tempo, staccato and deep like people imitating drums with their voices.

Seven

Replete, Susanna and Gilles Lagreze had been sitting in silence for several minutes at opposite ends of the ornately carved ebonized table (carried from the house specially for the occasion and placed in what Gilles described as his 'English bower – or approximating such') listening to the distant sounds of Port au Prince – a muddled cacophany of music (rock and roll shouldering steel-band tintinnabulation to one side), cries, laughter, something that sounded like heavy machinery grinding into the earth – carried on low, surging waves across the bay. Above them, twining its way through the branches of an oleander that looked only mildly poisonous, an old and splendid jasmine scented the air with the heavy, sweet perfume it reserved for dusk, the tiny white flowers like minute stars in the light of the flickering candles in their glass globes suspended from the cross-beams of the pergola. From time to time large insects collided suicidally with the globes, producing an oriental chiming.

'This is absolute heaven!' Susanna said, breathing deeply.

Incredibly it was almost six weeks since she had come to Haiti, and the dinner had been in her honour, a sort of belated welcome.

Monsieur Lagreze gave her a melancholy look. 'Yes,' he agreed. 'But for how long, I wonder?' He stared at the dark, heaving ocean as though it might ease his reluctance to contemplate the future, or, at least, make some sense of it. He leaned forward and carefully placed his brandy glass on one of the small, circular lace mats, giving Oscar (who had left the table and was trying to outstare a lizard that had waddled from the bougainvillea) a tight, knowing smile; an unnoticed smile that dropped away as he closed his eyes briefly.

'For ever and ever,' Susanna declared, stretching with one arm, purring luxuriously.

The lizard released Oscar with a single, thoughtful blink. 'Nothing lasts for ever, darling,' Oscar said gratuitously over his shoulder.

'Some things do.'

'Do they?'

'Oh, yes. If you really want them to.'

Oscar felt a moment's paralysed confusion. He moved his feet and the lizard skittered to a safer distance, turned, and renewed their game. 'I'm afraid they don't – even if you *do* want them to,' he said quietly, aware that his response, a hopeful rebuttal of Susanna's mild accusation, was feeble.

An arc light from the white stone tower at the mouth of the harbour swept across the bay, picked out a fishing boat, its sails empty, then moved on, lighting the dark emptiness.

'I am reminded,' Monsieur Lagreze said, conscious of the sad insinuations and politely trying to waylay them, 'of the curious custom the Neapolitans have of prolonging their demonstrations of affection for their departed loved ones. Do you know of it?' He retrieved his glass, sliding the stem between his third and index finger, and swilling the vintage brandy.

'No,' Oscar said lazily, uninterested now that he had been lured back into competition with the tiny reptile.

'I seem to remember something.' Susanna gave a thoughtful frown, running a finger across her brow. 'Why yes! Goodness. Of course. It frightened me terribly when I was first told.'

– It had struck her as horribly portentous. The huge black and gold hearse, drawn by eight horses, plumed and draped in finery of black and silver – supplied and overseen by Gaetano Bellamuno, undertaker supreme, proud possessor of this most baroque of hearses, and, perhaps not so ironically, patron of the arts – lumbered past the Teatro Nationale where, in letters of gold that matched the scrollery (cherubs, lilies, defending angels) of the deathly transport, her name was emblazoned: COPPELIA. CON LA PRIMA BALLER-INA INGLESE (no matter that they got *that* wrong) SUSANNA LICHFIELD. To the side of that an enlarged photograph of herself on points, arms arched over her head, from *Giselle* as it happened, but that was irrelevant also. Unexpectedly one of the horses, usually so docile as if appreciating the solemnity of their calling, chose that moment to shy, and the cortège came to a sudden, shuddering halt. Susanna, on the point of leaving the Teatro, exhilarated by the success and passion of the final rehearsal, froze on the sidewalk: it was as though (and the thought was to crop up again and again through the years, leaving her with the same terrified, cold sensation) the hearse had come to fetch her talent from the boastful placard and cart it off –

Susanna shivered.

'Ah, you are cold?' Monsieur Lagreze was already rising from his chair, one arm outstretched as if to ward off the chill or shepherd her towards the warmth of the house.

'Oh no. No. I was just thinking.'

'Ah yes,' Monsieur Lagreze said with a sigh that suggested he fully understood, and settled back in his seat. 'It is disquieting, is it not, yet comforting nonetheless?'

'I suppose it is.'

'*Les mémoires tristes ne sont que la mémoire des moments joyeux.*'

'Yes.'

It was Oscar's turn to cede defeat to the lizard. 'Will one of you tell me what on earth we're talking about?' he demanded without looking round, his voice bantering.

Monsieur Lagreze cleared his throat.

Immediately Susanna held a finger to her lips and shook her head.

Oscar swung his feet to the ground and stood up. 'Well?' he asked, taking his chair by the carved back stretcher in one hand and carrying it, swinging, back to the table. He sat down, looking from Susanna to Gilles, his eyes quizzical and a little amused.

Susanna gave him a wan, tired, smile. She had folded her arms across her chest and her breasts stood up under her chiffon dress embroidered with flowers and impossible foliage and imaginary birds, not unlike the dress she had been wearing when Oscar had first met her. (How ridiculous the introduction had been! A party. The host – or hostess? God alone knew. 'This is Susanna – some day we will say her name with awe! And this, my dear – this divine man is Oscar. You two are just made for each other.' That had made them laugh!) Once again he felt the pain in his heart and looked away, fixing his eyes on one of the swaying flames, narrowing them to slits as though averting hypnotism; why, oh why had she come to Haiti? Why did he still love her so? What was the point? He peered surreptitiously at her again, perhaps for encouragement that there *was* some point, some hope – something.

'I think I *will* get my wrap.'

'Allow – '

'No. Please, Gilles. I can get it myself. You stay and entertain poor old Oscar.'

She felt the eyes of both men follow her as she made her way across the patio (her heels ticking like some delicate clock on the alabaster) towards the house, her arms folded again, her back very straight, her neck arched.

– To continue, Signor Bellamuno said (for it was he no less who took Susanna protectively by the arm and guided her towards the Cafe d'Angelo for the espresso she had requested), it may well appear gruesome to those who cannot understand the deep need we have to nurture the affection we perhaps neglected to demonstrate fully when our beloved ones were alive. So it is that when the flesh has turned to dust we disinter the bones and wash them in scented water and wrap them in winding sheets of white linen and place them in marble lockers with respect. When we feel lonesome we can remove them, and fondle their bones as, indeed, they must have fondled us (as children, as parents, as lovers) and tell them again of the love we have for them –

'You look so grim!' Oscar's voice caught up with her. She was about to turn and explain away the accusation when Monsieur Lagreze replied, 'I apologise.' Feeling oddly cheated Susanna crossed the drive and entered the house.

Oscar moved his eyes from Gilles's face and, staring at Susanna's empty chair, reached blindly for his glass. 'So, Gilles – ' He tossed his head to replace a wisp of his thinning hair that had been blown across his forehead by a sudden slight breeze; his expression, as he kept the glass to his lips without drinking, managed to be both speculative and indifferent. Nonchalantly he continued, 'What's all this I hear about Duvalier?'

Monsieur Lagreze winced, although he kept his eyes vague. His voice was overly casual as he tossed back a question. 'And what is it that you have heard about our good President?'

Oscar snorted. 'Good President! Bloody maniac.'

Monsieur Lagreze shrugged. 'The term is relative. What have you heard about him?'

'That he is preparing to abandon Haiti for healthier climes.'

'Indeed?'

'Indeed.'

'You are better informed than I.'

Oscar eyed him askance. 'Come off it, Gilles. You know every damn thing that goes on.'

Monsieur Lagreze wagged a finger. 'It is better – at the moment – to know nothing.'

'Ah. Then there *is* some truth in these rumours?'

'I did not say that.'

'No. Of course not.'

'In fact we are not even having this discussion.'

Oscar grinned. 'What discussion?'

Monsieur Lagreze was lighting a cigar. He returned the grin as he waved away the gathering smoke from in front of his face, waving quite vigorously as though to disperse contamination. The click of his lighter as he snapped it shut seemed to jolt him into sudden alertness. He stood up and walked to the parapet, gazing down and about him in silence. Again the light flared across the bay; the small fishing boat was gone, perhaps sunk, sucked into the deep by some fantastic monster, and the possible tragedy of the boat made him feel immeasurably sad. Behind him Oscar was helping himself to another drink.

'What exactly have you heard, Oscar?' he asked seriously, turning and sitting, or rather propping, himself on the parapet.

'Just the rumours.'

Monsieur Lagreze waited.

'Rumours that we could be about to get an approach from Duvalier to help in his safe exit.'

Monsieur Lagreze nodded. 'Yes,' he said. 'Yes,' he said again. He heaved himself to his feet, and looked for a moment as if he was about to toss his cigar down the cliff; he changed his mind and returned slowly to the table, sitting down heavily. 'If such an approach should be made I have been told already that it will be I who will make it.'

'I thought as much.'

'And your reaction?'

Oscar grimaced. 'Hardly up to me, is it? No doubt we would do everything possible to help.'

'Would you?'

'I should think so. If only because it would suit our interests to see the back of Jean-Claude.'

'You would give him sanctuary in America?'

'You're probing.'

Monsieur Lagreze inclined his head.

'Possibly – for a while. He would hardly want to stay in America, would he? A bit too close to home, I would have thought.'

'He might have to.'

'Oh?'

Monsieur Lagreze took a deep breath. 'The President had hoped to avoid the indignity of asking for any assistance but there seems there might be no alternative.' He stubbed out the cigar angrily, making the ashtray rattle on the table. 'I can tell you that he almost left two weeks ago, but his plans were thwarted at the last moment. Switzerland rebuffed his request for asylum.'

'I see. Like that, eh? Still, there are other countries, surely, who would welcome an influx of his loot.'

Monsieur Lagreze smiled bitterly. 'You believe so?'

'I would have expected so.'

'So did we. Greece, Spain, Morocco, Jamaica, even Gabon – ' Monsieur Lagreze gave a disparaging snort ' – they all regret that the time would be inappropriate to welcome the Duvaliers for any lengthy stay.'

A nocturnal bird, the size of a pigeon, flew overhead and sent an embittered cry ricocheting over the bower. Oscar looked up.

' – time is so short,' Monsieur Lagreze was saying.

'Ach, there's time enough.'

'Ever since Gonaives – and I tried to warn him about that but he would have none of it.' Monsieur Lagreze seemed to be arguing with himself. 'I warned him that once the Church lent its support to the opposition he would have to act quickly. Alas, he believed that with the Archbishop dead things would change. But – ' He shrugged with an air of hopelessness. 'The trouble with absolute power is that those who have it mistake it for divinity. When that error becomes apparent it is always too late.'

Oscar leaned forward and planted his elbows firmly on the table, cupping his chin in his hands. 'This approach, Gilles. When do you expect it to be made?'

'I have not the faintest idea. It will, I hope, be soon. Before the Lenten festival. I fear that by that time it could already be too late. The President, you see, has little stomach for an all-out campaign of violence to bring the country under control. He has, I think, convinced himself that he is in no real danger. With Port au Prince quiet under the thumb of his troops and police he distrusts our reports that the rest of the country is in open revolt. He will, as usual, leave everything until the last minute. And while his wife agrees with us, his mother, the senile thing, does not.'

'But you are certain he will leave – eventually?'

Monsieur Lagreze resorted to his favourite shrug. 'It is, my friend, quite inevitable.'

'What is?'

Susanna's gay, light-hearted voice, giving lie to the seriousness of her question, left both men, for an instant, speechless. She stared at Oscar gravely. 'You look so grim, darling.'

Oscar was forced to laugh. 'I said that to Gilles a minute ago – without the endearment.'

'Yes. I heard. For a second I thought you were talking to me.'

'Oh.'

'So tell me: what is quite inevitable?'

'That night must follow day?' Monsieur Lagreze suggested in a futile effort to evade the issue.

'Really, Gilles. I'm surprised at you.'

'I do think we should tell her,' Oscar said quietly, leaning back. Unconsciously he had been watching her: her tanned neck and arms – rather bony and used a good deal to emphasize her words – the sable stole (the only luxury she had willingly accepted from Solomon) draped over her shoulders, her black hair swept severely back this evening and fashioned in a bun at the nape of her neck to give her cheekbones an added sharpness, her eyes that he always thought of as smouldering, set wide apart, huge. He yearned suddenly to reach out and touch her, just touch her gently: his hand momentarily stretched out but only to pick a crumb from the table and squeeze it between his fingers, then drop it.

Monsieur Lagreze looked dubious.

'Tell me what?'

The two men stared at each other.

'Oh, for heaven's sake, come on you two.'

Still they stared in silence.

'What is so mysterious? What is the dreadful thing Oscar thinks I should be told?'

It fell to Gilles Lagreze to explain. He spoke slowly, his voice pedantic, a little condescending, as though he was dealing with a child. How could he possibly explain? How could he make her, or anyone else for that matter, understand the appalling tragedy that was about to be heaped upon them? What words could he find to express his fear that the heart was about to be torn from the country he dearly loved? More to the point, how could he make her appreciate what precisely he had meant by 'inevitable', since the fantastic power and potency of the houngains was something well beyond her ken? Even to think of trying made him uncomfortable. In truth he was embarrassed: it irked him that he, a man of the world, educated, refined, cultured, should have to admit to being possessed of the same uncanny fear of the dark powers that controlled Haitian thought, as shackled the uneducated, deprived masses. Yet it *was* so. Monsieur Lagreze, for all his worldliness and panache, knew that within him lurked that very real terror which mesmerized all Haitians. So, choosing his words with elaborate care and skilfully avoiding all reference to endemic sorcery, he confined himself to underlining the more obvious dangers that would ultimately stalk all foreigners still in Haiti should the President finally depart.

'What I don't understand is why he has to leave at all,' Susanna remarked almost petulantly, as though subconsciously blaming the President for inconsiderately jeopardizing the country's tranquillity.

'He is – in a word – getting the push,' Oscar said flippantly with a tolerant smile.

'By whom? I thought he was unpushable.'

'By fate,' Monsieur Lagreze interposed. 'By the hostile spirits,' he heard himself say; immediately he looked away, reaching up to pluck a sprig of jasmine.

'Really, Gilles. I *am* surprised at you. Hostile spirits indeed!' Susanna giggled. 'You're not, I hope, about to tell me that poor little Jean-Claude is being ousted by some voodoo hugger-mugger?'

Monsieur Lagreze buried his face in the jasmine, shifting uneasily in his chair. He crossed his legs to disguise his unease, and blinked his gratitude as Oscar came to his rescue.

'It's not all *that* weird an idea, my love,' he said, not looking at her, studying instead the label on the brandy bottle. 'This isn't the good old U.S. of A., you know. There *are* things that happen here which are pretty well inexplicable.'

Susanna gave him a scathing stare. 'Not you too, Oscar. Honestly!'

Oscar felt himself blush.

'You believe it impossible?' Monsieur Lagreze asked.

'That voodoo can play some part in deposing a President?'

'That our ancient spirits might dictate the fate of our people,' Monsieur Lagreze corrected.

'Well no – not *impossible*, I suppose.' Susanna pulled her wrap closer about her. 'It just seems so terribly silly to hear two grown men talking about – well, about witchery as if it was . . . Oh, I give up.'

Monsieur Lagreze discarded the jasmine, placing it carefully on the table before him like an offering. Looking at it he nodded kindly. 'It must indeed seem absurd to you. Most things we cannot comprehend are either absurd or frightening.'

'I didn't mean to belittle you.'

'I know you didn't *chère* Susanna. There have been times when I myself have suspected the wisdom of believing in the magic our houngains possess.' He took up the jasmine again. 'But when the beliefs of centuries have been born within you, when fanatical adherence to the superstitions and dark heresiarchy are made to appear more important than any imported religion and bear greater retribution than any foreign God, it is impossible to dismiss them just because they strike others as absurd. Each night – even now, at this moment – somewhere on Haiti a ritual that would probably horrify you is taking place, a ritual that to most of us is no more sinister than the cryptic supposition of transubstantiation. The spirits of the dead are being consulted. Zombies are being created. Gods of an unimaginable world are being worshipped.' Monsieur Lagreze's voice went hoarse, and he looked away.

As though to endorse the veracity of his odd words a deathly silence enveloped the garden. The noises from across the bay ceased. The waves lapped eerily as though made of cotton wool. The flames from the candles no longer blustered: they reached to the top of their receptacles straight and narrow and unwavering. The insects that such a short time before had been drawn towards the flames simply vanished. The jasmine, it seemed, momentarily lost its perfume, or withheld it as though it was its breath. Then, away in the distance, away behind the mountains that piled up behind the house like godly fortifications, a curious tapping commenced. At first it was erratic: like the sound of a blackbird watchfully evicting a snail from its shell on a stone. But shortly the beat became consistent and regular as if the player, after warming up, had found his stride, and, in the unnatural stillness, it was oddly menacing and sinister.

'What – ?' Susanna began, stopping at once and cocking her head.

Another sound, a similar tapping to the first but of a deeper timbre, tumbled from the mountain. Then a third, more resonant and sombre still, joined in.

'What on earth *is* it?' Susanna asked in a whisper, trying Oscar, but he was no help whatever. He shrugged and grimaced, the contortions on his face indicating bafflement and something that suggested a rather comic awfulness – spooky, he might have said had he spoken. They both looked towards Monsieur Lagreze.

However, Monsieur Lagreze, it appeared, had worries of his own. He had slumped down in his chair, his hands folded across his stomach, his head bent forward, his eyes closed. He was frowning deeply, the furrows on his forehead rippling and jerking as though nervous of what they interpreted. – Above all you must evade the call made by the signals of *les Cochons sans Poils* –

Monsieur Lagreze shifted in his chair. A small moan escaped him. His eyelids quivered as though trying to open but forced closed by an assailing weight. It was as if he was asleep and dreaming, and in a sense he was. – Above all you must evade the call made by the signals of *les Cochons sans Poils*. His nursemaid's warning echoed in his brain, urgently trying to drown the hypnotic drumming that throbbed now, like an enormous heart, from the mountains behind him. It was probably these two warring factions demanding his attention that imposed his trance-like state: and it was his nurse, old and wizened, her skin like crumpled brown paper, who still stood by his side, huge and fat and toothless, filling his mind with terrifying hocus-pocus; and then it was his father, thin and straight as a rod, vastly wealthy yet retaining many of the idiosyncrasies of earlier poverty (his rumpled clothes, the collar of his jacket frayed, his shoes soled and resoled, his Panama with its once brilliant scarlet band, now a dull maroon, unravelling), deeply Catholic yet riddled with native, meddling superstitions, his arm, brittle but strong, about his shoulder. But even that protective arm, that arm sinewed cord-like from gathering coffee and cotton, from heaving gigantic planks of timber, had been pretty ineffectual, of course: the comfort was spoilt by the ominous cautioning of the nurse's words, words which he himself might have spoken (did speak, did he not?), spoken shamefacedly as though they were a last-ditch effort, a mournful, hopeless attempt to guard his only son against the inevitable. Nor yet the reassurance that by education and income he, Gilles (at that time eighteen and about to leave Haiti for Paris) stood a better chance of shrugging off the ghastly strictures of daemonic credulity. No help either, later, the sad, coyly persuasive Emily Saker, her gaunt, abused countenance suggesting that she had been deprived even of that one inalienable right of all women: the right, at some time, if only for a moment, to be beautiful. One bitterly cold January evening he had met her, or rather been accosted by her as she hunted for customers, her moulting, waist-length, moleskin coat small protection against the keening wind that hurtled up the length of the Seine, the only prostitute out and about on such a night. All she wanted, it became clear, was company, someone, anyone by her side if only to prove for a few nomadic hours that she was not totally alone; someone to hear if not to heed her dreary tales – affection an emotion long since banished. And the moment, that moment which should have been ecstatic, when he lost his virginity with her, had been tawdry and unfulfilling.

No, not even the forlorn Emily Saker (how truly extraordinary that her name, mentioned only once in passing and in a tone that hinted strongly it was one of her own devising, should remain so clear and challenging in his mind) had been any use, even though months, almost a year later, she had offered him a curious proof of redemption: he was certain he had spotted her, groomed and coiffed, stepping from a black Citroën, and elegantly making her way on the arm of an elderly *roué* across the pavement and into the Plaza Athenée . . .

Monsieur Lagreze suddenly sat bolt upright, peering at his two guests (who waited hopefully for an explanation, Oscar still fondling his glass, Susanna, her hands clasped behind her head, swaying slightly from side to side) a little sheepishly through half-open eyes.

– So, it had all been for nothing then, this grand education, this careful tuning of the mind to manipulate the intricacies of the law? For nothing this widening of his horizons, this bombardment of culture, this secular enrichment that made all things spiritual smack of treason, of a wicked denunciation of some integral, if profane, part of his being? It certainly appeared that way, although what on earth his beloved father had expected of this untraditional exile, what he himself had expected, was never made particularly apparent: an arbitrary fortification of the soul against his native cultish eccentricities perhaps, a befuddlement of the crowing dark spirits at least. And so far as his father was concerned the experiment had been a success: the years Gilles had spent in France had certainly released him from any passive acceptance of the oppressive, reckless connivance heaped upon Haitian natives by bokors and houngains, rendering them helpless pawns in a sinister tradition. And it had to be admitted that, up to a point, it *had* worked (even if the immediately apparent benefits had wavered slightly on his return to Haiti, their application suddenly redundant), allowing him, with a newfound Machiavellian skill, to slither and slide his way through two régimes of equal unpredictability, pretending – although this pretence, he was reluctantly prepared to admit, was often somewhat less of a duplicity than a wilful self-deception – to agree whole-heartedly, smiling benignly to boot, with the ruthless imbecilities of the old Doctor and the less vindictive if more idiotic whims of his son . . .

Somewhere inside the house a radio blared for an instant before the volume was hurriedly lowered; time only for the Miami station to warn of a hurricane, the words gabbled with such speed one gained the impression the reporter himself was in imminent danger of being blown from his perch. And from the wavelengths of the past other warnings no less dire reached Monsieur Lagreze's mind, all in foreign tongues commentating on the plight of Haiti, all uncensored, all, alas, true. How the world gorged itself on the misfortune of this small country! How they resolutely refused to participate in its salvation! And in the coming turmoil how gleefully they would see their most horrendous predictions come to pass!

'What on earth *is* it?' Susanna's question, still hanging in the air, finally forced his response. '*Les Cochons sans Poils*,' Monsieur Lagreze heard himself say.

Susanna gave a small, hysterical giggle. 'Really, Gilles! Hairless pigs? You must be joking.'

But Monsieur Lagreze was in deadly earnest. This was it, this was always it, the voice of disbelief and mockery that dismissed evil and allowed it to continue unmolested; as, indeed, those who recognized the true and villainous potency were dismissed as crackpots. Septimus Roach suddenly popped into his mind, looking cheerful enough, presenting himself, as it were, before the selection board as an applicant for the post of lunatic supreme. But, Monsieur Lagreze suddenly saw, there was more to this grotesque and pathetic priest. His very craziness, in this fantastic, disbelieving world, gave him a curiously rational air as he pranced about, waving his niblick. His unexpected and devil-may-care appearance brought other reflections of some curiosity to Monsieur Lagreze's mind: hints and shadows that had been unidentified until now, conversations heard but hitherto disregarded as rantings, like, for example, that extraordinary encounter between the late Archbishop Gidron and the President. 'Downfall' had suddenly become the theme, although whose was not quite clear.

The Archbishop, looking particularly frail, hunched in his wheelchair, wrapped in three tartan rugs of varying tribal allegiance. He was manoeuvred into place (slightly to the left of the President's garish ormulu desk) by Patrick (who looked suitably overawed in the presidential presence, probably only pretending to be, his white shoes startlingly at odds with his black suit). He had been summoned by Duvalier to explain what was deemed to be a lack of allegiance tantamount to treason, an accusation the Archbishop scotched by closing his eyes and feigning exhaustion, leaving the President stranded in his fury. Yet, when sensing the tantrum to be on the wane, the old man had miraculously awoken, and smiled a gentle smile which captivated even Duvalier, provoking a smile, tentative and strained admittedly, in return. The Archbishop announced mysteriously, 'The saviour we have been expecting has arrived,' with that mischievous twinkle of his in eyes otherwise pain-filled as he watched and enjoyed, dangerously, the President's nervous discomfort. Strangely enough, despite evident unease, no one in that vast, sumptuous office found the statement in any way outrageous. It was accepted as a bald, irrefutable statement of fact, and the Archbishop's unimpeachable character lent it a dire weight even if his detractors had been warning of his senility for some considerable time. But be he senile or not, the President was not about to take any chances: always keeping his prudent and more-or-less genuine leaning towards the more macabre deities of his country foremost in his mind (much of their potency the work of his enigmatic father, who had found that fear of the spiritually unknown was far more satisfactory and versatile a weapon against rebellion than any physical terror), he maintained an almost Celtic dread of God also. (The old Doctor, of whom Jean-Claude, despite his pampered childhood, was in terrified awe, had posed for a portrait with the image of Jesus Christ clapping him on the shoulder with some approval.) When the Archbishop spoke, regardless of what one thought of him as a man, regardless too of his peculiarly erratic spirituality, he spoke for God. Added to this, of course, was the myth, promulgated at some distant time by a few far-seeing Bokors, that a redeemer was on the way: shrewd and wily men, they had been quick to notice the advantages the early missionaries gained with their promises of 'another life' and the threats meted out by a zombie-like being they called Jesus. Adapting their own 'redeemer' to their specific needs, they were cunning enough to make this eventual saviour nicely vague, even to the point of evading any hint of what he might be about to save anyone from. Hence the superstition flourished that redemption would be from whatever one wanted: poverty was pretty high on the list, of course, as was hunger, but the promised coming also had political clout, hovering threateningly over the island's insecure ministers, over Jean-Claude also, whose insecurity rose persistently from the ever-nagging ghost of his father. So it was no great surprise that he was dismayed when the old Archbishop announced that, finally, the saviour had arrived.

Susanna's ironic giggle still rankled with Monsieur Lagreze. 'It is but their name that is, perhaps, amusing,' he said seriously, opening his eyes. 'They are a most potent band, sending their members into the night to spread evil.'

And it was certainly the whiff of evil (up to that moment unrecognised but revealed by the mere mention of it) that now pervaded the otherwise delightful setting. Oddly enough, it was Oscar who appeared most affected by it; his body stiffened, his eyes stared, his nostrils twitched as though assailed by some nauseous stink. While through his mind a curious tableau unfolded, stilted in its re-enactment as if the players were puppets rather than humans, their limbs jerking in extraordinary contortions – a tableau that he had witnessed on his own insistence following a half-intentional invitation from Gilles barely a month after he had arrived in Haiti. Up to now he had logged it as but another primitively frightening custom to be added to the collection he had amassed during his stints in foreign lands.

– So, you believe all this I tell you is nonsense? Monsieur Lagreze had asked, in no way offended, more amused as if he had won a little bet with himself.

– I didn't say that. What I said was that, like many native customs, its potency lies only in fear. So, not being particularly afraid – not yet, at least – I doubt I would be terribly impressed.

– Ah, impressed.

– You know what I mean.

– Of course. You would like, nevertheless, if I read you right, to attend one of these unimpressive little ceremonies?

– Yes. Why not?

– But just out of curiosity?

– Exactly.

– Very well. I shall arrange it.

And he *had* arranged it, and with a facility that somehow lessened any twinges of foreboding, although first an introduction had to be effected: a rather profane audience with one Maximilian de Voire. Boisterously nervous, tetchy under Monsieur Lagreze's saturnine gaze, Oscar accompanied his friend to the appointed rendezvous. Some three miles further down the coast from Gilles's own house, a porter met them at the gate of what once must have been an exquisite estate. The dishevelled, entangled garden gave evidence of having been spectacular, the exotic flora still soldiering on under the weight of thorny brambles whose tendrils clasped the smaller shrubs in wicked embraces and reached upwards to encumber the mightier trees, failed to humiliate them and fell backwards to form barbed arches under which one passed, it seemed, at one's peril. A stone nymph, from whose ewer, hoisted and precariously balanced on one shoulder, water must have tumbled, stood headless, dry, scaling as if diseased. Paved walks ran cracked and weed-strewn, almost invisible, the neatly laid, patterned brickwork erupting, forced from its foundation by tufts of coarse, spiky grass. The statuary, fake Roman, lay toppled, lesser gods and buxom goddesses lying like white corpses in the lush undergrowth, idols condemned to eternal rigor mortis.

The man led them to a small outhouse on the edge of the property, a revamped building that had probably once housed slaves but was now refurbished and transformed into what Oscar immediately thought of as a temple, instantly admitting to himself that the word was far too grand. Inside, reclining on a sheepskin covered chaise-longue, surrounded by a motley collection of amulets and trinkets, mostly African although one or two bore a distinct Oriental cast, the air thick with the scent of stale, lingering incense through which the sun, plummeting through a skylight, barely penetrated, was Maximilian de Voire. Whatever Oscar had expected it was certainly not this. The man had extraordinary presence, and was totally unlike the ridiculous witch-doctor image Oscar had stupidly, if forgivably, fabricated in his mind: he was tall and debonair, almost majestic, dressed in flowing white, gold-embroidered robes like a kaftan, the deep creases in his skin *suggesting* great age but his eyes, bright as burnished bronze buttons, proclaiming an alliance with everlasting youth. He rose, smiling as genially as any Washington host, and came forward, pavisanding, in those few strides enhancing his regality . . .

The drumming ceased, although for several seconds its echo lingered, vibrating even more forlornly down the mountain as though some wanton god was reluctant to diminish its potency. Susanna gave a small shudder. 'I'm glad that's over,' she said tightly, as Monsieur Lagreze tossed her a look that suggested there was little enough to celebrate.

'It is, isn't it? Over, I mean?'

Monsieur Lagreze nodded. 'The drumming, yes.'

'Good. It was beginning to get on my nerves.'

. . . Yet, despite the geniality and apparent generosity there was something distinctly unnerving inherent in Maximilian de Voire's smile: So this is the American you spoke of, he observed, manifestly refraining from permitting emotion to enter his words.

– This is my friend, Monsieur Lagreze replied pointedly.

Maximillian nodded tolerantly in the manner of a man making paternal allowances for another's lack of judgment or taste. And why, he asked, his voice bantering, why should our – (pausing now for a moment but not, it seemed, to seek an appropriate word, but rather using the brief silence further to unsettle Oscar, and succeeding) – why should our practices be of such interest to your friend?

Before Monsieur Lagreze could reply Oscar, peeved at being spoken about as though he was not there, or there but in some way incapable of speaking for himself, decided to defend himself. For knowledge, he said simply, grasping one word he had imagined as being signified by his awesome host.

– Ah, Maxmilian sighed.

Monsieur Lagreze raised an appreciative eyebrow.

– Or banal curiosity? Maxmilian then suggested with narrowing surly eyes.

Oscar nodded honestly. That too, of course. But not idle, I think.

– Ah, Maximilian sighed again, tucking his hands up the sleeves of his extravagant robe and taking on the appearance of some exotic monk, the jutting chin, the proud head slightly raised, the eyes now glazing with that expedient shimmer favoured by visionaries, instantly conjuring up a remembrance of a black saint for whom Oscar's mother had shown an uncharacteristic preference. But there was nothing beatific about his voice when he rounded on Oscar and demanded: And supposing I conceded to your request, what use would you make of all that you learned? –

'What's happening now?' Susanna's question, whispered as though expecting a remonstrance from someone sitting behind, seemed oddly irrelevant.

'You don't want to bother your pretty head with that,' Oscar heard himself reply, aware that his answer approximated neatly what he had time and time again said to himself.

Susanna bridled. 'Don't be so condescending, Oscar,' she snapped.

'I'm sorry. I – '

'Why does everyone have to treat me like a child?'

'I said I was sorry.'

'Words are easy.'

What looked like developing into a rather infantile bickering was brought to an abrupt, astonished halt by the sudden appearance of Septimus Roach on the patio: he did not arrive, he simply materialized, it seemed, looming into the small circle of light cast by the candles like a dishevelled ghost.

'Father Roach!' Oscar was the first to give tongue.

Septimus gave a little jerk as though startled at being recognized.

'*Mon Père!*' Monsieur Lagreze bayed, rising.

Septimus gave another twitch.

'Why – ' Monsieur Lagreze began, moving round the table and making for the unexpected visitor, leaving the word to survive on its own.

Septimus looked puzzled. He kept that bewildered look on his face as Monsieur Lagreze, taking him by the arm, guided him gently towards the table.

'Here,' Oscar offered, standing and pushing his chair forward.

Septimus sat down.

Only Susanna appeared unabashed. 'Hello, Father,' she said, her voice calm and friendly.

Septimus bestowed a tentative smile upon her.

'What brings you here?' Susanna then asked, while Oscar and Gilles Lagreze exchanged glances and kept their silence, standing quite still, almost as if they felt movement of any kind would break a particularly intriguing spell.

Septimus allowed his puzzled frown to deepen. 'I don't quite know,' he confessed. Then he gave a small embarrassed cackle. 'I thought you called me,' he added.

'Me?' Susanna stiffened.

Septimus nodded. 'I think so.'

Monsieur Lagreze came slowly back to the table and resumed his seat, easing himself into it, his eyes fixed on the outlandish priest.

'But how did you get here?' Oscar asked for some reason.

Septimus turned in his chair. 'On my bicycle,' he said.

The ridiculously simple reply made Oscar laugh – somehow he had anticipated a rather more miraculous mode of transport – and his laughter seemed to jolt Gilles Lagreze. He opened his mouth to speak, even leaned forward to stress the importance of his words, when he was forestalled by the sudden intrusion of renewed rumpus from across the bay; the insects reappeared on their suicidal bombardment of the candles, which had resumed a tempestuous flickering in their containers. It was most strange: it was as though the intrusion of Septimus Roach had obliterated all that had appeared threatening and unholy; as though, in some inexplicable way, the priest's presence had purified the moment and enfolded them in an aura that guarded them from harm.

'I *didn't* call you, Father,' Susanna said.

'No,' Septimus conceded. 'Unless – ' He shrugged.

'Unless?' Susanna quizzed, determined to get one straight answer.

'Unless someone called for you.'

It was Gilles Lagreze who spoke, resolutely avoiding everyone's gaze, staring at his huge hands that opened and closed (opening and closing as if hopelessly grasping at some truth) on the table before him.

'Oh, Gilles!' Susanna protested, certain that she was about to be hoodwinked out of a civil explanation.

Septimus nodded. 'Perhaps,' he said blandly.

Susanna, without wanting to, without meaning to, giggled. 'And who, might I ask, would do that?'

'Who can tell?' was all that Septimus had to offer.

'It *is* said that each of us has a guardian,' Monsieur Lagreze offered.

'Your guardian angel,' Oscar put in, trying to make light of this conversation that was developing such grim undertones.

Seriously, Septimus Roach agreed. 'Yes,' he said. 'Your guardian angel.'

Irked that his jocose suggestion had been taken seriously, making him, to his way of thinking, appear impertinent, Oscar snorted.

'*You* find the suggestion absurd?' Monsieur Lagreze asked him quietly.

'Of course. Well – I mean – the whole idea – '

'Yet Father Roach *is* here, is he not? And the' – he spread his arms wide – 'the atmosphere has altered, has it not?'

'Yes. But – '

Monsieur Lagreze was in no mood now to tolerate buts. 'You really must learn to open your mind, Oscar. I have spoken to you so many times about the inexplicable powers that exist in Haiti. I have let you witness some of them for yourself. Yet still you will not believe.'

'I believe you,' Susanna interrupted, alarmed by the uncharacteristic anger creeping into her host's tones. 'I think it's very nice to know someone, somewhere – or *something* is keeping a watchful eye on me.'

Rebuffed, Oscar struck a pouting pose. 'Have it your own way,' he said, annoyed with himself.

'Alas,' Septimus said forlornly, 'that is something none of us can ever have – things our own way. We are, I think, here to be manipulated.'

'Oh, lovely,' Oscar muttered sarcastically under his breath.

Septimus took to nodding again. 'For some, yes. For some it can be indeed lovely. For others – ' He stopped and stared at Monsieur Lagreze, their eyes holding and seeming to share a secret.

In the strained silence that followed Oscar found himself becoming thoroughy vexed, reduced, as it were, to a mocking infidel. What irritated him most was the fact that he *knew* there were powers that existed which were well beyond his ken. He had seen them in operation. He had witnessed Maximilian de Voire in action, create a zombie . . . involuntarily he shuddered. He decided, however, to persist with his derision. 'Well, now that you have performed your little act of salvation, perhaps we had better be making a move.' He walked round behind Susanna, and held her chair as she rose. 'We can give you a lift if you like, Father. Your bike will fit in the trunk.'

Monsieur Lagreze watched the car move down the gravel driveway at a sedate pace, its lights glowing redder as Oscar touched the brakes before swinging out on to the road. He stood there, staring, long after the sound of the engine had died away. Finally he shook himself and stretched like a man just waking from a long sleep, turning on his heels and walking towards the house. Why, he thought, why, oh why, did so many otherwise sane and intelligent people treat the incomprehensible as just so much infantile jibber-jabber? Why could they not learn to accept that there *were* powers beyond the human conception, powers for good as well as evil, powers not necessarily confined to the Christian ethic? He shook his head sadly. Ah, well, they would learn in the end, as everyone learned. He closed the door behind him. It was certainly curious how the priest had arrived on the scene just, as Monsieur Lagreze well knew, just as doom had started to saturate their minds; curious, too, how his concern had been, it seemed, only for the delightful Susanna Lichfield. There was, of course, only one explanation: yet how could she fit into the scheme of things; in what possible way could she have a role to play in the tragedy that so blatantly hovered over the wretched priest's head? He shook his head again and heaved himself upright, crossing the hall with cumbrous, heavy steps. Perhaps the priest knew: perhaps only he was *meant* to know; perhaps – Monsieur Lagreze climbed the stairs and made his way to bed.

Eight

Whether only he was meant to know hardly mattered. Septimus Roach did not know, he had not the foggiest idea what had made him abandon what he was doing, hastily mount his trusty Modestine and hurtle along the road to the home of Monsieur Lagreze; yet the impulse, while definitely puzzling, had in no way caused him anxiety or alarm. It was not the first time such an inexplicable overwhelming had taken hold of him. Far from it. He could, he freely admitted be said to be prone to such impulsive excursions, some of which, it was true, took place in his dreams, yet even these proved to be a mere foretaste of reality since they inevitably re-occurred and were undertaken, with equal bewilderment, at some time in the future. But there had been no forewarning of his visit to Monsieur Lagreze. He had been in the hospice, comforting, as he saw it, a young man riddled with disease (although what consolation his extraordinary sophistry could have been was hard to tell) when he was forced – there was no other word for it – to make the journey.

'And where have you been off to?' Sister Mary had demanded, worried, on his return, but kindly.

For the life of him Septimus could not answer. It was not that he could not remember, nor that he did not wish to reply. It was as though he had not actually been anywhere, had never left the dying young man. Yet he must have gone somewhere or Sister Mary would not have missed him, nor would he have been obliged, gratefully, to accept a lift home in that luxurious American motorcar. Yet the young man had died in his absence and Septimus knew he had been with him at his death, holding him in his arms, rocking him, easing him as best he could into a frightening eternity, placing him on God's generous lap. 'Out,' he said finally.

Sister Mary gave him a disapproving glare. 'The boy has died,' she told him, indicating the still figure on the bed.

'I know.'

Sister Mary did not appear to find anything untoward in this knowledge. 'It was a peaceful passing he had,' she said.

Septimus nodded. 'I know,' he said again, staring at the motion-less corpse. 'I was with him.'

Sister Mary froze, while the bandage she had been rolling un-ravelled and curled itself into a white snake at her feet.

Septimus gave a high-pitched, nervous giggle. 'In spirit, Sister. In spirit.' Sister Mary relaxed and resumed her monotonous rolling. 'Although,' Septimus continued, looking impish as he spotted the nun start to go rigid again. 'Although it could have been my spirit that went out.'

Suddenly his statement seemed to take on a sobering aspect, and Septimus frowned deeply, and took to mouthing to himself. Then he shook his head violently. 'But if that was the case you wouldn't have missed me, would you?'

Sister Mary gave him a baleful look.

'I mean,' Septimus went on, mostly to himself, although gazing at the corpse as if anxious to include it in the conversation, 'I couldn't very well be in two places at the one time, could I? Or could I?' His face brightened as his eyes twinkled. 'Could I, do you think?'

Sister Mary closed her eyes dismissively, and clamped her mouth tightly shut.

Left alone to flounder hopelessly in his confusion and seek an answer to his ludicrous riddle, Septimus lowered himself gently on to the narrow bed still occupied by the dead boy. Yet, after all, was it such a ludicrous riddle? Could anything that had happened to him so many times before be dismissed so lightly, be classified as merely ludicrous? And it certainly had happened many times before, this strange and eerie diversification of self – had it not? Certainly it had.

And now (while outside the hospice night clung to the city like a fraught mother, shrouding it in a protective blackness, starless, that hid its shame and wretchedness and fear, while mischievous imps like churls flitted through the minds of sleepers implanting images that would be recalled and acted upon when daylight came, while some men plotted and others cringed in their despair) sitting there on that metal cot that still, obscenely, seemed to heave and twang with the rasping, laboured breathing of the slowly stiffening corpse, Septimus saw himself, in his mind's eye, lying spreadeagled in the stony culvert, and heard again clearly the muttered Paraguayan voices overhead. And while a natural fear of death kept him motionless (although even this had an odd undertone to it, the rigidity in no way of his own devising but more as though his body, each fibre reacting in unison, had anticipated the logical sequence in his mind) his spirit – yet not only his spirit, for it appeared that some second body, or some body impersonating his, clearly visible and susceptible to pain alas, transported itself as though on metaphysical wings, gliding rapturously, to another place, but a place more grim and terrible than the abyss in which he lay. It was a strange effect, like being gloriously drunk, or hypnotized, or perhaps in some way dead although not totally dead, more a dozing death; resembling a vision in which oneself participated, in which only oneself was tangible, in which only oneself suffered . . .

– The tiny battered body lay crumpled on the floor, the horrific impact of its head crashing into the stone wall still sending shunting echoes about the cell, these and a low whimpering the only sounds for several minutes. Nobody moved: everyone stared at the child, transfixed, Septimus curiously detached, wondering only where the whimpering came from, then realizing it was from within himself, then feeling it swell like a terrible vomit and burst from his lungs as a manic, despairing scream, a contagious scream it seemed for the woman now threw back her head and screamed like an animal in horrendous pain. Yet there was a difference in the two sounds: the women screamed words, wild accusatory words, words that ripped into Septimus because he knew them to be true. 'You killed my child. Our child,' she screamed over and over but each time less shrilly until finally it was no more than a strangled whisper, a whisper more damning, more wretched than her loudest cries. Septimus heard himself fall silent. He felt himself curl into a huddled posture. He felt himself clamp his hands over his ears. But there was no escape: other voices, familiar but not quite identifiable, took up the clamour, relentlessly bludgeoning his mind.

– Take her out, Colman ordered. And that, he added, pointing with his crop at the child.

It was Delgado who bent and took the dead child by one leg and removed it, swinging it like a piglet's carcass, from the cell. Then, for the moment, Septimus was alone. At first he stayed where he was, crouched, shivering uncontrollably, his teeth chattering, sweating, sobbing, every nerve aching. And it seemed as though it were these same nerves that eventually moved him from his corner and eased him painfully to the spot where the child had fallen. Then suddenly, crazily, he was washing himself in the child's blood, patting the small pool of blood with the palm of one hand and smearing it on to his face, all the while muttering to himself something about washing away the guilt, something about exonerating himself from the outrage that had taken place. Finally he lay prostrate, his cheek on the blood. He stopped trembling. He seemed almost peaceful, almost as though he had fallen asleep –

'Oh! I'm sorry, Father. I didn't mean to wake you.'

'You didn't, dear lady. You didn't. I wasn't asleep . . . well, actually I was but I shouldn't admit to it, should I?'

It was noon on the day after the momentous dinner party at Monsieur Lagreze's home, and Susanna, on an impulse, had called at the hospice again, catching Septimus partaking of a nap. 'Be generous and convince yourself you found me meditating.'

Susanna laughed. 'Very well.'

Septimus swung his feet off the bed on which he had been lying and found himself face to face with the crucifix, the black countenance of Christ staring at him but, oddly enough, with what appeared to be a twinkle in His eye as if He had enjoyed the mild subterfuge.

'I was just passing,' Susanna lied, recalling for an instant the surprise of the taxi-driver's face when she had told him where to take her.

'Aren't we all,' Septimus said, turning to face her and peer over her shoulder towards the cot from which the corpse had since been removed.

'So I thought I'd pop in and see how you were.'

Septimus spread his arms and struck a pose, offering himself for examination.

Susanna laughed again. 'I can see you're fine.'

'And you?'

'Me? Oh, I'm fine too.'

Septimus nodded. 'Good.'

'Father – ' Susanna began, breaking off after just the one word and looking, casually she hoped, away.

Septimus waited uneasily.

'Father, will you tell me something?' Susanna asked quietly without turning round.

'If I can.'

'Why – what really made you – what did you really mean last night when you said you thought you heard me call you?'

Septimus felt his mind start to fidget. 'Just that,' he said.

'But why on earth should you have thought such a thing?'

Septimus shrugged. 'Who can say?' he said, hoping his rhetorical reply would somehow waylay further interrogation: but it was not to be.

Susanna persisted. She shook her head. 'I need an answer, Father. I *truly* need to know what it was that you meant.'

'A sensing,' Septimus put it.

'Of *what*?'

Septimus walked to the doorway, passing Susanna but not looking at her (she, in turn, not looking at him) and stared out at the dismal street. Of what indeed! If only he knew. Someone to his left, out of sight, coughed and spat hugely. Of tragedy, perhaps? No, that did not quite seem to fit. The lady, he noticed from the corner of his eye, was studying him with curiosity and apprehension. Two dogs started to fight, snarled a disgruntled treaty and parted, moving away from each other, bristling, casting macho glances over their shoulders. Of unbearable sadness? But that was the lot of every human. A woman, passing, suckled a child, humming to it as it sucked eagerly at her enormous breast, filling itself with warm life. Of incalculable loneliness? Yes, that was more like it. For there was, was there not, behind the carefully cosmeticized eyes, that puzzled hurt that only loneliness could shed? Burdened men, two of them, backs bent double under the weight of their loads of charcoal and ice, plodded past him barefoot. But if that was, in fact, the case, how could he, Septimus Roach, the loneliest of the lonely, possibly help?

'Father – I need *help*!'

– And *Help*! Septimus heard himself whimper but only long after, possibly hours after Colman and his henchmen had driven off in the requisitioned fruit lorry. Help! the feeble plea was no more than a breath of supplication, something only the hard earth could have heard, or God. And it must have been God or one of His spotters who heard, for suddenly Septimus was surrounded by faces peering down at him, yet not quite faces: shadows, more, clustering about him, pulling at his limbs, trying to help him to his feet. But he didn't want to get to his feet. He wanted simply to lie there and let life shiver from him with its extraordinary precision, let it drip slowly and methodically from his veins into the succouring earth. A compassionate face, round and olive-coloured and unsmiling but gentle nevertheless, emerged from the gathering mist that blurred his vision. 'Padre,' it began, but if it uttered more it was lost, devoured by the anxious babble of other voices.

'*Mi amigo.*'

'*Americano*, eh?'

'*No.*'

'*Que haceis aqui?*'

'*Veo que la terra anda*,' Septimus heard himself say, and despite his confusion, marvelled at his brilliance.

Another face, not unlike the first but older, less round, the cheeks sunken as though some artificial padding had been removed, pressed close to him. 'I am Domingo,' it told him in a tone that suggested it expected to be recognised. 'You will be hokay now, Padre,' it assured him. 'You will be very hokay now, Padre.' Which was very nice to know. Then he was making his way towards a beautiful garden through which a small stream ambled, a garden, he could just make out if only by squinting, planted with the most incredible flowers which preened themselves and flaunted their colours in a gentle, caressing breeze filled with the strains of music – Respighi, it sounded like. He was alone. The attentive, consoling faces had vanished. Ah, not quite alone, it seemed. Infinitely forlorn tableaux appeared and dissolved before him, peopled with old familiars who eyed him with something approximating suspicion, although there was one character Septimus could not recognise, a gangling creature who it seemed was doomed to be lost for eternity but cried: Save me, save me. And, perhaps through repetition, the word 'salvation' took complete possession of Septimus's mind. Salvation! The promised reward for all those sacrifices he had promised to make and had not. Still, for the moment, it seemed as though he might be on the point of salvation. But the encouraging moment soon passed. Will you not help me? the forlorn wail went up again. Will you not help me? –

'Will you help me, Father?'

Suddenly, in what was truly a blinding flash, Septimus realized that what he had hoped for ever since their first encounter, preposterous though it might be, was that this woman, so far removed from all his own experiences, would come to *his* rescue as, if the supposition was not too blasphemous, Mary Magdalen had come to the rescue of Christ; if only to lead him by the hand, so to speak, through the gathering hordes of whiffmagigs that jostled him relentlessly, and away along that worn, cobbled road which for all the world resembled the grey broad back that God had turned upon him. Instantly (helped by renewed growling between the two dogs, their treaty in tatters) Septimus dismissed God from his mind. It ran through his head that he could, perhaps, create a diversion that would distract Susanna from her need, but he did nothing about it. Instead he drew strength from the circling, belligerent hounds and faced up to the demand. Turning he presented to Susanna a face filled, he hoped, with the promise of deep concern and compassion. 'How can *I* help you?' he asked simply.

Thus confronted, Susanna shook her head. 'I don't know. I'm frightened,' she confessed. '*Really* frightened.'

'Ah.'

'Can you understand, Father?'

'Understand? Oh, yes. Fear affrights me like the adder's tongue. Or was it touch? Yes, touch, I think – and probably not an adder. Of what?'

Susanna twisted her fingers. 'I don't know,' she said again, and smiled weakly, blushing a little at her vagueness.

But Septimus didn't seem to mind the obscurity. Indeed, from the way he nodded sympathetically and pursed his lips one might have suspected that half-glimpsed loomings were something he understood far better than stark clarity. 'Not of me, I hope?' he asked but only for want of something to say.

'Good heavens no.'

Septimus permitted himself a tiny, almost coquettish toss of his head. 'Well, that's something.'

'At least, not of you directly.'

Septimus looked away immediately, his eyes settling on a pile of dirty sheets he had faithfully promised Sister Mary he would arrange to have washed, but had not. So he *was*, after all, to be implicated. He peeped at Christ on the crucifix for inspiration, trying desperately to think of something purposeful to say: Christ was adamantly mute and, alone, Septimus could locate nothing in his mind which made sense of the prickly situation. Fortunately, as it turned out, nothing was expected of him.

'Ever since I came here – no, ever since I first met you, you remember, at the hotel with Oscar and Monsieur Lagreze? – I've had this weird feeling that – ' Susanna stopped abruptly. Now she too eyed the pile of dirty linen, and far back in her mind an embittered voice requested: – Will you bring down the sheets?

– Of course.

– I don't want to see them.

– Very well.

– I don't want to see anything of his.

– As you wish, mother.

– How could he *do* such a thing to us?

– Daddy didn't mean to hurt *us*.

– The humiliation of it!

– For God's sake, mother!

– And don't you keep on trying to defend him, young lady. Oh, it was just so typical of him. Cruel. Selfish. Just thinking of himself. No matter what became of me. No matter that I would be left to put up with the sneers and hintings.

Anway, while her mother had made a meal of the tragedy, she had gathered up the sheets and the pillowcases from Daddy's bed (a camping trestle-like affair he had erected in what he had rather grandly called his 'study' wherein he had taken to locking himself, often talking to himself aloud, perhaps even plotting the details of his suicide), and held the bundle close to her, moving her head back and forth so that her cheek brushed against the linen where his cheek had lain, his smell still there, all that there was left of him that could not be defiled by her mother's angry tongue or grasping fingers. And she had taken the linen to the beach, to the spot where she had found his shirt and jacket and trousers, and burned it, making of the pyre a small, pathetic ceremony, imagining the smoke to be a sort of incense offered to some unidentifiable deity that would understand her father's decision.

' – strange feelings,' Septimus Roach was saying.

'I'm sorry?'

'We are all of us prone to – from time to time that is – strange feelings,' Septimus repeated.

'I suppose you're right.'

'Another person's.' Septimus was hurrying on as though to permit any interruption might call his bluff. 'Or our own but as another person, some imp that has filched part of us and set up house next door the better to tantalize us, would you think?' he rattled on, his puzzled expression waning. 'Yes, that would make sense,' he added, his puzzlement deepening again and indicating that it made no sense at all. '*Nihil est in intellectum quod prius non fuerit in sensu,*' he remarked darkly as an afterthought.

'I'm afraid I don't understand, Father.'

'Nor I,' Septimus put in quickly, regretfully.

'What I was trying to say – ' Susanna tore her eyes from the sheets and fixed Septimus with a sad, lamenting gaze. 'What I was trying to say was that ever since I met you I've had the oddest feeling that I was *meant* to meet you.' She gave a small embarrassed laugh as she noted the appalled expression that folded itself over Septimus's face, but ploughed on nonetheless, even clearing her throat before adding: 'It's as though – and I *know* this will sound crazy – as though something . . . something momentous is going to happen. To *me*. But it will be because of *you* it happens.'

Septimus didn't like the sound of that. Not one whit did he like it. It frightened him to death. '*Imaginare flagrans,*' he heard his voice – it was *his* voice, was it not? Certainly it sounded very much like his voice – say. 'It's a rummy place,' his voice went on, apparently trying to make some sense of the moment. 'Haiti. Affects people. Many places do, you know. Makes them – '

'You don't understand, father.'

'I *am* trying.'

'I know you are. I'm sorry. I'm probably just being silly. It's just that I – '

'Not silly, no.'

' – that I – '

'The other side of the coin being that most of us in our isolation and confusion try to shift our imminent calamities – but never our pleasures, which is interesting, you must admit – on to others, blaming them, in a sense, for whatever befalls us.'

'That's *not* what I mean,' Susanna snapped vehemently. 'I'm not *blaming* you for anything, Father,' she added, her voice oddly repentant.

– and not even the chance to repent, someone said, her mother most likely.

– Maybe he saw nothing to repent, Susanna answered.

'I know you're not,' the priest's voice cut in.

'Thank you.'

'Not intentionally anyway. But that, as they say, is another story.'

'Father, please help me – please?'

Septimus swung away from Susanna's pleading face and concentrated on the road once again. Who was it had asked him for help before? He could not remember. Opposite stood a single motionless woman, the fringe of a ragged awning obliterating her face; by her side, curled on the ground, was a child, unmoving in slumber. The afternoon was filled with strange, menacing noises, like those of uneasy sleep filled with the miscalculations of dreams lumbered with the intrusion of nightmares: the grating, roaring engine of the bus that made its way to the centre of the city, stopping briefly at the intersection far to the right, was the drum-roll of someone condemned; a howl down the street, perhaps animal, perhaps human, was someone being murdered most foully. A fault in the electric cables crisscrossing the road like some disintegrating trampoline sent a twitch of lightning shooting skyward to rival the brilliant sun. A scuffling at his feet made Septimus glance down: the crippled cobbler grinned up at him, his eyes alert as though awaiting a response to some request he had made. 'How can I help you?' Septimus asked again, spreading his hands in acceptance of some sorrowful words he could vaguely recall.

'I don't think you can, Father.'

'Ah,' sighed Septimus; hurt, but more relieved than he was hurt. He moved back into the hospice and stood looking down at Susanna's bowed head, waiting for her to speak again. For the moment she was distracted, her eyes fixed on the huge crucifix in the corner, her brow furrowed. Then: 'In fact I *know* you can't, Father,' she confessed morosely, speaking, it seemed, to the figure of Christ.

Septimus felt his head nodding in abject agreement and made as if to speak, opening and closing his mouth in a peculiar masticating gesture. His eyes were overflowing with tears and there was not a damn thing he could do about it. As though to distract his attention from this predicament he took to plucking threads from the frayed cuffs of his cassock, letting each thread float singly to the floor by opening his fingers extravagantly wide, waiting patiently for each to land safely before continuing the unravelment. Then he began to shake, violently: dreadful, heavy shudders, such as he himself had witnessed at gravesides as relatives faced with the inexplicable finality of death strove to contain their sorrow. Yet through his tears, surmounting the almost unsurmountable obstacle of his trembling body, Septimus watched in amazement as he managed a little joke:

he held aloft a single fibre and surveyed it studiously: 'A wisp from the rudder of Tam-o'-Shanter's mare, would you think?' he asked. Then he flopped down on the nearest bed, leaned forward, his elbows on his knees, and buried his face in his hands.

Instinctively, Susanna began to reach out towards the sobbing priest, but her reaction was cut short. Slowly, unbelievably, it was her father leaning forward on the bed, his long fingers gnawing at his temples, weeping painfully. – I wanted so much to help you, he was saying through his fingers, the words drowned to a whisper in his plight. But: 'I'm so *sorry*,' Septimus said, looking up and dredging a smile from his anguish.

'Oh no, Father. It was my fault. I shouldn't have asked. I didn't realize, you see – '

'No. Of course not,' Septimus reassured her, his smile broadening as he felt safer on the mutual ground of half-admitted failure. 'How could you have?'

'Anyway, I guess it's time I started to sort things out for myself.'

Septimus said nothing. He did not move. Yet he somehow managed to express approval of the decision.

'It's time, too, that I went back to New York.'

That, it appeared, was a very different kettle of fish: the reaction it yanked from Septimus was extraordinary. He was on his feet in a flash. Gone was all trace of approval, of understanding, of, more to the point, moroseness. He strode up and down between the beds, flapping his arms. His eyes gleamed wildly. 'Go back to New York?' he demanded, his voice rising to a high shrill.

'Yes.'

'You cannot,' Septimus told her, coming to a halt.

'I *beg* your pardon?' Needled, Susanna drew herself up stiffly.

'I'm sorry. I'm sorry. I'm sorry.' Septimus apologized profusely, jumping about from foot to foot. 'But don't you see?'

'No I don't, Father.'

'No. Of course not. How could you,' Septimus said, the words sounding familiar and making him frown for a second, making him pause, making him wonder if this conversation was actually taking place or whether he was simply recalling it from another time . . .

'It really was quite terrifying,' Susanna admitted to Oscar later, downing her drink quickly as though the memory was just about as terrifying as the event.

They were sitting on the veranda of the Ollofson waiting to go in

and have dinner. It was late evening and the lights overhead made
the darkness beyond their reach appear infinitely black. At the far
end of the veranda two men, one with a guitar, the other with a
saxophone, both perched on high stools, sipped beer from cans
as they rested between numbers, the saxophonist perspiring, the
guitarist, a red bandanna about his forehead, looking cool, his fingers
flexing all the while as though eternally strumming a soundless
instrument. There had been distracted applause when they had
stopped playing, but for the most part all those seated had continued
talking, and there was an urgency about the way they spoke, men
leaning forward, their heads almost touching, some drawing what
appeared to be diagrams on the table with their fingers, all, if their
resolute nodding was to be believed, in consummate agreement.

'He's mad.' Oscar condemned Septimus and dismissed Susanna's
appeal for sympathy in one swoop. 'What in heaven's name made
you visit him in the first place?'

'I wanted to see him.'

'Whatever for?'

'To ask him something.'

'What?'

'Just something.'

Oscar shrugged. The duo in the corner started to play again, a
sad, lilting version of 'My Baby Just Cares For Me', the saxophonist
carrying the melody huskily, making it, almost, a spiritual.

'Another?' Oscar asked, indicating with a glance, Susanna's
empty glass.

Susanna shook her head.

'Oh. I won't either then.'

Suddenly Susanna was talking. She was talking about Septimus
and how for a second he had become her father. She was talking
about the strange dallying compunction she had felt to visit the
priest, explaining how some inexplicable force had made it seem
that she was to be irrevocably linked with the priest. She was talking
of the awful loneliness she felt, a loneliness that apparently only the
befuddled priest could erase but by what possible magic was unclear;
talking about the weird feeling of impending disaster which in some
way she was to be instrumental if only as a peripheral agent; talking
about the sadness she felt that the love she and Oscar had once
shared, could not be revived; talking about – But there was some
mistake. Susanna was not talking. She had not uttered a word. She

had been staring into the darkness in silence. It had all been an illusion, an extraordinary exorcism from which emerged her voice saying clearly, 'I'm thinking of leaving Haiti and going back to New York, Oscar.'

If she had expected a lover's protestation (and she had, had she not?) none was forthcoming. Although tiny lines of sorrow appeared at the corners of Oscar's eyes, and the eyes themselves seemed to gaze forlornly at some receding vision, he only nodded his head and tapped the rim of his glass with his thumbnail. 'That would probably be best under the circumstances,' he said quietly, without looking up.

'Oh.'

– My baby just cares for me –

'Oh,' Susanna said again. And then, as if suddenly struck by a possible significance, a meaning that would excuse Oscar's blandness, she asked, 'What do you mean – under the circumstances?'

Oscar folded his arms behind his head. 'Well, things are going to get pretty hairy here soon. We've agreed to help Duvalier leave. Gilles made the official request. As soon as it's known he *is* leaving all hell will break loose, and I don't want you here when that happens.'

'Oh,' Susanna said yet again, oddly disappointed with the reason.

Actually Gilles Lagreze had not made the official request. No *official* request had been made. Gilles Lagreze had just 'dropped in', saying, 'Good afternoon, my friend,' as Oscar's prim secretary closed the door behind him. He twisted his Panama hat in one hand by releasing it as if to drop it, then catching it again further along the wide brim, mopping his brow with the handkerchief held in his other hand: 'Before they freeze to hailstones in this stupendous air-conditioning,' he explained, beaming sardonically, as the beads of perspiration were absorbed in the immaculate linen. 'You are busy perhaps?'

Oscar shook his head. 'Never too busy for you, Gilles.'

Monsieur Lagreze gave a small bow to acknowledge the compliment.

'Glad of the interruption to tell the truth.' Oscar threw the pen he had been using on to the desk. 'Bloody paperwork. Nothing but bloody paperwork these days,' he said with a grim smile. 'Sorry, Gilles – do have a seat,' he added, pointing to a chair and half rising as if this action exonerated any impoliteness, then sitting back again and reaching for a cigarette which he lit with extreme care, using a match ripped from a book advertising a San Francisco Pizza Parlour. 'You?'

Monsieur Lagreze declined to smoke but settled himself on the chair (first moving it an inch or so closer to the desk), and placed his hat on the floor beside him.

Oscar exhaled a lungful of smoke. 'And to what do I owe this pleasure anyway?'

Monsieur Lagreze cleared his throat and waved some of the smoke to one side, using the time to give Oscar a slightly cunning look. 'I have an appointment with the Ambassador in' – he glanced at his watch, making a great show of removing it from his pocket, opening it, studying it, closing it, returning it to his pocket again – 'twenty-five minutes. I thought I would just – you knew, of course?'

'Knew?'

Monsieur Lagreze smiled indulgently. 'Of my appointment.'

Oscar felt himself flush and hid his embarrassment behind another cloud of blue smoke. 'Yes,' he admitted finally.

Monsieur Lagreze nodded and took to observing his friend in silence for a few moments. Strange, he thought, how different the man who sat across from him at the chess-table to the man who now sat across from him at the desk, the diplomatic hat donned, pretending – well, perhaps not quite pretending – that he was unaware of the reason for this visit.

'And you know, also, the reason?'

Oscar nodded. 'I think so.'

'And?'

'And?'

Monsieur Lagreze smiled again. 'And how will it go, do you think?'

Oscar stubbed out his cigarette. He retrieved the pen and started to doodle. 'That depends.'

'On what?'

'On what *exactly* you want.'

'You know what I want, Oscar.'

'Not *exactly*.'

Monsieur Lagreze gave a chuckle. 'So evasive even to a friend?'

'I'm not being evasive. Careful.'

'I understand.'

Oscar stopped doodling and looked up. Suddenly he laughed.

'What the hell! You know as well as I do that you'll get what you want, Gilles. To tell the truth it's not helping you to get Duvalier out that is causing the concern. It's what happens *after* he's gone.'

Monsieur Lagreze nodded. 'I can appreciate that.'

'What will happen, Gilles?'

Monsieur Lagreze shrugged. 'Who can tell?'

'What do *you* think will happen?'

'I, like everyone else, can only guess.'

'Make a guess then.'

Gilles Lagreze decided to take his time about guessing. It was a dangerous exercise, guessing. Still, he admitted to himself, he had guessed his way through life pretty successfully thus far. 'There will, of course, be difficulties.'

'I like that, Gilles. Difficulties!'

'There will be a period of unrest,' Gilles went on, unsmiling.

Oscar, however, found himself forced to smile. 'I bet there will.'

'Rioting. Looting. Killings.' Monsieur Lagreze listed the words, but with a curious casualness as though seeing them as being of small consequence.

'But then . . .'

'Then?' Oscar prompted.

'Then we will get back to the business of living our lives, of course. Those of us that *are* still alive, that is.'

'You don't think *you're* in any danger surely?'

Monsieur Lagreze looked shocked. 'Me? No. No, I doubt that I will be considered of any great importance in the scheme of things. No threat to those who seek power at any rate. I was thinking more of – ' Monsieur Lagreze paused, his huge, expressive eyes suddenly dimming, their lids half obscuring them . . .

'And what about you?' Susanna asked, repeating the question as if suspecting the dinner gong, rung with such gusto from within the hotel at that moment, had obliterated it. 'What about you, Oscar?'

'Oh, I expect I'll be all right. We – embassy staff – usually are, you know,' Oscar replied with a tight smile.

'And what about Father Septimus?' Susanna asked suddenly, her tone imperative as though she foresaw disaster hovering over the image of the wayward priest that flickered in her mind.

The smile dropped from Oscar's lips. 'Why do you ask about him?' he asked flatly. 'Why should anything happen to him?'

'I don't know. I worry about him, that's all.'

'You too.'

'Why? Who else?'

'Gilles.'

'Gilles. What does he think will happen?'

'He doesn't know either.'

'What did he say, Oscar? Tell me, please.'

'Not much, really. You know Gilles. He never says much.'

'What *did* he say?'

Oscar grimaced. He finished his drink. 'Only that he was worried about old Septimus.'

That, however, was hardly a fair interpretation of what Gilles Lagreze had said: after several minutes during which he sat motionless in his chair, all the while with his eyes half-closed, he went on; ' . . . of the priest. *Père* Septimus.'

Oscar was flabbergasted. 'Septimus? That lunatic? Why on earth would anyone want to harm him?'

'They would not, I think, of choice,' Gilles explained, opening his eyes, showing them to be as mournful as his tone. 'But there may not be a question of choices, you see.'

'No I don't see, Gilles.'

'You do not, do you, Oscar, believe in fate?'

Oscar believed he had heard faith. 'Yes I do,' he protested. 'Up to a point,' he qualified, adding a small snigger. 'If I didn't have faith, Gilles, I wouldn't be – '

'Fate, Oscar. Fate. Destiny.'

'Oh, *fate*. Sorry. That's a different matter.'

Monsieur Lagreze raised his eyebrows and waited patiently.

'No. I cannot honestly say I have too much truck with fate.'

Monsieur Lagreze nodded benevolently. 'That, you see, is where we differ. Not just you and I. I don't mean that. But all of us. Our two cultures if you like. Our peoples. We, here in Haiti, believe absolutely in fate. It is something we share with most of Africa. I sometimes think it is the only thing that keeps many nations from going mad. If it is fate we must accept it, regardless of its goodness or evil.'

'Give over, Gilles. I know you far too well to believe you subscribe to all that claptrap.'

Monsieur Lagreze raised a hand, shaking his head, smiling pleasantly. 'You only know what I have let you see of me,' he pointed out, widening his smile. 'Just as you have only shown me the side of you that you wish me to see. You see my clothes and you see that I am educated. You recognize my wealth. You respect, I hope, my intelligence. But of me – inside all these, these, trappings – of *that* you know nothing. And it is *that* me which worries about the priest.'

'You've lost me, Gilles,' Oscar said almost angrily, and took refuge behind another cloud of smoke, sucking on his cigarette as though he hoped the nicotine would make him see some light. For Oscar, despite his irked admission, had a very clear idea about the matter to which his friend referred. Possibly because he had spent so much of his adult life abroad, away from that uniquely stultifying American God, he had often felt that there was indeed a power – nameless, seething, mesmerizing, immensely potent – that plotted the passage of man's existence, scuppering his best-laid, most arrogant plans, so that there was little if anything one could do about it . . .

'Ready to eat?' Oscar now asked Susanna.

They were almost the only ones left on the veranda: Pavlov's dinner gong had worked its charm. The musical duo had taken up their positions in the dining-room and played unobtrusively: nothing recognizable, although from time to time Oscar thought he detected snatches of 'I'm Gonna Sit Right Down and Write Myself a Letter', and, amazingly, 'Greensleeves'.

'If you're hungry,' Susanna answered.

'I'm starving.'

'Well then, let's eat.'

It was not until later, after they had finished eating and returned to the veranda for coffee (joined by the musicians, who struck up 'My Baby Just Cares For Me' again with minor variations) that Susanna's possible departure was mentioned once more.

'Can I ask you something?'

'Of course.'

'Did Solomon suggest you leave Haiti?'

Susanna shook her head. 'Uh-huh.'

'You have spoken to him, though?'

'Yes. I ring him most nights.'

'Oh.'

'It's the least I could do.'

'If you say so.'

'He's worried, naturally.'

'Naturally.'

'Don't be supercilious, Oscar.' Then: 'There's really no need to be so jealous.' And: 'Solly *is* very special to me but not in the way you've led yourself to think.' Susanna was surprised to hear herself make these admissions. They were, of course, true. There had never been anything but a friendship of the most platonic species between them. Solly, ugly, basked in her beauty; shy, he positively wallowed in her exhibitionism; tending towards meanness, he fought against this by being absurdly, lavishly generous towards her; lonely, he dallied delightedly in her companionship. And Susanna, for her part, used Solomon not quite as a father figure but as a sort of guru, allowing him to guide her, to teach her and, certainly, to worship her from a distance. At times she detested him, detested his doting meekness, his humility, his enormous patience, but always she returned to him shamefacedly, ever finding a curious comfort and peace in his company.

'You *are* coming back, aren't you?' Solly had asked on the telephone last night.

'Of course I am, Solly.'

Solly waited to hear when.

'Soon,' Susanna told him.

'How soon.'

'Soon,' Susanna repeated.

'I see.'

'Don't worry so, Solly.'

'Of course I worry.'

'There's no need to.'

Solly sighed.

Susanna felt obliged to add, 'Whatever there was between Oscar and me is over.'

Solly sighed again, deeper.

'Truly.'

'If you say so.'

'I do. Anyway, that has nothing to do with why I'm coming back to New York.'

'Oh?'

'They say there's going to be trouble here.'

Solomon sucked in his breath. 'What sort of trouble?'

'Political.'

'Oh. Who says that?'

'Everyone. Oscar. Gilles – you know.'

'What does he say?'

'Who? Oscar?'

'Gilles?'

'I don't know first hand.'

'What does Gilles think?' Susanna asked Oscar now.

'About what?'

'About what will happen.'

'You know Gilles.'

Susanna found the answer annoying. It was the second time in the space of a couple of hours that Oscar had tried to fob her off. 'What has he told you?' she demanded.

'What has he told me? Well, he would agree with me that it would be safer if you left.'

'That's not what I asked you. What exactly has he said – for heaven's sake why don't you just tell me?'

'I'm sorry. I'm sorry.' Oscar, surprised at the sudden anger in Susanna's voice, tried to recall the exact words Gilles had used. 'He said there would be a "period of unrest",' he quoted wryly. 'That there would be rioting and looting and – and some killings.'

Susanna stirred her coffee thoughtfully. 'Is that all he said?'

'All? Hah, I would have thought that was enough.'

'Was it all?'

'All that matters.'

'But he did say something else?'

'Really Susanna, you are – '

But whatever Susanna was remained unsaid. In one corner of the veranda a woman screamed and everyone went silent, slowly turning their heads to stare, perplexed, vexed, in the direction of the interruption, picking the woman out, their eyes following the finger with which she pointed. Below the veranda, on the gravel that surrounded it, caught in a particularly brilliant circle of light shed from one of the bulbs of which the shade had been broken, doing a grotesque sort of pavane to the rhythm of the music, was the crippled cobbler. Highlighted in the surrounding darkness he looked almost daemonic as he rotated himself on his buttocks, his tame chicken racing along the perimeter of the circle, its wings spread. Startled by the scream he stopped his dance and stared in bewilderment at all the ogling faces. Then he opened his mouth wide and imitated the scream, clearly enjoying himself. He tried it again and again, each time louder, shriller before tiring and rolling away into the blackness.

'Jesus!' Oscar exclaimed, just as 'Jesus!' he had exclaimed when Gilles Lagreze, nodding as though convincing himself of the veracity of his words, had said, 'It is believed, you know, by many, that the priest has been sent as a redeemer.'

'Jesus!'

Monsieur Lagreze gave a wicked chuckle. 'It frightens you?'

'I think it's bloody stupid.'

'You think it not a possibility?'

'Septimus Roach? A redeemer? For God's sake, Gilles. The man's a raving lunatic. He couldn't redeem a bad debt.'

'Perhaps it is his very madness that is his greatest force.'

'Oh boy. Terrific!'

'. . . him before,' Susanna was saying.

'Hmmm?'

'I've seen him before. The cripple. Several times.'

'Poor bastard.'

'I sometimes think he's following me.'

Oscar gave a tentative laugh. 'You imagine it.'

'Maybe. Did Gilles say anything about Father Septimus?' she asked suddenly, watching Oscar.

Oscar, his cup almost to his lips, gave an uncontrollable twitch, slopping his coffee. He used a paper napkin to mop the liquid from the tabletop, carefully avoiding Susanna's gaze. 'Why should he?'

'Did he?'

'Well yes. As a matter of fact he did.'

As happens sometimes, for no obvious reason everything went quiet. Nobody spoke for a moment. The music stopped playing briefly, and it could, of course, have been this saxophonic hiatus that caused the lull in conversation. Into that silence Susanna bellowed, 'What did he say about him?' The spell was broken; everyone went on talking again; the music resumed – a gay little number, an improvization it sounded like, but on what was anyone's guess.

'He's worried about him,' Oscar said cautiously.

'Is *he* – Father Septimus – going to leave?'

'I've no idea.'

'He can't leave, can he?'

'I don't see what's to stop him.'

'No. I don't suppose you would, Oscar.'

Oscar ignored that. 'Anyway, it's you *I'm* worried about. You will go back to New York, won't you?'

'If I can.'

'What's that supposed to mean?'

Susanna leaned forward and let her fingers trace their way down Oscar's cheek. 'You wouldn't understand, my love. Not in a million years,' she told him quietly.

'Try me.'

'You'll only laugh.'

'I won't. I promise. Here,' Oscar said, putting his hand on his heart. 'Hand on heart and hope to die.'

'Don't *say* that!' Susanna slapped her hand on the table. 'I'm sorry, Oscar. I'm all of a jitter.'

'That's why you should get away.'

'I know.'

'Good.'

'But – oh, Oscar – I'm so afraid.'

'There's nothing to be afraid of, darling. Look: leave everything to me. I'll book you a ticket and see you off safely. Once you're away from here everything will be all right.'

But Susanna was shaking her head. 'That's not what I mean.'

'Well, tell me what you *do* mean. I only want to help.'

'I know you do, Oscar. I know you do.'

'Tell me then.'

Susan started to shake her head again, but stopped and looked hard into Oscar's eyes. 'Very well.'

And in his eyes she saw her eyes; and in her eyes she saw the slightly bloodshot, pleading eyes of Septimus Roach, yet it was as though she saw them through the eyes of a third party, familiar but nameless. There was activity in the priest's eyes: she seemed to be swimming in them, or trying to, but was always on the point of drowning, blinded by a curious light. 'Your eyes, Father,' she heard herself say with remarkable calm under the circumstances, 'they glare so.' And to oblige he blinked. She was no longer drowning. The water was still there certainly, but trickling delicately into a pool, a mosaic swimming-pool the diving board of which had been snapped in half, the broken half floating on the water, moving about on the tiny waves created by the little waterfall, while she, distracted, drew designs with the toe of her shoe in the dust that had gathered on the tiles surrounding the pool, swinging her leg sideways extravagantly from time to time as though limbering her muscles. There was no noise, not even from the tumbling water. She stamped her foot – still silence. Then the broken board took on a life of its own, bobbing up and down, sinking a little deeper each time, whooshing upwards, clearing itself of the water before plummeting down again, deeper again. Incredibly it called to her: Help me! Save me! It was her father. But there was something else: it was not her father's voice, it was the priest's.

– Help me! Save me! the voice cried.

– Yes. Oh yes. Here, take my hand.

She reached out. She imagined she heard music, a guitar and a saxophone, but this was soon obliterated by the stale thudding of drums. She grasped the outstretched hand: she *tried* to grasp the outstretched hand but that hand and hers passed through each other.

– Help me! Save me!

– I cannot.

– You must.

– I cannot.

– You must. If you do not save me you yourself cannot be saved.

'Susanna?'

The sharp, anxious voice of Oscar calling her name made her jump. The other people on the veranda (fortunately half-empty by now) were eyeing her curiously.

'Are you all right?'

'Yes. Yes. I'm fine, Oscar.'

'You're sure?'

'Of course I'm sure. Why are they looking at me that way?'

Oscar grinned boyishly. 'They weren't exactly expecting to hear someone yelling for help.'

'I did that? I called for help?'

Oscar continued to grin. 'You surely did. At the top of your voice. Put the fear of God into most of them. Myself included.'

Mortified, Susanna nonetheless tried grinning back, managing quite well. 'I am sorry, Oscar. I didn't realize. I – '

'What were you thinking about?'

'About my father, I think. And Septimus.'

'Him again.'

'Yes. Him again.' Susanna turned her head and simpered an apologetic smile to those eyes that were still probing her. She even made a fluttering little gesture with one hand that she hoped indicated temporary lunacy.

'The sooner we can get you away from here and you forget all about that old fool the better.'

'I don't think that's the answer, Oscar. I'm sure it's not.'

'I'm sure it is.'

'I think I'm supposed to stay here and help him.'

'You *what*?' Oscar exploded, he now becoming the subject of surreptitious stares.

'I think I'm supposed to stay here and help him,' Susanna repeated.

'What in God's name makes you think that?'

'I don't know.'

'And help him with what, for Christ's sake?'

It was uncanny: suddenly a tiny voice, her own voice but from years back, the voice she could so clearly remember using as she called wildly to the ocean to return her father, crept from her mouth. 'To die, I think.'

Nine

Oblivious to all the morbid interest being taken in him, Septimus Roach sat in the convent chapel and thought about praying. It was curious, he told himself, how it was drummed into one from an absurdly early age that one *should* pray when in church. It was, one was told, the right, the proper, the *only* thing to do. But this surely wasn't the case at all. In fact, Septimus had a theory that it was the last thing anyone should do: one should only listen, sit quietly and listen. One was, after all, in God's house and it was up to Him to do the talking. Which was all well and good when God was in one of His better humours. On the other hand there was little to be pleased about when the Almighty was in the throes of a temper and took to scolding, which, as far as Septimus was concerned, seemed to be most of the time; it was certainly the case on this particular morning, despite the fact that more people than usual had attended his mass, many coming, admittedly, more out of a fondness for the priest than for God. So, Septimus thought about praying, using his prayers to keep God quiet, preventing God from getting a word in edgewise. Who was it who said 'Prayer is useless unless we listen in silence for the response'? Bishop McKewen probably. It sounded like the sort of sentiment he would express, he being on particularly chummy terms with God. Perhaps he pulled rank! The idea cheered Septimus up and he gave a low cackle. Alas, even this spartan cheerfulness was short-lived. It was as though all his familiars, all those nice, sane, understanding people who had crossed his path as he trudged his way through life, had banded together to admonish him. But their well-meaning, considered chastisements seemed to run off him like water off a duck's back, which was a good thing. It was as if, he thought (concentrating with considerable effort on the thought, using its growing potency to obliterate the gibberings in his brain), as if he had been declared mad and been placed in a region of intolerable unreality, an asylum where only he was insane.

Yet there was a ridiculous solace in the moment: a tranquillity similar to the one he had felt when Patrick had appeared at the hospice and said, 'The pain will cease soon.' At least that was what Septimus had chosen to hear; what Patrick had actually said was rather more mundane: 'The rain will cease soon,' he had forecast, shaking his multi-coloured golfing umbrella on the porch and leaning it against the jamb of the door before coming in.

Delighted and unsuspecting, Septimus had said: 'Good.'

'Yes,' Patrick had agreed. 'But only for a short while,' he added.

Dejected again, Septimus made no reply.

'But we must expect such downpours at this time of year, must we not?'

'Must we?'

'Indeed we must.'

'Oh dear.'

'And you? You are well, *mon Père?*'

Septimus made a gesture, a shrug that expressed that he was passably well.

'Excellent,' Patrick said. 'Excellent,' he said again, glancing at the huge crucifix and back to Septimus again. 'Excellent,' he repeated.

Confronted with such an abundance of excellence Septimus felt suddenly uneasy. He felt, it dawned on him, like some poor beast being scrutinized and proclaimed excellent, the only reward for such excellence being slaughter. Septimus stood perfectly still staring at the floor while the enormity of the analogy passed into his soul. Still, someone was on his side, it seemed; someone capable of putting the wind up the suave, unflappable Patrick, to boot. That someone chose that precise moment to come to the rescue: drenched and bedraggled but smiling away nevertheless, in scuttled the crippled cobbler, coming to rest at Septimus's feet, tugging at his soutane and peering up at him winking encouragement, steam already rising from his ragged clothes, the chicken, as though awakened brusquely from a particularly pleasurable snooze, peeping from under his jacket, blinking and uttering hoarse clucks that sounded like mordant laughter. Septimus smiled benignly on the cobbler and patted his head. Patrick glared furiously at the squatting cripple, pulling his elegant raincoat closer about him as though to shield himself against any possible radiated deformity.

'I must go,' he announced coldly.

'So soon?' Septimus loaded the question with impishness.

'I have many things to do.'

'You are such a busy man, Patrick. You know, I can honestly say I have never known such a busy man as you.'

'This is true,' Patrick agreed, pleased for some obscure reason that his busyness had been recognized.

'It must be gratifying to be so important – or to feel that one is so important at least.'

Patrick assumed a humble expression. 'It is not I who am important. I am a mere messenger.'

'So was Judas,' Septimus could have sworn he said, but apparently hadn't, since Patrick (who would surely have taken offence) was still looking humble, self-effacing, still talking for that matter, saying, ' – but a servant of those who – '

'What, what?' Septimus, his mind off at a tangent, had been thinking still of Judas, for whom he had a soft spot really; unfortunate Judas, who had simply fallen victim to greed, and who could blame him; or been terrified out of his wits, and that was pretty blameless also; or possibly been misrepresented through the ages, turned into an ogre, the entire guilt for the crucifixion lumped upon his shoulders, when he was probably quite a nice chap, trying to make ends meet as it were. Anyway, if *he* hadn't done it someone else would, would they not, if only to precipitate what was presumably inevitable? However, the word 'servant' did penetrate his strange ruminations, and 'Cervantes,' Septimus said without thinking.

'Exactly,' Patrick agreed, somewhat to Septimus's amazement: try as he might – and he was certainly trying, despite the distraction of the cripple grabbing his hand and licking it in the manner of an animal seeking salt from the pores, making strange guttural noises to boot – he could not for the life of him envisage an even remotely logical connection. And no explanation was about to be given it seemed, for Patrick, sidling past, keeping Septimus between himself and the guzzling cripple, was taking his leave.

'Extraordinary,' Septimus exclaimed after he had gone.

The cripple, satiated, nodded wildly in agreement, and scuffled alongside Septimus as he moved towards the doorway.

The rain had ceased. The street was awash. Patrick, his umbrella like an exotic mobile flower in the surrounding grey drabness, tiptoed an erratic, irritated route away from them, his free hand outstretched as though to keep his balance, as though the only pathway through the mud and slime was a swaying tightrope. Children emerged from the shacks that lined the street to splash with delight in the unexpected luxury of abundant water, their small white teeth glistening with glee in their round black faces; their mothers, standing in doorways, seemed charmed by the childish escapades. Men, too, came from indoors and settled on the wooden planks that served as a footpath: they lit pipes and cigarettes, and smoked, some talking in low voices, some just staring into the nicotine haze they had created. The sun suddenly blazed, and in the twinkling of an eye the sky was blue; in a matter of seconds, or so it appeared, everything was dry again. And everything returned to life: the voluptuous flowers (for even in that dismal street flowers abounded), whose riotous colours had somehow been dimmed by the rain, gleamed and flashed in the renewed sunlight. Pots and pans rattled. Transistor radios filled the air with their wavering cacophany. Voices were raised. Yet, surveying all this, surveying, too, the cripple who had followed him to the doorway and now sat on the stoop contentedly picking termites from his chicken, Septimus felt utterly saddened. It was these people – *his* people as he had come to think of them – who would suffer; they always did, the poor, the defenceless, those least wanting upheaval in their lives. Even Monsieur Lagreze had agreed with him on that point, which gave it a certain irrefutability.

They had bumped, quite literally, into each other, Monsieur Lagreze, lost in thought and not watching where he was going (although later, when he thought about it, he admitted there had been no reason for the hurry, and even that had been curious since hurrying was not his wont), had all but bowled Septimus over. What made the incident amusing, causing them both to laugh albeit somewhat speculatively, was that there was not another soul within miles, none that was visible at any rate. Why they had both chosen that particular day and that precise time to visit the ruins on the outskirts of Petionville was anyone's guess. It was Monsieur Lagreze who seemed most surprised. 'Again, *mon Père*, you appear so very unexpectedly,' he said, pleasantly enough.

Septimus nibbled the tip of one of his mutilated fingers and frowned, as though seeking to uncover any darker meaning that might be lurking in Monsieur Lagreze's bland observation. Luckily he could find none. He took to nodding. 'So it would seem.'

'A remarkable coincidence!'

'Perhaps. Unless – '

Monsieur Lagreze waited for Septimus to continue, passing the time by gazing about him, pretending that he was in no way anxious; gazing at the murals that depicted the auspicious day, January 1st, 1804, when Jean-Jacques Dessaline had proclaimed independence and Haiti had readopted its Indian name meaning 'mountainous country'. The artist had gone slightly haywire, depicting the scene as a sort of ethnic inferno, Dessaline raised aloft on a cloud of his own importance, and at his feet the people represented as toil-weary peasants – but frightfully noble peasants, of course – wielding toolery of the soil but even then with a preference for the vicious: scythes, sickles, axes. And as he looked Monsieur Lagreze had the feeling that these stony figures were once again banding together: in a flash they had become one gigantic, menacing creature staring back at him. Monsieur Lagreze looked hastily away.

'Unless, of course, it was plotted that way,' Septimus was saying matter-of-factly.

'Plotted that way?'

'Hmm. Haven't you ever found that? Suddenly, for no reason – none that one can possibly envisage, that is – you meet up with someone or simply see something, hear a sound, get a whiff of some long-forgotten smell – hay, for instance – and it always seems so *right*, so *absolutely* right that it should happen?'

'Well . . .' Monsieur Lagreze began doubtfully.

'I don't mean good, of course. Right yes, but not necessarily good. Usually not, in fact.' Septimus gave an enormous sigh. 'That's been my experience.' He paused for a moment to shake some irritant from his sandal. 'So, what would you say is about to befall us, eh? What catastrophic cataclysm is about to engulf us, would you say? What god is about to smite the both of us?'

Monsieur Lagreze decided it prudent to shake his head and hold his tongue.

'Come now,' Septimus encouraged, feeling he was getting into the swing of things, 'surely *you* can throw a little light on the subject?'

Two young men, looking like tourists, looking like lovers for that matter, their arms linked, their glances ardent, strolled past. One of them made as if to speak but changed his mind and went back to admiring his companion, who studied a small guidebook assiduously. Below them, on the road that wound its way in a complete circle about the ruins, a coach shuddered to a halt, and from it a chattering batch of Americans descended, women mostly, all elderly, all determined to be consumed with culture. Septimus and Monsieur Lagreze watched them. '*This* could be it – your catastrophic cataclysm,' Monsieur Lagreze suggested with a twinkle.

Septimus took him seriously. 'It could indeed.'

The tourists formed a neat crocodile and started to climb the narrow path of loose stones towards them, their voices floating up in the sweltering air.

It was Monsieur Lagreze who made the first move. Tugging at the brim of his Panama he started to move away from the ruins, Septimus amiably following, down the rough track. The tourists obligingly, or perhaps fearfully, since the two men undoubtedly presented a bizarre duo, edged to one side to let them pass, keeping their eyes averted but nudging each other as if to alert one another to the possibility that Septimus and Monsieur Lagreze were part of that native culture they were determined to master. Monsieur Lagreze's car was parked in the shade, the only shade in the desolate place, under the awning of a makeshift canteen. 'I may drive you back?'

He may indeed. Septimus settled himself comfortably into the air-conditioned vehicle, but not before emptying both his sandals carefully, taking them off and shaking them. The action irritated Monsieur Lagreze. Like so much else about the priest he found his blatant, excessive poverty accusing. He reversed the car rapidly, spinning the wheel, swinging it in a wide loop; then he slammed the automatic transmission into forward and sped off towards the city.

They had almost reached it, the spire of the convent chapel gleaming white amid the conifers that surrounded it, when they came upon a roadblock. Monsieur Lagreze braked the car to a skidding halt. Instantly it was surrounded by swaggering, sullen Tontons Macoutes. Septimus was petrified; uniforms still terrified him. Faces changed but the cruelty they performed was still dressed in uniforms. And these were no different: they seemed to ignore Monsieur Lagreze and concentrate totally on him, making him quake. 'Do not speak,' Monsieur Lagreze told him from the corner of his mouth, lowering the window and speaking rapidly to the face that peered in.

'Ha! Monsieur Lagreze. Hokay. *Allez*.'

Miraculously the men drew back. Two Land Rovers parked nose to nose across the road jerked to the verge. Barrels were rolled away. Monsieur Lagreze drove on, smiling broadly, cheerfully waving one hand.

Just beyond the blockade, to their right, a dozen or so young men lay face downwards on the road, two soldiers with rifles standing over them. Septimus stared at the prostrate bodies: some were barefoot, a few had shoes but the soles were worn through, wedges of cardboard protruding from the holes. Their upper garments had been removed and their torsos glistened with sweat. To one side, out of reach, their shirts and pullovers were piled, thrown there like oddments for a jumble sale.

'Always the poor,' Septimus muttered.

'Oh yes. I do agree with you.'

'Why *is* it always the poor who suffer?' Septimus asked, his voice drifting away as though not expecting an answer.

'You think the rich should suffer?' Monsieur Lagreze asked.

'A little, perhaps.'

Monsieur Lagreze chuckled. 'We do – a little.'

'But it is the poor who pay.'

Monsieur Lagreze nodded. 'Yes. It is always the poor who pay. It is only the poor who *can* pay, you see. The rich . . . ' Monsieur Lagreze shrugged. ' . . . with what would they pay? All they have is money. And it is not money that is required in these circumstances. It is the souls of men. Only the poor have souls left to them.'

. . . It was in that way that Monsieur Lagreze had explained his agreement. And now, still standing in the doorway of the hospice (alone, since the cripple had taken off, bouncing down the street on his stubs, waving happily back at the men who mocked and jeered him) Septimus saw the street down which he stared vanish and re-emerge as an abyss from which he was being lifted and carried in strong arms to safety; saw it vanish again and waver back into view as a river, a torrent down which he was being swept; saw it vanish again and become a cobbled pathway that weaved its way between small, flat-roofed, white houses from the windows of which people in curious garb leaned, and shouted at him, but what they shouted he could not understand. Again the scene changed: now it was a track up a hillside and he was being forced to ascend it, carrying some load on his back; now it was a village square and someone was trying to sell him a newspaper, pushing it close to his face, forcing him to read the headlines: ES INEVITABLE LA MUERTE DEL PADRE SEPTIMUS!

'Father Septimus!'

Someone had grabbed him by the shoulders and was shaking him violently. 'Father Septimus! What *are* you screaming about?'

Blearily Septimus turned and stared at Sister Mary. 'Screaming?'

'Come inside and let me – '

'*Es inevitable* – '

'What?'

'Nothing.'

'Come inside. Please.'

'Was I really screaming?' Septimus asked, allowing himself to be pushed down into a chair.

'You most certainly were,' Sister Mary told him, giving him a tight, encouraging little smile now that the crisis was averted.

'Good heavens! And what was I screaming?'

'Just nonsense.'

'Oh.'

Sister Mary busied herself brewing coffee, glad that she had got away with her fib. But as soon as she heard Septimus clear his throat she knew retribution was at hand. 'What nonsense?' floated towards her, and she turned her back on it. 'There's only one sort of nonsense, father,' she said trying to make her voice light and airy.

The coffee started to boil, froth rising to the top of the can. She took two mugs from the shelf over the stove, rattling them together as though to obliterate the voice (it, too, coming to the boil) that cudgelled her.

'What is nonsense for the goose is not necessarily nonsense for the gander,' it said.

Sister Mary put two heaped teaspoons of sugar into one of the mugs and stirred it.

'Funny things, geese,' Septimus went on. 'Guardians of the Styx. Most vociferous. Come in all shapes and sizes. Still, they don't really deserve to have their gullets stuffed, do they? What did you say I was screaming?'

This time there seemed to be no escape, no way of avoiding the question. Sister Mary turned and stared at Septimus. 'Father, why have you forsaken me?'

That made Septimus blink. 'Forsaken you? My dear Sister Mary, far from forsaking you I have – '

'That is what you were screaming.'

' – ? Really? How strange . . .' Father, why have you forsaken me! Another voice, yet still a woman's, now took up the plangent cry he was accused of uttering, and Septimus felt himself start to tremble. Will you not help me, Father? someone else put in as Septimus groped his way towards recognizing the first voice. And somewhere on the fringe Sister Mary (and who but a fool could mistake her voice?) was adding her tuppence worth, chiding him kindly for making 'a show of himself', for 'acting the maggot', whatever that meant. He listened, and, as if it had become another moan-filled night outside, the hospice grew darker to his eyes, and he heard a single, rumbling voice above the muted cries of abandonment and need: 'Septimus Roach, this is what it is like to die. No histrionics. No great drama. Just this, a blurred perception of the pleadings you ignored and a far clearer awareness, alas, of the fact that you could, had you put your mind to it, have done something about the agony of others. Here – drink this, it will do you good." Even in his turmoil Septimus realised there was something odd about this. He shook himself, and felt inestimable relief as Sister Mary, holding a steaming mug of coffee before him, repeated her command. 'Here – drink this, it will do you good.'

'Ah,' Septimus said, taking the coffee and guzzling it, peering over the rim of the mug at the nun who had now moved away from him and was sitting on one of the beds, one without blankets, watching him. 'Delicious,' escaped him.

Sister Mary merely nodded.

A spider the size of a small octopus legged its way up the wall, seeming at all times to be on the point of tripping itself up but never doing so. It vanished, squirming its way into a crack below the roof. Septimus wondered if there was perhaps a crack in the roof of the world into which he could escape. Well, whatever about that there was no escaping the din of the sudden furore that started outside on the street.

Sister Mary was the first to move, bustling towards the doorway, muttering, 'Now what has your screaming started?' Smarting with a mixture of affront and guilt, Septimus followed her.

'*Cochons! Cochons! Cochons!*'

The chant, singularly musical (as everything, even death, seemed to be on Haiti) and as yet without too much venom, reverberated down the muddy space between the shacks, gaining volume in its echo. Everyone was on the street and giving tongue from the rotting wooden sidewalk, all baying. Even the dogs (and there seemed to be a massive population of these of a sudden) joined in, mostly sitting on their bony haunches, heads thrown back, yodelling at the unexpected excitement. A pair of asses, temporarily left to their own devices but still laden with huge green barrels, one on either side of their narrow backs, bared their teeth and added their highly distinctive insults to the din.

An old American jeep made its way with menacing sullenness towards the hospice. But it was not the vehicle that was the butt of the outcry. From each end of the street, advancing towards each other with uncharacteristic precision, machine-guns at the ready, were two groups of Tontons Macoutes, a dozen or so men to each group, their faces impassive.

The jeep stopped at the hospice, not directly in front of it but a couple of yards from the doorway. Septimus watched, mesmerized. He saw the man beside the driver step out. He noted that he was heavy-necked, a prize-fighting-fisticuffs-bare-knuckled type of man with receding hair (his cap, peaked, and with enough braid for an Admiral of the Fleet or a Venezuelan corporal, in one hand) and a bullish, swashbuckling manner. He was joined by another man who leaped nimbly from the back of the jeep, a tall, slim Caucasian in a pale-blue, drip-dry American suit with a worried face and crew-cut hair the colour of a dormouse. They stood by the jeep, glancing towards Sister Mary and Septimus, speaking in undertones. The Dormouse (as Septimus instantly christened him, even managing a mental snigger despite the overpowering sense of dread that had overtaken him) looked vaguely familiar, and Septimus racked his brain to recall where he might have seen him before. He was no nearer a solution when the Admiral disengaged himself and strode towards the porch. He placed himself, feet apart, in front of Sister Mary, and then, with one hand and gently enough, moved her to one side. Septimus, finding himself face to face with him, instantly became aware of two things: that the street had become deathly quiet, and that he wanted to be sick. His stomach heaved. His hands sweated. He started to tremble again but in an odd way: he trembled from *inside*.

The Admiral wasted no time in coming to the point. He placed one enormous hand on Septimus's shoulder and asked in a friendly, smiling tone, 'You a spy, no?'

Septimus, speechless, felt the fingers tighten on his shoulder. He could summon nothing but the foretaste of vomit to his mouth.

The hand started to rock him. 'Why you no answer me?'

'Of course he's not a spy!'

Without moving his head the Admiral transferred his stare to Sister Mary. 'I speak to heem.' The eyes flicked back to Septimus again.

Septimus no longer wanted to be sick. He wanted to laugh. To throw back his head and roar with laughter. Or wake up: to dismiss what was undoubtedly becoming a nightmare by switching on his consciousness. He settled for laughter, but laughter of a feeble enough breed, a chuckle that could just as well have been a groan. That didn't please the Admiral: not one little bit did it please him. He removed his hand from Septimus's shoulder and waggled a thick finger in his face. 'This matter not *amusant*,' he said, his anger not in his tone but in his eyes.

'Perhaps I . . .?' The Dormouse came forward, his face more worried than before. 'Perhaps if I explained to Father Roach . . .?'

The Admiral guffawed suddenly, with real merriment (although Septimus, who had heard such laughter before and under pretty similar circumstances, could gauge its quality to a tee), slapping Septimus jollily on the biceps with the palm of his hand. 'He good man,' he announced, indicating Septimus with his braided cap, and stepping a little to one side to allow the Dormouse closer access. 'He talk to us for sure,' he added, making it clear that there was nothing of which he was more certain.

'Father Roach, Sister,' the Dormouse began, politely including Sister Mary (who all the while had stood transfixed, her lips quivering as though in prayer, her fingers twiddling the big wooden beads of the rosary that dangled from her side) in his address. 'I'm sorry about this. I'm Gillam – Lester Gillam, American Embassy. The Colonel here . . . internal security . . . Oscar – Oscar Nicholson – you know him, I think – asked me to – ' The litany peppered Septimus's brain.

The face of the admirable Colonel began to glower, and he took to slapping his own thigh.

Lester Gillam threw him a quick look. '*Un moment*, Colonel. *Un moment*,' he said. '*Peut-être seuls?*' he suggested. '*Le prêtre et moi – seuls?*' he explained with a flick of his eyes towards the interior of the hospice and a twitch of one hand.

After a little thought the Colonel nodded curtly in assent and folded his hands behind his back, watching closely as Gillam took Septimus by the arm and steered him inside. 'I'm sorry about all this, Father,' he apologized again in a whisper.

Septimus simply stared at him.

'They're getting very nervous. *Very* nervous,' Gillam explained, and explained who *they* were by jerking his head, almost imperceptibly, in the general direction of the porch. 'There are things happening, you see. Changes taking place – about to take place. Everyone – most especially all foreigners – is, well, regarded with suspicion.' He took a deep breath. 'They think you might be a spy,' he concluded abruptly.

It took quite some time for that to sink in. 'A spy? Me?' Septimus asked finally.

Gillam nodded.

What followed seemed a fair enough question so Septimus asked it: 'For whom?'

Gillam shrugged. 'It doesn't matter for whom. Just a spy.'

Septimus spotted the logic in that. 'I see.'

'Have you – I'm sorry, Father – have you been – '

'Spying?' Septimus shook his head thoughtfully. 'No. At least I don't think so.'

Gillam sucked in his breath in one long, continuous hiss. 'What do you mean – you don't think so?'

'Not in the way you and the Admiral – teehee' – Septimus heard himself titter and could hardly believe it – 'you and the Colonel mean.'

Gillam began to lose his patience. 'This isn't any laughing matter, Father.'

'I know. Oh, I *do* know. Forgive me. I know it isn't.'

'We heard at the embassy,' Gillam was saying, somehow giving the impression that everything worth hearing was heard at the embassy, 'that they were going to arrest you and Oscar – Oscar Nicholson, you *do* know him, don't you? – asked me to try and find out what it was all about and to try and avoid any such unpleasantness.'

Unpleasantness! Septimus felt the urge to laugh again but

managed to refrain. Almost instantly he wanted to cry. It was all starting again. He lowered himself on to the nearest bed. Starting all over again. He looked at his hands and felt once more the searing pain in his nailless fingers. Well, at least they couldn't inflict that particular torture on him. There were always the toes though, which wasn't such a happy thought; he wriggled them in his sandals. Slowly a strange calm descended on him. He looked about him as if awakening from a deep, untroubled sleep. He smiled. The peaceful blanket of submitting to the inevitable was wrapping itself about him. He widened his smile, and was still smiling when the name Lichfield penetrated his calm. He frowned and cocked his head as if to hear something that had escaped him.

'It would be much better if you told *me*, Father.'

With an effort Septimus pulled himself together. 'I'm sorry. I was – never mind. Tell you what Mister . . .?'

'Gillam.'

'Yes. Gillam. Tell you what?'

'What Miss Lichfield was doing here?'

Septimus looked baffled.

'Why did she come to this . . . ' Mister Gillam looked about the hospice as though seeking an adequate name for it.

'I don't really know,' Septimus told him. 'For help, I think. Although why she should come to me for help I cannot imagine. I am the last person in the world, Mister Gillam, to be in a position of offering help, particularly, you will appreciate, as I am in dire need of that commodity myself.'

'What sort of help?'

'Painless,' Septimus replied without knowing why.

The Colonel was stomping up and down on the porch, peering in the doorway each time he passed, his footsteps sounding like small claps of thunder in the attentive silence.

'Leave that. What about Monsieur Lagreze? You do know a Monsieur Lagreze, don't you? A Monsieur Gilles Lagreze?'

Septimus nodded affably. 'Oh yes.'

'What's your connection with him?'

'Connection? Ah, well. Now. *I* go to *him* for help. Maybe that makes him the spy in the ointment, would you think? The – forgive me – the nigger in the woodpile.'

'Father!' Mister Gillam's voice was a strangled shriek, perhaps brought about less by Septimus's perfidious ramblings than by the fact that the Colonel at that moment decided enough '*seul*' was enough and strode into the hospice. 'Ah, Colonel.'

The Colonel stared fixedly at the crucifix, not abandoning it when he asked, 'That. What he do there?'

'He watch,' Septimus answered pleasantly.

'Watch?'

'Hmm. Watch. Lookey lookey,' Septimus went on, aware that he was dangerously close to impertinence but no longer really caring.

'Lookey lookey?'

'I spy with my little eye.'

'You spy?'

It was getting tricky again.

'Oh, no.'

'It's a game,' Mister Gillam volunteered. 'A child's game, Colonel.'

'No game. Very serious.'

'Yes. Of course, Colonel. I meant I spy with my little eye – it's the name of a children's game.'

The Colonel was as bewildered as any man who had never played a game in his life. But he decided for his own reasons to let the matter drop. He walked stiffly across to the crucifix, turned, and struck a pose that indicated his fearlessness before God. Then he looked from the crucified effigy of Christ to Septimus, several times. He gave Mister Gillam a broad wink. 'Good this game,' he said.

Now Mister Gillam was getting confused.

As was Septimus, although for a different reason. It was as though the Colonel was referring to crucifixion, sizing Septimus up for inclusion in the next game. Which wasn't to be just yet, it appeared, since the Colonel moved across the room and threw an arm about Gillam's shoulder. 'He tell you everything?'

'Father Roach? Oh yes.'

The Colonel nodded. 'No spy?'

'Definitely not, Colonel.'

The Colonel beamed. 'Good. Good. Very good. He *good* man like I say you before.'

'Indeed,' Mister Gillam affirmed.

'You see, priest? We like you.'

Septimus smiled weakly.

The Colonel shook his head and laughed uproariously. 'Lookey lookey,' he said. 'We go now,' he announced, hugging Mister Gillam closer to his bosom and making for the door. 'Lookey lookey,' he kept repeating, and said it again as he took his arm from about Mister Gillam and pointed to something on the street that also amused him.

Septimus, standing beside Gillam, bent sideways and peered from behind the bulk of the Colonel. The Tontons Macoutes stood shuffling their feet in a circle in front of the hospice, mostly looking bored. Inside this circle, forming another, was a band of disconsolate youths, sitting back to back, their hands tied behind them. They seemed angry rather than frightened: some singing, some shouting.

'More spies?' Septimus whispered in Gillam's ear.

Gillam shrugged. 'He has to go back with something.'

'Why these?'

'They were handy. No – they're students probably. Students can always be labelled as troublemakers.'

'Ah.'

'Thank God they're not my problem.'

'Whose problem are they?' Septimus wanted to know.

Gillam looked perplexed. 'Not mine,' he said finally.

'But – ' Septimus began to protest, almost shouting the word, making the Colonel give him a momentary glance.

'Don't interfere,' Gillam hissed. 'Just be grateful you're not out there on the ground with them.'

Perhaps feeling some explanation was necessary for his glance the Colonel turned and beamed. 'We go,' he said, and made as if to do just that. Indeed, he had one foot in the jeep when he changed his mind. He waited for Lester Gillam to take his seat, waited deliberately, before returning to the porch, his arms outspread. 'You good man,' he roared with tremendous emphasis, and Septimus found himself clasped in a gargantuan embrace. 'You friend,' the Colonel bellowed. 'You *good* friend,' he added.

Septimus, almost breathless, nevertheless got the giggles. It was so ridiculous. One minute he had been scared half to death and the next, now, he was being clasped to the massive bosom of this gigantic Haitian who spoke English in the staccato gibberish that Hollywood allotted to its Redskins. And it was contagious, it seemed. 'You good friend too,' Septimus was saying, even daring to pat the Colonel on the back.

'I come again,' the Colonel promised, releasing Septimus at last if not entirely, holding him at arms' length by the wrists. 'Soon I come again.'

'Oh.'

Then the Colonel *was* gone, striding to the jeep and vaulting into his seat beside the driver with incredible agility for such a huge man, turning his head to Septimus one final time, calling, 'Lookey lookey soon.'

Septimus instinctively smiled and waved and watched as the jeep was driven slowly away, followed by the bound students (who now that the full impact of their predicament had sunk in, were strangely silent, gone the bravado, gone, too, all vestige of hope) who were forced to trudge in single file behind it, Tontons Macoutes on either side of the sad, silent line, these looking decidedly unmilitary as they slouched and shuffled along.

It was only when the procession turned left towards the Carrefour at the end of the street and disappeared from view that Septimus became aware of everybody staring at him. And it was not just that they were staring: his eccentricity made them do that most of the time and he had become impervious to it. No, now there was some element in their eyes that was quite different. At first he could not make it out. Then an old woman spat on to the street and with her spittle came the realization that the eyes upon him were hostile. Gone was all trace of their tolerant joviality that customarily accompanied their stares, the looks that told him, Yes, we know you are mad, we know you are crazy, but you are trying to help us in your own way and you are almost our friend.

And he had certainly tried to be their friend. More, he had attempted as best he knew how to show them the love and compassion of which they had been for so long deprived. Their squalor and disease held no terrors for him; he rejoiced, almost, in being able to hold them in his arms as they died, showering them with understanding and consolation. And what was extraordinary was that in those moments his madness fell from him, and he became a true minister, administering the love he had always presumed emanated from Christ. Day after day, night after night, he would tramp through the district seeking out those in need, washing the infirm, feeding those too weak to feed themselves, or just sitting with those who longed for nothing more than company in their last hours.

'You better come in, Father,' Sister Mary told him, touching his elbow.

'Yes.' Perhaps she had noticed the change also. 'Did you see – '

'Yes, Father. Come along in.'

'But why?' Septimus sounded terribly upset.

'It's just a mistake they're making.'

'A mistake?'

'Yes. A mistake. They don't understand.'

Neither did Septimus. Sister Mary busied herself clearing up the mess that Septimus's overturned coffee-mug had made on the bedclothes. As she stripped the bed she talked. As she talked she clucked a lot. She was being motherly. She was being chatty. She was reassuring him. She was explaining that those people out there were pretty ignorant and didn't understand. They didn't think, you see. They only really believed what they saw no matter how much they might profess to believe in their gods. And what they had seen was the Colonel embracing Septimus. And what they had seen was Septimus patting the Colonel on the back. And what they had seen was the Colonel striding off in great good humour to his jeep. And what they had seen was Septimus smiling and waving after him as though to a beloved friend. That was what they had seen: so naturally they would be a bit moody. But there was nothing to worry about. In an hour, in less time than that, they would have forgotten all about it. And would he please be so good as to get her a pair of clean sheets, if there were any, from the cupboard?

Blindly Septimus went to the cupboard. The full implication of what the nun had told him not yet registering, he nodded as though accepting everything she said as reasonable.

Sister Mary humphed. 'I did ask for sheets, Father,' she said, but took the pillowcases anyway.

'What else could I do?' Septimus wanted to know. 'I had to pretend.'

'Of course you did. And quite rightly too.'

'They cannot possibly believe – ' Septimus sat down.

'I told you they wouldn't.'

'Maybe he did it on purpose – the Colonel, I mean.' Septimus stood again. 'You think that could be it?'

'Maybe. But it doesn't matter. Just you put the whole incident out of your mind. I have.' Sister Mary finished making the bed and put her seal of approval on her handiwork by patting the pillow. 'There. That's better. Now, have you eaten?'

Septimus couldn't remember; nonetheless he said, 'Yes.'

'You're sure?'

'Quite sure.'

'Then all we have to do is wait for the poor unfortunates to arrive.'

But no one came that evening. Sister Mary kept going to the door to stare up and down the street like a harlot touting for trade. And the street itself was eerily quiet and dark. 'I don't understand it,' she kept saying, mostly to herself.

'Perhaps if I were to go?' Septimus volunteered.

'It's got nothing whatever to do with you, Father. I'm quite sure of that,' Sister Mary insisted, although she sounded none too certain.

'I think I will go, however.'

'Well, you could certainly use a good night's sleep.'

'Sleep, perchance to – yes. Anyway, I may as well. Will you – ?'

'I'll manage fine by myself.'

Feeling like a thief in the night Septimus left the hospice and walked up the dark street. With a slow-burning pain of apprehension he felt how lonely, how isolated he was, that all around him, in spite of the assurances that he was a good man, in spite of the promise that no man was ever really alone since God was always at hand, in spite of the dog that now raised its head and growled at him, stretched a solitude through which he alone must pass. A path of treason, someone, he could not remember who, had called it, and perhaps they had known something he didn't. Traffic lights, slung overhead at the intersection, blinked mischievously in the distance. It ran in his head that he could perhaps make his way to one of the little bays that indented the island, jump the lights, so to speak, and steal one of the small boats that always lay anchored in the bays, and sail away by himself, unnoticed and painlessly. But the idea disintegrated almost immediately, shattered by an odd whispering sound that seemed to come from the houses and shops that lined the dingy street:

– You spy.

– You fathered that bastard.

– Your kind not care for life.

– We won't make a martyr of you, priest.

– You'd like that, no?

– Lookey lookey you spy.

Septimus stopped dead in his tracks, listening. No: he had, yet again, been mistaken. There was no whispering, no sound at all for that matter apart from the distant rumbling of traffic, and the occasional dull booming that could have been thunder, or an explosion, or the Colonel striding in his dreams. Even the dog had decided its growls were futile and gone back to sleep. Septimus gave a small shudder as though someone had trodden on his grave. Suddenly, above him and to his right, someone drew back a curtain and showered him with brilliant instantaneous light; then, almost instantly, they drew the curtain shut again and left him once more in darkness.

He moved on. Why, he wondered, was he feeling so furtive? More to the point, why was it that, even though he was walking down the street towards the still blinking traffic-lights, they seemed not to come any closer, seemed, indeed, to recede the nearer he should have come to them? Another illusion. He consoled himself with that thought for several strides. Like life itself, the thought continued rather less consolingly. Still, the analogy held. No matter how one strove the goals always remained just beyond one's finger-tips. – It is not the achievement that is our goal. It is the fact that we continually try to achieve a state of holiness – Bishop McKewen, generous as ever, had decided to accompany him part of the way. And Septimus was heartily agreeing with the pronouncement. 'Quite right,' was what he answered, and answered it aloud. 'Quite right,' he said again and meant it, even though he knew that he was readily agreeing only because, as he well knew, it was so much easier to defraud oneself into believing that one was continually striving, whereas actual failure to achieve was something far more difficult to explain. But the Bishop had foreseen this duplicity, it seemed. 'But we must not try and fool ourselves – '

'Indeed not.'

' – by explaining away our weaknesses as human frailty, and thereby giving ourselves licence to blame God.'

'Good heavens, no.'

But, alas, that was exactly what he *had* done, was it not? Septimus was thinking long after Bishop McKewen had taken his leave. And there had been no limit to his ingenuity either. The most potent and final obstacle to reaching that state of oneness with God (which he had dearly longed for) was the facile let out that it was never his fault when things went wrong, always someone else's. It is not my fault that I find myself in such or such a predicament; if so and so had not done that then I would not have been forced to react thus; and ultimately, if God had not made me in this way I would have had the strength and wisdom to – aaaaaaah! Septimus dismissed the presumptuous philosophizing with a prolonged groan. The last thing in which he wished to indulge at the moment was self-examination. All he wanted, he told himself, was a friend, a kind, uncomplicated friend, someone who would listen to him, to understand him, to console him. And such a friend seemed to be making his way towards him in the shape of the crippled cobbler who bounced along in the gloom, a bag of plastic netting filled with discarded fruit and scraps of meat slung from his shoulder. But he did not stop to listen to Septimus, did not pause to console him. He bounced past as though he did not even see him. And it was when Septimus turned to watch what he now thought of as his last forlorn hope of friendship vanish into the dark that the excrement hit him in the face. It came from nowhere. Septimus was stunned. He clawed the mess from his eyes. He was grievously pained. He used the hem of his soutane to wipe his lips. He was frightened. And he was suddenly running, racing wildly, stumbling, falling over, clambering upright and running again, waving his golf-club before him as though blinded yet able enough to ward off impediments. He skidded to a halt only when he reached the intersection, leaning against a pile of cardboard boxes filled with garbage, gulping for air. He felt his knees buckle, and slid slowly to the ground. It was oddly comfortable there. He closed his eyes, which was a mistake. So this is what you have come to, Septimus Roach. How much now for your grand schemes? And believe you me there is nothing symbolic about this whatsoever. You, to whom every possible chance was given, have ended up where you belong. You are finally rejected. You are as nothing . . . You are unwell – that sounded odd. Septimus opened his eyes.

'You are unwell?'

Very odd. Septimus blinked. And perhaps that was all it took to clear the mind, for now he could see the two patent-leather black shoes that humiliated his ridiculous sandals. He looked up as the question was repeated: 'You are unwell?'

'Ah. Patrick. As ever to the rescue. No. I am not unwell. Tired, I think. Weary might be a better word.'

'You cannot be seated there,' Patrick told him in a voice over-loaded with annoyance.

'No. I suppose not.'

'Give me your hand.'

Septimus held out his hand.

'Now – up.'

Septimus was on his feet. 'Thank you, Patrick.'

'I am glad that it is only I who saw you like this.'

'Yes.'

'I will now take you home.'

'You are very kind.'

Patrick produced a handkerchief. 'You have dirtiness on your face.'

'Yes.'

'You may use this.'

'Thank you.'

'No. No.' Patrick refused to take back the soiled handkerchief, even stepping back a pace in disgust. 'Throw it there,' he said, nodding towards the pile of rubbish.

'You must now be most careful,' Patrick also said, but later.

He had walked Septimus to the gates of the convent, a protective arm thrown about his shoulder. He stood quietly as Septimus fumbled for his key, fumbled and wondered why he felt there was something sinisterly significant about the word 'now'.

'Must I?'

'Indeed yes. I have heard, you understand, of the episode this afternoon.'

'I expect you have.'

'He is very clever, the Colonel.'

'I'm sure.'

'Also very dangerous.'

Septimus nodded and sighed gratefully as he found the key.

'But he has a fear of you.'

'Of me?' For a moment the idea pleased Septimus.

'Oh yes. A considerable fear.'

Septimus started to giggle.

Patrick regarded him gravely. 'You do not even yet understand?'

'No. I'm afraid I don't. Understand what?'

'Why you are here.'

It was ridiculous. It was a game. A merry charade. 'Tell me, Patrick. Why *am* I here?'

'To die,' Patrick told him quietly.

Ten

The Ambassador was flapping. His expectation of wielding the baton for Uncle Sam in this godawful backwater had never materialized. All his million-dollar contribution had brought was bloody exile in a land where everyone screwed anyone or was screwed by anyone for a couple of bucks. And now what little power he had imagined was his was being usurped, and for days he had been taking out his wrath on his staff.

'God damn it, Nicholson, I should have been told.'

'You were told, Mr Ambassador. I told you myself.'

'I'm not talking about that. I'm talking about tonight. I should have been told long ago that they were sending a plane to take the little bastard out.'

'Maybe they didn't know themselves until this morning. I mean, it was probably impossible for them to fix an exact day. Duvalier has changed his mind several times in the last couple of weeks.'

Slightly mollified, the Ambassador asked, 'Any fear of him changing it again now?'

Oscar shrugged. 'There's always a chance with him, but I doubt it. I think it's been made clear, even to him, that if he does he's on his own.'

'And you've got everything under control this end?'

'I believe so.'

'Well, that's something,' the Ambassador allowed grudgingly. And then, as if his next thought embodied something that struck him as potentially dangerous, he went on, 'That other guy. That friend of yours. The big Haitian, what's his name – ?'

'Gilles Lagreze?'

'Yeah. Lagreze. That's the one. What about him?'

'What about him?'

'What's he up to, dammit?''

Oscar shrugged again. 'Nothing that I know of. He's known

Duvalier most of his life and he was asked to act as intermediary. I don't imagine he's *up* to anything.'

That was not, however, acceptable to the Ambassador. He started to shake his head and lit one of his cigars, which was a sure sign of an argument to come. 'Oh, he's up to something all right. You can bet your balls on that. I can sniff them at it. Mark my words, Nicholson, he's up to some damn thing.'

'I can't think what. Anyway, knowing Gilles, it wouldn't be anything that would affect us.' Oscar laughed suddenly. 'You can be sure if Gilles is getting anything out of this he's already got it. He's not the sort to take a chance and wait to view the aftermath.'

'How the hell you could have got mixed up with – '

Oscar cut the Ambassador short. 'I like him.'

The Ambassador gawped. 'To each his own, I suppose.'

'Exactly.'

An explosion, one of many during the past few days, rattled the embassy windows. The Ambassador swore, and mumbled something about fucking Commies.

'Will that be all, Mr Ambassador?'

'Huh? Oh. Yeah. Yes, that's all, Oscar. Just see to it that I'm kept fully informed.'

'Of course, Mr Ambassador.'

'See that you do,' the Ambassador insisted forlornly.

Oscar Nicholson fumed quietly as he made his way down the long bright corridor lined with potted plants and framed photographs of the present and past Presidents. He had, he decided, far more important things to deal with than the Ambassador's gigantic, if gradually deflating, ego. Most importantly there was Susanna to consider. If, as now seemed certain, Duvalier *was* about to leave, there would be undoubted turmoil and the last thing Oscar wanted was for Susanna to find herself embroiled in the inevitable reprisals. She had changed her mind again: she would not be leaving; she felt she *had* to stay. Yet, when pressed (and, God knows, he had pressed her hard enough) she could advance no explanation for this obtuse necessity. Somehow, usually by some flimsy coincidence, Septimus Roach crept into her reasoning, and there was some inexplicable logic in this that worried Oscar to death.

He had just about reached the door of his office when his secretary popped her head out of hers. 'Oh, Mr Nicholson. Mr Lagreze is in the waiting room. He would like to see you.' She held a yellow pencil to her lips, using it like a finger to impress some obscure need for secrecy. 'Shall I – '

'Yep. Show him up, Valerie.'

Valerie didn't move, however. She took to tapping her slightly protruding upper teeth with the pencil, looking as though at any moment she might burst into tears. Oscar seemed not to notice. 'Yes. Show him up,' he repeated somewhat gruffly.

'Mr Nicholson?'

'Yes?' Then he was aware of his secretary's distress. His voice eased itself into a state of concern. 'What's the matter?'

'Are we going to be all right?'

'All right? What do you mean, all right? Of course we're going to be all right.'

'Everyone's saying there's going to be terrible trouble.'

'Nothing we can't deal with.'

'They're saying – '

'Look, would you just stop worrying about what "they" are saying? We're not in Africa,' Oscar told her condescendingly. 'You'll be perfectly safe. Just show Mr Lagreze up, will you?'

'Yes, Mr Nicholson.'

'And stop worrying,' Oscar stressed, a little more kindly.

'Yes, Mr Nicholson.'

There was, however, someone else in a similar frame of mind. 'It is a worrying time for us, is it not, Oscar?' Gilles Lagreze said as soon as he was seated, indeed starting the lament before he had settled in his chair.

'We'll cope.'

'I'm sure you will.'

'He is going to leave this time – definitely, I mean?'

Gilles Lagreze nodded, albeit somewhat hesitantly. 'Oh yes. All is packed and ready for the departure. It took a little persuading, I will admit. Madame, you see, is not at all anxious to surrender her comfortable way of life.'

'But he is going?' Oscar put in rapidly, something like panic in his voice.

'Oh yes.'

Oscar slumped back in his chair, flapping one hand in front of his face to express exaggerated relief.

'However – '

Oscar was upright in a flash. 'Oh God – what now?'

Monsieur Lagreze smiled impishly. 'For public – what do you say? – consumption, no? – our President is insisting that he is not leaving. He intends to motor through the streets of the city – to expose himself, as he so delicately puts it, to see and be seen by his people.'

'Christ above! He must be mad.'

Monsieur Lagreze seemed to agree with a slow positive blink.

'Doesn't he have any idea what's happening out there?' Oscar waved a hand towards the splendid gardens which protected the embassy from any contact with the squalor.

'He has heard, of course. But he does not believe it. Does not *want* to believe it, which is perhaps worse.'

'Some lunatic will shoot him as sure as God.'

'Oh, I think not. The drive is a masquerade. He knows that without protection his life is not worth a gourd. He will be very protected, I assure you.'

Oscar began to smile sinisterly. 'Mind you, Gilles, if someone *did* top the bugger it would make life a lot easier for me.'

'No doubt. But it will not happen.'

'Pity.'

'Perhaps.'

Oscar rose from behind his desk and moved towards a filing cabinet. 'Coffee?' he asked, producing a thermos from the top drawer. Monsieur Lagreze declined. 'It's my own. Sure?' Monsieur Lagreze still declined. Oscar poured coffee into a plastic mug and returned to his desk.

'Right. So, let's take it that he is going. Who takes over, Gilles?'

'Ah . . .'

'You, perhaps?' Oscar enquired, smiling.

Monsieur Lagreze looked horrified. 'Me? Dear me, no.'

'Who then?'

'A junta, I believe. A five-man junta.'

'Who heads it?'

'Henri Namphy – if my information is correct.'

'You know him?'

Monsieur Lagreze smiled enigmatically. 'A little.'

'And what's he like?'

Monsieur Lagreze took refuge in another shrug. 'Now, he seems a quite reasonable man. In a year . . .?' He spread his hands.

Oscar was forced to laugh. 'You're so bloody calm, Gilles.'

Monsieur Lagreze smiled. 'There will be enough hysteria, I assure you.'

'I'm sure there will.'

'There is to be a curfew, I understand.'

'Inevitable, I suppose.'

'But whether it will be heeded – ' He spread his hands again.

'God, I wish it was this time tomorrow.'

'It will come soon enough, my friend. Perhaps – who can say? – too soon.'

'Never too soon, Gilles.'

'We shall see.'

'Is there something you're not telling me?'

'No.'

'You sound as if you're expecting something.'

'One must always be expectant in these circumstances, wouldn't you say?'

'Of what?'

'Why, of the unexpected, of course.'

'Hah!'

'Of that which one should have foreseen,' Monsieur Lagreze added, raising his eyebrows.

'You *do* know something.'

Monsieur Lagreze shook his head. 'I have told you everything I *know*. I speak now only of what I do *not* know. Of what I cannot know. Of what no one can know until it is too late.' He sounded, suddenly, very sad.

'Gilles, I'm desperately worried about Susanna.'

'Yes,' Monsieur Lagreze said solemnly.

'I couldn't persuade her to leave.'

'No.'

'Oh, for God's sake, Gilles, say something besides yes and no!'

Monsieur Lagreze said nothing.

'I'm sorry. It's just she's been so damned odd lately. Says the weirdest things.'

Monsieur Lagreze prolonged his silence, waiting.

'You know what she told me?'

Patiently, Monsieur Lagreze waited to be told.

'That she *couldn't* leave.'

Monsieur Lagreze seemed to be giving that some thought.

'I'm sure it's got something to do with that damn priest – Septimus.'

Monsieur Lagreze began to look a trifle perturbed.

'If I didn't know better I'd say he'd hexed her.'

'Hexed?'

Oscar gave a nervous titter. 'Bewitched. Hypnotized – some damn thing.'

'Oh.'

'She keeps talking about him, says – you won't believe this, Gilles – says he needs her.'

'Perhaps he does,' Monsieur Lagreze suggested.

'Don't you start, Gilles.'

'It's all part of what I was trying to explain earlier. The unexpected. The incident recalled, the word so seldom recognized, so often unnoticed that shapes our destiny.'

'Oh, great. That's another thing. *She's* on the fate and destiny kick too.'

'And you are unpleased?'

'Damn right I'm unpleased – displeased.'

'Because against it you are helpless?'

'That has nothing to do with it.'

'If you say so.' Monsieur Lagreze sounded sympathetic. 'Anyway,' he continued, rising and straightening a small dent in the brim of his panama, 'I must, as you say, away.'

'Mind how you go.'

'I will, Oscar. How I wish all this was over and we could again have our games of chess.'

'We will soon, Gilles.'

'I hope you won't be disappointed, my friend.'

And probably he wouldn't be. Monsieur Lagreze drove from the embassy grounds, acknowledging the salute of the marine as though accustomed to such pomp. That, he reflected, was the real tragedy of all uprisings, of all wars: in the end nothing much changed, everyone slipped back into old routines and spoke wisely to each other of how things used to be as if to convince themselves things *had* changed. The rich (fortunately, he thought, with a wry smile) would still be rich if not richer; and the poor would certainly still be poor if not poorer. Someone was deposed; someone took his place and waited for his turn to be deposed.

On an impulse Monsieur Lagreze made a tricky u-turn and aimed

his car in the direction of the Ollofson. A quiet drink by himself
before the pandemonium began. A small indulgence. Who could tell,
perhaps within the next few days the dear old Ollofson itself would
fall victim to some well-aimed petrol-bomb. Not, Monsieur Lagreze
allowed as he parked his car in the shade, that its demise would be
of earth-shattering importance, but that was another thing that
made the expected revolution so sad: in their effort to destroy what
they saw as evil the hot-heads would erase most of what was good,
blasting indiscriminately at anything that smacked of what they had
never been able to savour or attain. Equal rights for all was a noble
enough sentiment but it was as fallacious and misleading as –
Monsieur Lagreze stepped from his car and locked it behind him,
coughing as he started to walk towards the hotel entrance, all the
while trying to conjure up a suitable comparison – as, perhaps,
power to the people and all the other slogans devised to secure
authority for the few and beguile the multitude into a totally fake
sense of achievement. The eternal quest for utopia, he was thinking
when he heard his name being called. Monsieur Lagreze shielded
his eyes from the glaring sun with one hand and looked towards the
voice.

'Here. Over here.' Susanna Lichfield was waving a small handkerchief at him from the veranda. 'Oscar's not with you, I
see.'

'Eh – no.'

'Is he coming?'

'I think not. I have just left him at the embassy. He is most busy.
Most busy.' Monsieur Lagreze noticed the pain in Susanna's eyes,
and it prompted him to add. 'He mentioned that he is most concerned for you.'

Susanna gave him a sceptical peep from under her eyebrows.

Monsieur Lagreze held up one hand to proclaim his honesty. 'He
is very concerned for you,' he insisted.

'There's no need for him to be.'

'You are – ah, my dear Hispo, yes, a little *crème de menthe*, thank
you. Susanna? – just the *crème de menthe* then, and, Hispo, *plenty*
of ice. You are certain?'

'Quite certain.'

'Oscar also mentioned – no, no matter. I intrude.'

'What, Gilles?'

'It is really not my affair.'

'Tell me, Gilles. Please.'

'He mentioned that you felt an – an alliance – is that the word? – with *Père* Septimus.'

'Oh.'

'Thank you, Hispo. Is that true?'

'Not an alliance, no.'

'That was my inadequate word. What would you call it?'

'You'll laugh at me like Oscar did.'

'Oh, no, my dear Susanna, I will indeed not laugh.'

Susanna studied her companion's face for a moment. 'No. No, I don't think you will. Well then – you really want to know?'

Monsieur Lagreze leaned forward. 'I am most anxious to know if you care to tell me.'

'All right.' She gave a small titter. 'Now I don't quite know how to explain it. A feeling isn't right. More a sort of intuition. It's so silly really, but it's rather like as if someone had actually told me – years ago – that I was going to be . . . involved, I suppose, with Father Roach, and it was only recently, since I came here – since I *met* him that I remembered it.' Susanna could feel her expression pleading for understanding. However: 'Now you can laugh,' she said harshly.

Monsieur Lagreze shook his head slowly, sympathetically. 'I do not laugh.'

'You're too damn polite, Gilles.'

That made him laugh: a slow, sedate rumbling as one does when accepting a compliment with embarrassment. And Susanna laughed too: a nervous tinkling poised to be severed the instant the mood changed. But the mood held.

'Did you make any sense of it, Gilles?'

'It is, perhaps, one of those – those incidents of which only you are intended to make sense.'

'But I can't. God knows I've tried.'

'It may be that it is not yet time for you to understand.'

'I don't follow.'

Monsieur Lagreze interlaced his fingers to make a church and pressed the steeple against his lips. His expression was pained as though Goethe's famous church bell was resounding in his mind pursuing, this time, not the child but some rather more rarefied truant. Susanna was winding her watch – or perhaps she was moving the hands forward. Possibly it was this that made Monsieur Lagreze say, making it sound like a warning, 'One cannot hurry these things.'

'But that's just it, Gilles. *What* things?'

Monsieur Lagreze longed for the power to explain, and with that explanation to clarify matters for himself. For in truth he was as much in the dark as the charming lady who sat opposite him holding a strand of her hair in her fingers and twisting it round and round. Well, perhaps not quite as much in the dark. It was, as he now thought of it, irritating. He knew precisely what 'things' he had referred to; they were old familiars: they had had their knees under the table of his mind on many occasions, had hung up their hats and made themselves at home like old friends making periodic if unexpected visits. But how – how in heaven's name to explain them? Impossible! One simply accepted them. Accepted them as one accepted such equally inexplicable concepts as faith and hope – and God, for that matter. Yet while faith and hope – and God, for that matter – were deemed vital to the human condition, let that other phantom 'destiny' be mentioned and hands were raised in alarm, brows furrowed in disapproval, souls shielded against the diabolic. Anyway, Monsieur Lagreze, taking his hands from his mouth and demolishing the church, spreading them on the table before him, decided to take the bull by the horns. 'Your destiny,' he said simply, hoping the simplicity of his tone would waylay the complication of his intent. Not so: at least, not quite so. He was, however, gratified and relieved to hear that Susanna embraced his words without the expected consternation, merely lobbing the words back at him with only a trace of a tremor: 'My destiny?'

'A matter common to us all.'

'You *believe* that, Gilles?'

'But most definitely.'

'Even though – what I mean is – I thought destiny was something hidden, secret. Something you discovered only as you went through life.'

Monsieur Lagreze nodded ponderously. 'For most of us. Some, however, for reasons we do not know, have a power to foresee.'

From the bar the scratchy strains of a tango reached them. Looking over Monsieur Lagreze's shoulder Susanna could just make out in the gloom the figures of two people dancing: they swayed, they coiled themselves about each other, they dipped, they straightened, they dipped again, all the while gazing into each other's eyes. How could anyone dare to enjoy themselves let alone be so obviously in love when she, Susanna, was . . . She felt her eyes brim with tears, only her grief was for something quite different:

– I'm burying him now.

Her mother's flat face pronounced the flat objective in a flat voice.

– How can you, mother? They haven't found Daddy's body.

– I'm burying him anyway.

And she had done just that. She dug a circular hole in the back garden and into it she threw every photograph of her husband that existed. Then she covered them with soil, stuck the spade in the ground, and wiped her hands on her apron to mark her satisfaction with a job well done. At first Susanna was aghast, then all she could feel was sadness at her mother's bitterness; but it was a sadness of a macabre sort tinged with a brittle humour, insofar as her father had finally, dramatically escaped his bondage. No, her true grief overwhelmed her suddenly when she realized that life went on as before. Standing there in the garden, her mother still beside her staring at her handiwork, Susanna was torn asunder by the trivial details that continued to be important to her. Above the wooden panelled fencing an electrician climbed a pole to check a fault in the overhead cables; he waved to her and winked. Children on roller-skates roared down the sidewalk, invisible, yelling with joy; a woman's high-pitched voice called for a dog to come to her and squealed with delight when it did; canned laughter rattled from a television set; a small, single-engined plane flew low overhead trailing an illegible slogan in its wake; a radio blared Nat King Cole singing, 'When I Fall In Love' . . .

'Then you *can* change them – I can, I mean.'

Monsieur Lagreze shook his head. 'I think not.'

'But surely if, as you said, I can foresee – could I not do the opposite and get away with it?'

Monsieur Lagreze smiled sadly. 'Fate, my child, is not what we do. It is what is done to us.'

And something was being done to her now, although not in the manner which Monsieur Lagreze had intimated. She was being jostled and bumped by a swarm of journalists who suddenly stampeded from the bar and raced towards the car-park, some vaulting the parapet in their anxiety to get there. Hispo, who had been watching the exodus with a stony face, came to the table and apologized for what he termed 'this discomforture', whisking invisible crumbs from the table with a white napkin, and enquiring (one suspected with an eye to profit since, unpaid, he received a small sum for each drink consumed on his territory) if another drink would be desirable for the composure, perhaps?

'*Pourquoi pas?*' Monsieur Lagreze agreed, ordering by waving his hand over the two empty glasses.

'I shouldn't,' Susanna said, but only after Hispo had departed.

'Neither should I.'

'I wonder where on earth they were all rushing to – do you know, Gilles?'

Monsieur Lagreze chuckled happily. 'It is most likely they are chasing another rumour.'

'Oh. About Mr Duvalier?'

'Most probably. At present all rumours seem to concern Mr Duvalier.'

'Is it true he's leaving?'

Monsieur Lagreze nodded.

'How sad.'

A great honking of horns started up as the journalists' cars (not that many and all grossly overloaded) were stymied at the gates by a charabanc filled with jeering Haitians, some squatting perilously on its roof, that had stalled, steam hissing from its radiator.

'How strange,' Monsieur Lagreze observed.

Susanna glanced about her, tossing her head back as her hair fell over her eyes. 'What is?'

'That you should find the Duvalier departure sad.'

Everyone had left the charabanc and was pushing and heaving at the vehicle which, for the moment at any rate, refused to budge, while those on the roof had, as if by magic, produced a variety of brass instruments and were playing, not a tune exactly, but a sort of rhythmic beat that encouraged, like a galley-drum, the straining bodies on the ground.

Susanna absent-mindedly put on her sunglasses. 'I don't really know why I said it.' She gave a small laugh. 'I was probably thinking of something else.'

Monsieur Lagreze inclined his head sympathetically.

'Oscar wants *me* to leave, you know.'

'Yes. He did tell me.'

'Should I?'

'If you can.'

Susanna jerked her head, sending the sunglasses slipping to the end of her nose. 'Oh – he *has* been telling tales.' She took the glasses off, folded them, and put them back in her handbag.

'As I said, he is concerned.'

'Poor Oscar. He's so, so – '

– Soso:

Erik Arcado had materialized from nowhere and was taking her by the hand, guiding her up the steps of some spectacular building the outline of which resembled the mountains that rested on the clouds. Then they were inside, but the interior was far too small to be that of the edifice they had approached. It was tiny. Square. Gloomy. Lit only by the dim light that came from a circular window set high in the thick wall. That wall was unadorned: white with flaking plaster. The other three walls, however, were covered by primitive paintings. Erik was pointing to them. A succubus reclined in an oyster shell and gestured provocatively to a man who seemed to be drowning but who smiled contentedly nonetheless. Crude trees arched across the ceiling, their roots firmly planted in the foundations, and in their branches, leafless and seemingly brittle, grotesque creatures with human bodies and monkey-like heads cavorted, the males with penises erect but oddly curved like bloated gherkins. Two lovers reclined naked by a river on which black swans floated: they seemed to be sleeping, or about to sleep, or about to awaken, their legs entwined, their arms outstretched in a curious somnambulistic attitude, their fingers clenched as though they held in their palms the total pathos of love . . .

' – so gallant.' It was Monsieur Lagreze who finished the sentence.

'Why not? It does suit him rather, doesn't it. Gallant. I do believe he *does* sometimes rather see himself as the knight in shining armour.'

'And you the maiden fair?'

'Once.'

'Not still?'

'I think not.'

The bus had been moved and the brass band trumpeted the victory. The cars eased their way past it and sped off down the road. The neglected tango ground forlornly on. Hispo arrived with the drinks. Someone in a room upstairs coughed. Water gurgled down a drainpipe. What sounded like a chainsaw came to life, spluttered and died again. Plates were rattled as the tables were set for lunch.

'If you were me, Gilles, what would you do: go or stay?'

'If I were you,' Monsieur Lagreze said thoughtfully, aloud but to himself. 'If I were you I would go upstairs, pack and be on the first afternoon flight out of here.' He finished his drink almost in one go, swilling the ice in the glass and swallowing the last drop. 'I regret that I must now leave you,' he said, before wiping his mouth with the paper napkin Hispo had provided.

'I understand, Gilles. You must be up to your eyes.'

Monsieur Lagreze rose heavily. 'You will,' he said, taking her hand and holding it tenderly, 'whatever your decision, be careful?'

'You're starting to sound like Oscar. Of course I'll be careful. I'm not going to do anything. I'm going to finish my drink and have lunch and think about what you said. Now *that* can't land me in any trouble, can it?'

'One would think not.' He kissed her hand.

Alone (all alone as it happened since those few residents who had not taken off with the reporters had taken off and reported for lunch) Susanna put her sunglasses on again and watched Monsieur Lagreze make his way to his car. Rose-tinted spectacles: the thought loomed, hesitated, vanished. But there was nothing rosily tinted. Everything, like the mood that now descended on her, was bleak. As was the outlook, she decided without quite knowing why. Maybe it was her damned destiny to find all things saturated by bleakness.

She sipped her Campari: the tart's drink, someone had told her, and the memory made her smile to herself. Instantly the whore's dream (she had been told this too, possibly by the same person who had disparaged the Campari) began to take shape in her mind: an idyllic hideaway far from the ravages of hectic, economic life. An absurdly romantic cottage, rose-covered with great thick bushes of lavender bordering the flagstone path that led to the latticed door. But it was more, far more than just a place to which she could escape: it was a home that stood on a bluff overlooking some great heaving sea, a grey cold sea in which she swam every day, diving deep into the watery stillness, her eyes peeled for –

'Madam will lunch?'

' – ? Oh.' Startled, she shook her head. 'No. No lunch, Hispo. Thank you. I have to go out.'

'Madam will take care?'

'Yes, madam will take care,' she answered vaguely.

And it was with care that she prepared herself for what was assuming, in her mind, the guise of a 'fateful' journey, changing into flat-heeled shoes, tying her hair in a ponytail and clipping the tip of the tail to the top of her head, covering the lot with a silk scarf (with seahorses rampant) tied under her chin. The jacket she chose was linen, and she filled the pockets with items from her handbag. Half way down the driveway of the hotel she once again put on her sunglasses and shoved her hands as best she could into the stuffed jacket pockets, strutting with a grandly raffish air. She had no idea where she was going: Destiny, she decided (even her thought tinged with sarcasm) would take charge and hence responsibility for her Fateful walk.

As she turned out of the ornate iron gates, one of them tugging its hinges from the unpointed stone pillar, and into the dusty roadway her stride shortened, her swagger evaporating, making her feel childishly guilty at having adopted it in the first place. The road was totally empty. It was uncannily still. The eucalyptus trees, their leaves weighted with that unique and pungent odour, appeared petrified, a feeling heightened by the coolness they shed. Nothing stirred. The large winged insects and small shining reptiles that usually abounded were nowhere in sight. So daunting was the silence that, quite consciously, she found herself almost tiptoeing. It was as if she had found herself on the pathway to a magic place, a place such as Alice might have found, a place that charmed children and terrified adults, a place where dragonflies were harnessed with silken bridles, where ladybirds pulled little silver ploughs, where moths delivered letters, where daffodils the size of snowdrops blossomed, where – suddenly she stopped in her tracks and laughed. Erik Arcado again! How odd that the land he had created for her, just for her, should come so vividly to mind now. She walked on slowly. But how beautiful it had been. And how she had clung to that make-believe image!

She reached the main thoroughfare, a narrow enough road that did not widen until it became the Carrefour, and stopped again. This, too, was deserted although she could now hear noises coming from the centre of the city: they seemed to sweep up the road and pass her like goblin traffic but in waves of sound as though from time to time they were halted by some fairy traffic-lights. God, she must be going out of her tiny mind! But if she was it didn't perturb her; she crossed the road smiling, something of the old jauntiness returning to her step. And she was still smiling when it came sailing out of nowhere: an improvised rickshaw affair, a low wooden cart on large narrow wheels drawn by a bicycle. The cyclist, head bent to his chest, barefoot and wearing only a snazzy pair of purple shorts, perhaps dreaming he was participating in a particularly important Tour, ignored her; but waving gaily from the cart, looking for all the world like a potentate, a pretty ragged and woebegone potentate it was true, was the crippled cobbler, his chicken, perched on the tubular metal rail that ran the length of the back of the cart, waving too with its wings. Yet there was something more to all this than a mere greeting. The cobbler seemed to be beckoning her to follow, and there was an urgency about the gesture. He still had a hand in the air as the contraption turned left and disappeared.

Susanna hesitated, telling herself not to be so silly. Actually, she was making a tremendous effort not to follow the cripple. What she could not have explained was that she was being drawn relentlessly towards the street up which the rickshaw had been pedalled, the 'street of the hospice' as she called it privately. But she would not be drawn. She would resist. She would turn on her heel and make her way back to the hotel. She would collect her book – *Bleak House*, as it happened – go to the river and read. She would play no part whatever in this demented plot. She would certainly not call on Septimus Roach again – that was for sure.

'Good heavens!' Septimus greeted her.

'Hello, Father.'

'Good heavens!' Septimus exclaimed again, slurring the words a little as though mildly intoxicated. 'Another visitor.'

'I'm sorry – I – ' Susanna faltered. She glanced about her and into the hospice: there was no one else there.

'I was just saying to the Bishop that his comparison of myself to Ryder was altogether spurious. Quite without foundation.' Septimus had paused and was drawing a circle in the air with one finger. 'It really is unforgivable how one is *always* compared to someone else, and usually someone for whom one has no regard – or no knowledge of at all for that matter.'

He stopped talking and tried to grasp the circle in his other hand, apparently succeeding and stowing it away in his pocket. 'For example, had this Ryder fellow never existed – and you must remember that for me at least he never did exist until the bishop here created him – the comparison could not have been made. Now, I ask you, would that make me non-existent, or would I then be compared to some other unfortunate mortal, making me another person, a shadow of my former self?'

' – '

'Or in order to comply with these outrageous facsimiles must we acquire a certain, I won't say technique exactly, but a falsehood, a dubious disguise, at any rate, that sublimates our original right to detachment?'

'I don't – '

'Good. Neither do I. Not for one minute.' Septimus was looking in triumph towards an upended fruit crate that lay at the far end of the porch. 'You see,' he told it or some phantasm using it as a seat, 'you are outnumbered two to one. An adequate majority. The vote being taken. The die cast. However,' he continued, turning to face Susanna, although whether he was actually looking at her was difficult to tell since his eyes were obliterated by the sunlight glinting on his spectacles, 'as in everything – and I do admit this – there might just lurk an element of truth in the assumption that each of us resembles someone else. You, for example' (he was, having moved his head a fraction, definitely looking at Susanna) 'could, I suppose, for the moment at least, be quite reasonably compared – what's that? – Oh, no – You think? – Rather more biblical, I thought – ' (he was arguing with the seated phantom, and getting the better of it into the bargain) – 'I was sure you would – compared to – ' (he was back to Susanna again) 'to Mary Magdalen – '

'*What?*'

'Or is it Maudlin – I seem to recall – never mind.'

'Father – '

'How nice to see you.'

He had, it seemed, shaken off whatever insanity had possessed him. He was standing up, offering his hand to be shaken. He was smiling benignly in the manner of a man without a care in the world. He was being utterly charming. He was a gracious host. He was fooling her completely – or so he was telling himself. In fact, although certainly there was something charming about his manner, he was not smiling. He looked inexorably sad. And he had not in the least bamboozled her. As the grim realization of this swamped his tattered mind he turned away, muttering darkly to himself, leaving Susanna, quite literally, speechless. It was several moments before she managed, weakly, her brain already creating a thousand excuses for a hasty retreat from all this, 'I shouldn't have come.' Yet she stayed where she was.

Septimus, on the point of walking away, stopped. He stopped his muttering too, and swung round. 'Why did you come?' he asked.

'I have no idea. I was walking – ' Susanna stopped abruptly and looked about her, searching the street for the cobbler. He was nowhere in sight. There were other people though, standing in small groups, huddled almost, occasionally casting surreptitious glances in the direction of the hospice, but mostly talking among themselves, some with arms thrown round the shoulders of companions in a sort of scrum, assiduously plotting whatever it was they were plotting. They were all men, Susanna noticed, and all wearing hats of one kind or another; all serious as though their conversations were momentous; and all – was furtive the word? yes – and all furtive as if their meeting should really be taking place in the dead of night. Deliberately she forced herself out of the moment; she tried to stop thinking, to make her mind peacefully blank, and she had almost achieved this state when Septimus interrupted, clearing his throat and saying mysteriously, 'I was, of course, expecting you.'

'You can't have been.'

'Or someone else.'

'Oh.'

Septimus hummed. 'An inevitable advent,' he said, and found the phrase to his liking. '*Adventus inevitabulus*,' he added, nodding.

Susanna took one pace backwards, putting her foot on the top step of the rickety flight that led down from the porch, looking like a bird about to launch itself into flight. Indeed, she wanted nothing more than to fly, or flee, but Septimus's doleful stare seemed to transfix her, just as the conversation (of a sudden clearly audible if unintelligible, and the more frightening for that) of the men on the far side of the street seemed to press against her back like a great, restraining hand. Their murderous-sounding plotting was now complete, one could suppose, since they were, although still gesticulating and nattering, now standing in a line, their hands in their pockets, staring towards the hospice, their words shot from the corners of their mouths.

' – you,' Septimus was saying. 'Or the Colonel. You've met the Colonel, have you? No? Charming man – in the manner in which Lucifer is said to be charming, of course – although I wasn't really expecting him until later.' He sucked his lower lip pensively, and leaned forward to inspect a small biplane that flew low overhead. 'Pilate,' he said darkly. 'Or Biggles,' he suggested, brightening. 'Or Herod,' he added, becoming morose again, frowning.

'Biggles most likely,' Susanna heard herself say.

'You think? Well, that's a relief then, isn't it? Not that I had too much doubt about it but one cannot be too careful, especially with those Pharisees congregating over there.' He raised himself on to his toes and peered over Susanna's shoulder at the men lined up opposite. 'The end is nigh,' he sighed, rocking on his heels. Then he walked slowly into the hospice and shut the door.

In an impatient, angry gesture Susanna snatched off her headscarf, released her hair from the ponytail, and shook it free. She was suddenly furious. She was also frightened, the more so since the men, unobserved, had silently moved closer and were now in the centre of the street. They had also stopped talking, and only stared at her, their mouths slightly open, their attitude expectant; but expectant of what was not something Susanna intended to find out. She must have run very fast for the next thing she knew she was back at the gates of the hotel, gasping, leaning against one of the pillars with one hand, her chest heaving, one shoe missing, one stocking laddered from the knee to the ankle. But at least she had made up her mind. She was going straight to her room; she would pack, and take Monsieur Lagreze's advice and scram. How could she have been so misguided as to believe, even for an instant that her destiny was in any way involved with that stupid, stupid, stupid priest? She sank to the ground. Damn him to hell. She folded her arms about her knees, sobbing.

It was there that Oscar found her, driving past her in fact on his way out of the Ollofson, then spotting her, braking and slamming the car into reverse, jumping out almost before the car had come to a halt.

'Where in the name of Christ have you been?' he demanded. Then, slowly becoming aware of her condition, adding, 'Jesus, Susanna, what happened?'

'Nothing happened.'

'Something's happened.'

'Nothing's happened, dammit.'

'I've been going frantic. Where have you been?'

'Out.'

'Where?'

'For a walk. Oscar will you stop – '

'By yourself?'

'Yes. By myself.'

'Are you out of your mind?'

Yes, I'm out of my mind, Susanna wanted to scream at him. Totally and utterly crazy. So completely demented that I imagined, just for a second, mind you, so perhaps I'm *not* so utterly and totally crazy, that I was getting involved, for once, in something that would have some meaning, something that would fill that void with which I have lived for more years than I can recall.

'Don't you know – Christ, I tried hard enough to warn you – that you could have been in very real danger out there on the streets by yourself? Especially now?'

'I wasn't in any danger, Oscar.' She sounded remarkably patient. No danger that he would understand, anyway.

'You damn well were.'

'All right. All right. *All right.* But I'm not now, am I? I'm here. Safe and sound – well, reasonably sound. Damn.' She addressed damnation to her stocking, holding her leg out, balancing on the other as she surveyed the damage.

'How did that happen?'

'I tripped and fell, Oscar. Perfectly innocent. Nothing sinister. I tripped and fell. It does happen to me, you know.'

'You're sure?'

'Sure of what?'

'That that's all that happened?'

'Of course I'm sure. Don't nag me so.'

'I'm not nagging. I was bloody worried.'

'Well now you can stop bloody worrying. I'm perfectly fine.'

Later, in her room, showered and pampered by scented powder, Susanna almost regretted the way she had treated poor old Oscar. He looked so lost and pathetic sitting on her bed, his head hanging. If only he wouldn't – oh, drat him. If only he wasn't always so damn *nice.* Anyway her mind was made up, which was a good thing. 'I've decided to take your advice, Oscar. I'm leaving for New York.'

'When?'

'Now.'

'*Now?*'

'Yes now. You told me I should leave as soon as possible.' She took her suitcase from the trestle by the wardrobe and tossed it on to the bed.

'How come the sudden decision?' Oscar asked, standing.

'I've told you. I simply decided that you were right.'

'Oh.'

'You did say I should leave?'

'Yes.'

'Well then.' She opened the suitcase and removed the sheets of tissue paper she used to wrap her silk dresses and blouses. 'You also said I could leave everything to you, remember? Tickets, and all that.'

'Yes. I remember. You want me to see to it?'

'If you would,' she said matter-of-factly, aware that she was being purposely offhand and brutal.

'Okay. I'll do it right away. I know there's a flight to Miami at five, will that do?'

Susanna glanced at the small travelling clock beside the bed. 'Fine.'

As soon as Oscar had left the room, Susanna flopped on to the bed and lay back, staring at the ceiling. Away she was going from this grim and menaced place. Away from Oscar too. She ran her fingers through her hair. Well, probably it was best to end it this way.

– The end is nigh.

So clear, so near, so sad was the voice that she heard it made her sit bolt upright. She was shaking. She was holding herself tightly to stop the shaking. But she was still shaking when she went to the window, and held back the curtain, gazing out. At first she saw nothing untoward. A slight breeze had risen and the leaves of the distant eucalyptus shook and rattled against each other. A pied cat stalked across the driveway, its eyes fixed on something unseeable by mortals. The journalists had returned and their voices could be heard, loud, frustrated, and a little drunk. Then she spotted the cobbler. He was looking up at her, mouthing words she knew she did not want to understand. With a small cry she stepped back and let the curtain fall. She stood there, quite still, whimpering in her mind.

Eleven

Dawn came as it always came at that time of year: bright and burning and golden and almost without warning, the only herald the sound of seabirds.

After a long and sleepless night (during which, for no immediately explicable reason, the spectres of Rudolpho and Mimi held centre stage in his mind) Gilles Lagreze lay in his bed watching that dawn, impervious to the tragedy that had been proclaimed, smoulder into glory. He felt very gloomy, unusually morose. The history to be enacted that evening would soon be forgotten by those conniving meddlers who had precipitated it, and poor dear Haiti would be the only sufferer. But – he swung his legs out from under the single sheet that covered him and sat on the edge of the bed, his head in his hands – perhaps a country thrived on its sufferings, and upon the sufferings soon to be inflicted on Haiti's soul it might not only thrive but flourish and prosper. He scratched his armpit absent-mindedly. It was a promising thought and it temporarily revived his habitual sang-froid. He scratched his other armpit, his eyes staring out of the enormous window that ran the full length of one wall, and coming to rest on the somewhat over-voluptuous caryatid atop the column that supported the jasmine in the bower. A telephone shrilled downstairs, stopped for a few seconds, and took up its strident demand for attention again on the table beside his bed. He let it ring a few times before answering it, loath to be dragged away from the carefully contrived peace that surrounded him. As though in a vain effort to maintain that peace he did not speak; a series of grunts were all that he transmitted down the wires, their variations of pitch and accentuation left to convey his meaning.

That over, he stretched and yawned and groaned as his muscles and nerves strained. So, it had begun. The summons to the palace had come, a summons hesitantly issued by some underling already jangling with fear at the prospect of what the immediate future might have in store. And with reason, Gilles Lagreze reflected as he showered and dressed. The jittery voice could well be eternally silenced before the day was done. As, indeed, might his own. He dismissed the thought by slamming the bedroom door loudly behind him. Strangely (coming downstairs and rejecting the offer of coffee but ordering a taxi to be called) he was, for the moment, less concerned about himself than he was for the beautiful artefacts he had so lovingly collected. He told himself with cold logic that he was replaceable: his treasures were not. Perhaps all that really mattered in the end was the preservation of the beautiful, which must be an indictment of something. But maybe not. Glancing at his reflection in the hall mirror, he smiled at himself to improve his image, or more likely to bolster his flagging spirits. And it seemed to work. He felt much more light-hearted as he left the house and made his way through the garden to the taxi that waited at the gate. He spotted a bud on the rosebush Peace, found it melancholically appropriate, and stuck it in his lapel. Then, like a man who detests goodbyes but cannot resist the pain inflicted, he turned cumbrously, swivelling his heels on the gravel, and stared with an aching heart back towards his house. His Miramar, he fantasized but without too much exaggeration. *His* beloved Miramar mirroring, he most ardently hoped, the glorious Mexican edifice rather than the tragic imitation in Trieste. Still, there was no lonely, unhappy Carlotta here to be driven (as he was about to be driven by the taxi-driver who was already making impatient clicking noises with his tongue) helter-skelter into insanity; unless the face that regarded him from the upstairs window could be taken as a Carlotta of sorts, certainly looking wild enough, although, he admitted and raised his hat, his beloved mistress always did look thus at such an hour of the day. He climbed into the taxi, not without some difficulty. He was getting too fat; he was already too fat. He folded his hands over his stomach and stared out of the window.

They passed what had started out, with fanfare and high intent, to be a model farm: it had long since abandoned any such pretence, the only reminder a swinging wooden sign, hung over the gateless entrance, that bellowed the legend CHAROLAIS, all other words, had there been any, flaked and peeled away. The fields where cattle dreamed of roaming were brown and arid and cracking in places; the ditches were dry. The hills beyond glowered in purple disgust.

The first building came into view, a *blanchisserie*, gutted by recent fire, its amber-coloured walls blackened by the smoke that still rose from the debris. Then the cemetery, its monuments gleaming spick and span, its occupants content in the knowledge that they were beyond the anger of any revolution. A handful of young people, all male, their heads tied in bandanas of the sort popular with kung-fu practitioners, were shaking the massive gates of the cemetery, trying to break in. It struck Gilles as comical that anyone in his right mind would try to enter such a place by force. It was a passing reflection; he thought no more about it, suddenly distracted by a small mob, wielding machetes and clubs, pitchforks too, like Marxists in propaganda pictures, chanting, dancing, waving, looking villainous but seeming to be in good enough humour and enjoying themselves. Which they probably were and would continue so to do until that first, perhaps unintentional blow was struck, until the first blood ran, until the massacre began. And verily it would soon begin. Monsieur Lagreze imagined he could already smell it. He wrinkled his nose. How soon would the first life be taken, and whose would it be? Oddly enough it never occurred to him, not at this moment at any rate, that it might be his own. It was not that he actually believed he was immune: it was more a case of the other chap getting the dreaded disease, the other chap being cuckolded, the other chap giving up the ghost. Always the ghosts.

Four men rushed on to the road in front of the car, making it swerve and the driver swear: leering they jumped to one side in the nick of time and made off dragging behind them what looked like an effigy, of whom it was impossible to tell. Monsieur Lagreze took his handkerchief from his inside pocket and wiped his brow. When he lowered the handkerchief the American Embassy was in focus.

. . . Death was on Oscar Nicholson's mind as he mentally strangled the Ambassador, but smiling and nodding as though murder was the furthest thing from his thoughts.

'Run through it again for me, Oscar,' the Ambassador demanded, putting his boot-shod feet on his desk and lighting a cigar which he smoked with the noise of a suckling pig. And Oscar obligingly ran through it for the third time, pointedly speaking slowly as though to a fool.

'I get it,' the Ambassador got it, almost. 'When's the plane coming in?'

'It's here already, Mr Ambassador. A C-141 Starlifter. A cargo plane, I'm afraid, from Charleston.'

'The bugger won't like that.'

'Probably not, but it's what they sent.'

'And departure time?'

Oscar shrugged. 'Whenever Mr Duvalier and his entourage get there.'

'Can't you be more specific?'

'No. As long as Mr Duvalier is vague, I have to be vague.'

'And he's given no hint?'

'Only that it will be sometime today. Or tonight. Personally I think it will be tonight, but that's just my guess.'

'And meanwhile we just sit on our asses and wait?'

'Precisely, Mr Ambassador.'

That, at least, was what Oscar prayed the Ambassador *would* do: sit on his ass and keep well out of the way. But that was probably asking too much. In a fit of outrageous whimsy Oscar created in his mind a picture of the Ambassador being bundled unceremoniously aboard the cargo plane, FREIGHT stamped on his ass, instead of Duvalier, but even this small and farcical joke brought him little comfort. He was (and the realisation came like a blinding migraine) desperately worried. Fortunately he did not have to worry about Susanna, safely gone, but he was worried about his friend, Gilles Lagreze. He was worried about the accursed priest, Septimus Roach. He was even a little worried about himself. And, while every fibre in his body told him he should concern himself only with the matter of Duvalier's impending departure, it was Septimus Roach who dominated his thoughts for the moment, fragments of the conversation that had taken place between them last evening still bouncing round his brain. Deciphering the meaning of what the priest had said was a tease, and it still rankled like the final word in an otherwise completed crossword that, although known, would not come to light.

Oscar lit a new cigarette from the one he'd been smoking, doodling with the smoke as he exhaled, making of it an outline of Septimus which only he could recognize and appreciate. 'It'll have to be quick, Father. I'm up to here in work,' Oscar had said, hopefully pre-empting any rambling discourse, holding one hand over his head.

'Very quick,' the priest had promised, but there was a look about him that suggested the promise was there to be shot at.

'I'm all ears.'

'I am to die,' Septimus told him quietly.

Refusing categorically to read anything ominous into the statement, Oscar nodded, casting his face into adequate sympathy. 'As we all are, Father,' he said. 'It's one of the hazards of living – or so I'm told.'

'You don't understand.'

Oscar stubbornly, wittingly, rejected the lure of battle. 'What is there to understand, Father?'

'My death, you see – may I?'

'Please.'

Septimus sat down. 'My death, you see, will be seen as murder.'

'Oh. Murder.'

'But it won't really be – murder, I mean.'

'Good.'

'It will be an expiation.'

Oscar decided to nod.

'Although at this moment I'm not yet quite sure of what.'

'No. Well, one wouldn't be.'

A small yellow light glowed on the telephone just before the buzzer sounded. Oscar grabbed the receiver. 'Who? . . . Oh, right . . . Yes I'll speak to him. Yes – Hi – when did that happen? – Shit – Yes I have – It's his decision – we *can't* – You're sure? – Okay – It gives *us* a breather although what the crew will say . . . I wonder what brought that on? – Yes, I'll deal with it – Yeah, thanks. Thanks a lot and up yours too. 'Bye – Sorry, Father,' Oscar apologized either for the vulgarity or for keeping him waiting, and stabbed another button. 'Valerie, get hold of Jarrow and Stephenson and tell them to meet me in the Ambassador's office in' – he glanced at his watch, glanced at Septimus too – 'five minutes. Make that ten. He's *what*? When? – Where's he gone, for Christ's sake? Well, tell Jarrow and Stephenson to come here then. Thanks . . . Sorry about that, Father. Where were we?'

'Dying.'

'Yes. So you were. Look, Father, could we – it's not that I'm heartless, but could we talk about this some other time? I really *do* have – '

But Septimus wasn't listening. He had gone to the window and was gazing out, cupping his ears in his hands as though concentrating on pitch. And perhaps he was. It was difficult for him to tune his mind to the orchestra of voices that waltzed into his consciousness.

But for once there was nothing sombre about their tones: lilting more like, gay almost, definitely encouraging:

– Cheer up, old bean!

– Nothing is ever as bad as it seems, sport!

– Keep your chin up!

– Lookey lookey for the silver lining!

But it was too good to last. Gradually the timbre of the voices changed, getting darker, hinting that the silver lining might merely be tinfoil.

– Mind you, I wouldn't like to be in your shoes, sonny!

– There is, of course, a path through hell, as Blake well knew, but, dear me, it is *so* difficult to find. I doubt you'll ever make it, friend.

– Perhaps, dear boy, like Goethe's horse, you should suffer yourself to be –

Now there was a cold aloofness in the voices, accusatory, pointing fingers, wearing black caps. And they were no longer talking to him but among themselves.

– He has only himself to blame.

– He is so useless, so ridiculous.

– Look at him! I ask you! Have you ever seen such a clown?

A wail arose that drowned the voices, sending them scudding into oblivion. Septimus was appalled when he realized the wail was his own; more shocked than even when he felt Oscar's arm about his shoulder, felt himself being guided like an invalid back to his chair. 'I'm perfectly all right, you know,' he protested.

'Sure you are, Father. Look, you're living at the convent, aren't you? Why not let me get someone to drive you back there, and you get some rest?'

'Rest? I don't need rest. What I need is – ' He couldn't think what he needed.

'You look awful – '

'I always look awful. What I need – ' Again what was needed escaped him.

'Look, let me, as I said, have someone drive you back to the convent. You needn't rest. Pray, or read, or do handstands. Just stay there until tomorrow morning. Then I'll come and we can have a good talk.'

'Oh, I couldn't do that.'

'Whyever not?'

'It wouldn't fit. Don't you see? It wouldn't fit at all. Besides, there's the woman to consider.'

'What woman?'

'The beautiful American woman.'

Oscar was getting uneasy. 'What American woman?'

'The dancer – No! The ballerina. She who could have launched a thousand ships and – '

'You mean Miss Lichfield?'

'Is that her name?'

'I'm asking you.'

'I have no idea. Strange, isn't it? There she is about to play the most enormous role in my downfall and I do not even know her name. Maybe I did once. Anyway, it's gone. Things do, you know – go. Slip away. Through one's fingers. Through one ear and out the other. Through gaps in one's soul. Rather a dirty trick, wouldn't you say? Hmmmm.' He paused, humming. 'But what's in a name?' he asked after his breather.

'Well, if it is Miss Lichfield you're talking about, I'm afraid you'll have to arrange a stand-in. She flew to Miami this afternoon.'

'Miami?' Septimus sounded puzzled.

'That's right.'

'This afternoon?'

'Yep. I put her on the plane myself.'

'You're certain?'

'Oh, I'm certain all right,' Oscar replied grimly, remembering the pain he felt as she mounted the steps and disappeared into the plane without a backward glance, without a wave, without anything to which he might cling.

'But that means – ' Septimus began, only to stop and frown.

Oscar waited. But whatever it meant must have slipped through one gap or another. Septimus stood up and drew a rough outline of Ireland on the carpet with his niblick. He stood back and thought about it; leaned forward and added a few finishing strokes. Then, abruptly: 'I must go to the palace immediately.'

'You what? You'll do no such thing, Father.'

'But I must.' He sounded reasonable.

'Don't you know what's going on?'

'Of course I know what's going on.' He erased the invisible republic from the carpet with the toe of one sandal. 'That's precisely why I must get to the palace and have a word with – '

'You cannot go within a mile of the palace,' Oscar interrupted, surprising himself with his vehemence.

Septimus seemed to surrender. 'Oh,' he said. 'I see.'

'Just go back to the convent. Or to your hospice. Stay indoors and out of the way – please?'

'The way,' Septimus repeated. It seemed to trigger off a battery of ways. 'The way forward,' he said to himself. 'The way back. The way of the world. The way things are. The way things will be. The way of the – Yes. Well. I will – teehee – a-way!' He tried a more substantial laugh but it had a hollow sound as though the part of his mind which dealt with humour recognized it essentially as a fraud.

Anyway, away he went. Outside the embassy compound he stopped, listening. Somewhere in the distance a clock was striking; Septimus stood there motionless, adjusting his mind to the falsehood of the thought that had struck him. The cock croweth, he had thought. But it was no cock, not yet at any rate. Just a clock striking, but striking somewhat wildly: seventeen, eighteen, nineteen. Nineteen o'clock. But it was not yet over: the clock struck thrice more, and Septimus shuddered. The silence that followed was filled with melancholy moanings: not I, not I. Denial was what it meant.

Septimus felt dizzy, his face grey as a pile of ashes. He leaned against the railings, aware that the marine sentry was regarding him with the utmost suspicion. As the dizziness fell away he began to be afraid, the more so since he could not quite pinpoint what it was that frightened him. The sentry had looked away. The clock had fallen silent. His brain was tranquil. Yet he was shaking. And, dear God, who was this scudding like tumbleweed along the road towards him if not the crippled cobbler? He closed his eyes and groaned to himself; when he opened them there was no sight of the cobbler, just himself and the sentry and a few innocent enough passers-by going about their business.

'You look like the death!' The ground had opened and disgorged Monsieur Lagreze.

Septimus blinked. 'Gracious me!' He reached out and touched Monsieur Lagreze on the cheek. 'You *are* there.' He withdrew his hand and smiled.

'Certainly I am here.'

'I wasn't sure. So many – yes. Well, How fortuitous.'

'I may help?'

'Indeed. As someone who knows everyone. I was on my way to the palace. You could tell me – '

'I think not – '

'I'm sorry?'

'Not the palace. Not just now.'

'No?'

'Definitely no.' Monsieur Lagreze spoke kindly, paternally.

Septimus was wagging a finger towards the embassy. 'That man – Mister Nicholson? – he was saying also – why not?'

Monsieur Lagreze was hesitant. 'There is confusion,' he tried.

'Ah.' Septimus tapped the side of his nose and gave a conspiratorial, knowing wink. 'Yes, I shall take your sound advice and return immediately to the convent,' he all but shouted, following Monsieur Lagreze's gaze, though the sentry was out of earshot and was paying them no heed in any case. 'Why?' he whispered, further disguising his question with a cough.

Monsieur Lagreze lowered his voice too. 'Just believe me, *mon Père*. It would be most unwise for you to visit the palace just now.'

Septimus seemed to be enjoying the conspiracy. 'Oh. Right. The both of you cannot be wrong. Did you hear the clock strike?'

' – ?'

'Three times it struck – after some mechanical confusion, of course. Trying to strike up a conversation, perhaps? A friendly warning. Not unlike your own. Well-meaning. For my own good, of course. Bishop McKewen – you don't know him, I think – he was here the other day: in spirit, as they say – he was a great one for suggesting remedies for my own good. Ah, well. Dickery, dickery dock, the warning came out of the clock, the clock struck three – I wonder why they all found the number three to be so very significant. I mean, why not two – or four, for that matter? Come to think of it that particular number looms up again and again, does it not? Even for poor old Judas. He should have stuck out for forty – that would have put the cat among the pigeons!'

Monsieur Lagreze stared vacantly.

'Perhaps you don't agree,' Septimus concluded, taking the silence for rebuttal.

And it was during that silence that Septimus walked silently away, running his niblick slowly across the bars of the railings, counting the metallic resonances. And for a moment he was a child again, racing from the concreted playground of Belvedere College, his satchel on his back, a ruler (wooden but with a thin metal strip embedded in it) in his hand. He was running the ruler along the black railings that kept the tall house wherein the Jesuits dwelt from being burgled at the dead of night. He was hop-skipping down the road towards Finlater's Church, or, more correctly, towards the confectioner's shop on the corner to devour ice-cream, to buy Woodbines with money saved from bus-fares, explaining one's late arrival to an anxious mother as being due to an extra hour spent studying for a mythical examination or, better still, to a visit to the school chapel which always evoked forgiveness.

– Did you pray for Mammy?
– Of course.
– A big prayer for Mammy?
– A huge one.
– Ach, you're a darling.

So even then he had used God to swindle his way out of difficulty! Septimus became conscious of the extraordinary activity which everywhere suddenly surrounded him: as if in a trance he had made his way without incident, he hoped, to the palace and now stood opposite it. Between him and the shining edifice were, or so it looked, hundreds of Tontons Macoutes, armed to the teeth, holding back a good-tempered crowd, a crowd that was silent for the most part, a crowd that had come, it seemed, simply to stare. To stare at what was not discernible unless it was the jeep that had stopped within feet of Septimus and from which stepped the Colonel, his spruce, decorated uniform looking somewhat baggy and with great patches of dark perspiration under the arms and halfway down the back. But he was beaming broadly, which was a good thing possibly, as he came up to Septimus and embraced him in a ferocious hug. He stepped back, keeping one hand on Septimus's shoulder, and scowled at him banteringly. 'You come spy on *me*?' he bellowed, and followed this with a roar of laughter. Then, slipping the hand behind Septimus's neck and on to the other shoulder, he was guiding him across the road towards the gates of the palace, the Tontons Macoutes looking bemused as they passed, unsure whether they should salute or not but settling the matter by coming to a shuffling sort of attention.

Why the Colonel had taken Septimus with him was unclear. When they reached the gates he removed his hand and started to talk rapidly in a low voice to two men (one a civilian, the other in a white uniform that glittered even more with braid than his own, a couple of oversized medals dangling from his chest) who approached him with quick, nervous steps, rubbing their hands together but not from any satisfaction that one could detect. Then off he went ahead of them, back into the palace without a backward glance, leaving Septimus stranded, alone, wondering what on earth to do. By now he had forgotten why it was he had wanted to come to the palace in the first place. He tried to remember. He failed. But he decided to go in anyway. Or try; failing in this too as his way was blocked by a slim young guard with beautiful features and cruel eyes who placed himself in front of him, the rifle in his hands held lengthwise.

Septimus accepted the situation. He shrugged and smiled, and turned away. Confrontation was not his strong suit. Anyway, there was something he had to do – if only he could remember what it was. It would come to him, no doubt. Just as the curious sound of hissing came to him now. Most odd. He shook his head as though to dislodge the atmospheric interference in his brain, and started to push his way through the crowd. But the static grew louder. It was not in his brain. It was in his ear, both ears; everyone he passed was hissing. Then someone on his left pushed him, and someone on his right pushed him back. He was pushed from behind. He was pushed from the front. Someone was shouting. Several people were shouting. The hissing was fading. He was standing alone. He was not standing alone. He was surrounded by blue uniforms who were clearing a way for him, who were accompanying him along the clearway, who were escorting him to the edge of the crowd, who were urging him to 'Vas! Vas! Vas!' and *vas vite* into the bargain.

In his mind, thoughts coiling through it like serpents, he was standing outside the American Embassy again, as he had done some time ago, only it was not the American Embassy but the Hotel Ollofson, and he was out of breath again although that 'again' applied to yet another time, he knew, another race run; but he was always running from something, was he not? Yet he was not the only one: a chameleon ran up a tree (a eucalyptus that threatened to topple and crush the boundary wall of the hotel) and met a fellow chameleon running down; a smoke-coloured cat with a tail so long is brushed the ground raced from the gateway and darted up the road, a small bird dangling from its mouth; a leaf, mysteriously propelled since there was no wind, flew away from him, every so often lifting itself a little higher; a huge butterfly, its wings veined as the leaf had been, hurtled towards the wall, tried to vault it, made it, and vanished. Septimus felt better. Company, even in disgrace, was a comfort. Small comfort, but comfort nevertheless, and he was prepared to settle for that. He would settle for a mug of Sister Mary's coffee too. Just what the doctor ordered. Just what Bishop McKewen ordered. No – that was tea. Tea and Beatrix Potter. Poor little Peter Rabbit. Poor Peter! Cocknapped at the third stroke . . . at the third stroke it will be . . . *que sera sera* . . . or won't be. It won't be long, Father. Who said that? Septimus looked sharply about him. No one, and just when he was beginning to feel better.

'. . . better come with me and sit down.'

'Better not, you mean.'

'I've been watching you.'

'I spy with my little eye.'

'I thought you were about to faint.'

'Faint hope.'

It was only then that Septimus realized he was truly speaking to someone. 'Oh,' he said apologetically.

'Come, *mon Père*, allow me to buy you a drink,' Patrick coaxed.

Septimus hesitated.

'It is recommended.'

Well, if that was the case . . .

Patrick took him, not, as he had expected, to the hotel, but past the gates and further up the road to a run-down sidewalk café. Outside on the grass verge were two metal-topped tables, four plastic chairs set about each. Septimus sat down while Patrick went to get two beers, and it was while he was sitting there that he realized the change that had taken place in Patrick. Oddly, he seemed to have shrunk a little; his elegant clothes didn't quite fit as well as they might; there was a distinct gloominess about his expression; his shoes, while highly polished, looked as if they should have been down-at-heel, and somehow emphasized the man's despondency. Septimus made a mental note to enquire as to what could be the matter, but by the time Patrick arrived back at the table, carrying two cans of lukewarm beer, he had forgotten about it. They sipped their beers, Septimus awkwardly, Patrick considerably more deftly. Under other circumstances, in other guises, they could have been mourners recently returned from the graveside, their eyes sad as only the recently bereaved are sad.

Then Septimus was nodding desperately, removing his spectacles, remembering that he had eaten nothing for quite two days, although why this should suddenly become important was beyond him. 'Abstinence,' he said aloud. Patrick stared intently at him, his head cocked on one side. Not that Septimus noticed; without his spectacles he could see practically nothing, and certainly nothing very clearly, an incapacity, he had once remarked, that had distinct advantages from time to time. The sunlight dazzled him, misshaping everything, transforming even Patrick, with an uncanny sleight of vision, into an outline of someone kneeling, someone gazing upwards at something that fascinated and horrified, hands clasped, the face expressing the agony of others . . . Hastily he put on his spectacles again. No one had noticed. Patrick still gazed at him. The owner of the café had come from inside his mobile sweatbox and was contentedly urinating against one of the wheels, directing his jet on to the hubcap so that it sprayed ornamentally. An insect, striped orange and black as though wearing a knitted jumper, was hovering close by. He had got away with it. He reached out and lifted the can to his lips, gulping its contents, then set it back on the table again, set it back precisely on a ring made of some previous liquid.

– Always put things back exactly where you got them.

– Yes, Mammy.

– That way you'll always know where things are, won't you?

– Yes, Mammy.

– And you won't have to be rushing about looking, will you?

– No, Mammy.

– Come sit on my knee.

– Yes, Mammy.

– Now, you know when Baby Jesus made the world He put everything in the right place?

– Yes, Mammy.

– Well, that's what you have to do with your life, son. Put everything in the right place.

– How will I know?

– What the right place is? Oh, you'll know. You'll certainly know that. There'll be your own little special angel to tell you.

Well, if there was, the little devil had been off duty for longer

227

than Septimus cared to remember. He and Patrick exchanged a look of understanding, and with the look calamity moved closer.

A terrific detonation somewhere behind them in the city shook the café and sent birds skywards from all over the area.

'*Tiens*,' Patrick exclaimed with remarkable calm.

Two dogs, terrified by the din raced up the road, their tails between their legs, then turned and ran back again, bewildered, long tongues hanging.

'The bell that tolls,' Septimus said before he could stop himself.

'True,' Patrick said.

The echoes of the explosion swept back from the mountains, and sweeping back, too, came the birds, their flight erratic, seeking escape from this horrific cage of sound. And above them other flying creatures, four small military planes, like avenging angels, their wings almost touching as they zoomed dangerously low over the café, over the Ollofson, over the city.

' – annoyed with me,' Patrick was saying, sounding at the same time bemused and bitter.

'Indeed not,' Septimus replied, trusting to luck, Patrick's words catching him on the hop and signifying nothing. 'Why on earth should I be?' he added, since luck appeared, for once, to be on his side.

'Oh, not you, *mon Père*,' Patrick told him with a small, supercilious smile, '*L'Administration*,' he explained, sounding grim.

'Oh, dear,' was all that Septimus could muster. He was at somewhat of a loss as to what he was supposed to make of the information. He made a face, instantly decided it might give the wrong impression (although what the *right* impression might be never occurred to him) and changed it, making another, changing that too, but settling for a third: a grimace he seemed to recall getting him out of more than one tricky situation. Amazingly it seemed to work again.

'So what do I do?' Patrick asked.

Ah, so there was a catch! He had missed something. His brain, as it were, had missed a beat. Several beats by the sound of it. So what, then, was he supposed to tell Patrick to do? He wanted to raise his head and protest: Now hang on there just a minute my fine feathered friend, I cannot possibly be expected to advise you. I am as befuddled as you. I am a fool!

'Fools!'

Septimus lurched, knocking the leg of the table with his knee,

228

sending Patrick's can of beer tumbling to the ground. Patrick seemed unworried. He leaned forward, appearing almost grateful that a space had been cleared, and planted his elbows on the table. 'To dismiss me like that!' He snapped his fingers. 'As if I was an insect. Or some vermin.'

Septimus slowly began to catch on. 'You have been dismissed?'

'Like that.' Patrick resnapped his fingers. 'Like as if I had been of no service.'

'Oh, dear,' Septimus said, resorting to his stock phrase of sympathy. 'Oh dear me.'

'So what do I do?'

Septimus frowned and valiantly tried to think of some solution; it was, it turned out, a wasted effort. Patrick didn't really want to know. He had already made up his mind. 'I'll tell you what I will do, *mon Père*,' he confided.

'That's a relief,' said Septimus quietly.

'I am to return to Belladere, to where I was born,' Patrick continued, some of his pride returning, his voice expansive.

'They have ordered you to go back to – '

'No,' Patrick snapped. 'I am returning there of my own choice. I *wish* to be there. Back to the source, you see.'

'Yes, I see,' Septimus said, but clearly didn't.

'Good.'

'And who knows, perhaps it is for the best,' Septimus suggested resignedly, continuing, as he noticed Patrick about to disagree, 'Mind you, as a general rule that is, there always being the inevitable exception to everything, but as-as-as-as a general rule, or so they say – and they do know despite what the anti-theys may think – where was I? – oh yes – as a general rule they say things only happen to us because they are meant to happen, and that it is up to us to adapt each new situation to our own needs,' Septimus was saying; or thought he was saying; until he realized he was not saying it; he was thinking it which was much the same thing. In no way discouraged he continued, aware that he was off on a tangent, 'As in times of great tragedy, there is always another person who thinks for you. Some generous being. Unknown but at the same time familiar, who tidies up the appalling distortion in your brain, my brain. Puts everything away. Locks all the mental doors. Closes the windows. Draws the curtains. All save one. An escape hatch through which one can crawl back to sanity.'

And it was through some such hatch that Septimus was now crawling. It was most odd. He was on his hands and knees crawling, with Patrick bending over him.

'You are injured, *mon Père?*'

'Hmm? Oh, no.'

'You should be more careful. Give me your hand.'

'A hand in need is a handy deed.'

'You are sure you are not hurt?'

'Only my pride, the pride – teehee – that comes before the fall. Most apt, wouldn't you say?' Septimus was upright again, looking none the worse for his tumble, grinning broadly at his little witticism. 'What happened?'

'You tripped over that.' Patrick indicated the niblick.

'How silly of me. Tripped on my own petard. That doesn't sound right. Never mind. Where are we?'

'Here.' Patrick swept an arm over the area. 'I was walking you as far as the junction. You said you wanted to go home.'

'Home?'

'Back to your hospice, you said.'

'Home . . . how strange.'

'To the hospice,' Patrick repeated, watching Septimus closely as he swayed from side to side with his eyes closed.

'Ah, the hospice. Not a hospice any more, I'm afraid, my dear Patrick. No one comes there anymore, you know. Not since – it must be a terrible thing to die alone. I mean *really* alone, and feel that out there' – Septimus jabbed his niblick at the sky on which black clouds had now daubed their outline – 'that out there innumerable spirits, gods of every hue, are vying for your soul. Anyway, as I said, no one comes to the hospice now. Only Sister Mary and myself – and you, of course – you have been there? Yes, I remember. Only us. Oh, and Miss Lichfield, only she's in Miami, I understand. It's all my fault, of course.'

Wary, and reluctant to become involved in any mystifying obtuseness, Patrick cleared his throat, and said quickly, 'It would be my opinion that it would be better for you to return to the convent – go where you live, *mon Père.*'

Septimus gave him a puzzled look. 'Where does anyone live? In communicado. In cognito. In esse. In finity. In hell?'

Patrick was holding out his hand. 'I must leave you.'

'You too?'

'– ?'

'Just thinking. First that dear lady. Now you. Leaving me.'

'It is so meant. As is known we must adapt.'

'I said that a moment ago.' Septimus laughed. 'No, I thought it. Sorry. And perhaps you're right.'

Patrick was shaking him by the hand. 'I will have you in my mind, *mon Père*.'

'Ah,' Septimus sighed.

'I will, in a sense, be with you.'

'Ah,' said Septimus again.

'You will not be alone.'

But he was certainly alone now. He was standing at the junction. He was making his way gingerly towards the hospice. He was feeling a little cowed, a little anxious. But there was more to it than that, he knew. Much, much more. He was making his way towards something that defied control; something that had been foretold but which had slipped his mind; something that, now he was becoming more aware of it, terrified him. It was not a place towards which he journeyed, although he could only think of it in those terms, if only to stabilize his whirring brain. It was as though he could feel his sanity finally slipping away from him, but they were parting on friendly enough terms, which was civilized.

Black clouds crashed against each other and thunder growled as he made his way down the narrow street. It was, inexplicably, very crowded, and already growing dark; which was infinitely more perturbing since but a moment ago, three strides ago, it had been bright and clear. There seemed to be a pall of smoke, but perhaps it wasn't smoke, perhaps it was – he couldn't think what else it might be. Fairy lights strung along one side of the street shed miniature rays of coloured brightness into the gloom; many of the lights were missing, leaving dark gaps. Then he was being jostled; he was almost being knocked down; he was being helped upright again. A large man on a large chestnut horse passed close to him, and he could smell the sweat on the horse's flanks: Goethe's horse, no doubt, being ridden to death for its pains. Someone shouted, possibly at him. Everything was getting very chaotic. People pressed up close to him and peered into his face, people he almost recognized, people who moved away again with looks of stern disapproval. A group of dancers encircled him, dressed in long cloaks on which the signs of the zodiac had been sprayed in luminous paint, flapping their cloaks like the wings of gigantic scavenging birds. He was transfixed within the circle. Like dervishes they whirred about him, tossing their heads. The hood slipped from one and it was Bishop Matthew McKewen, no less, who was uncovered, and came forward, warning him to mind his step, and with that warning vanished. Then they had all vanished, and Archbishop Gidron (how well he looked! Fit as a fiddle or almost) was sturdily manipulating his wheelchair through the throng. 'It is how you perceive yourself and all that you deem important,' he shouted, laughed, and was swallowed up in the crowd. Or in a puff of smoke. There *was* smoke hanging low over the street. Septimus felt his eyes start to water, his throat go dry. And in the distance, not too far distant, there was the jaundiced flickering of fire, was there not? He couldn't be positive. It was so difficult to be positive with the curious crackling noise that sounded in his head, like gunfire from far away. It ran through his mind that all this had happened before, so perhaps he wasn't quite as mad as some supposed. Perhaps he was asleep.

Just as he was becoming accustomed to that idea a cry went up. Everyone seemed to be running away from him (past him, bumping into him, shoving him out of the way, striking out at him, but away from him nevertheless). This was certainly no dream.

'*Il va partir!*' a man's voice yelled, or something that sounded like that.

'*Il va partir,*' another voice screamed.

'*À l'aéroport,*' someone else shouted.

That too was taken up. '*À l'aéroport.*'

It became a chant. A war cry. '*À l'aé-ro-port. À l'aé-ro-port.*' Feet thudded to the rhythm, the original pell-mell running subsiding to an organised trot with Zulu undertones. Soon, however, it was fading, drifting away. Suddenly Septimus found himself totally alone. The street, still shrouded in smoke, stretched emptily before him, except – except that someone was now walking towards him, calling his name in a high-pitched, choking voice, futilely trying to wave the smoke from in front of both of them. 'Father . . . Father . . . Father,' the voice called.

'Gracious me, Sister Mary. You look – '

'They've burned the hospice.'

' – as though you've been . . . burned the hospice?'

'I tried to stop them,' Sister Mary wailed. 'I tried to stop them.

But they held me. They wouldn't even let me save the medicines, or the – '

But Septimus was no longer listening. He was walking towards the hospice. He was standing in the midst of the charred ruins. He was sobbing uncontrollably. He was looking about him. He was shaking. He was kneeling. He was holding the scorched figure of Christ in his arms, rocking it. He was comforting Christ as he had so often prayed that Christ might comfort him. He was saying crazy things like 'don't worry' and 'it's not the end of the world' and 'these things are sent to try us'.

'Why Father? Why would anyone *do* such a thing?' Sister Mary wanted to know, calling her question from the street.

Septimus heard and shook his head.

'It's so cruel,' Sister Mary decided.

'I'm sure they didn't think of it so.'

'All we ever did was try to help them.'

'I know. I know,' Septimus offered in comfort. 'But perhaps in helping we offended.'

'We cared for their sick and their dying,' Sister Mary insisted, possibly to defend herself against the vaguely insinuated offence.

'Yes,' Septimus agreed.

'So why?'

Septimus had no answer to that; none that he could forward at any rate. In an odd way he had not been surprised when she had told him of the arson. For some reason it seemed to fit: into *what* it fitted was still a puzzlement, a puzzlement that lined both their faces as they stood side by side in the debris, listening to the chanting mob who by now were far away, their voices severed and clipped like echoes, listening too to the raucous cry of the bizarre nightbirds that swarmed in from the sea each evening: small birds, ugly and menacing, something like jays, something like starlings, those harbingers of death; cowardly.

Septimus took the nun's hand and patted it affectionately. 'You trot along back to the convent,' he told her kindly.

'And you?'

'I'll just stay a little while. Just a little while – then I'll be there too.'

He stayed all night, keeping a solitary, pathetic vigil. He knew he was in mourning, but for what he had no idea exactly. Yet he felt strangely at peace, or enchanted, as once he had felt enchanted and at peace in an innocent friendship with Christ. He sat on the still warm ashes and fondled the image beside him. It struck him that perhaps there was something significant in the fact that the two of them were sharing this mournful night. Once he spoke aloud: 'If I am to survive I need your help,' but to whom he addressed this plea was a mystery even to himself, and at the moment he spoke, as though by some diabolic providence, his words were drowned by the roaring of aircraft flying low overhead in ragged formation, their lights blinking like bloodied stars.

Septimus lowered himself to the floor, toppling, and lay down beside Christ, gazing skywards. How clear it had suddenly become, all threat of the storm now gone. How bright the stars. And how close. How terribly, infernally close. He reached up as though to pluck one. Then a shadow of immense fatigue crashed on to him. He stole fretfully into sleep.

Twelve

'What in God's name is keeping them?'

Oscar's irritable question, lobbed across the darkened tarmac of the François Duvalier International Airport at no one in particular, was fielded by Gilles Lagreze. 'Nothing, I think, in God's name,' he replied with a dark, admonishing smile.

'They should have been here hours ago.'

'A few hours will seem little to our President as he faces a future without power.'

'It's after two, dammit.'

Monsieur Lagreze shrugged.

'Don't tell me he's changed his mind again?'

'Oh, no. He will be here. He is . . .' Monsieur Lagreze paused and turned away, staring back into the distance.

'He's *what*, Gilles?'

'When I was last with him he was saying goodbye to his closest friends.'

'What time was that?'

'About midnight.'

'Christ, it can't take him *that* long to say goodbye. He can't have *that* many friends,' Oscar decided sarcastically.

'It is a relative world,' Monsieur Lagreze pointed out.

'I bet.'

'There will be many who feel they are being left – well, unprotected.'

'Ha.'

Monsieur Lagreze turned back to face Oscar. 'Old habits die hard,' he smiled, making of the words both a cunning apology and mild accusation.

The time seemed to pass incredibly slowly, probably due to the unnatural quiet. All civilian planes had been grounded, incoming flights cancelled. Only military aircraft were allowed to take off and land. The small knot of American diplomats and lesser Haitian dignitaries waiting on the lightless tarmac grew increasingly edgy. Many of them paced up and down, glancing frequently at their wristwatches. Oscar stamped his feet as though feeling cold despite the humidity. At least, he thought, he had been spared the presence of the Ambassador. Not that he had not wanted to come. He certainly had. Had been looking forward to it no end. Oscar managed a malicious chuckle to himself as he recalled the Ambassador's face when he had been told not to attend the departure.

– Dammit all, Nicholson, I *want* to be there. Why shouldn't I be there? I'm Ambassador, godammit.

Oscar felt like telling him that Washington didn't want him to be there in case he made a fool of himself. Well, *sir*, he said instead, it's *because* of your position that Washington thought it would be better if you did not attend. They feel it wouldn't be proper for you to be seen affording any honour to an ex-President.

– Oh, that's the reason?

– Of course.

The Ambassador preened himself. Yes, he allowed, I can see how that might be misinterpreted.

– Exactly.

– Pity though. I'd like to have been there to see the bastard off.

– I'm sure you would, Mr Ambassador.

And Oscar, still stamping his feet, would willingly at that moment have exchanged places with the Ambassador. 'Well, Gilles,' he said. 'I'm not hanging about here like this. Let's go and see if we can at least get a drink.'

Monsieur Lagreze glanced towards the others.

Oscar winked. 'Just you and me, Gilles. It's time *they* earned their keep.'

The departure lounge was, of course, deserted and gloomy. The head waiter, an elderly man with pointed, angular features, welcomed them with obsequious suspicion, betrayed by his fumbling courtesy. As he led them to a table there was a curiously effeminate lilt to his gait; he was heavily perfumed and impeccably turned out in black trousers and a scarlet jacket with brass buttons cut to remind Oscar of hunting pink.

'Bourbon,' Oscar said, preoccupied, not following the waiter but making for a table that overlooked the runway. 'We can keep an eye on the activity from here,' he told Gilles.

Monsieur Lagreze nodded and sat down opposite him. '*Un demi*,' he ordered, then corrected himself. '*Non. Un soda.*' Oscar raised his eyebrows. 'To keep the brain clear.'

'I've never known yours to be otherwise.'

'That is because you do not truly know me.'

'I thought I did.'

'Better than most, perhaps.'

The major domo strutted out through the doorless doorway (the aperture screened by alternate lengths of bamboo cane and multi-coloured beads, making of it the sort of entrance one might expect in some rather demoralizing dancehall).

Oscar hesitated: 'What difference is this' – he looked towards the runway – 'going to make to you, Gilles?' he asked seriously, clearly genuinely concerned.

Monsieur Lagreze beamed. 'It is not a great worry. To me it will make little difference – for the while at any rate. Namphy, who is to take over, is – shall I say? – an old friend of mine.'

'Ah.'

'Indeed.'

'You're a cunning bastard.'

'Careful, Oscar. Just careful. Of course much will depend on for how long Henri can actually maintain his power. He could, you see, be overthrown in the twinkling of an eye. And then . . .'

'And then?'

Monsieur Lagreze beamed again. 'Well . . . by then I will have to be sure that the new incumbent is also an old friend of mine.'

Oscar laughed, cutting short his laughter almost immediately to ask, 'Jesus, what's keeping them?' Whether this applied to the drinks or the presidential entourage was unclear.

'And you?' Monsieur Lagreze enquired. 'What difference will it make to you?'

'No more than usual. When things quieten down I'll probably be shifted to some other godforsaken spot. Chad, or Ethiopia, or Beirut, God knows. I can tell you one thing: if I am shifted I'll miss you, Gilles.'

'And I you, my friend. But – ' Monsieur Lagreze stopped talking and leaned back as the drinks were placed on the table before them (little paper doilies first, a bowl of nuts, a bowl of olives: *très exacte*), and produced a cigarette. Instantly the waiter had a flaming match cupped in his hands and offered it to him. He sucked on the cigarette, letting the smoke seep slowly from his wide nostrils, before concluding, ' . . . but it has not come to that yet.'

'No. Not yet.'

'And much can happen.'

Oscar grimaced. 'You can say that again!' Then he frowned as though he had just caught sound of something, or become aware of some underlying gist. 'You said that as though – ' He shook his head. 'Forget it.' He took a long drink.

'As though?' Monsieur Lagreze insisted, holding his cigarette upright in two fingers, jabbing the air as if trying to create smoke-rings.

'As though nothing. It's this waiting. It's getting on my bloody nerves.'

'Of course. But there is something else, no?'

'Where *are* they?' Oscar was on his feet, blinkering his eyes with both hands and peering out of the plate-glass window. Beyond the airport, between it and the city, any number of small fires had been lit. Oscar fancied he could see figures dancing round them but, he conceded, it was probably his imagination. He thought he heard a crowd roar, but when he listened intently he could hear nothing, nothing but Gilles Lagreze who had swallowed some smoke and was now coughing vigorously. To his right there was a sudden blinding flash, followed almost immediately by two more, all of which he knew should have heralded explosions but he could not hear these either.

'Something else?' he asked, as though the question had only now penetrated his brain.

Monsieur Lagreze, recovered, spread his hands. '*La femme*,' he said, purposely making the words sound theatrical.

'Oh. Susanna, you mean. That, as they say, is over and done with, I'm afraid. It was over years ago really. I just didn't admit it. Actually, between you and me, that's what I found so hard to take. Admitting it – finally. It was so – what's the word? – so reassuring, I suppose, to think or believe that I was in love all those years when really I was just covering up a loneliness. Ever been in love, Gilles?'

Monsieur Lagreze shook his head.

'Well, keep it that way. It's a killer.'

'Perhaps you expected too much.'

'Perhaps.'

'Or demanded too much?'

'Who knows.' Oscar came back to the table. 'Who bloody well cares? Jesus, I'd love to get roaring, stinking drunk.' He emptied his glass. 'I'm going to have one more anyway.' He raised a finger to summon the waiter. 'You?'

Monsieur Lagreze eyed his soda balefully. 'I think perhaps not. Later I will have a little wine – with you, maybe?'

'It's a date . . . Oh, another bourbon. Thanks . . . At least it was me who convinced her to go back to New York.'

'Yes. She told me.'

Oscar smiled at the tone of Monsieur Lagreze's voice. 'Oh, she did, did she?'

'Yes.'

'And she asked you if you thought she should go?'

Monsieur Lagreze smiled and nodded.

'And you said?'

'I said if it was me I would go immediately.'

'Ah.'

'But she would have stayed if you had wanted her to.'

'I know.' Oscar sounded suddenly sad. 'But there was no point. Besides, she could have been in danger.'

A telephone jangled behind the bar making them both jump; it stopped ringing before anyone had time to answer it.

'I *was* right, wasn't I, to tell her to leave?'

Monsieur Lagreze frowned. 'How can *I* say?'

'But you told her – '

'I told her only what she wanted to hear.'

The door of the lounge was thrown open and a worried-looking man, clearly American, clean cut and smacking of an advertisement for Old Spice, stuck his head round the jamb. He looked across at the two men, seemed relieved, and said, 'Just checking before the fun starts,' and left, leaving the door to heave itself to on its compression hinges.

'Will there *be* much trouble, Gilles?'

'Much fun?' Monsieur Lagreze parried with a smile before answering seriously, 'I imagine there will. Freedom breeds its own special sort of mayhem, does it not? Those who have been held in bondage feel that need to prove that they are truly free, or to prove what they believe is true freedom, by destroying what they believe has been responsible for their lack of it.' Monsieur Lagreze finished his soda. 'So the politicians get murdered. The rich get murdered. The servants of the politicians and the rich get murdered. But then – then, you see, there is no one left who can justifiably be murdered. Only, alas, the taste for murder has been acquired. They cease to be selective. Old family quarrels are settled in the name of freedom. Lovers are killed for being unfaithful; a man who overcharged a pittance for some vegetable, a woman who slighted another's husband, a bus driver who refused to stop – all these are killed in the euphoria of freedom.' Monsieur Lagreze emitted a huge sigh.

'You, personally, Gilles – are you – ?'

Monsieur Lagreze stopped him with another shrug. 'Perhaps, but I do not believe so.'

'I hope you're right.'

'You would be sorry?'

'Of course I'd be sorry.'

'Well, if anything should happen I will die happy in knowing that one person at least will regret my demise.'

'Don't be so – shit, Gilles, they're here!'

. . . It was three thirty when the headlights of the cavalcade pierced the darkness. The gleaming silver BMW with the ousted President at the wheel stopped by the plane just as Oscar and Monsieur Lagreze (the former out of breath but Gilles remarkably unflurried) reached the boarding steps. Beside the President sat his dazzling wife, Michèle; in the car behind were his mother and four children; in other cars seventeen more people, making up the appropriate entourage for an ex-President for Life.

Monsieur Lagreze looked strangely puzzled. What should have been momentous or, at the very least, moving, was neither of these things. History, it seemed, was being made with the minimum of fuss, which, the thought struck him, is, in fact, how all great history *is* made. He watched Duvalier move towards the military aircraft, stopping to bestow a few words of thanks on the row of neat khaki-clad guards who had protected him in the final months of his presidency. Two grim-faced men, the taller in uniform, the other in expensive, well-cut civilian clothes, members of the five-man junta in whom the abdicating president had entrusted the leadership and welfare of Haiti, observed the departure without emotion;

Duvalier passed them without a glance. He reached the steps and hesitated, looking back towards Port-au-Prince as all exiles must surely look back, taking that final impression of the place they thought they loved away with them. For a moment he looked despondent; then he spotted Monsieur Lagreze and brightened a little, a flicker of an apologetic smile in his eyes. He gave the impression he was about to go to him, longed to go to him, but changed his mind. Instead he gave Monsieur Lagreze a long, penetrating stare, a stare filled with an emotion he expected his old friend to appreciate. He raised one hand in a gesture part farewell, part benediction, part absolution, furtive tears welling up in his eyes. Then, abruptly, he mounted the steps and disappeared into the plane.

At three forty-six the Starlifter took off; watching it, Monsieur Lagreze half expected to see it circle the city, but it did no such thing. It flew thunderously away, a dull-green monster merging with the dark-blue hues of dawn, and the poignant moment was over.

'Well,' Oscar was saying, rubbing his hands together more to warm them than from glee, 'that's that.'

'Yes,' Monsieur Lagreze said sadly.

'All over bar the shouting.'

'As you say.'

'Let's get the hell out of here.'

Together they moved away, Monsieur Lagreze instinctively linking his arm through Oscar's. 'Monsieur Lagreze!' someone called. They stopped and looked round. 'Ah,' Monsieur Lagreze said. 'Pardon me one small moment, will you?'

Oscar watched his friend make his way back towards the two men Duvalier had so pointedly ignored. He saw him shake hands with the one in uniform, giving the other a cold, polite bow. He saw them talk, nodding in agreement; only once did Monsieur Lagreze shake his head in dissent. He saw a uniformed arm being thrown about Monsieur Lagreze's shoulder; and he watched, somewhat amazed, but more amused, as Monsieur Lagreze was suddenly embraced and kissed on both cheeks.

'That was all very friendly,' Oscar remarked later as they made their way towards their parked cars.

Monsieur Lagreze chuckled but said nothing.

'Nothing like a kiss to seal a truce,' Oscar persisted.

There was a bitter edge to Monsieur Lagreze's response. 'There are, as you know, my friend, kisses and kisses.'

'Oh. One of those.'

'One of those.'

'Still, better than a slap in the face, eh?'

'Many kisses *are* a slap in the face.'

'Oh. I'm sorry, Gilles.'

Monsieur Lagreze gave a tired little laugh. 'No, it wasn't like that. Not quite. I was – how do you say? – being buttered?'

'Ah.'

'My advice was requested.'

'Oh-ho!'

'And, of course, rejected. But that was to be expected. They were, you see, just making the required gesture. Very important that – especially here in Haiti – the gesture. Just in case, you understand,' he added mischievously, cocking his head. 'Poor Henri – '

'You make it sound as though you don't expect him to last all that long.'

'I never expect anyone to last all that long.'

'The Duvaliers did.'

'They were somewhat different. I think it will be a little more difficult for Henri. He has made the bad mistake of having his closest friend, Prosper Avril, seconded to the junta. Alas, dear Prosper is not a man to play the second fiddle for very long, I fear. A year at most, I think.'

'But you said he was Namphy's friend.'

Monsieur Lagreze smiled bitterly. 'That is exactly what I said. Yes.'

Their cars were parked side by side and they stood between them, Oscar resting an arm on the roof of his, Monsieur Lagreze searching in his pocket for his keys. Finding them he opened the door. 'That glass of wine – ?'

Oscar hesitated. 'I should get back to the embassy.'

'Ah, of course.'

'The Ambassador will want a full report.'

'But yes.'

'And he'll be expecting *me* to tell him.'

'Naturally.'

'Oh, hell. A few hours won't make any difference.'

'You are sure? I would not like to be responsible should you be admonished.'

Oscar hooted with laughter. 'I won't be admonished, Gilles. And even if I am I think I know how to handle our Ambassador.'

'Oh, of that I am certain.'

'Come on, let's have that wine.'

'Very well . . . we will, I think, take my car.'

'Right. Yes. I'll get someone – ' Oscar looked about him. 'I'll ask Jarrow,' he decided. 'Jarrow!' he called, and moved off to meet the man who had 'just been checking' the lounge while waiting for the fun to start, returning almost immediately. 'That's settled. Jarrow will take my car back to the embassy. Also,' he added after a slight pause, 'he will tell the Ambassador should he ask for me that I'm still out here sniffing around.''

'Excellent.'

'But that means you'll have to drive me back, Gilles.'

'It was my intention.'

'Thanks.'

. . . Sitting there in the great, high, lavishly furnished room, sipping a superb vintage from shimmering crystal, Oscar let the wine roll around his tongue before swallowing. 'God, that's good, Gilles.'

Monsieur Lagreze smiled his appreciation. 'A little special, yes?'

'Nectar.'

'Hardly that. But a *little* special.'

'Can you tell me what Namphy had to say?' Oscar asked, some time later. They had consumed one bottle and Monsieur Lagreze was in the process of opening another. His back was to Oscar, his body crouched as he carefully extracted the cork, trying not to shake the bottle that was viced between his legs. He sniffed the cork with a sigh of approval and refilled both their glasses before answering. He had reseated himself in a high-backed, winged armchair and crossed his legs (carefully shifting the crease in his trousers to one side) when he finally spoke. 'Only that he would appreciate my – my co-operating, as he said.'

'And will you?'

Monsieur Lagreze smiled benignly. 'I will not be unco-operating. I am, as you know, never unco-operating. Although I cannot see that anything I may or may not do could be significant. I did tell him I thought he was in error to impose an immediate curfew.'

'Oh, there's to be a curfew?'

'Yes. From this afternoon.'

'Well, that's par for the course, isn't it. What makes you think it's such a mistake, Gilles?'

'Because no one will obey it! So he is setting off his reign – if I may use that word – with instant civil disobedience, and from there, well . . .' He lapsed into meditative silence.

'Did you explain to him why you thought it was wrong?'

Monsieur Lagreze gave him a mildly horrified look. 'I did not think it was – eh – politic to elaborate on my view.'

Oscar grinned. 'No. I get your point.'

'It would be galling, don't you think, to have your first decision described as stupid?'

'I imagine it would. So you let it go?'

'I just frowned and hummed a little, and left it at that.'

'And that was all?'

'Almost.'

Oscar waited.

'It was most unexpected.'

Oscar continued to wait.

'He – and I will admit it came as something of a surprise to learn that Henri even knew of him – he expressed a concern for Father Septimus.'

Whether it was the pale blue dawn, looking unusually icy through the huge window, or whether it was the mention of the priest, Oscar shuddered. He placed his glass on the table by his side and stood up, hesitated, then walked to the window. A formation of birds flew across the skyline, long-necked creatures, swans or geese, he supposed, graceful as spirits. The sea below them, below the window, was calm, mirroring their flight. A fleet of small fishing smacks moved silently over it, the accompanying thudding of their diesel engines inaudible to him, making them oddly sinister as though they were up to no good, burying bodies at sea perhaps, or ferrying their souls to another world. Sea of Tranquillity, he thought. Or Sea of Darkness.

' – in the dark,' Monsieur Lagreze was saying.

'I'm sorry, Gilles?'

'Rien. Rien du tout. I was just musing, thinking that the priest was not someone who could be kept in the dark.'

'I still don't see – '

'Why *should* I have been surprised? Everyone on Haiti knows of the famous Father Septimus.'

'Oh. Yes. I see,' Oscar said, sounding as if he didn't.

'It's not as if his coming here was an accident.'

Oscar was becoming more confused; there was something in his friend's quiet pronouncement that seemed to be shouting at him, a presence that took on a life separate from the mere words. Monsieur Lagreze, meanwhile, had continued to talk. 'I'm sorry, Gilles,' Oscar apologized again. 'I wasn't listening.'

'It was not important.'

'I'm sure it was. What – yes, just half a glass.'

'It would seem fanciful,' Monsieur Lagreze said, giving Oscar half a glass of wine and filling his own. 'You might think it is – hah – *le vin qui parle*. But you would be wrong, you know. Quite, quite wrong.'

Oscar, with one final longing gaze at the sea (the birds, the boats gone) returned to his chair. 'I don't know what to think until I know what you're talking about,' he said.

'About the thing you have dismissed so easily in the past, my friend. About destiny and fate.'

'Oh God.' Oscar groaned and stretched. 'Not again, Gilles. Not tonight at any rate. I tell you what: give it a week for things to settle down and then we'll have an all-night debate about destiny and fate, all right, eh?'

'I will win, you know.'

'Maybe.'

'But for certain. I will, you see, by that time have the proof.'

'Proof of what for God's sake? I'm beginning to believe you *are* half drunk.'

But it was Monsieur Lagreze's turn not to listen: not to Oscar at any rate. Yet he did seem to be attempting to hear something, his head on one side, his eyes staring but unseeing, his body motionless. It was as though whatever motivated his great frame had taken off, abandoned him, for the time being at least, to seek – peace? knowledge? redemption? – in another place, a place excluded to the body, a place peopled by souls. And in a sense this was true. For Monsieur Lagreze was no longer sitting comfortably in his winged armchair sipping wine. He was again with his nurse, standing before the great houngain, watching that indiscernible spectre walk towards him, trying desperately to put a name to the grey and lined and infinitely sad face.

'It was him!' Monsieur Lagreze heard himself shout in a hoarse whisper.

Fortunately at that exact moment Oscar had decided to speak: ' . . . telephone Susanna?' Monsieur Lagreze registered, covering his discomfort by nodding vaguely and reaching for his wine.

'Thanks. Where is it – the phone?'

'Oh. Ah. There is one in my study – just across the hall.'

. . . Strangely enough, although the ghostly vision had made an indelible impression on his mind, on their first encounter, when he had toppled the priest from his ridiculous bicycle, Monsieur Lagreze had not immediately recognized him as the forlorn spirit of his childhood; nor, indeed, later, when he had been harassed by the priest for funds for his wretched hospice, had he equated the two. It was only when he had caught the whiff of the curious stories circulating, when he had noticed the strange, tense elation among the houngains, that he had recalled fully the features he had seen and matched them to Septimus Roach. Yet even then he was sure he was making a ludicrous mistake: how on earth, by what possible stretch of the imagination, could this absurd priest be the one for whom everyone waited?

'She sends her love.' Oscar told him, bouncing back into the room.

'How kind.'

'She had a dreadful flight.'

'Oh dear.'

'Anyway, she's safe and sound.'

'Yes. Good.'

'And glad now to be away.'

'Understandable.'

'Hmm.'

From his tone one might have suspected that all had been well on the telephone. It hadn't. To begin with Solomon had answered from Susanna's New York apartment, and Oscar had willingly detected a certain smugness in his tones. And Solomon had played a wicked little game with him, toying with him, saying Susanna was lying down and could he, perhaps, call back at a more convenient time? He would hardly expect him, Solomon, to disturb Susanna now, would he? Yes, he damn well would.

– Hi, Oscar, Susanna's voice, tinkling like a bell, making it clear that she had been in on the game, came down the line.

– Hi, yourself. I'm sorry to disturb you.

– You didn't. Solly was acting the fool.

– Oh. How are you?'

– Recovering from the flight. It was dreadful.

– I'm sorry.

– It wasn't *your* fault.

– No. Still . . .

– How are you?

– A bit tired.

– We heard on the television that Duvalier left.

– Yep. He's gone.

– That must be a relief.

– It is.

– And Gilles, how's he?

– Oh, fine. I'm with him now. Phoning from his house.

– Give him my love.

– Sure.

Then there was silence, almost as if the line had broken down.

– Hello? Susanna?

– Yes, I'm here.

– Oh, I thought we'd been cut off.

– No.

– Yes we have, Oscar wanted to shout.

– Oscar?

– Yes?

– Will you please do something for me?

– Of course, if I can.

– Will you check and make sure Father Septimus is all right?

– If you want, but I'm sure he is. Why?

Susanna gave a small, nervous laugh. I don't know. A feeling.

– You and your feelings. Sure I'll check. Don't worry.

– Thank you, darling.

And then the telephone link was cut: poltergeists gibbered down the line.

'She also asked me to check on old Septimus,' Oscar told Monsieur Lagreze. 'Some *feeling* she had,' he added, half expecting, half hoping his friend would scoff at the idea.

But he didn't. Monsieur Lagreze looked distinctly worried. 'Did she explain?'

'What?'

'The nature of the feeling?'

'No. Of course not. It was just a silly feeling, that's all.'

'I wonder.'

'Oh, for God's sake don't start again, Gilles. I couldn't stand any more mysteriousness tonight.'

'No. I do apologize.' He administered the apology reasonably. 'Just the same . . . would you mind terribly if we did, as Susanna requested, check that the priest is well?'

'If you want,' Oscar said resignedly.

'Just to be on the safe – ' He stopped as the telephone rang.

Oscar, his mood turning sour, watched Monsieur Lagreze leave the room. Damn the bloody priest. More to the point, damn Solomon Gross! He would have damned Susanna too had his mind not demurred. It struck him that it was, in fact, he who was damned, and he was about to elaborate on that promising theme when Monsieur Lagreze hurried back into the room, looking alarmed. 'There has been trouble, I fear.'

'Oh Jesus. Already?'

'A nun has been found murdered, and they have burned the priest's hospice.'

'Oh shit! Sorry, Gilles. And Septimus?'

'We do not know. He hasn't been seen since midday, or sometime in the afternoon. He was noticed drinking beer in a café near the Ollofson.'

'Drinking beer?' It sounded so inappropriate.

Monsieur Lagreze nodded abstractedly. 'With someone.'

'Who?'

'We do not know.'

Something about Monsieur Lagreze's tone made Oscar regard him intently. 'Gilles, what is it? What's going on that I don't know about?' Oscar asked quietly.

'First we must find the priest. You will come with me? It is not the time for explanations.'

'Of course I'll come with you.'

'We will go to the hospice first, I think.'

'Whatever you say, Gilles.'

At first it seemed as though the drive into the city might prove uneventful. Between Monsieur Lagreze's home and Port-au-Prince one would have been forgiven for believing it to be just another day, a day when people went about their business. True those people who did pass seemed to be in a hurry, mostly running, and all headed for the city centre. It was only when Monsieur Lagreze swung his car left-handed on to the Carrefour that the extent of the chaos was revealed. Tens of thousands of people were out on the street, chanting jubilantly. 'He flew away! He flew away!' they screamed, waving flags of red and blue, the colours of Haiti's flag before Papa Doc had replaced it; waving the Stars and Stripes too, and calling, inexplicably, *'Vive l'Amérique!'*

'Christ,' Oscar swore. 'We'll never get through that lot.'

'I think not.'

'It looks like the rest of the way on foot.'

'I'm afraid it does. You are unafraid?'

'Damn right I'm unafraid.'

'There is a road which would circumvent this.'

'Well, come on then. I thought *you* were in a mad hurry to get to the priest, Gilles?'

'Preferably in safety.'

'We'll be safe.'

Monsieur Lagreze turned the car into a side street, and together they set off on foot like thieves, clambering over the piles of litter, the crates, the cardboard boxes, even a dozing cat, that obstructed their way. Somewhere a woman's voice called *'Aidez-moi, aidez-moi'*; somewhere else, unbelievably, a guitar twanged out the tune of 'Layla'. Down September 22nd Street they trotted, Monsieur Lagreze stumbling and almost falling on the rubble strewn about the tin-roofed house, now ablaze, where Papa Doc once lived. Then, turning right, moving parallel to the Carrefour, passing other buildings that burned furiously (only one of which Oscar recognized, a property owned by the departed President's father-in-law, who had used his government connections to make millions in imported automobiles) they brushed past small groups of men who seemed to want no more than to pat them on the back, to thank them, to dance with them, to share their joyous moment with them.

At last, breathless, their sides heaving, they reached the Cité Brooklyn, and made for the narrow street where the hospice was situated. They were still some twenty yards from it when Monsieur

Lagreze grabbed Oscar by the wrist and restrained him. 'We are too late,' he said. With an almost imperceptible gesture he invited Oscar to follow his gaze.

Ranged across the street, not exactly lined up but clearly blocking any entrance, were some eight men. At first glance they could have been thought to be merely loitering; it gradually dawned on him that there was something sinister about their presence. It was as though they had no need physically to block the way, the aura of menace they exuded did that. 'Who are they?' Oscar asked, surprised to find himself whispering.

'Houngains Macoutes,' Monsieur Lagreze replied.

For some perverse reason this irritated Oscar: in his mind he equated them with such pooh-poohable figments as ghosts, the devil, the good fairy, even Santa Claus. 'So?' he demanded.

'So we cannot pass them.'

'Oh for God's sake, Gilles, come *on*.' He made as if to walk forward.

'We cannot.'

'Well *I* bloody can!'

Before Monsieur Lagreze could stop him (although, surprisingly, perhaps, he made no attempt so to do) Oscar was advancing steadily towards the assembled houngains, putting on a brave face. No bloody witch-doctors were going to stand in *his* way. Certainly not. The houngains barely regarded him, allowing him to come within a few feet of them. Then Oscar felt someone tap him firmly on the shoulder. He spun round. There was no one there. The houngains were still several feet to his front, Monsieur Lagreze the same distance behind him looking both frightened and powerless. Oscar faced the houngains again. They seemed to be smiling at him, and there was a gloating in their smiles. Again Oscar tried to make his way closer to the houngains; again a hand was placed on his shoulder, this time definitely restraining him. He felt suddenly afraid. All his bravado drained from him. He was consumed by a terrible premonition. A tiny voice, faint, too faint to be recognizable, called, 'Help me, help me!' Then, as though someone had struck him over the head, he felt his knees buckle. He fell in a heap on the ground. Looking up he could see that, still, there was no one near him. He tried to call out, the words echoed in his brain but they made no sound. He tried to get up, but he could not move. A great sleepiness came over him. 'Help me, help me,' the voice called again, but fainter now. Blackness enveloped him. Now everything was fading from his vision. For a terrible second he thought he was dying; then he collapsed into unconsciousness.

Thirteen

'It is time,' said Septimus Roach.

He had crashed into sleep and now, waking with an effort, unaware that it was the aircraft of the Duvaliers departing that had aroused him, he observed the face of Christ glaring at him with stern foreboding. He pushed himself up on to one elbow and bravely glared back at the wooden image with which he had slept, holding it in his arms.

The roof gone, the hospice was open to a clear dawn sky; there in the ashes it could have been, he thought, that he was lying in a sepulchre, feeling peaceful enough, the great and awful weight of living lifted from him. Yet a sepulchre should be silent, and this place certainly wasn't. It was filled and humming with sound: scorched timbers creaked, two sheets of twisted corrugated iron screamed against each other, his heart thundered. Farther away, yet seeming to come from beneath him, there was another sound, one that came in waves, an organized, methodical chanting, lapping and receding, occasional words, like stranded shells, discernible. But one voice predominated, soaring over all the others; a woman's, filled with grief, begging to be helped. For one small moment Septimus thought he recognized it; he was on the point of energetically putting a face to it when deliberately, maliciously, his brain obliterated all thought of it. He lurched to his feet, tottered and fell back again, and the more immediate voices fell silent.

He groped in the ashes for his faithful niblick, found it, and used it to heave himself upright. He gazed about him, taking his time. In that corner where the crucifix had stood a rat the size of a small beaver balanced adroitly on its hunkers and cleaned its whiskers, looking to Septimus's weary eye for all the world like an old woman applying makeup, exhibiting the same air of resigned detachment. One of the beds had been twisted by the intense heat into a fantastic shape, its tubular steel contorted to a Dali brainstorm; against it

252

(for some reason, perhaps divine, only superficially charred), the cross on which his rigid, glaring, sleeping-companion had been hung, a blackened coffee-pot like a billycan beneath it. On the other side of the room, the steel medicine cabinet had exploded, and hanging from it like jewelled stalactites, the melted glass bottles and pots that had contained Sister Mary's lotions and potions and pills. Along another wall the shelves had collapsed, but only at one end, and sloped crazily to the floor: the infamous downward slide, thought Septimus vaguely. The long mirror (so useful when he had felt the need to argue with himself, always with the comforting thought that he would win) was shattered, but the glass remained within the frame; eyeing it, he was appalled to see eight gaunt, bespectacled images of himself eyeing him back. He blinked, making of his eyes shutters in the vain hope that they might photograph some rather more pleasant scene, but the unholy octet remained steadfastly at their post, cheekily blinking back; he turned quickly away. Sighing deeply, too deeply as it turned out and thumping his chest with one fist as a fit of violent coughing overtook him, Septimus returned to squat on the floor at the feet of the wooden Christ, removing his spectacles and wiping his streaming eyes awkwardly with his sleeve. He was, he knew, waiting for something, and he felt oddly safe amid the ruins of his sad little hospice; it was, he told himself, a place that had been built out of love, and only in such a place could any man find sanctuary.

Behind him on the road a man, a rent-collector, stopped and stared at the gutted building. He took, after a while, a small notebook from his pocket and wrote something down, licking the pencil-lead before writing. Septimus regarded him balefully, casually noting the baggy, ill-fitting suit, the two-tone shoes, the fedora, the calculating look, wondering what thoughts could be passing through the rent-collector's head. Perhaps he had already rebuilt the hospice in his mind, making of it a hotel, or a bar, which would be more profitable, or a brothel, more lucrative still; it could have been, however, that he was merely totting up the loss of income the fire had caused, finding only economic tragedy in the ashes.

'Phoenix,' Septimus said to himself as the rent-collector sauntered away: not that much would rise from these ashes. Except himself, he thought, and with a wistful smile he rose shakily to his feet and shuffled out on to the road. It struck him for the first time how deplorably sad it was that the street didn't even have a name, none that had ever been mentioned at any rate. Rue des Pauvres, he tried. Rue des Inconnues. Calle Tottenham Court. Via O'Connell. Via Dolo . . . It turned out to be a fruitless pastime; no name, not even his grimly jocular ones, could alleviate its squalor or lift the melancholy street from its depressing decay, deserted now apart from the rent-collector who had moved smartly down its length and was banging with his fist, with evident frustration on the shuttered *boulangerie*, just as God had hammered for admittance to his soul. Septimus walked mentally down the road making of it his own abysmal path through life, through the burgeoning foliage of youth that had promised so much, through the starker landscape of early manhood that had promised rather less, passed the signs he should have followed but had ignored, to – the rent-collector had stepped back into the centre of the street and was yelling abuse at an upstairs window.

Septimus turned away. He felt a sudden surge of sadness for the rent-collector, friendless as *he* was friendless, and weighed down by this awful friendlessness if the jib of his shoulders was anything to go by. Septimus, from the corner of his eye, watched him abandon his attempt to gain entry and make off down the road, disappearing finally round the corner. And who could tell? Perhaps from around that very corner, that corner around which life always waited, help would come. Something was certainly coming. Septimus squinted. Not help, alas. Not unless help had adopted the guise of the crippled cobbler, for it was he who now shunted his way towards Septimus, faster than was his wont, waving as he came. Or perhaps it was being carried in abundance on the shoulders of the men who followed him, the ragged platoon that swung into the street and advanced, also waving, towards the hospice. Their grim faces did not look all that helpful, however. Still, one could never tell; help often came from the most unlikely places, did it not? God worked in mysterious ways, did He not? Yet there seemed to be little that was exactly mysterious about the men who strode doggedly towards him, and suddenly Septimus knew again what it was like to be afraid. Help, he thought vaguely with a timid glance towards the wooden Christ; the painted eyes stared back, still grimly stern.

Someone was tugging at his leg. The cripple's bloodshot eyes gawped up at him, but there was pity in those eyes too, which was promising. He reached down to touch the upturned face, but the cobbler pulled away with a small cry of alarm, terror replacing whatever pity had been in his eyes. Septimus felt hurt. He wanted to explain that his action had been of the most benevolent kind, that he shared the cripple's affliction, that he fully understood how cruel life could be. Further, he wanted to reassure him that things were never as bad as they seemed, that there was always light at the end of the tunnel, that every cloud had a silver lining even though, all the while, he was aware that he was really trying to convince himself and failing.

A small breeze curled itself down the street and rustled the ashes, whipping them away from the wooden image, and for a dreadful moment Septimus thought Christ had moved. The cripple, though, had certainly moved several yards away and was stroking his chicken, watching the other men move closer, slowly, as though the wind propelled them too. Then, for a second, everyone remained motionless, a painting, a fresco; then someone shouted a single Creole word which Septimus could not understand. It seemed vital that he should, however, and he was still puzzling about it when the men surged on to him, knocking him to the ground.

Incredibly, the fear that moments before had consumed him vanished, and Septimus felt a curious calm filter into his brain. He lay on his back staring up at the faces that stared back down on him. He wanted to laugh; they *did* all look the same! The faces pushed closer: no, they did not all look the same, and he no longer wanted to laugh. He wanted, quite simply, to fall asleep. He closed his eyes. He was being very brave. He was accepting everything with the dignity anyone would expect of him. He was being very foolish, but courageously foolish and that was the important thing. He was taking everything in his stride. He was playing it cool, which allowed him to pick out the snippets of advice being whispered in his ear by voices that seemed to come from far away:

– You must not show fear, Padre.
– You must pretend you *want* to die.
– When you can take no more you must pretend you *are* dead.
– You must play possum.

Play possum? Surely nobody said that? Septimus opened his eyes again. A round black face was pressed close to his, the mouth slightly open, the breath smelling of cashew nuts. Instantly it withdrew and was replaced by another, this one topped by a natty cap of Black Watch tartan; then it too was withdrawn. He decided it was time to stand up for his rights – well, stand up on his feet at any rate. And he nearly made it: he had got to his knees, had even got one foot firmly planted on the ground, when someone placed a boot on his buttocks, shoved, and toppled him over again. Then the boot kicked him viciously in the ribs. He rolled over and sent a mute appeal for help in the direction of the hospice, but no such thing was forthcoming. He was definitely in this on his own, and he caught the first scent of the tangibility of his danger. He was being kicked again, methodically, as though everyone in the crowd was taking their turn. 'They will try to soften you, Padre,' someone had told him, was telling him, so maybe that was what they were doing. They were taking their time about it too. And enjoying it . . . What Heuxos! call thy father for I will sport tonight! . . . A young man with the face of an angel grabbed him by the shoulders and yanked him to his feet. He looked so kind, this young man, that Septimus thanked him: 'Too kind. Too kind,' he said, and reached out to shake him by the hand. But the Angel stepped back as though struck, and then lunged forward, furiously hitting Septimus with all his force across the face, sending his spectacles flying, making his head reel. Again he sent out a distressed supplication towards the wooden Christ, but his look was arrested and landed on the cripple who sneered at it, grinding his gums.

'You friend Tontons Macoutes,' someone very close to him shouted.

The accusation, bewildering, sent a slow burning pain of terror through Septimus. He tried to deny it, shaking his head, but someone, perhaps the Angel again, started to shake him, screaming at him, ripping his threadbare soutane, then pushing him into the waiting arms of someone else who took to shaking him also, pulling the soutane from his shoulders, leaving him naked but for a singularly ragged vest and a pair of pale-blue trousers secured to his waist with an Etonian tie. Any lingering hope of deliverance was stripped from him too. The mood, part real, part mischievous, that had sustained him with its tricky deception vanished completely. He realized that all along he had placed his hope in the expectation that someone would come and save him; he had no idea who, could not conceive of anyone, but someone, anyone. Now he sensed no one would come. It ran through his head that he had never felt quite so alone, despite the multitude that surrounded him; never quite so abandoned, despite some half-remembered promises a once familiar God had made; never quite so helpless, despite the fact that he had (once that he could clearly remember) been far more helpless. He felt the chill of mute resignation sweep into his soul: this was a feeling he had experienced before also. He knew, horribly, what it signified; he buried his face in his hands.

'You friend Tontons Macoutes!'

The accusation hit him as brutally as the fist that knocked his hands away from his face. Someone was forcing them behind his back; a small bone near his elbow seemed to crack. The man in the Black Watch cap undid the Etonian tie, guffawing (how they all guffawed!) as his trousers slipped to the ground, and knotted it about his wrists.

'*Regardez!*' the Angel screamed, pointing to Septimus's shrivelled, drooping penis, taking his own from his jeans and waving the great black virile organ in glee, and they all guffawed the louder. Perhaps accidentally (for he was doubling up and rocking with laughter) the Black Watch pushed Septimus in the back: he tripped on the trousers about his ankles, and crashed to the ground. Four pairs of feet shod in tennis shoes kicked him to his feet again. '*Aux pieds,*' one shouted, while another grabbed him and pulled him upright by his hair. 'On your feet, friend of Tontons Macoutes.'

'I have no friends,' Septimus heard himself say, and was surprised at the depth of sadness in his voice.

'*Le Colonel* your friend. We see.'

'No.'

'He kees you.'

'He *love* you,' the Angel said, still holding his penis and now grinding his hips, thumping his loins back and forth.

Although he had no recollection of having been keesed by the Colonel, and despite the fact that he could now taste the ominous bitterness of blood in his mouth, Septimus, for one infinitesimal moment, grasped the word 'love', monstrous though its context was, and clung to it, letting it suffuse his entire consciousness. For was it not –

'For the love of God – '

– ah, indeed, was not everything done for the love of that God . . . But wait just one minute! Had not someone very real put forward the irrefutable conception? Someone he knew? Or, at least, whose voice he could certainly count as familiar? He peered about him. If only it wasn't all so damnably blurred.

'For the love of God, stop it!'

The voice was somewhere to his left and behind him, shrill, almost a scream: strange how only he seemed to hear it . . . 'Father,' it called now, and at last he could put a face to it. Sister Mary! An odd choice of avenging angel to say the least. Still, one never knew . . . For some reason he repeated the word aloud: 'Father!' That was a mistake; the men also seemed to find the word to their liking. They took it up and started to chant, injecting the word with a curiously venomous mockery. 'Fah-theeer, fah-theeer, fah-theer!' And suddenly it was as though they were dancing about him, but perhaps it was only his mind that was whirling. 'Father!' Sister Mary's voice (now sounding as though it came from a great distance, as if she had never really been there, as if he had merely imagined her proximity) tried to console him. Alas, it did no such thing, and, admitting its inadequacy, it wasted away and was heard no more, replaced by Angel's suave tones as he placed his mouth close to Septimus's ear and muttered something in Creole. It must have been something significant for a great cheer went up, and Septimus felt himself being pushed forward, manhandled down the street a little way, before being jolted to a halt beside the two donkeys tethered to the shafts of an upended, painted cart. All about him the men were whispering in the manner of men about to perpetrate some act of which they themselves were afraid, some act that might bring dreadful retribution but worth performing nevertheless. Someone grabbed him by both ears from behind, pulling his head sharply back. It was this awkward position and not pain (for he was, he knew, almost beyond that particular sensation now), that made him open his mouth wide: immediately the halter from one of the asses was thrown over his head, the bit jammed between his teeth. The rancid taste of saliva and congealed vegetation made his stomach heave. He was, indeed, on the point of vomiting when Angel leapt on to his back, jerking the reins cruelly with one hand, whacking him on his bare buttocks with the other, his long legs crossed about Septimus's loins, his feet thumping him agonisingly in the testicles as he urged him forward. 'Vas!' he yelled. 'Vas!' his companions yelled. And, incredibly, Septimus found the strength to go round and round at a stumbling trot, prevented from falling only by the hold Angel had on the reins.

It was great fun, it seemed. Everyone wanted to have a go, and they took it in turns to mount him, each one goading him on harder than the one before as though they needed his humiliation and agony to prove their manhood. Finally, after being ridden number-less times around the jeering circle, Septimus collapsed. And lying there, face down, his arms feeling as if disjointed from his shoulders, it was most curious that he could see in his mind's eye what certainly appeared to be a spirit, his own spirit, grow more free, more emboldened as it made its way into the light above him. No longer was it the dried-up, pathetic thing he had always surmised it to be; it shone and seemed oddly noble and proud. And perhaps all this was not so ludicrous. When, as a young and eager man, he had striven to attain what was then described as a state of grace, he had always imagined his soul as being noble, something in which he could take considerable pride; and now (starting to tremble, some demon trying to implant the possibility of yet further torment in his mind) it was as though, briefly, he had shed the years, those long and awful years of which he was genuinely ashamed, and was absurdly young again, and it was from this long-since forgotten youth that the curious spirit rose.

And he himself was rising, dragged unceremoniously upright by large, coarse, greedy hands. Standing unsteadily, the first thing that struck him was the sudden devastating silence. He peered about him cautiously. The men were still there, but their attitudes had altered: the grins that previously had edged out the intrinsic wicked-ness of their monstrous sport had vanished, superseded by a grim, downward turn of mouth that presaged expectant cruelty. Their eyes, too, had lost that occasional flicker of childish pleasure which Septimus had beheld and had hoped would redeem him from further torment; now, almost glazed, they portrayed that furious intensity which precedes the prospect of awful tragedy. It was as though, Septimus thought, as though collectively and at the same instant, they had conceived a diabolical plan and as if each was waiting for another to make the first move.

It was the Angel, perhaps inevitably, who made it. Unobserved by Septimus, he had entered the gutted shell of the hospice and was now wrenching the Christless crucifix from the debris. He carried it from the hospice and stood, holding it before him, over Septimus, one leg either side of his prostrate body, the foot of the cross by his knees, planted, possibly by chance, so that it cast its shadow directly on to him.

Perhaps it was the appalling realization of what was about to befall him that made Septimus scream, or perhaps it was the fact that this realization was already inflicting its mysterious, unbearable pain. Or perhaps it was neither of these things: perhaps it was just that dreadful cry which those who consider themselves lost or damned send winging towards whatever god is theirs when all human aid is witheld from them.

For whatever reason, it was a rending scream, a horrible shriek that left his throat like vomit. Incredibly he could hear it streaking away. It was, he imagined dazedly, like an India-rubber ball, tossed from the phantom of one familiar to another, occasionally dropped, bouncing, caught again, passed further down the line, passed hurriedly as if it burned those who touched it, or as if it contained his soul which nobody wanted anything to do with, or as if to hold it would condemn the holder to a damnation such as his own. 'Ayeeeee,' he thought he heard himself scream again. And it was, alas, no longer a mere ball that was being constantly rejected; it was himself, spurned and scorned, denied, it had to be faced, the chance to make excuses, each familiar (dear God, how angry they all looked, particularly Bishop Matthew McKewen whose anger was deepened by disappointment) all but denying any knowledge of this vagrant spirit, raising their eyebrows in shock as though astonished anyone might have the temerity to imagine they had ever had anything whatever to do with him. Then, suddenly, the eerie progression was halted. He was static in the air; suspended, waiting, but waiting for what he had no idea. Soon, however, that became clear. From nowhere a long woebegone line of pilgrims appeared, filing past him in silence, heads bowed like criminals defying recognition. There was a strange sameness about them all, yet it took Septimus an extraordinarily long time under the circumstances to realize they were cartoons of himself, each encumbered by some monstrous deformity that revealed itself only in their eyes, eyes that flickered upwards towards him as they passed, sad, mournful eyes, eyes that did not accuse, eyes that merely reproached. And he witnessed himself, some fatuous notion of disguise crossing his mind, attempt to pull some clothing over his head only to discover he was naked – something he would have sworn he had not been moments before. And lying there on the street he tried the same gesture until he realized he *was* naked, and those ethereal fractions of his being had disappeared.

The pain returned; and he could hear what he could only think of as moaning; and black, sweating faces were peering down at him;

and hands were taking him by the shoulders and by the feet and raising him a little off the ground; and then they were lowering him again on to something hard, something quite warm, something uncomfortable that hurt his spine; and both his arms were pulled sideways and manoeuvred from one position to another as if he was being fitted for something, and the same thing with his feet only here his ankles were crossed, one over the other; and the men had crowded closer, bending, craning their necks, leaving only a tiny sphere of blurred light into which he might gaze. It crossed his mind that into that light he might escape, although something seemed to be advising him against any such action; as Kafka had generously pointed out, it was safer to be in chains than to be free. Which was an interesting point of view, and one which he really must deliberate upon at some time in the future.

Septimus was, in fact, mustering his thoughts along those Kafkaesque lines when the first nail penetrated the palm of his left hand. Oddly enough, for the moment, he felt nothing; his whole consciousness was consumed by a curious hissing noise like a massive, multitudinous intake of breath, but more, it seemed to him, like that strange, encouraging sibilance his mother had used to calm his childish anxieties, a shushing sound made between the teeth as she held him on her knee, saying, 'Shush now, laddy. Just one little prickeen of the good doctor's needle. And Mammy promises you that you won't feel a thing.' But, he remembered, he had felt the prickeen; just as now, suddenly (the fractional delay it had taken to be transmitted to his brain somehow increasing the agony) he was aware of the searing, burning pain in his hand. Instinctively he tried to withdraw his hand: he felt the flesh rip, and the pain increase, yet he felt too, which was very odd, a reassuring calm settle itself upon him. It was as if, for a split second, he had been made aware that the time for conjecture was over; that what was happening to him was inevitable, a culmination of suffering to illustrate to him how lightly he had got off previously; that he was being offered a chance, although a chance for what was locked in some other being's imagination – expiation loomed into his mind. And sacrifice. And redemption, which was encouraging. 'It is only through suffering that we can hope to achieve redemption.' What fool had said that? Septimus was still trying to puzzle that one out when Angel, crouched above him, put one knee on his right wrist and hammered in the second nail. It was far more painful than the

first, and before he could stop himself, before, indeed, he had time
to think about it, Septimus screamed again.

– Shush now, my laddy.
– You must pretend to be dead.
– You won't feel a thing, Mammy promises.
– They always want you to die slowly.
– You must play possum.

Trying to make sense of the snatches of encouragement and advice
that whirled within his brain, Septimus stopped screaming. And
miraculously the pain also ceased, or rather it became continuous,
familiar, bearable. Foolishly he decided to smile. It crossed his mind
that by smiling he might convey his willingness to forgive, since
somehow, now, forgiveness and redemption seemed to go hand in
hand.

Alas, as it turned out, Angel was in no way interested in forgiveness, and the smile infuriated him. He was nailing Septimus's feet,
making a thorough job of it. He worked in the manner of a man
accustomed to wielding a hammer, and took pride in his work,
testing the feet frequently, adding additional nails as the fancy took
him. He held the unused nails between his lips, removing them one
by one as he required them. Finally he stood erect and looked about
him as though for applause, or at least approval. This took quite a
while to come; the others, now that the deed had been committed,
seemed less sure of its wisdom. They seemed reluctant now to be
part of it. They shuffled their feet. They glanced, pretending not
to, at each other. Some of them made as if to back away only to be
dissuaded by curiosity. What had started, for some, as an outrageous
prank had somehow got out of hand. They were clearly afraid,
and the smell of that fear was pungent and overpowering. Even
Septimus, lying there, still bewildered, could smell it. He recognized
it immediately, and thinking it was his own, became surprised.
Strangely enough he felt anything but afraid. Not yet anyway. True,
he *had* been earlier, but not any longer. His mind was quite coherent
and was ticking away logically. He was being tortured, certainly,
but he had been tortured before and had survived. Soon, he told
himself, he would be saved. Something would happen. He was
being tested. And just when he reached the limit of his endurance
he would be saved. Of course he would. Incredibly he felt himself
relax.

And something certainly was happening, although it appeared to have little to do with salvation. He was being lifted aloft and carried high above the heads of his tormentors. The pain became excruciating as he was rocked from side to side with each step his bearers took. He was moving away from the hospice and down the mean, filthy street. He could just make out the topsy-turvy roofs of the shacks as they passed. He spotted an open window; crazily he wondered if he might escape through it, but it was swept from his vision before the idea could find foundation. For a moment the crucifix was tilted to one side, and Septimus caught sight of a familiar face looking up at him. Instinctively he tried to raise an arm in a friendly wave of recognition: he cried inwardly as the pain shot up his arm, yet it hurt him more that the crippled cobbler looked away, disowned him, rejected his implied, heartfelt friendship. Yet there was one person who was not, it seemed, intent on rejecting him; someone who stood transfixed apart from the jostling crowd in the shadow of a doorway, the doorway of what was always referred to simply as 'Dominique's' wherein Dominique mustered her vacuous-eyed girls for economic pleasure (as he himself had stood in the shadowed doorways of a thousand misericords mustering something that had nothing to do with pleasure). Both hands were raised to her face, a face contorted in disbelief and horror. Well no. Not transfixed after all, for she was moving along the boarded sidewalk, keeping pace with the crowd, still clutching her beautiful face with both hands, her lips quivering, perhaps restraining tears, perhaps mutely talking to him. Behind her the cripple scuttled, and behind him others loomed for a moment as familiars, then disintegrated into strangers, then took on the shape of familiars again, striding purposefully. Trying desperately to focus his bleary eyes, Septimus drank in these macabre people. He could just make out that they were busily talking to each other, and quite jovially at that, although their stern countenances belied the levity of their words. Through the eerie, portentous moaning of the crowd, through the monotonous, sepulchral beat their feet made on the dusty roadway as they now broke into a jog-trot – increasing a thousandfold the pain he had believed could get no worse – through the booming distant explosions, through the occasional jubilant cries that seemed to swing in at him from all directions, words emerged, spasmodic and jerky:

– I always said he would come to –

– A monastery is the place for you, Septimus.

– always giving himself the licence to blame God –

– You know, he told me he actually asked to come here –

– He must have known –

– How could he?

How could he indeed? Find himself in this calamitous situation, that is.

They had almost reached the intersection. By turning left they would eventually arrive at the Hotel Ollofson, by turning right they would enter the heart of the city. In fact they did neither. Those carrying him halted suddenly, and were instantly surrounded by a mob that appeared to have been anxiously awaiting their arrival. Septimus felt himself being lowered again, and placed flat on the ground. Only this time nobody seemed to be looking at him. Angel was busily talking, gesticulating as he spoke, to a tall thin man with a shaven head: and everybody was watching them. They were certainly arguing, and the expression on the thin man's face showed clearly that he was not accustomed to having his authority questioned.

Septimus became aware of someone else lying on the ground; someone dressed in a suit, someone whose upturned face he knew he should recognize. He raised his head. He was on the point of putting a name to the face when suddenly flies began to swarm about his own face; then, scenting the blood, they moved as one and feasted on the wounds in his hands. Mercifully the cripple, squeezing his way between the legs of the mob, settled on the ground beside him and, in a gesture of friendliness, waved away the flies with, amazingly, a polka-dotted handkerchief. Then, tiring of this activity, he deputized his chicken to guard one hand, placing it carefully so that it could peck at any flies that attempted to land. Septimus smiled his thanks, but the cripple wasn't looking. A sudden commotion had broken out; voices were raised. Someone was protesting, shouting loudly in a voice that was decidedly familiar to Septimus, but he was being shouted down. 'Help me,' Septimus heard himself say pathetically, trying desperately to see whoever it was had come to his defence. Then it dawned on him that perhaps this great protector might not be there to defend him, but rather to goad the others on. He tried again to raise his head. Yet try as he might he could distinguish nothing: it was all still a blur. But he was being defended all right; heartening words filtered into his consciousness:

– You cannot –

– It is not as it was –

– There will be serious repercussions –

Alas, interspersed was the other side of the argument, which seemed to be presented with much more authority, in flat voices that smacked hugely of fatalism:

– We must –

– Nothing has changed –

– We can only obey what is destined –

Suddenly he was being hoisted in the air again, but not before someone placed a ridiculous flat cap on his head, making everyone laugh; everyone except Septimus, who, recognizing the true humiliation of the gesture, wanted to cry. On one side he could make out the Angel, looking grim; on the other side Black Watch, capless, and looking the more menacing for it. And it had become quite a procession. People had gathered from their special hiding places and surrounded him, talking in low, desperate voices, shuffling along rather than walking. What was it Joyce had said? 'They moo and make brute music with their hooves.' Yes, that was it. Recklessly Septimus giggled. Immediately he regretted it. Preposterous things were being said between Angel and Black Watch, things without adequate reason, things that were like questions he was supposed to answer in order to save himself, questions, however, that had not been asked but which nevertheless hung suspended in the air, his life depending on him deciphering them. Strangers appeared beside him from time to time, peering, and went away again nodding as though they had definitely identified him. All thought of escape, of salvation of any kind even, vanished from Septimus's mind. His will and any glimmerings of hope were paralysed; and time too. He started to babble, trying, it seemed to him, to keep his spirits up. He had not the least idea what he was saying. Oddly, he could not even hear his own words; nor could anyone else, apparently, or if they could they ignored them. 'It is always the poor who suffer. It is therefore the poor we must save,' he thought he was saying. 'I have nothing to say,' he was also insisting. 'I am playing possum but even for that it is too late.' Someone carrying the foot of the crucifix seemed to stumble, and Septimus crashed to the ground. But that wasn't it at all. He had been deliberately dumped on the ground. Brilliant pain seared his wounds. The mocking cap slid from his head. The sun scorched his eyes, yet for a moment, above him, he could just make out the monument to Jean-Jacques Dessaline, although those toil-weary peasants on the mural appeared to be moving in the most extraordinary manner, squirming almost, all trace of inflicted nobility removed from their faces. Then he realized there were people standing in front of the mural, and it was these who were moving, these who tried so hard to wriggle out of their anxiety. Something was beating rhythmically in his head: no, it was outside his head, bouncing on his skull, a drum of sorts. Or someone's heart. It was, unbelievably, remarkably soothing. Septimus was just getting used to its hypnotic, dull tempo when he was hoisted high in the air. It was most odd. He could suddenly see quite clearly. Looking down, he found himself quite objectively watching the bent backs of the men as they secured the foot of the cross in the ground, making something of a hash of it too. All pain had left him, replaced by a curious sense of relief. Now, finally, he realized that he was about to die, or be left to die which amounted to the same thing. He realized too that he was losing control. His tongue was lolling out from one side of his mouth and he could not withdraw it into his mouth. He felt urine trickle down his leg. 'I am so sorry,' he said quietly, yet his voice was so sorrowful the apology could hardly have been applicable to his mishap. But there must have been something about the words that appealed to him: 'I am so sorry,' he said again, and for a moment he closed his eyes.

Images gathered in his waning consciousness, doing nothing, merely curious, watching as life hesitated before finally departing, watching what he could only think of as his spirit as it fearfully, tenaciously clung to his body, terrified of what might await it. But why, he suddenly wondered, should his spirit be so afraid? What could await him that could be so truly terrible? He thought he heard the clock near the American Embassy striking its uncontrolled time. But that was impossible. Yet there was something chiming, a tiny bell. 'This is my body,' he heard himself say, wondering why the words struck him as so significant. 'This is my blood.' Only it wasn't his. It was the child's and lay uncongealed on the floor, and he was dipping his finger in it, hunched, moaning, appalled at the realization that he had sacrificed the child, his child, so wantonly.

He felt his body start to jerk in the spasms of imminent death. His immediate need, it seemed, was a drink. He was parched. His tongue, still lolling grotesquely, felt swollen, felt hard as leather. He opened his eyes as best he could. Strange . . . he could see his old niblick wavering before his face. With an effort he moved his eyes down the shaft and spotted the cripple holding it, pushing it towards him, towards his face. Something was attached to it. It touched his cheek. Cool. Moved away. Returned and settled on his mouth. So cool. And damp. And soft. Septimus realized it was a sponge, or some cloth soaked in water. He sucked on it hungrily. Then it was withdrawn. He tried to look down again, to thank the cripple, but his vision was clouding rapidly. All he could distinguish was a mask gazing up at him and he made it into a compassionate one; this small act of generosity made him feel happy. He settled down to die, leaning his head back, even moving it from side to side until he found a comfortable position.

. . . And he was drifting away from this sorrowful place, his departure accompanied by a lilting Paraguayan folk-song played on the guitar as Jośe Asuncion Flores might have played it, the strumming turning, suddenly, to the sound of thundering water cascading over granite rocks, rocks that somehow became pliable and formed themselves into shapes, familiars who moaned and groaned as though in the throes of love.

He was entering a tiny hut, following someone, an overpowering urge surging in his loins, which seemed particularly queer since he was really following Bishop Matthew McKewen down some steps, the bishop in front of him, turning, warning, 'Watch your step.' 'I am watching my step.' 'I should jolly well hope so,' the bishop retorted with a friendly enough smile. 'Once a boy a rose espied,' his mother was singing, bouncing him on her knee, jazzing the song to suit her rhythm. 'You spy?' another voice enquired. And with that he was alone, although he suspected it wouldn't be for long. Bits seemed to be flying off him as though plucked: he watched them float away like feathers. So *this*, he thought, is what it is really like to die: then, from the corner of his mind's eye, he noticed that the objects were not, in fact, pieces of himself at all. They were something far more sinister than that. They had life of their own. They were tiny, shrivelled beings. They did not have life of their own. They were puppets. Their arms and legs stuck out at awkward angles as though their maker had been distracted while in their creation. And they had their backs to him, which he found disturbing. He tried to see who was controlling them; he could find no one.

Now he was being hauled from an abyss. How wonderful! Just

when he thought he was being totally abandoned someone had come to his rescue. But then these kind samaritans too were gone and he was left clinging to a spindly shrub, a cactus probably, the cruel spikes of which were penetrating his palms. His weight was drawing the roots of the plant from the dry, rocky soil. He could hang on no longer. He was exhausted. He was falling. Hurtling down, down and down to the farthest reaches of the abyss that seemed to have no bottom, all the while thinking that no one could possibly help him now even if there was someone kind enough to consider so doing. He would never be found. He would lie abandoned in the air that rushed past him for eternity. Although not quite abandoned, it seemed. He would have company: the puppets, or something approximating to them, had returned. They faced him, their countenances stern. Instantly he recognized them. Archbishop Gidron was to the fore, jouncing about on the end of his strings, his wizened face telling him 'I told you so' by its bland expression. And Patrick, Patrick was certainly there, he, too, with a smug sort of look. Odd that the cobbler should be hanging about in the background; odder still that he appeared totally cured, no sign of his crippling evident. But Matthew McKewen was also there, which was a relief. He would surely come to his defence, would set the record straight. Not so, alas. For now they were all laughing at him, pointing, their little bodies convulsed in uproarious mirth.

In an effort that seemed to drag every last ounce of strength from his body, Septimus opened his eyes. At first he thought he had already died and was in some strange sort of paradise, the landscape stretching flatly away from him until it reached the mountains, then surging up their great slopes on to their purple, mist-shrouded peaks. A dismal prospect, he reflected. Then he looked down, peering through hanging eyelids that got heavier by the moment. It took what seemed like a very long time for the merged faces to disassociate themselves one from the other. They ranged before him: Angel and the shaven-headed man he had been talking to; Black Watch, who had retrieved his cap and now wore it at a jaunty angle; the cobbler, still sadly deformed after all, nursing his chicken; Patrick, or someone very like him, who had smartened himself up again, who was chatting to Gandhi . . . Gandhi? Septimus groaned, and Gandhi vanished. The others remained however, unmoving, waiting, not, it seemed, with any great expectancy of surprise. Patience was written all over their countenances. It was as though,

Septimus thought, they were standing by, biding their time to witness the inevitable take place. Yet how kind they looked, as if they *would* do something if it had not already been taken out of their hands. But perhaps he thought this in a last effort to comfort himself. 'Thank you,' he tried to say, but his tongue strangled the words, only a hoarse, guttural noise escaping him. But the cripple at least seemed to understand. He gave Septimus a small wave and what passed for a smile.

. . . It was so cold. The blazing sun gleamed like an enormous frozen disc. Septimus stared to shiver. Then, quite lucidly, he knew it was life slithering away from him. His poor, tired spirit wriggling from its tiresome skin, he reasoned. Shuffling off the old mortal coil.

And for one wonderful, brilliant moment it was as though he could see his soul ascending into light, soaring, clean, forgiven, welcomed. He tried to call to it, to encourage it, to share in the joyous occasion. It seemed, for some reason, vital that he should keep an eye on things; seemed that should he fail to do so all would be lost. But he was managing beautifully. In no time at all the God he had tried so hard to please would reach down and –

. . . Something distracted him. It sounded like a crack of thunder. Instantly everything went black.

Epilogue

The mortuary stank of violent death. Great weals of congealed blood whipped across the walls, some taking on the shape of sinister crosses like evil monuments to those who had been tortured and slain there. A canvas stretcher on trestle legs had been placed in one corner, and on it, covered to the neck by a sheet that had been mended with fisherman-stitching across the centre, lay the body of Septimus Roach. An off-centre, naked light-bulb shone almost directly on to his face, and on his face, too, was a puzzled look. Yet he appeared peaceful enough, as though whatever had confused him had been, to him at least, of no great importance.

Far more distressed was Oscar Nicholson's expression, although there seemed to be little sorrow in his eyes; he looked furious. But there was a certain embarrassment also, as if his anger was directed mostly at himself. Nor, indeed, was there much in the way of sadness to be detected in Monsieur Lagreze's gaze. He appeared more to pity Septimus than mourn him, and there was a flickering in his eyes that hinted at triumph, but this could reasonably have been attributed to the manner in which he had dismissed Oscar's rebuke: 'You knew what was going on, Gilles. You should have stopped it,' he had said a moment before.

'That was not possible,' Monsieur Lagreze had replied with a grim finality that had whittled away the potency of any further accusation.

Oscar turned the attack to himself. 'Dammit, *I* should have done something.'

'There was nothing you could have done,' Monsieur Lagreze told him, making as if to give his friend a consoling pat on the shoulder but changing his mind and tugging his own earlobe instead.

'I bloody could have if I hadn't blacked out.'

Monsieur Lagreze let that pass, and looked away.

'I could have sworn someone belted me on the head, you know,' Oscar persisted, instinctively feeling his pate.

'No. No one touched you, Oscar. You just collapsed.'

'Bloody odd.'

Monsieur Lagreze didn't seem to think it was all that odd, however; a small, knowing smile appeared for a second on his lips. But he said nothing, and they stared in silence at Septimus for a few minutes.

The thick windowless walls made the mortuary virtually sound-proof, and the single fly that had managed to invade the room flew across it with the noise of a Spitfire, settling somewhere in the gloom.

'And another thing,' Oscar went on finally, his voice loud and abrasive, then falling to a whisper. 'This secrecy. It's all wrong, Gilles.'

'It was an agreement made between your Ambassador and our new Interior Minister,' Monsieur Lagreze pointed out politely. 'It was taken out of our hands,' he added, and sounded pleased that it had been.

'I know it was, damn you. But it's still wrong.'

Monsieur Lagreze shrugged. 'It would be better, you think, if everyone was told how' – he glanced at the corpse – 'the priest died?'

'Yes. As a matter of fact I do.'

Monsieur Lagreze made a noise that could have been a hastily suppressed little laugh. 'That is just the man in you talking. Not the diplomat. Believe me, Oscar, it is truly for the best that *Le Père* Septimus died in an accident,' he said quietly, now deciding that his gesture was appropriate and patting Oscar on the shoulder.

'Better for Namphy, you mean.'

'Better for everyone.'

The fly zoomed down and landed on Septimus's face, and Oscar leaned forward to drive it away. It plunged upwards into the lightbulb and flew off again into the shadows, dazed, its engine pinking.

'It would, you see – the truth, I mean – take too many lies to explain,' Monsieur Lagreze added.

'So nobody is to be held responsible?'

'We are all, in our way, responsible.'

'That's not what I mean, Gilles. Dammit, he was murdered.'

Monsieur Lagreze flinched. 'Not precisely.'

'How precisely, then?' Oscar demanded.

'If I told you it was simply something that *had* to take place, would you accept that?'

'No.'

Monsieur Lagreze smiled sadly. 'I thought not.'

'You could hardly expect me to.'

'No, but that, my friend, is how it was.'

'Oh, I see.'

'You don't really,' Monsieur Lagreze said without reproach.

'Oh but I do. Some poor old bugger gets murdered and you calmly palm it off on fate or destiny or some other such crap.'

Monsieur Lagreze looked genuinely hurt. 'I do not, as you say, palm it off on fate or destiny. It is not for me to do any such thing,' he said humbly. He took a deep breath. 'It was simply the way he was *meant* to die. And he knew that, I think.'

'Oh, great. Well, he can hardly argue the point now, can he?'

Monsieur Lagreze made a small clicking noise of distaste with his tongue, turning to face Oscar and eyeing him balefully.

'I'm sorry, Gilles.'

Monsieur Lagreze accepted the apology with a bow of his head. 'It is best, you know, sometimes, if you do not *try* to understand. Just accept.'

'The easy way out, eh?'

Monsieur Lagreze looked surprised. 'Oh no, Oscar. That is something in which you are quite mistaken. It is, in fact, the most difficult way. Acceptance without full understanding is most difficult. It is the gift of saints, you know.'

For a moment Oscar looked amazed, then amused, but there was sadness in his amusement. He shook his head slowly before asking, 'Who knows? Maybe you're right, Gilles.' He moved away from the stretcher. 'Come on. For God's sake let's get out of here,' he said, already striding towards the door.

Before following, Monsieur Lagreze pulled the sheet over Septimus's face, pausing for a moment before actually covering it to smooth the priest's ruffled, wispy hair. It was a gesture not immediately associable with a man of his bulk, filled with delicate kindness. And there was a reverence about it that seemed somewhat out of place. It was a caress almost, expressing something approaching mute gratitude.

'Good God! What the hell – ?'

Monsieur Lagreze, walking along the narrow corridor that led to the exit, almost stopped in his tracks as Oscar's exclamations registered.

'Gilles, come and look at this.'

Monsieur Lagreze joined his friend at the door and looked. It was an astounding sight. In the small concrete courtyard that separated the mortuary from the road, and in the road itself, and beyond, almost, it seemed, as far as the eye could see, people had gathered and were sitting quietly on the ground, mostly cross-legged. They did nothing; just sat there, their faces expressing no emotion. They looked not sad, not happy, not expectant, not inquisitive. Yet they seemed oddly peaceful, almost as though some great burden had been lifted from them.

Oscar felt Monsieur Lagreze's hand on his arm, and 'Come,' he heard him say. They picked their way slowly through the crowd, everyone obligingly leaning sideways to let them pass. Once Oscar hesitated; he spotted the crippled cobbler, chickenless, in the shade near the gateway. It struck him that there was something different about the cripple. His grotesque perkiness had gone; even in his awful deformity he appeared to have assembled a dignity that made him seem whole. Oscar looked quickly away. 'What on earth were they *doing*?' he asked minutes later as they made their way without thinking towards the Hotel Ollofson.

Monsieur Lagreze looked embarrassed.

'Come on, Gilles, tell me.'

'Waiting,' Monsieur Lagreze said simply.

'Waiting? For what?'

'Just waiting.'

Oscar stopped walking and rounded on his friend. 'For what?' he demanded

Monsieur Lagreze smiled patiently. 'Just waiting with the priest, Oscar. Keeping him company, you might say. In Haiti we do that, you know, when we are in the debt of someone who dies.'

The rain that had hung in the heavy air all morning started to fall, gently now, building itself up into the downpour that had been threatening for days. A man in ragged clothes and a Mexican sombrero rushed up to them trying to sell obscene postcards. No sooner had Monsieur Lagreze brusquely sent him on his way than another man appeared, younger than the first but equally dismal of aspect, offering them matches. A melon tumbled on to the road from a passing lorry and exploded: immediately scores of children appeared and scooped handfuls of the juicy mess from the dust, devouring it gleefully. A woman screamed as though being murdered. Someone else laughed. A truck loaded with soldiers thundered towards the palace; a dog chased it, snapping at the wheels, then abandoned the chase and settled down to scratch itself thoroughly.

'Life, as they say, goes on,' Oscar observed wryly as they turned into the garden of the hotel.

'Oh yes,' Monsieur Lagreze affirmed. 'Oh yes,' he said again, pausing and gazing into the distance, towards the mountains. 'Oh yes,' he said once more.

BRIDIE AND THE SILVER LADY

M. S. Power

'They planned the killings together, secretly. That is what Bridie tells the nice young doctor in the crisp white coat who questions her. "Lady said it was the only thing to do. My Silver Lady. She just couldn't see any other way out."'

Retreating to the country with her children, Kathleen Lynch believes she can escape the nightmare of their past. But there is no escape from the damage wrought by incest, no sanctuary from the pain which still echoes relentlessly.

At only eleven years old, young Bridie Lynch has been touched by an evil capable of stirring the darkest recesses of a child's mind. A chilling, malignant force she no longer has the power or will to resist. For she has become the prey of the Silver Lady – a spirit of awesome guise and prodigious strength. And in the terrifying emotional twistings of a disturbed child's soul, the Silver Lady is the power that summons Bridie to kill . . .

0 349 10090 X
FICTION

A DARKNESS IN THE EYE

EYE

M. S. Power

Seamus O'Reilly, 'Godfather' of the Provisional IRA, was a ruthless, vicious man. But he found the times demanded such an attitude. He was also thoughtful, humble and tired. Tired of always losing in the struggle for peaceful, political solutions. Now the British Army is determined to infiltrate and exploit an angry new splinter group rising up within the Provos. O'Reilly's superiors make their decision, and the pale image of a settlement fades out of his grasp again.

This final novel in M. S. Power's haunting trilogy about Northern Ireland takes O'Reilly closer to defeat than he had believed possible. It carries us directly to the heart of an eerie world of shadows, ghosts and muddled beliefs, where another war is fought; against the stupid, who misunderstand the very nature of power, and against the ignorant, unable to value a future beyond the thrill of their own violence and revenge.

0 349 10029 2
FICTION

LOVING AND GIVING
Molly Keane

In 1904, when Nicandra is eight, all is well in the big Irish house called Deer Forest. Maman is beautiful and adored. Dada, silent and small, mooches contentedly around the stables. Aunt Tossie, of the giant heart and bosom, is widowed but looks splendid in weeds. The butler, the groom, the land-steward, the maids, the men – each has a place and knows it. Then, astonishingly, the perfect surface is shattered; Maman does something too dreadful ever to be spoken of.

'What next? Who to love?' asks Nicandra. And through her growing up and marriage her answer is to swamp those around her with kindness – while gradually the great house crumbles under a weight of manners and misunderstanding.

Also by Molly Keane in Abacus:

GOOD BEHAVIOUR
TIME AFTER TIME

0 349 10088 8
FICTION

A BORDER STATION

Shane Connaughton

'Presented as a developing series of stories, playwright Shane
Connaughton's first sortie into fiction is, in effect, a novel of
refreshing originality and authority. Its unifying motif is the
growth to maturity of a boy who remains nameless through the
seven stages that mark his development. His father is a Garda
sergeant dangerously frustrated by his posting in the murderless
village of Butlershill in Cavan. The boy's mother, who is the
heart of the book, is witty, good-humoured, sensuous; when it is
said of her that people love her, it is not hard to believe it.

At first glance it is familiar terrain, but, happy to say,
Connaughton is his own man. There is nothing secondhand
here. The originality arises from two sources; first the author's
acute eye and ear for the objects and sounds of the world he is
describing; and secondly his sharp playwright's and
screenwriter's sense of the dramatic. Remarkable . . . a highly
recommended read'

Irish Times

0 349 10193 0
FICTION

Abacus now offers an exciting range of quality fiction and non-fiction by both established and new authors. All of the books in this series are available from good bookshops, or can be ordered from the following address:

Sphere Books
Cash Sales Department
P.O. Box 11
Falmouth
Cornwall TR10 9EN.

Please send cheque or postal order (no currency), and allow 60p for postage and packing for the first book plus 25p for the second book and 15p for each additional book ordered up to a maximum charge of £1.90 in U.K.

B.F.P.O. customers please allow 60p for the first book, 25p for the second book plus 15p per copy for the next 7 books, thereafter 9p per book.

Overseas customers, including Eire, please allow £1.25 for postage and packing for the first book, 75p for the second book and 28p for each subsequent title ordered.